Selected praise for Catherine Asaro

"Fans of fantasy romance: Run, don't walk, to the
bookstore to get *Charmed Destinies*. You will not be
disappointed. Truly original plots, amazing writing, and
touches of humor made this anthology a wonderful
read.... 'Moonglow' by Catherine Asaro is the most
amazing and beautiful love story I have read this year....
I loved 'Moonglow' so much that the first thing I did
when I finished it was to read it again. The world of
Aronsdale and the characters of Iris and Prince Jarid
are wonderfully developed...it took my breath away.
It's a perfect balance between fantasy and romance,
and I am now wondering why I took so long
to read Catherine Asaro."
—*Fantasy Romance Writers*

"Asaro has created a magical world in 'Moonglow.'
It will leave readers desperate to know more
about these enticing characters."
—*Romantic Times*

THE MISTED CLIFFS

Catherine Asaro

LUNA™

www.LUNA-Books.com

LUNA™

First edition July 2005

THE MISTED CLIFFS

ISBN 0-373-80226-9

Copyright © 2005 by Catherine Asaro

www.LUNA-Books.com

Printed in U.S.A.

CONTENTS

To my nephews
Nathan and Owen
With love

I would like to thank the following readers for their much-appreciated input. Their comments have made this a better book. Any mistakes that remain are mine alone.

For reading the manuscript and giving me the benefit of their wisdom and insights: Aly Parsons, Jeri-Smith Ready, Connie Warner and Al Carroll. For their critiques on several scenes, Aly's Writing Group: Aly Parsons with (in the proverbial alphabetical order) Al Carroll, John Hemry, J. G. Huckenpöler, Simcha Kuritzky, Bud Sparhawk and Connie Warner. To my editor, Stacy Boyd, and also to Mary-Theresa Hussey, for being editor goddesses; to Kathleen Oudit, Julie Messore, Laura Morris, Jenne Abramowitz, Dee Tenorio and all the other fine people at LUNA who helped make this book possible; to Stephanie Pui-Mun Law, the artist who did my gorgeous covers; to Binnie Braunstein, for all her work and enthusiasm on my behalf; and Eleanor Wood, my excellent and much-appreciated agent.

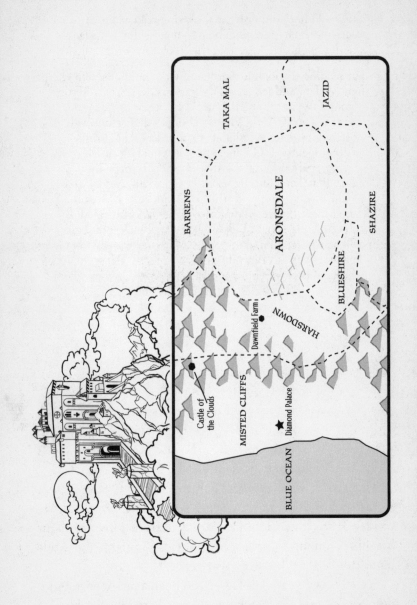

1
Citadel of Rumors

They called him the Midnight Prince.

Cobalt the Dark, the only son of Varqelle Escar, stood on a ridge and looked out across the Barrens. In the distance, the blurred towers of a half-hidden fortress made black silhouettes against the darkening sky. The Citadel of Rumors. It guarded a bleak, northern landscape.

This sunset would finish far more than one day. An era would soon end. For the last eighteen years, the people of Aronsdale, Harsdown, and the Misted Cliffs had lived without hostilities among their three countries. Tonight, the Midnight Prince would destroy that peace.

For eighteen years, his father had been a prisoner in these desolate Barrens. For eighteen years, Varqelle, the king of Harsdown, had lived in the Citadel of Rumors against his will, captured by the Aronsdale king, guarded by Aronsdale cavalry and troops, locked here in isolation while an imposter sat on his throne in Harsdown.

Now that would end.

Cobalt mounted his horse, a powerful charger. He had left Admiral, his travel horse, back in camp. This one stamped and snorted, straining to run. His advisers had cautioned him to wait for morning, but Cobalt had waited and planned for years. He would delay no longer. He drew his sword and stretched his arm straight up with the blade pointing at the sky. Behind him, six hundred warriors would be leaning forward in their saddles, ready to charge. His men would thunder out of the crimson sunset like avenging angels.

He intended to free his father—no matter what the price.

Melody Headwind Dawnfield went by the name Mel, and woe to anyone who called her Princess Melody. She sat astride Tangle, a horse from the royal stables, and rode through the orchards on her family's estate in Harsdown. The practice sword at her hip had interlocking polygons engraved on its hilt. Her yellow hair caught leaves, and she knew she ought to tie it back. She would have preferred to cut it off, but she had promised her father to reconsider.

Mel sighed. Her father was an admirable king, a great army commander and swordsman, but he cared about fashion too much. She preferred to tramp about the orchards and hike in the woods. Her behavior would be considered scandalous for a woman of the royal court in Aronsdale, the country of her father's birth, but here on their farm in Harsdown it was only odd. Her father often grumbled about her lack of decorum, but Mel knew he enjoyed her free spirit. Although she had no desire to conform, she also wished to do well in her role as heir to the throne. Someday she would have to follow the dictates of protocol more closely, but for now she had the liberty to be herself, and she relished that freedom.

She reined Tangle to a stop under an apple tree rich with green and gold autumn leaves. She loved this fertile country far more than the stark mountains to the north or the humid southern climes. The horse snuffled and shook its head, then settled down to nibble at straggles of grass. Mel sat in the saddle and braided her hair. The last rays of the sun slanted through the trees, and many shapes showed in the patches of light and shadow on the leaf-strewn ground, a triangle here, a circle there. One caught her notice in particular, an almost perfect square. It glowed with light, so bright she had to squint. Oddly enough, it had a red tinge—

The leaves within the square caught fire.

"Hai!" Mel swung off Tangle and stamped on the flames. The horse stopped grazing, but otherwise didn't seem concerned. This wasn't the first time he had witnessed her mishaps. Fortunately, only a few leaves caught fire, and she easily put out the small blaze. Tangle went back to grazing.

Mel winced. "Sorry about that." At least a horse didn't chastise her for losing control of the spell. It was more than she could say for Skylark, the elderly mage mistress who was training Mel.

She knelt by the ashes. Apparently she had exerted more control than she realized, for the fire had burned in an exact square. She focused on the square and thought of the color hierarchy of spells, from lowest to highest level: red, orange, yellow, green, blue, indigo—like the rainbow created when light shone through a prism. She imagined the next color after red—and the square glowed orange, adding its luminance to the fading light of a gorgeous autumn day. Refocus-

ing on yet another spell, Mel imagined the orchards in a sea-
son when their trees were thick with green leaves and green
foliage carpeted the hills. The light within the square turned
green—and suddenly Mel *knew* how much Tangle enjoyed the
succulent grass.

"Hey!" Mel grinned at the horse. He lifted his head to look
at her, then returned to his meal. She sat back on her
haunches. Amazing. Would Skylark believe Mel had felt the
mood of a horse? Green spells worked mainly on human be-
ings, revealing their emotions. They might conceivably work
on an animal, but usually only an experienced mage could
achieve that level of nuance. Mel had come into her abilities
relatively late in life, only within the past few years, and she
had a great deal to learn.

"What do you say?" she asked Tangle. "Shall I try a blue
spell?" Mel doubted she could go as high as blue, the color of
healing. She struggled when Skylark worked with her on such
spells and had yet to create one. Mel's mother, Chime, was a
green mage, one color below blue, and Mel suspected green
would be her highest color as well. Her father, King Muller,
was an indigo, but he could use only flawed shapes. They
damaged his spells, with unpredictable results. For that reason, he rarely called on his power, lest his spell go awry and
hurt someone.

She attempted the blue spell, with no result. Well, she was
only eighteen. Perhaps she needed more time for her mage
talents to finish developing. Skylark had her own theory about
why Mel couldn't do blue spells. The mage mistress claimed
it was because Mel preferred "hefting swords and dashing
about on horses" to the more serene pursuits of healing and
meditation. The theory aggravated Mel. A swordswoman
needed the ability to heal just as much as did a scholar or mys-

tic, and she deeply regretted that she couldn't manage the blue spells.

In ancient times, mage queens had ridden with the army. Sometimes a wildness stirred in Mel, deep in the night, and the fire of those ancient queens burned within her. In her dreams, she thundered across the land on a charger with her sword held high. Her people had fought no war for eighteen years and had no reason to think they might soon, but she was the only child of the king and queen of Harsdown, and regardless of what she did with her mage heritage, the day would come when she inherited the title of mage queen.

Mel had been born only months after the war with Varqelle Escar had ended and he lost his throne. Her parents became the king and queen of Harsdown. Mel had known a life of warmth and serenity, and she loved it here. Sometimes she chafed at the weight of her duties, but she also savored the challenge of her future as heir to the Jaguar Throne of Harsdown. Such a startling name, though; jaguars weren't native to the settled lands but had been brought here by sea merchants long ago. The great black cats stalked the warmer regions of southern Harsdown, rare and deadly, far too cruel a beast to symbolize her family. When she became queen, perhaps she would call it the Sun Throne.

Her mood dimmed. She would become a queen only after her parents died, a thought she never wanted to entertain. They were the suns in her life. For all that they often exasperated her, they were also the two most loving people she had ever known.

She couldn't imagine her life without them.

No scouts had detected Cobalt's company as they crossed the desolate northern lands. They had come east from the

Misted Cliffs and ventured through remote passes in the Escar Mountains. Then they traversed the icy northern tundra and headed into the Barrens. They started out each morning before dawn. During part of the day, they rested themselves and the horses, both those mounts they rode for travel and the chargers they used in combat or when chasing bandits in the Misted Cliffs. Each evening they headed out again and rode in the fading light, hidden, covert, silent.

Cobalt's spies had determined that no "mages" defended the Citadel of Rumors. It didn't surprise him. He had thought long on the subject and listened to the scholars in his grandfather's royal court. He had weighed their debates about the validity of mage powers and come to the conclusion shared by many of his people. Mages were tricksters.

The country of Aronsdale—deceptive, treacherous Aronsdale—claimed only six mages of any significant power: King Jarid and Queen Iris; their cousins, Muller and Chime, the false king and queen of Harsdown; and two elderly mage mistresses. Such claims added mystique to tales of their royal House, but none of them fooled Cobalt. Perhaps they might manage a few minor spells, but he suspected they were adept at herbs and chants rather than magic. Even if they had genuine powers, it didn't matter. He was resolved to see his father given justice, and he would overcome a thousand witches if necessary.

His army gave the Citadel of Rumors no warning. They came hard and fast out of the dusk, six hundred shadows. The men at the fortress responded with admirable speed, given the surprise, but not soon enough to stop Cobalt's men from wheeling in their battering ram. Arrows rained on the invaders from the walls above, volley after volley, and then flaming oil, but it was too little and too late. Cobalt's archers returned the volleys even as his other men assaulted the massive gate. They brought it crashing down as dusk spread its cloak across the Barrens.

Cobalt's cavalry thundered into the stronghold, hundreds of mounted warriors, and also his lightmen, the riders who carried torches. As they engaged the Aronsdale forces, his troops strode behind them, their war cries ringing off the walls. They broke through to the central building and smashed open its great doors, toppling the stone dragons that had guarded the entrance for centuries. The statues shattered on the flagstones.

Cobalt's cavalry rode straight into the hall beyond. Pillars filled it, hundreds of them. Each pair of columns rose up over ten feet, then joined in a circular horseshoe arch. The circle shape supposedly focused the power of a mage, if one believed the tales. Glistening mosaics covered the arches, and red crystal spheres hung from their apexes on gold chains. Row after row of arches filled the hall, a forest of columns. Very few of the Aronsdale defenders remained and most seemed to have reached this hall. They faced the invaders, swords in hand, desperate in their final stand.

The battle raged among the pillars, and the exquisite arches toppled. One of the larger columns that held up the ceiling also fell, and a portion of the ceiling collapsed to the floor.

When several of the defenders retreated toward the far side of the hall, Cobalt's pulse leapt, for he knew they would kill his father rather than let Varqelle escape. He went after them, but a giant warrior on a black horse blocked his way. Fired with battle rage, Cobalt swung his blade through the air in a wide arc. Their swords clanged, and the force of the blow shook through his arm. Although the man had good training and fought well, Cobalt had more than just training. He had spent years leading his men while they tracked, fought, and captured the bandits and killers that made their living in the mountains and borderlands of the Misted Cliffs.

His opponent delayed just a second—and Cobalt's sword found its target. His challenger jerked from the thrust through his chest, his mouth opening as if he couldn't believe it had happened. Cobalt yanked back his sword, and the blade smashed a column covered with gilded mosaics. Broken tiles flew into the air and added their debris to the wreckage on the ground. Dust swirled. The Aronsdale man toppled from his horse and collapsed on the floor, then lay crumpled amidst the shattered tiles.

Breathing hard, his heart pounding, Cobalt looked around. No Aronsdale man remained standing. Cobalt mourned the death and destruction they had wrought here, but the courage of his opponents and the beauty of this citadel had hidden a crime too heinous to allow.

Now that would change.

Cobalt rode deeper into the hall, accompanied by eight of his men. His charger stepped over debris and bodies. He passed under a large arch and into a wide corridor. His spies had mapped the citadel, and he had memorized its layout as he had memorized every fact they gleaned about this place. He had a good guess where he would find the man he sought, for he had read everything ever written about his father and questioned anyone he could find who had known Varqelle. His father was a renowned sovereign, infamous after his failed invasion of Aronsdale. Although Cobalt had never met him, he knew more about Varqelle Escar than most anyone else alive.

It took only moments to reach the Hall of Arcs. King Jarid, the Aronsdale sovereign, gave audiences here when he was at the citadel. Now Jarid was many days' ride to the south, at

Castle Suncroft, the hereditary estate of his family. The hall should have been empty.

Cobalt rode through the great entrance. The Hall of Arcs stretched before him, its walls, ceiling, and floor built from rare violet marble and engraved with interlocking circles. At the far end, six steps led up to a dais, which supported a cushioned bench where Jarid would sit with his queen or advisers during an audience. No one sat there now—but Varqelle stood in front of it, his head lifted, his eyes dark, his shoulders broad. Black hair swept back from his forehead and fell to his shoulders. The years had added streaks of gray.

Although Cobalt had seen portraits of his parents at the Diamond Palace where his grandfather lived, he had never met his father. But he had no doubt whom he faced. He rode down the hall, aware of silence behind him. His men waited outside. They knew this meeting was only for the father and the son.

As Cobalt neared the dais, he saw Varqelle more clearly, the gaunt face with a strong chin and nose, the dark eyes and brows, the high cheekbones of his royal heritage. Lines creased his face. He wore a dark gray tunic and leggings tucked into black boots, and a gray cape. A warrior's sword with a massive hilt hung from his leather belt. Cobalt knew then that he and his men weren't the only ones who had killed today; Varqelle's captors would never have willingly allowed the deposed king such a weapon. If they had tried to kill Varqelle, as Cobalt feared, then they had died instead.

Varqelle watched him with a dark, unreadable gaze. Sweat broke out on Cobalt's forehead. Would his father recognize him? Varqelle had no way to know who had attacked; neither Cobalt nor his spies had managed to send a warning. Varqelle had never known his son. Dancer, his queen, had deserted him only months after Cobalt's birth and fled with her child back to the Misted Cliffs. Cobalt had been fifteen by the time Varqelle had built up his army enough for an invasion, but his father still hadn't had sufficient force to take on the Misted Cliffs. Dancer believed Varqelle had attacked Aronsdale because he perceived it as the weakest country among the settled lands, that when his army was strong enough, he would march on her country. Someday Varqelle would have come for his heir. Instead he had lost his throne and his freedom— until now.

Tonight the son came for the father.

Cobalt reined in before the dais, then dismounted and dropped the reins. He knew this horse enough to trust that it wouldn't desert him within these walls.

Then he walked to his father.

Varqelle watched him with no emotion on his ascetic face. His hand rested on the hilt of his sword. Cobalt kept his arms at his sides as he climbed the dais. At the top, he was four steps away from Varqelle. He stood a head taller even than his father, who had a height greater than most men. It was hard for Cobalt to imagine his pale, delicate mother as queen to this man. The years had weathered Varqelle and added to his aura of power. He would crush those he deemed weaker than himself.

Varqelle said, "Well done, my son."

Cobalt's breath stopped. The silence of the citadel seemed to roar in his ears. *His father knew him.*

Cobalt had anticipated this moment for decades. He knew Varqelle's notorious reputation, knew his mother's fear of her husband, knew his grandfather's distrust. But Varqelle was the only father Cobalt would ever have, and in the parched emotional fields of his life, his need to know this man had become a compelling force in his life.

Cobalt went down on one knee, folding his immense frame before his sire. Then he said the phrase he had practiced in his mind a thousand times, since he had been old enough to long for a father.

"I pledge to you my loyalty," Cobalt said.

"I accept." The king's voice rumbled. "Rise, Cobalt."

He stood, and a crystalline power seemed to fill him, as if the cold northern air seared his lungs and heart clean of emotional debris he had accumulated over the decades. He felt strong.

"I have many men," Cobalt said. "We will take you to the Misted Cliffs. King Stonebreaker offers sanctuary."

Varqelle's gaze darkened. "Why? He has no love for me."

Cobalt spoke with suppressed bitterness. "Grandfather has no love for anyone." It had taken him years to convince the king of the Misted Cliffs that Varqelle would be of more use to him free than in prison. "He also has no male heir—except me. If you regain your crown, then someday I will inherit the thrones of both the Misted Cliffs and Harsdown. What matters to Grandfather is that the power of his house will double."

Varqelle's eyes glinted. "As will mine."

"Yes."

The king paused. "And your mother?"

Unease stirred in Cobalt, the one hesitation that had plagued him through his years of planning. He knew the rumors, that his mother had fled her husband's brutality. Dancer had never told him what happened, despite his many questions. But neither had she tried to stop him from following his drive to know his father.

"She is well," Cobalt said. "I would see that she remains that way."

"I also." Varqelle's gaze never wavered. "The Jaguar Throne awaits us."

As much as Cobalt wanted his heritage, he had his doubts. He didn't believe the Misted Cliffs could defeat Harsdown and Aronsdale combined, and he had no desire to embark on a war that would lay waste to three countries. Would they repeat the mistakes of history? Two centuries ago, Jazid and Taka Mal had attacked the Misted Cliffs and nearly destroyed all three countries. They had severed the Misted Cliffs in two, but they couldn't hold their subjugated lands. Harsdown absorbed some of the conquered territory and the rest became a new country, Shazire. It had taken many generations for their realms to recover. It could happen again, this time with the Misted Cliffs attacking two other realms. Cobalt had no wish to precipitate such a ruin.

Yet no matter what his wishes, he couldn't have rescued his father without his grandfather's help. So he had made a devil's bargain. Nor was he certain who to name as the devil—his grandfather...or himself. A dark spirit drove him, restless and wild, full of anger, quenched only when he was riding hard with his men, sword in hand. He wanted to avoid war—but if it happened, he would gladly go into battle with Varqelle.

Varqelle spoke in a shadowed voice. "I accept the offer of my wife's father for sanctuary in the Misted Cliffs. But never forget, my son, that the Jaguar Throne is your heritage. We will reclaim your legacy—no matter what it takes."

2
Cobalt the Dark

Night had fallen by the time Mel finished tending her horse and returned to the house. Her parents could have chosen to live in Castle Escar, the fortress of the Jaguar King high in the northern mountains, but they preferred the sunnier climes and milder countryside here in the lowlands. Their sprawling farmhouse had many wings, all built from sunbask wood, so warm and golden it almost seemed to glow.

Mel went in a side entrance, into the boot chamber. She smiled, thinking of how her mother, Chime, found "boot chamber" so amusing. Born a commoner, Chime had lived on a farm until she was Mel's age. She often told her daughter stories of how they all tramped straight into the kitchen after working in the orchards.

That had been before the mage mistress of Castle Suncroft

had come searching for mages—and found Chime. Mel had heard the story so many times, she knew it by heart. The princes of the Dawnfield line were expected to wed the most powerful mages they could find among the eligible women of Aronsdale. So a reluctant Chime had agreed to marry Prince Muller, cousin to the king, and after a rocky betrothal, they had come to love each other. Then Varqelle had invaded Aronsdale. Mel shuddered. Had he succeeded eighteen years ago, he would have executed her father, possibly her pregnant mother as well. Mel would never have been born. It disquieted her to know Varqelle still lived, imprisoned far to the north.

While Mel cleaned her gear from her training with the army earlier that day, she mulled over the fate that had put her father on the throne. Varqelle had commanded a more powerful military than Aronsdale, but Aronsdale had mages. Legends told of armies backed by a mage queen, and those tales strummed a chord within her. In both a literal and figurative sense, mages gave light. Red spells brought warmth, orange eased pain, yellow soothed emotions, green read emotions, blue healed injuries, and indigo healed emotions. A mage had a maximum color she could use, and she could do spells with that or any lower color. Red and orange mages were most common, though they numbered only in the twenties. Yellows were rarer. The only known greens were Chime and the mage mistress at Castle Suncroft. Skylark, the mistress here, was the only pure blue. Iris, the Aronsdale queen, was a rainbow, with blue as her strongest hue. Muller, Mel's father, was the only living indigo, and legend claimed King Jarid was a purple mage. Together, they had all helped defeat Varqelle.

"Lucky for them I wasn't involved," Mel muttered as she put away her practice sword. Fighting was easier. It frustrated her that she could do so little with her magecraft. She wondered if she would ever figure out her maximum color or shape. Geometric shapes determined the strength of a spell. The more sides to the shape, the more power it gave. A triangle offered less than a square, which was less than a pentagon, and so on. A circle was essentially a polygon with an infinite number of sides, which made it the most powerful two-dimensional shape. The sphere was the highest form of all, a three-dimensional polyhedron with an infinite number of sides. A mage could draw on any shape up to her maximum. Most used only two-dimensional shapes, and that was all Mel had ever managed.

She sighed. Skylark kept insisting Mel would master at least some three-dimensional shapes. Mel admired Skylark. Really, she did. But the mage mistress exasperated her no end, always pushing, pushing, *pushing* her to make spells Mel couldn't manage.

Mel admired her mother, too, an accomplished green mage who used three-dimensional shapes with up to twenty sides. But Mel feared she would disappoint her. At age nineteen, barely a year older than Mel was now, her mother had ridden with the Aronsdale army. A green mage could neither heal nor add health, but she could make someone *feel* stronger. She could pour confidence into soldiers, firm their wills, raise morale—and during battle that often made all the difference. She could also judge the moods of their enemies, if she could get close enough without being caught, which helped her to predict their strategies, often with considerable accuracy.

When it came to magic, Mel felt more kinship with her father, though he was an indigo, for he also struggled with his spells. Indigos did more than soothe; they could actually give someone a stronger will, a happier outlook, an easing of grief. Legends of such mages were a thousand years old, from a misty age with few historical records. In modern times, no one had believed they existed—until Muller. Usually only women showed the traits of an adept, but after so many centuries of marrying powerful mages, the Dawnfield men had them, too. However, Muller's power responded only to flawed shapes, and it made his spells crooked and erratic, as likely to injure as to heal. In the war, his abilities had been invaluable, but now he rarely used them.

With a grimace, Mel braced her hand against the wall and tried to tug off her boot. Her flaws weren't only in her spells. People tended to ascribe larger-than-life traits to the royal family and wear blinders when it came to their faults, but her parents never missed anything. They always noticed her misbehavior, including her less-than-royal apparel and her penchant for sneaking out late at night to explore the orchards. Mel's mouth quirked upward. Her mother might seem a paragon of queenly elegance now, but Mel's grandmother delighted in telling tales about how wild Chime had been in her youth, running about the farm and causing mischief.

As Mel worked on her boot, she told herself she wasn't bothered by her struggles to make spells. Just as her skill with a sword improved with practice, so would her magecraft. Both pursuits satisfied needs within her, one physical, the other mental. When she trained with the army, she felt strong, not only in her body, but also in her character; when she learned mage skills, it strengthened her mind. But it was discouraging that her talent was taking so long to mature.

The blasted boot wouldn't come off, either. Mel yanked— and her foot popped free. She lost her balance and stumbled. She could have fallen, but with so much flexibility, she easily twisted around and caught a hook on the wall. She grinned. All that daily exercise came in handy.

"You look smug," a good-natured voice said.

Mel spun around to see her father, the king of Harsdown, leaning casually against the door frame with his arms crossed. Gray streaked his yellow hair. At forty-six, Muller Dawnfield projected maturity and experience, and the faint lines around his eyes added to that impression. It contrasted with the portraits Mel had seen from his youth, when he had been so beautiful that people had called him pretty. They never said it to his face, though, given his expertise with a sword.

Mel had never understood why it embarrassed him that he had a lithe physique and wielded a sword with grace. She wished she had his art. She didn't care about looking tough; she never would with her slender build. She just wanted to fight well. Part of that came from her drive to feel she could protect herself and her people, and part from the satisfaction it gave her to excel at military disciplines. Chime encouraged her interest, determined Mel would grow up strong. Her instructors praised her skill and said she had a natural talent with the sword. Perhaps it was her Dawnfield blood or the indomitable spirit she inherited from Chime that made her feel such kinship to the warrior queens in her ancestry.

However, Mel still lacked her father's style with a sword. Ironically, the same could be said about their clothes. He was dressed impeccably today in a gold tunic over a white shirt and darker gold leggings tucked into knee-boots. Embroidery edged his shirtsleeves, and topazes and opals studded his finely tooled belt. He was without doubt the best dressed warrior in Harsdown.

"Hello, Father," she said.

"Where have you been?" Muller said. "We expected you at supper."

"I was doing field exercises with Lieutenant Windcrier."

Muller didn't look convinced. "He and the others were back over an hour ago."

"I also went riding in the orchards," she admitted.

"What about your studies?" He endeavored to put on a stern expression. "Your tutors say math is the only thing you aren't behind in."

Mel held back her smile. No matter how hard he tried, he could never manage to be mad at her. "I like math."

"Yes, well, you have other subjects, you know." Bewilderment tinged his voice. "And why do you dress that way? You're a lovely woman, Mel, but you act as though you think you're a boy."

She walked over to him, her gait uneven with one boot on and one boot off. Going up on tiptoe, she kissed his cheek. "I'm sorry I missed dinner, Papa."

His attempt to look strict melted. "Ah, Mel." Then he remembered himself and frowned. "You need to behave," he added.

"The orchards were beautiful today." Mel stepped back and braced one hand on the wall while she pulled off her other boot. "I lost track of the hours."

Muller sighed. "I don't know what to do with you."

She gave him her most angelic smile. "How about letting me do whatever I want?"

"For flaming sakes," he growled. "You're just like your mother was at your age. She always smiled at me like that and I couldn't think straight. And she never listened to me back then." He squinted at her. "I'm not sure she does now, either. She is just better at making me think she does."

Mel laughed softly. "What a difficult life you have, Papa."

His answering laugh was kind. "You minx." Quietly he added, "I would hope for you no greater difficulties in life than a father who grouses about your clothes."

She set her boots on the tiled floor. "You seem pensive tonight."

"I feel odd. I don't know why."

"Make a mood spell."

He blinked. "For who?"

"Yourself." Mel went to the wall opposite the door and took her shoes off the shelf. "It might surprise you." She often tried such spells. Sometimes they gave her unexpected insights into her own thoughts.

"I already know how I feel," he said. "Besides, my mood spells aren't reliable."

Although his tone was casual, Mel knew what it cost him to make that admission. She turned around, a shoe in each hand. "They are just different, Papa. So powerful! You're the only indigo alive."

His face gentled. "A powerful mess. But thank you."

"What does Mother say about your mood?"

"She thinks I worry too much."

Mel walked over to him in her socks. "You do."

"Is that so?" He cocked an eyebrow. "When did you become an expert on the royal moods?"

"Everything will be fine," she assured him. "You will see."

He offered her his arm as they walked out into the hallway. "I hope so."

Mel didn't see any reason to worry. Her parents had been successful with Harsdown. King Jarid had been clever to put two farmers in charge of this country, where farming was the most common way of life. Chime had spent her youth learning to run her family's orchard; Muller's family made their living from their lands and supported the farms of their tenants. Both Aronsdale and Harsdown exported crops and the wares of their craftspeople and imported many of the other goods they needed to live.

During Varqelle's reign, the people of Harsdown had suffered under heavy taxes and a lack of education. Many families had teetered on the edge of poverty. Muller and Chime had instituted wide-ranging programs designed to teach people improved methods of agriculture and animal husbandry, and they had restructured the taxes to be less of a burden. They also started guilds to train teachers and encouraged villages to set up schools. Mel thought it appalling that Varqelle had wrung so much from his country to support his war efforts while so many of his people struggled. Even now, some considered him the rightful sovereign, but in her eyes he had forfeited any right to his title when he put personal ambition before the welfare of his country.

Over the years, Mel had seen the standard of living and education rise among her people. Orchards thrived, crops grew thick in the fields, shops were booming, and merchants came often now to Harsdown.

She couldn't imagine it would ever change.

Cobalt's men rode as hard as they dared with only moonlight to guide their progress. It would have been safer to wait until morning, but Cobalt didn't want to risk that extra time. He had lost men in the battle, men whose deaths he grieved. His force was now more vulnerable to attack. It would take many days to reach the Misted Cliffs, and the sooner they were away from the Citadel of Rumors, the better.

Varqelle sat easily on the stallion they had brought for him.

His confidence in the saddle suggested he had kept physically fit during his confinement in the Barrens. Cobalt had feared to find him broken in a cell. But then, if Jarid Dawnfield had been a brutal man, he wouldn't have let the deposed king live.

Dawnfield was a fool.

At the age of thirty-three, Cobalt was four years younger than Jarid, but he saw far more clearly than the Aronsdale king. Cobalt would never have allowed his enemy to live after vanquishing his army. Tonight was witness to the folly of that choice. But Cobalt was grateful to the Aronsdale king for his ill-advised compassion.

Cobalt had been fifteen when Jarid imprisoned Varqelle, and on that day, Cobalt had begun to make plans to free the sire he had never met. He had also wrestled with the knowledge that another person had taken his heritage, a supposedly masculine girl. He abhorred Melody Dawnfield, not for anything she had ever done—for he had never met her, nor had he any desire to do so—but because she would inherit the throne her family had stolen from his father.

Over the years, his spies had gathered information on the Citadel of Rumors. Aronsdale guarded the keep well, but Cobalt had persevered until he knew its vulnerabilities. He had also worked on his grandfather, Stonebreaker Chamberlight, king of the Misted Cliffs, convincing him to support the mission. As much as Cobalt had loathed asking his grandfather for help, his need to free his father had overcome even his burning resentment of Stonebreaker. When his grandfather had finally given him a force of men, Cobalt had trained them with care, taking time to know them, to assure himself of their prowess as warriors and their loyalty to his cause.

Cobalt had learned to command by pitting his small army against the mercenaries and criminals who roamed the badlands between the Misted Cliffs and Harsdown. These days, people called that territory the borderlands, for it had finally become safe to travel after Cobalt cleaned it up. His men rode with him tonight, brimming with the success of their mission.

Rock formations jutted all around like broken pieces of mammoth pottery. The land stuttered in natural furrows and ridges, and they had to slow their pace, enough to make conversation possible. Cobalt took his spectacles out of a protected sack in his travel bags and put them on so he could see the dark landscape better.

Varqelle smiled slightly. "Glasses?"

Cobalt flushed. It was hardly an imposing or convenient trait for a general. Fortunately, he needed them only for far distances or in the dark. He was a mediocre archer without them, but he didn't need them for sword fighting.

"I almost never use them," he said.

"Like your mother." Varqelle paused, then spoke with a nonchalance that sounded forced. "How is she?"

"Well." Cobalt vividly remembered her words before he had left on this mission; she made him swear that if he came back with Varqelle, he would protect her from her husband. He knew almost nothing about why his mother had left his father, and it greatly disturbed him that she feared Varqelle.

"Has she spoken to you about me?" Varqelle asked.

"Very little." Cobalt felt constrained in talking about her. To him, his father was a stranger, albeit one he very much wanted to know. But Varqelle had the right to ask. Dancer was his queen, though he hadn't seen her for more than three decades.

"She deserted me, you know," Varqelle said.

Cobalt shifted in his saddle. "I know."

His expression hardened. "In Harsdown, the penalty for such desertion used to be execution."

Cobalt stiffened. "You will not harm my mother."

Varqelle made a visible effort to relax. "I have no wish to harm her. But understand, son, I was angry for years. It is hard to forget."

Cobalt hesitated. "It has been a long time. Perhaps now you and she can find some common ground."

"Perhaps." Varqelle didn't sound optimistic. "Does Muller Dawnfield still rule in Harsdown?"

"Aye." It relieved Cobalt to change the subject. "He sits on your stolen throne."

"Castle Escar is the worse for it."

"He and Queen Chime don't live in the castle." Cobalt knew of the mountain retreat only through Dancer's descriptions. She said it reminded her of the Misted Cliffs. It sounded stark and remote, a fortress high in the mountains, away from the fertile plains and gentle countryside. Such a place could appeal to him.

"Where do they live?" his father asked.

"On a farm."

Varqelle laughed. "How dignified."

"It is a rich estate," Cobalt said. "Its output would increase your coffers if you were king again. As you should be."

His father gave him an appraising look, the planes of his face thrown into relief by the moonlight. "I am pleased you would have me back on the Jaguar Throne. But what army will put me there? I find it hard to believe that after eighteen years of letting me rot in the Barrens, the Harsdown army will come thundering to my side to overthrow that silly fop who thinks he is their king."

"Muller Dawnfield is surprisingly well liked," Cobalt admitted. "I don't see why. He seems weak. He is reputed to have talent as a military commander and strategist, but that may be Aronsdale propaganda." Judging from what Cobalt had heard, Dawnfield spent most of his time worrying about trees and clothes. The man's life had spoiled him with too many emotional riches. Strength came from learning to overcome the hells a person lived. Cobalt knew. His life had made him strong. Rage often filled him, too, and a hunger to ride and fight. Perhaps now that he had freed his father, his spirit would calm.

Varqelle spoke dryly. "The Dawnfields did manage to keep me locked up for all those years."

It felt like a rebuke, though Cobalt heard no censure in his father's voice. "I should have come sooner."

"You came when you could. And you did well." For the first time, Varqelle smiled with ease. "It pleases me. You are a fine son, a man to make his father proud."

A fine son. The unexpected compliment left Cobalt at a loss for words. He never heard such from his grandfather. Stonebreaker made no secret of his scorn.

Regardless of what his grandfather thought, though, he wanted Cobalt to inherit the Jaguar Throne. It would increase the influence of Stonebreaker's line. He had declared Cobalt crown prince to the Sapphire Throne of the Misted Cliffs. His daughter, Dancer, should have inherited the title; in lands where royals had only one child, women often held a throne. But Stonebreaker refused to consider her. He wasn't the first king to modify the expectation of "one heir" to "one son." But his queen had died, and he had never remarried. That left only Cobalt to inherit. No matter how worthless Stonebreaker considered him, the fact remained: if Varqelle regained the Jaguar Throne, they could unite

Harsdown and the Misted Cliffs and greatly increase their family's power.

The Chamberlight king, however, had no love for Varqelle. He claimed his son-in-law had sorely abused Dancer until she fled home to her loving father. Cobalt knew better. His grandfather disliked Varqelle because, for a short time, the Harsdown king had replaced him as the primary force in Dancer's life. Cobalt doubted his grandfather cared if Varqelle had taken a rough hand with his wife; Cobalt had felt the force of Stonebreaker's blows plenty in his childhood. So had Dancer. She and Cobalt had lived in fear. But she never told him *why*. In fleeing Varqelle, she had gone home to a monster, and however much Cobalt might love his mother, a part of him could never forgive her for the price her decision had exacted.

The day had come in his youth when Cobalt had fought back against his grandfather. It had enraged Stonebreaker, and he had beaten Cobalt harder. But Cobalt had continued to grow, and to train with a sword and in hand-to-hand combat. When he reached his full height and weight, he towered over all other men. He had become so large that even a man as physically powerful as Stonebreaker no longer dared hit him. Cobalt had sworn to his grandfather that if the king ever touched Dancer or him again, Cobalt would retaliate. Even now, Cobalt continued to train, obsessively, with single-minded determination, as if sheer physical power could overcome the nightmares of his youth. He hated himself for the violent fury that simmered within him, ready to flare, for he believed it made him no better than the man who had taught him that rage.

Stonebreaker had backed away from his worst violence, but his verbal attacks had never stopped. Cobalt suspected his grandfather supported this expedition in part because he hoped Varqelle would help him control his grandson. Or maybe Stonebreaker felt the years pressing on him. He had no other kin, and Cobalt's grandmother had died years ago from a fall in the cliffs. In his darker moments, Cobalt wondered if Stonebreaker had lost control during a rage and killed her. Cobalt hated him—but the king of the Misted Cliffs was the closest he had ever known to a father.

The one light in Cobalt's life was his mother. From her, he learned that love could exist within a family. Fragile and easily broken, it suffered always, yet somehow it survived. If not for Dancer, he might have become so hard that nothing human remained within him. Only she could have convinced him to call off this mission. She never asked that of him, and he could only guess at what it cost her. But she understood; he had to face his father if he was ever to appease the doubts that haunted his life.

Cobalt needed to know this man, Varqelle Escar, or he would never know himself. He had to come to terms with what it meant to be Cobalt Escar; otherwise, he feared one day he would snap from the brutal loneliness he called life and kill either himself or his grandfather.

3
Castle of Clouds

The messengers from Aronsdale arrived late in the day. They had ridden hard, and dust covered their horses and clothes. Mel saw them pound into the yard behind the farmhouse, in front of the stables. As they surrendered their exhausted mounts to stable hands, members of the house staff ran out to them.

Her parents met with the visitors in her father's study, and Mel waited in the antechamber outside. She had changed into blue silk leggings and tunic, more formal attire, for she had recognized the white and indigo livery of the riders. They came from Castle Suncroft, the home of her cousin, King Jarid.

After an hour, her father opened the door. His expression disquieted her; it was as if an avalanche were thundering out of the mountains and he saw no way to stop it from burying them.

"You can come in," he said.

Uneasy, Mel went with him into the study. Shelves with books and scrolls lined the walls, as did star charts and maps of Harsdown. The two riders were rising from high-backed chairs near the desk, with its clutter of scrolls and ink bottles. They bowed to her parents and to her, and then left the room. Muller closed the door behind them. It all happened with an eerie quiet that chilled Mel.

Her mother stood by an arched window across the study, her yellow hair loose, flowing down her back to her waist. Chime's vibrancy was muted today, and Mel had never seen her face so drawn. Sphere-General Samuel Fieldson stood with her. He was a burly man, strongly built, with graying hair the color of granite. He had been a Cube-General during the war against Harsdown and had helped lead Aronsdale to its narrow victory. Now he served as her father's chief military adviser.

Skylark, the mage mistress, was standing by the hearth. The decades had lined her face, but her blue eyes remained alert. Her braid hung over her shoulder, thick and full, completely white. Along with Fieldson and Chime, she served in the inner circle of the King's Advisers.

A portrait of the royal family hung above the fireplace. It had been painted when Mel was six. Curls tumbled around her shoulders and her blue eyes matched those of her parents. Right now, neither of her parents had anything resembling the serene smiles in that portrait.

"What happened?" Mel asked.

Muller walked over to the desk. He gazed down at a scroll held open by a paperweight sculpted in the shape of an ice-dragon. Chime pressed her palm against the window as she watched them.

"Father?" Mel asked.

He turned and spoke quietly. "Cobalt Escar led a company of men against the Citadel of Rumors. They wiped out most of the defenders and freed Varqelle Escar. King Stonebreaker has granted Varqelle asylum."

Varqelle free and the men at the Citadel dead? It couldn't be. Mel had heard tales about Prince Cobalt from travelers. Some called the Chamberlight heir a brute, others named him a demon, but none disputed his cruelty.

"What does it mean for Harsdown?" Mel asked.

Her father pushed his hand through his hair. "Varqelle will demand I return his throne."

Mel stared at him. "He cannot!"

General Fieldson spoke. "Then he will come for it himself. His son has a well-trained force and a reputation as a formidable military leader. Stonebreaker must have supplied the men for the strike against the Citadel of Rumors, which means he is willing to take an aggressor's stance now. I doubt they will stop with the citadel."

"You mean we will fight the Misted Cliffs?" Mel asked.

"I don't know," her father said. "We have lived in peace with them for centuries. They took no side in our war with Harsdown eighteen years ago. But Cobalt is King Stonebreaker's grandson and will be the heir of two kingdoms if Varqelle regains his throne. And he has had many years to convince his grandfather to ally with his father."

Mel absorbed his words. If King Stonebreaker supplied Varqelle with an army, they would ride against Harsdown. Her father would go to war. Maybe die.

"No." More loudly, she said, "No! It must not happen."

Chime came to the desk and laid her hands on it as if drawing strength from the place where she signed documents as the queen of Harsdown. "If he invades, we have no choice but to fight."

"We must prepare," Fieldson said.

"Can we survive against the Misted Cliffs?" Mel asked. "Their army is large."

Her father answered grimly. "It is more than strong enough to defeat ours. We will also have Aronsdale support, but even if Jarid and I combine our armies, we aren't evenly matched with the Misted Cliffs. If my men start deserting back to Varqelle, their former commander, we will be in trouble."

"Harsdown has been under your rule for eighteen years," Fieldson said. "Your army is loyal."

Skylark spoke. "And we have mages."

"No!" Muller's voice exploded. "I will not see my wife and daughter ride to war. Nor you, Skylark. Gods, you're a great-grandmother. You should be knitting on your rocking chair."

Skylark smiled dryly. "I would die of boredom."

Chime came around the desk to him. "I must go. The mage queens have always ridden with the army." Her melodic voice had an underlying steel. She was far more than the lovely vision in that portrait above the hearth. The painter had seen her as a golden-haired angel, but this strong-willed woman had a power beyond what he had captured in the picture.

Mel went over to them. "I will also go with the army." Although she had never faced anyone in genuine combat, she had always known, in the back of her mind, that her day-to-day training was preparation to kill. Until this moment, it hadn't seemed real. But she could never remain here in safety while her parents risked themselves.

Her father looked as if he were dying inside. "Were you my son, I could no more refuse you than I could myself."

"Son or daughter," Mel said. "It makes no difference."

"But it does to me," her father said.

Fieldson spoke. "Muller, your wife has gone into battle before. Her help was invaluable. And your daughter is as well trained as any of the junior officers her age."

Muller regarded him with a chill gaze that Mel hoped he never turned on her. "What man encourages another to send his wife and daughter to their deaths?"

"I would have *none* of you go into combat," Fieldson said. "Not Mel, not Chime, not you. But what would you have us do? You lead the army and we cannot win against the Misted Cliffs without other mages. Even with them, we might lose."

Muller scowled at him. Then he swung around to Skylark. "What say you, Mage Mistress?"

"If you go to war," she said, "someone has to stay here and govern Harsdown." She nodded to Chime. "The queen."

"Yes." Muller nodded. "You are right."

"And it is true I am elderly," Skylark said. "I would slow down the army."

Muller gave Fieldson a pointed look. "It appears my mage mistress does not agree with you."

"I agree about Mel," Skylark said. "She should go. She has the ability and the training."

"I will not send my heir to die," Muller said flatly.

Fieldson shook his head. "If only Jarid had executed Varqelle."

"Do not criticize my cousin and our king," Muller said. But he sounded tired. They all had to be having the same thought.

"It might have made no difference," Chime said. "Had Jarid executed Varqelle, Prince Cobalt probably would have raised an army anyway, to avenge his father's death and regain his throne."

"But why would Stonebreaker want a war?" Mel asked. "Surely he must see there would be no real winners."

"They will consider it a victory if Varqelle regains his throne," Chime said grimly. "No matter what they destroy."

"Jarid sent an envoy to the Misted Cliffs," Muller said. "Perhaps the situation can be resolved without combat." He looked around at them. "But we must prepare the army. Just in case."

The Castle of Clouds stood atop a massive cliff, part of a wall of cliffs that stretched to the north and south for many leagues. They towered over the lowlands and marked the western border of Harsdown with the larger country of the Misted Cliffs. Almost no one lived in that desolate region. The castle was inaccessible except to those few who knew the convoluted path to its apex. It took its name from the clouds that swirled around its parapets and walls.

Centuries ago, a Chamberlight king had built the castle for his wife. It consisted of towers—only towers—surrounded by a high wall. The white stone blended with the clouds. Spires topped the domes, and pennants snapped in the wind, each with a filled-in blue circle on a white background. The circle was drawn to resemble a sphere, the symbol of the House of Chamberlight. Flying buttresses braced the walls, and bridges arched among the towers. Two statues of ice-dragons guarded the path to the main gate. The keep had a courtyard and stables, but little else within its wall. No other construct existed like it in any of the settled lands, not in Shazire to the south, Jazid or Taka Mal to the east, Aronsdale and Harsdown in the central lands, or here in the western lands of the Misted Cliffs, which stretched from Harsdown to the western coast, where the Blue Ocean rolled to the horizon.

Above the castle, the River of Diamonds flowed through the mountains and fell in a long waterfall into the Lake of Ice. The land around the lake supported the only cultivated fields in this region. With its remote location, the castle had to sustain itself. It served as a sentry on the border, but nothing more; the royal court presided over by King Stonebreaker was in the Diamond Palace in the heavily populated lowlands west of the cliffs.

Dancer Chamberlight Escar lived year round in the Castle of Clouds. Cobalt knew she had chosen this retreat as a refuge from the court. He also loved the fortress. In his childhood, his grandfather had only let them spend part of the year here, away from him. Cobalt had treasured those times of freedom from violence and acrimony. Then he could almost put aside his bewildered anger. He had never understood why his mother had left Varqelle for the nightmare of Stonebreaker's violence, and she had always refused to discuss the subject. She claimed she was protecting Cobalt, and he never doubted she meant it. Why go to Stonebreaker, then? True, his grandfather would never have allowed her another retreat; he would have sent his army for her if she had fled to anyone else. But he had arranged her marriage. He wouldn't have ripped her away from her husband if she had chosen to stay.

Dancer would say only that he was better off here. Was his father such a monster? Varqelle's blood flowed in Cobalt's veins. Cobalt had freed him because it was a son's duty to his sire and king, but his wish to know his father often pressed on him more than those more traditional reasons.

Cobalt and his mother had agreed he would bring Varqelle to the castle first, instead of to the Diamond Palace. Dancer wanted to face her estranged husband in the safety of her retreat. It would be difficult enough for her to see him without also having to deal with Stonebreaker.

So Cobalt took his father to the clouds. Before dawn, they headed up a trail into the cliffs. As they went higher, fog curled around them, wet against his cheeks. Wind tugged his dark hair in its warrior's queue. His father constantly scanned the austere landscape, and Cobalt didn't doubt he was memorizing the route. Varqelle had never been here before; after Dancer left her husband, Stonebreaker had forbidden Varqelle to see her.

They reached the castle in the afternoon. Its wall stood four stories high and surrounded a wonderwork of towers. Sentries on top of the wall had watched their approach, and as Cobalt and his men arrived, the massive gate creaked open.

Varqelle tilted his head back to view the towers clustered at different heights. "Pretty."

"Yes," Cobalt said. The beauty of the castle soothed him despite its stark location, or perhaps because of it. He breathed deeply. This high up, the crystalline air was seared dry of moisture.

His father fell silent as they rode through the gate. They entered the narrow courtyard that curved around the base of the towers. The gatekeeper leaned out of his window in the small tower that flanked the gate and called down to the gatekeepers. Soldiers on horses patrolled the courtyard, and stable hands in the blue and silver livery of the House of Chamberlight hurried to attend the arriving company. Cobalt and Varqelle rode side by side through the commotion.

A slender man with wispy gray hair approached them, astride a dappled horse. He wore Chamberlight livery, and a large silver medallion with sapphires hung around his neck. Tenson Gray directed the castle staff and had served here for decades.

Matthew Quietland, a taller man in homespun clothes, rode at Gray's side on a chestnut horse. Matthew had been a stable hand with Dancer's household for as long as Cobalt could remember and oversaw the stables here. An odd sensation warmed Cobalt. Very few people evoked it from him. He wasn't sure what it meant, but he did know it pleased him to see the taller man. Matthew had offered an oasis of kindness when Cobalt had been a small boy running around these towers with smudges of dirt on his face.

Cobalt raised his hand in greeting to the two men.

"Hoy, there!" Gray made his way through the commotion of arriving warriors and running servants. "It is good to see you, Your Highness." His gaze flickered to Varqelle.

Cobalt turned to Varqelle. "Father, may I present Tenson Gray, our steward." Then he said, "Goodsir Gray, my father, Varqelle, King of Harsdown." He wanted to introduce Matthew as well, but protocol in the Misted Cliffs allowed introductions only for a servant of Gray's higher rank. Cobalt had little patience with customs that dismissed a man like Matthew, but he didn't want to risk offending his father, either.

Gray bowed from the waist. "I am honored, Your Majesty."

Varqelle inclined his head. "My greetings, Goodsir."

Matthew slid off his horse and bowed deeply. He could have spoken to Varqelle, but custom neither required nor encouraged it. Varqelle hardly even looked at him as he dismounted and handed him the reins, which were dyed the Chamberlight blue.

Cobalt swung off Admiral. As Matthew took the reins, Cobalt gave him what he hoped was a friendly expression. It felt stiff and unpracticed on his face, but he didn't want Matthew to think he shared Varqelle's dismissive attitude. Matthew's face gentled into a familiar smile. He nodded to Cobalt, then led their mounts around the towers toward the stables.

Varqelle craned back his head to look up at the walls. "An odd choice, that, a castle of only towers."

"But pleasing," Cobalt said.

Varqelle quirked a smile at him. "I rather like it."

Startled, Cobalt returned the smile. It stretched the muscles of his face in odd ways. Then he escorted Varqelle to a large tower on their right. Cliff-terns wheeled around its dome and broke the silence with their eerie cries. Cobalt felt his heartbeat in the veins of his neck, and sweat soaked his collar. He suddenly wanted to run and run until he exhausted himself. Unable to escape in such a manner, he instead escorted his father inside.

The base of the tower joined with two others to form a large hall three stories in height. Heavy beams held up its ceiling and clusters of gourds hung from the rafters. An arcade of white-washed columns painted with blue borders circled the hall and curved at their tops in scalloped arches that supported the balcony. The colonnade looked different today, though Cobalt couldn't place why.

Then it hit him; the architecture echoed the arches that he and his men had destroyed at the Citadel of Rumors. He felt heavy, remembering the deaths. But he had done what needed doing and his regrets wouldn't change that. What use was his remorse? It implied the hope of redemption, and he knew the truth, that his soul was parched of goodness. A man who had killed so many times—and who secretly entertained thoughts of murdering his own grandfather and king—was beyond salvation.

A figure appeared on the balcony.

She came forward and stood with her hands on the railing. Hair the color of a raven's wing, just barely streaked with gray, framed her alabaster face and fell over her shoulder in a braid to her waist. She had a slender, graceful build. Faint lines creased the corners of her large, dark eyes. Her delicate cheekbones and small nose gave her an ethereal aspect, one heightened by the white silk of her tunic and trousers. Cobalt had seen portraits done in her youth; she had been lovely at age sixteen, when she had borne her first and only child. The years had added maturity, elegance, and an indefinable quality that made it hard to look away from her face. Now, at forty-nine, his mother's beauty was devastating.

Her attention was riveted on the man at Cobalt's side, the husband she hadn't seen in more than three decades. Varqelle met her gaze, his expression guarded and unreadable. A sphere of glass seemed to enclose them and leave Cobalt outside.

Dancer broke the tableau first. She walked along the balcony to a spiral staircase and descended to the main hall. Cobalt was acutely aware of how slight she was compared to him and Varqelle, especially when they stood here in leather and metal armor and chain mail, with swords at their sides. How had Stonebreaker justified beating this frail woman? Cobalt didn't want to think what that said about Varqelle, that Dancer had chosen to live with Stonebreaker instead of with him.

She stopped before them with no welcome in her eyes and looked up at Varqelle. "My greetings, Husband."

Varqelle looked down at her. "Wife."

Cobalt waited. He wasn't certain what he had expected— perhaps explosions or some great revelation. Maybe secretly, in a deep place where he didn't want to admit the truth, he had hoped they might be glad to see one another.

None of that happened.

Dancer looked toward the entrance behind him and Varqelle. Cobalt could hear his men out in the courtyard; they were making more noise than usual. Probably they were excited to be home. He didn't turn around to look; this moment was too important to let anything distract him. He had told his men that under no circumstances was anyone to disturb him and his parents, not even if the castle were falling off the cliff or the sun out of the sky.

Dancer shifted her gaze to him. "Your men must be tired and hungry." Her tone was courteous. Impeccable. She was also so distant, she could have been encased in ice.

"We've had a long ride," Cobalt said. The rumble of his voice, deeper than that of other men, sounded threatening next to her soft tones. He wanted to reassure her, but he didn't know how.

"I will see that Goodsir Gray takes care of it," Dancer said.

"Thank you." Cobalt had never felt this stilted with his mother.

She spoke to Varqelle. "Perhaps you and Cobalt will join me in the Cloud Room? We could have—have tea. Wine." She caught her lower lip with her teeth.

Varqelle didn't look any more comfortable than his wife or son. Cobalt knew too little about him to judge, but he almost thought that behind his father's dark gaze and composed expression, he was...relieved? There had been no recriminations. Perhaps this might go all right after all—

"Ho!" a voice outside called.

Cobalt almost jumped. What the blazes? Surely his officers wouldn't come in now. As he started to turn, Dancer looked past him, her forehead creased—

The color drained from her face.

Puzzled, Cobalt shifted his focus to the entrance—and froze. No. It couldn't be. *Not now.*

Stonebreaker Chamberlight, king of the Misted Cliffs, stood framed in the archway.

4
Storm Tower

Mel whipped up her sword to parry a blow from Bricklayer. They were practicing on a field behind the stables, as they had done most of their lives, ever since the two of them had been old enough to lift the wooden play swords Brick's father had made.

Their relative abilities had varied over the years. They had been fairly evenly matched as small children, but they had only been playing with toys then. As they matured, they began practicing with blunted metal swords. In adolescence, Mel had grown faster than Brick, and she had almost always bested him. Then he had shot up like a cornstalk, tall and gangly. His voice deepened next, and his body beefed up with muscle. For a while during that frustrating time, Mel had lost every bout, unable to match his reach or strength. Gradually she learned to take advantage of the speed her smaller size and lithe build afforded her. Now they were evenly matched again, relying on skill and experience when they challenged each other.

However, today their bouts had changed. No longer was it just exercise, a game, a friendly competition. Their lives could soon depend on how well they trained. Brick would ride with the army if Varqelle invaded Harsdown. And Mel's parents had decided; if it came to war, Chime would rule Harsdown while Muller defended the country. Mel would serve as a mage and a junior officer for the army. She saw no other path she could take in good conscience.

After a few minutes, Brick sent her sword spinning. Mel glared at him and heaved in a breath, her hand clenched on the strap of her wooden shield, sweat soaking her tunic.

Brick raised his sword. "Ho!" He sounded tired and smug.

"Ho, yourself." But Mel smiled. "Well done."

"You, too." His crooked grin revealed strong, white teeth. He was a bulky youth, her lifelong friend, neither handsome nor plain, with brown hair that flopped over his ears. A friend who might soon die—and she could do nothing to stop this march of events toward war.

He rubbed his arm across his sweating face. "Long bout."

"Aye." Mel retrieved her sword from where it had landed on the packed dirt. "I guess I'm distracted."

He laughed amiably. "By my great swordsmanship, eh?"

"Hah."

They headed back to the house and parted with a promise to meet tomorrow. Mel tried not to imagine Brick in battle. She knew he would be a good soldier, but somehow that made it worse. He shouldn't have to risk his life because Cobalt Escar and his outlaws had murdered Aronsdale warriors to free a prisoner who should have died eighteen years ago.

Inside, Mel walked down the hallway, lost in thought. The sunbask paneling on the walls and the paintings of the summer countryside usually soothed her, but today nothing helped.

Her bedroom was large, all constructed in sunbask, from the parquetry floor to the walls, ceiling, and rafters. Rugs woven in blue and gold yarn warmed the floors. The four-poster bed stood across the room by one of the windows. Her favorite blue quilt lay fluffed on it, worn and freshly laundered. Shelves with her books took up one wall and her desk sat in the corner. It annoyed Mel that her parents expected her to study so much. She already had an education beyond what most people attained. Although her studies interested her, she felt she had done enough. By law, a person reached the age of majority at sixteen. At eighteen, she was more than old enough to decide her path in life.

As far as anyone knew, Mel was the strongest mage among the girls of her generation; as such, she was betrothed to Aron, her cousin, the crown prince of Aronsdale. About one year her junior, he had the Dawnfield good looks, dark hair, and dark eyes. He was supposed to marry the strongest mage in Aronsdale, not Harsdown, but no one quibbled over the detail. Although Harsdown was technically now a territory of Aronsdale, the two countries and their sovereigns operated on almost equal footing, and Harsdown had the larger area. Mel saw Aron once or twice a year and they wrote each other often. She could envision herself coming to care for him. But now, with the threat of war looming over them, her thoughts turned from romance to fear. As a newly commissioned officer, seventeen-year-old Aron would ride with the Aronsdale army.

Her betrothed could die.

A cry came from her bed. Startled out of her gloom, Mel squinted at the quilt. It looked normal. She went over and investigated, but found nothing on or under the covers. Crouching down, she peered under the bed.

Two yellow eyes blinked at her.

"Well, who are you?" Mel gently pulled out a small ball of fur, a powder-gray kitten. It resembled the stable cat, who had recently had a litter of babies fathered by a tomcat that prowled the farm.

The kitten mewed piteously.

"Are you lonely?" Cradling the small animal, Mel sat cross-legged on her bed. As she petted the kitten, the designs on her bedcovers caught her attention, all those chains of blue octagons on a lighter blue background. Mel loved the quilt. At age nine, she had figured out how to calculate the interior angles of each octagon and also its exterior angles. She liked geometry. Always she was coming up with relations to describe shapes. She often later discovered that her proofs had already been worked out in her books, but sometimes she came up with new ones. Someday when she knew enough, she planned to write her own book about geometry. It all connected to her magecraft. But it was hard to imagine turning her studies to the service of war.

The mathematics of death.

Mel bent her head, disheartened. As she brushed her hand over the kitten's front leg, it mewled in protest.

"What's the matter?" Mel murmured. She examined the leg and realized it was hurt, either sprained or broken. Dismayed, she looked around her room. The window nearest to the bed was open. The kitten could have climbed up a bush outside and tumbled inside the room. Its leg had probably already been injured. She doubted that short fall would harm an otherwise healthy kitten, but it could have made its leg worse.

"We'll get you help." Mel started to stand, but the kitten cried again. She settled back on the quilt, taking care not to jostle its leg. As soon as she calmed the animal enough to move, she would find someone who could set its leg. As she petted the kitten, the octagons on the quilt shimmered and their blue grew more intense. She filled with blue light. Beautiful blue light.

"That is a lovely animal," a woman said.

Mel surfaced from her reverie. Her mother was standing in the doorway, a slender woman in a glistening tunic and trousers sewn from layers of emerald and gold silk. Her luxuriant golden hair curled around her face, shoulders, and arms. It amazed Mel when people said she looked like her mother. Mel knew they were being kind, that she resembled a boy more than a girl. She would never have Chime's beauty.

"Didn't I close that door?" Mel asked. She tended to forget, which could be embarrassing given that she had just changed her clothes.

"You did. But no one answered when I knocked." Chime hesitated. "I felt your spell. I feared you were hurt."

Mel stared at her blankly. "What spell?"

"Your blue one. The healing."

Blue? "I don't know what you mean."

"May I come in?"

"Yes. Of course."

Chime came over and sat on the bed. "You aren't hurt?"

"I'm fine." Mel touched the kitten's front leg. "She hurt her leg."

Her mother examined the kitten. "She seems fine."

"What?" Mel gently probed the leg, but she found no trace

of an injury. This time when the kitten mewled, she sounded annoyed rather than in pain.

"Do you think I healed her?" Mel asked, bewildered.

Chime beamed at her. "It seems so."

Elation surged in Mel. "But why now? Blue spells never worked for me before."

"Never?"

"Sometimes maybe I would get a hint of something." Mel shrugged. "But no real spell."

"Did you do anything differently this time?"

"I didn't try. I just—well, sort of meditated." For Mel, it was a rare state. Usually she was too busy with her life to slow down and be contemplative.

"Perhaps you were pushing too hard before." Chime scratched behind the kitten's ear, evoking a contented purr. "You're also still maturing into your abilities."

"Maturing, pah," Mel grumbled. "When you were my age, you had already reached your full potential."

Chime spoke quietly. "That's true. And I've never made a blue spell in my life."

A tickling caught in Mel's throat, anticipation and nerves. "I will talk to Skylark. See what she says."

"I have been so proud of your talents." Chime's smile dimmed. "But of late I find myself wishing you had no mage-craft at all."

Mel's hand stilled on the kitten. "Would it matter? If Varqelle takes the Jaguar Throne, I doubt he will show us the same compassion Cousin Jarid gave him. At least if I go with the army, I'm *doing* something to protect us."

Chime took her hand. "We will manage. Somehow."

Mel squeezed her mother's fingers. Better to fight than to wait for retribution from a king bent on vengeance. Rumors ran wild now. They claimed Varqelle's monstrous son, Cobalt, the Midnight Prince, would lead Varqelle's army. Varqelle had never made it a secret that he considered Mel's family "weak, pretty pretenders." It made her skin crawl. Women weren't always killed by an invading army, but she would rather die in combat than have them touch her or her mother.

She saw that same fear reflected in Chime's eyes. The kitten rubbed Mel's hand, purring, fine now. She wished the wounds among their three countries could be as easily healed.

The Gales Chamber in the Castle of the Clouds took up half the third level in the Storm Tower. Its floor, curving walls, and domed ceiling were white marble. So were the thrones for the king and queen that stood on a hemispherical dais on the outer edge of the room. White cushions softened the marble seats and diamonds inlaid the high backs. Stonebreaker Chamberlight, king of the Misted Cliffs, sat in one throne. He wore the traditional garments of his station, blue trousers and knee-boots, and a snowy white tunic with a blue sphere on the chest. The Chamberlight sphere. Scholars claimed it symbolized the perfection of Chamberlight rule. A sapphire medallion hung around his neck on a gold chain. He was leaning slightly to the side, one elbow on the arm of his chair, his posture a study in regal carriage.

It didn't fool Cobalt. It never had.

He should have known Stonebreaker wouldn't respect Dancer's wish to face Varqelle in private. *Saints forbid you might show sympathy,* Cobalt thought, wishing he could pierce the king with his anger. Dancer should have sat in the queen's throne; as her mother's heir, she had the right. But she came nowhere near Stonebreaker. She stood by the door on the opposite side of the chamber, ready to escape.

Cobalt waited below the dais while Varqelle paced back and forth up by Stonebreaker. "Some of the soldiers in the Harsdown army would probably come over to us," Varqelle was saying. "I had good men."

"We cannot count on this," Stonebreaker answered. "It has been eighteen years. Many of them will no longer be in the army. Others may have genuinely changed allegiance to Dawnfield."

Varqelle considered him from the other side of the empty throne. "My men are loyal."

"It has been a long time." Stonebreaker tapped his fingers on the arm of his chair. "Muller Dawnfield is reputed to be a good commander. He also has Sphere-General Fieldson."

Varqelle didn't argue. Cobalt approved of his restraint. Stonebreaker detested people who challenged him, and neither he nor Varqelle had any liking for the other. However, Varqelle had no military force, nor was he likely to get one by angering Stonebreaker. If they did raise an army, Cobalt knew his father expected him to act as his general. Why else free Varqelle? Why, indeed. Cobalt wanted answers to questions that had driven him all his life. He was part Chamberlight and part Escar, and he needed to know what that meant. If finding answers meant he would sweep down from the Misted Cliffs at the head of an avenging army, so be it.

"Dancer." Stonebreaker beckoned to his daughter. "Come."

Cobalt gritted his teeth at his grandfather's condescending tone. He turned toward his mother, ready to intervene, but she shook her head slightly at him. She walked forward and her silks drifted around her body. Varqelle watched her with an intensity that burned. When Dancer came onto the dais, Stonebreaker glanced at Varqelle. Cobalt knew then why the king had come here; he wanted Varqelle to see that nothing had changed. Dancer belonged to the Misted Cliffs, not Harsdown. Cobalt wondered why his grandfather had ever agreed to any marriage, given how much he resented anyone taking Dancer's attention. If it was because he wanted an heir and couldn't get another one himself, no sign of that showed in his attitude toward Cobalt.

By tradition, royals had one child. In ages past, the custom had been slightly different: they had one *legitimate* offspring. With infant mortality rates so high, a king made sure he had plenty of progeny available. If something happened to his heir, he legitimized his favorite "spare." Historians placed the origins of the custom in a distant past when resources were few and a sovereign concentrated them on his heir. The supposed experts of those ancient times also claimed the blood of the king and queen was somehow purer if it wasn't "diluted" among more than one child. Cobalt thought his ancestors must have been daft to believe such a theory. More likely, they used it as an excuse to dally with their mistresses.

In this modern age of physicians and advanced herbal lore, children were far more likely to reach adulthood, and society was less tolerant of an adulterous monarch. Some royals had more than one legitimate child, such as King Jarid in Aronsdale. Cobalt would have liked siblings, a younger brother or sister he could love. But he always pushed away the thought. He would never wish his miserable childhood on anyone else.

Dancer mounted the dais and stood before Stonebreaker. "Yes, Father?"

He sat relaxed, his manner deceptively casual. "You have been quiet during this discussion."

"I have nothing to add."

"Really?" He indicated Varqelle, who had gone completely still, like a statue. "Have you no opinion as to whether or not your husband should reclaim his throne?"

Her face showed no expression. "My opinion is that you and my husband are better able to judge matters of war."

Varqelle spoke. "You have nothing to say?" More to himself than her, he added, "You never did."

Cobalt almost retorted that of course a woman of half a century would be more articulate than a sixteen-year-old child bride. But he held back. He knew Dancer; she would answer for herself or not at all. She often kept her silence for the same reason Cobalt kept his: Stonebreaker. Denied the chance to use his fists, the Chamberlight king turned his words into blows. They had long ago learned that fighting his verbal sallies only invited more. And despite Cobalt's warning, even now Stonebreaker sometimes became violent. Better never to speak. However, Cobalt remained on guard, ready to intervene if necessary.

"She has always prattled." Stonebreaker motioned idly at Cobalt. "At least he never talks. It is one of his few redeeming qualities."

Dancer flushed and Cobalt stiffened.

Varqelle looked from Stonebreaker to his wife, his gaze narrowed. Assessing. He spoke to Dancer. "If I regain my throne, will you join me in Harsdown?"

Cobalt felt suddenly shoved off balance. He hadn't expected that question. But he had hoped. Saints, he had hoped. Would they try again, incredibly, after all these years?

Dancer glanced at her father. His steel-gray eyebrows drew together. It was a simple expression, but Cobalt knew what it meant. In his youth, it had preceded the king's rages, when he used his fists. Now it warned of other retaliation, such as his coming here when Dancer had requested otherwise.

She turned to Varqelle. "I have my life here."

His voice tightened. "Thirty-four years ago you swore a vow to me, Dancer Chamberlight *Escar*. Hardly more than a year later you broke it. You have a chance now to make amends. I would think well before you refuse."

Why must you all threaten her? Cobalt thought. *Just tell her you want her back.*

Stonebreaker rose to his feet. "She has given her answer." He grasped his daughter's arm, his large hand clenching it so hard that Cobalt could almost see bruises form. Even as Dancer flinched and tried to pull away, Stonebreaker reached for her other arm.

Cobalt went up the dais, his step firm. He stood closer to Stonebreaker than custom allowed, deliberately intimidating with his height. Cobalt was one of the few people alive who could look down at Stonebreaker.

"I can escort Mother to her suite." Cobalt almost said *the queen,* but he stopped, knowing Stonebreaker would hear it as a taunt, a reminder that she "belonged" to Varqelle.

For an instant, Cobalt feared his grandfather wouldn't release her. Then Stonebreaker dropped Dancer's arm and turned to Varqelle, dismissing his daughter and grandson.

"You and I can continue this over wine," the Chamberlight king told his son-in-law.

Varqelle was watching them all closely. It was a moment before he said, "Yes. Certainly." He didn't look pleased.

Cobalt offered his arm to his mother. She set her palm on his forearm in the traditional gesture of a queen escorted by a male relative. Her hand shook, but his body hid it from the two kings. Cobalt and Dancer descended the dais and crossed the chamber, going past the guards, neither of them looking to either side. When they came outside onto the landing of the staircase, Cobalt closed the door, leaving the others in the room, and he and his mother out here in relative safety.

"Saints." Dancer leaned against the wall and closed her eyes.

"I should have guessed Stonebreaker would come," Cobalt said, angry with himself. "I should have taken Varqelle straight to the Diamond Palace instead of letting them come here to bother you."

She opened her eyes. "Don't castigate yourself. It isn't your fault that neither of them are easy men."

He grimaced. "To say Grandfather isn't easy is an understatement of magnificent proportions."

"I would have wished a different life for you." Moisture gathered in her eyes. "I can bring to you the Chamberlight Throne, the most powerful in these lands, but I cannot give you something as simple as the unfettered love of your family."

"Mother, don't cry." Cobalt spoke awkwardly. "You gave me yours. That is what matters."

She wiped her cheek and tried to smile. "When will you find yourself a wife? It is well past time. You need a lovely young sweetheart."

He couldn't imagine one that would want him. In fact, he could hardly imagine women at all. He had gone to courtesans in the past, but he found little comfort in it. He rarely interacted with anyone. In his youth, Stonebreaker had isolated him from other children, and Cobalt didn't know how to form friendships. He had grown up with no one to talk to except Dancer, Matthew, a few other servants, and the bodyguards who protected him from assassination. If only they could have protected him from the king. Although those days of violence had mostly ended, Cobalt sometimes thought words did more harm than blows. He had little to give to a wife, even if one would have agreed to endure his presence for the rest of her life, which he found unlikely.

"I would inflict myself on no woman," he said.

"Why do you talk like that?" She spoke firmly. "You are a fine man, strong and loyal. You should not lose confidence in your heart or your goodness."

"Goodness?" Only a mother would have such a deluded view of a man like him. "I killed many men to bring Father here. That is hardly goodness."

"You didn't imprison him. Nor are you responsible for his decision to invade Aronsdale." Her hand gripped the stone wall. "His sins are not yours. The same is true of my father, no matter how hard he tries to make you believe otherwise."

Cobalt couldn't talk about Stonebreaker. His emotions there were shards of glass that cut. "Why did you leave my father?"

She went rigid. "Please don't."

"You never answer me. Why?"

"I did what I believed best for you. This will always be my answer." She pushed a tendril of hair off her face. "My life with your father is private."

"You brought me here." To *hell*. "I deserve to know why."

"Because it was better here than there."

"Varqelle is no monster."

"Let it go, Cobalt."

"I *cannot*."

"I did my best." She took a shaky breath. "Someday you will be king, possibly of two countries. It is small recompense for this life, but it was the best I could do."

Cobalt didn't want to argue. It hurt too much. He gestured

toward the stairs. "Shall we go down? I believe the chamber musicians have a concert planned for this evening."

Dancer hesitated, searching his face. "All right." She stepped past, her silks rustling, and headed down the stairs.

Cobalt followed, brooding. Varqelle and Stonebreaker would plot and discuss, until finally they laid the plans for a war that would demolish all three countries, a war where Cobalt would go out and prove to Dancer beyond any doubt that he was, truly, the irredeemable monster the world believed.

The envoy from Aronsdale arrived at the Diamond Palace in the morning of a cool summer day. The fog had burned off and no longer shrouded the lowlands. Fertile countryside started at the base of the mountains on the eastern border of the Misted Cliffs and stretched out to the west in rolling hills of green. The palace sparkled on a hillside, hard and brilliant, its spires translucent, its gilded bulb towers reminiscent of Taka Mal, a country of scalloped architecture and bridges, or of Shazire, land of silk and silver.

Lord Brant Firestoke led the emissaries. He had lived all his life in Aronsdale, more then seven decades, and had served as an adviser for the last two kings. His shoulder-length gray hair swept back from his face, accenting the widow's peak on his forehead. He had deeply set gray eyes. His austere presence had made many a young man feel callow, but beneath Firestoke's sober exterior was a man known for his integrity, humor, and loyalty to the House of Dawnfield.

He rode with an honor guard from the Aronsdale army, thirty men on horseback in ceremonial armor. They wore the colors of Dawnfield, indigo and white. At the border between Harsdown and the Misted Cliffs, a company of fifty Chamberlight men met them, and escorted them through the cliffs to the lowlands beyond.

Now the travelers clattered into a courtyard of the palace, eighty mounted men armed with swords. Although no one had forced the Aronsdale warriors to disarm, the men in the Chamberlight company were at least as heavily armed and they easily outnumbered Firestoke's men.

So the representatives of Aronsdale arrived to negotiate with the Chamberlight king.

Stonebreaker met with the emissaries in the Hall of Sapphires. It was a larger affair than the Gales Chamber in the Castle of Clouds. Diamonds and sapphires encrusted the gilded chairs on the dais and left no doubt as to the wealth of the Chamberlight king, who sat on one of the two thrones. He reigned over a country rich in resources, including the farmlands where most of his people lived and the prosperous mines in the eastern cliffs. His country exported far more goods than it imported, and it was the only settled land with a seacoast and thriving merchant trade. Even after losing a third of its territory two centuries ago, the Misted Cliffs remained the strongest and wealthiest of the settled lands.

Today Stonebreaker gave the second throne on the dais to Varqelle. Cobalt had no doubt about the message his grandfather intended for the envoy: the House of Chamberlight considered Varqelle Escar a full sovereign. It also sent a private, colder message to Dancer. By rights, she should have sat in the second throne—and Stonebreaker knew she would have done so here in the Diamond Palace rather than lose face before the royal court. But he forestalled her. He would of course say he assumed she wouldn't sit with him after she had declined at the Castle of the Clouds. Maybe that was even true. But Cobalt suspected this was retaliation. Dancer had avoided Stonebreaker when he had wanted to make a point with Varqelle, so now he shamed her in front of the royal court and the Aronsdale emissaries.

Cobalt stayed in the columns to the right of the dais, near the wall, inconspicuous. One could learn much by fading into the background. Dancer stood by another column. She had draped herself in blue silks, and she wore a long silk scarf over her head. A veil covered her face. Although she had told him she could see through the veil, it hid her face from everyone except those who looked too closely for courtesy. She wore it often at the Diamond Palace, and it let her watch while she remained hidden.

Lord Firestoke came to the dais and went down on one knee to King Stonebreaker. After a pause that stretched out longer than necessary, Stonebreaker said, "You may stand."

Firestoke rose to his feet. He was lean and fit, with the well-developed shoulders and arms that implied he had wielded a sword often in his youth and continued to practice now. He had an aspect of intelligence, though Cobalt couldn't define exactly why. The best he could say was that the lines of Firestoke's face looked as if they had been set by a man who thought a great deal and acted on his principles.

"The Misted Cliffs bids you greeting," Stonebreaker said, giving a traditional response that indicated welcome tempered by wariness.

Firestoke inclined his head. "King Jarid sends his greetings and salutations."

Stonebreaker raised an eyebrow. "But not himself."

"He wished to come," Firestoke replied. "However, his advisers didn't consider it safe for him to travel."

Cobalt thought it an acceptable answer, neutral without

being coy. Everyone in this room knew why Jarid hadn't come. Even with a promise of safe passage, which the Aronsdale king didn't have, he would have been ill-advised to enter a country whose crown prince had just perpetrated an act of war against him.

Stonebreaker, however, narrowed his gaze. "How convenient."

Cobalt gritted his teeth. What did his grandfather expect, that Dawnfield would be stupid enough to come here himself? Fortunately, Firestoke didn't respond to the dig. He and Stonebreaker continued the formalities and expected protocols, always with subtle jabs from the Chamberlight king.

As a child, Cobalt hadn't wanted to believe his grandfather acted with malice. Every time Stonebreaker had given him some crumb of approval, his hope had surged. Perhaps the king would finally accept him, praise him, even love him. He knew better now. Stonebreaker lacked a crucial trait: He couldn't interpret emotions, neither his own nor those of others. That alone didn't make him cruel. But he also had no moral sense in how he treated people. Combined with his inability to judge the impact of his words or actions, it left him unable to comprehend the harm he caused. He simply didn't care. He was intelligent, however. He knew that to rule successfully, he had to deal fairly with his advisers, officers, and royal court. But he gained some perverse satisfaction in setting people against one another, perhaps because it drew attention away from his own flaws.

Cobalt doubted anything could prevent this war that couldn't be won. His father and grandfather wanted it too much. What unsettled him even more was that a darkness within him welcomed the specter of battle.

* * *

"The answer is clear," Varqelle told Brant Firestoke. "A pretender sits on my throne. If your king does what is right and removes his cousin, we will avoid hostilities."

Firestoke met his gaze. "Harsdown attacked Aronsdale without provocation, Lord Varqelle."

Lord. Not king. Cobalt could almost feel his father bristle, though Varqelle showed no outward reaction. They were seated around an oak table in Stonebreaker's Sapphire Chamber, a circular room deep within the castle. It had a recessed floor and maps of all the countries on the walls. Cobalt had met here with his men to plan his expedition against the Citadel of Rumors, and it was here where they would design strategy against Harsdown. This war was madness and they all knew it; Stonebreaker might have a bigger army, but not by much, and the Dawnfields had their cursed mages. Such an offense, that they sent women into battle; even worse, it worked. Cobalt didn't believe those women were sorceresses, but they did possess an uncanny ability to predict strategies of the opposing army.

"You lost the war," Firestoke told Varqelle. "Why, then, should we relinquish the throne?"

Varqelle answered in a shadowed voice. "You will not win another war. The Jaguar Throne has been held by the House of Escar for over a thousand years."

"No longer," Firestoke said.

"For now," Varqelle said. He and Cobalt had both worn black to this meeting: boots, heavy trousers, tunic, and shirt, all black. It was the color of the jaguar. Cobalt had never seen his father in any other color, except for the studs in his ears, the blue diamonds. They came from the colors of Escar, black with blue accents. Cobalt blue. It was the origin of his name. The colors would fly again in Harsdown when the House of

Escar regained the throne—if they didn't obliterate Harsdown, Aronsdale, and the Misted Cliffs in the process.

Stonebreaker sat back in his chair. "We are three old men arguing about a war that we are too old to fight." He waved at Cobalt. "There is your general. The Midnight Prince, a man without a conscience. The lord who never speaks." He leaned toward Cobalt. "What say you, Grandson? Shall we descend on Harsdown and destroy all the gains they have made in the past eighteen years?"

Varqelle stiffened and his jaw clenched. Cobalt shook his head almost imperceptibly at his father, hoping he understood the caution to restrain himself. Stonebreaker was perfectly aware he had insulted his son-in-law. Parrying his verbal sallies would only escalate the exchange. One of Stonebreaker's greatest "gifts" was the ability to manipulate other people into tearing each other apart while he sat back and listened.

Cobalt had never heard his grandfather admit he was wrong about anything. When Stonebreaker erred or hurt someone, he turned around and accused them. He was an expert at it. He could stir up anger until everyone believed that the person wronged had committed the offense. Cobalt had reached the point where he never responded to his grandfather unless it was absolutely necessary. His silence was his protection.

Now, however, he had to answer or lose face. He had set these events into motion and he would gladly fight for the Jaguar Throne, but he didn't want to wipe out Harsdown in the process. His father's people shouldn't have to die so they could become his people again. Unfortunately, Cobalt saw no alternative that would return the throne to the House of Escar.

Cobalt spoke quietly. "I have no wish to destroy anything."

"You refuse to lead your father's army?" Stonebreaker asked.

Cobalt gritted his teeth. Grandfather knew damn well that wasn't what he had said. He could tell Varqelle was growing angry.

"My father is a brilliant leader," Cobalt said. "I will support him however he sees fit."

"Will you?" Stonebreaker glanced at Varqelle, then at Firestoke. "It seems my grandson will ride on Harsdown."

Cobalt knew what Stonebreaker was doing. The king didn't want blame as the one who declared war, but neither did he want the House of Chamberlight to lose its claim on the Jaguar Throne. Varqelle couldn't retake the throne without an army, but if Stonebreaker supplied those forces, it would end centuries of wary peace between Aronsdale and the Misted Cliffs. The Chamberlight king wanted Aronsdale to believe other people agitated for this war. Not him.

Varqelle spoke to Firestoke. "You have our response for King Jarid. Return the throne or we will take it by force."

"You failed the last time you sought to break Aronsdale." Anger edged Firestoke's words. "Will you try again and destroy three countries?" He jerked his head toward Cobalt. "Aronsdale has already seen what violence your general is capable of."

Cobalt clenched his fist under the table, on his knee. He had set himself up for this, for it had been the only way to enlist his grandfather's support. Stonebreaker would get the power he wanted and his grandson would have the notoriety. Cobalt's large size and forbidding nature didn't help; just by themselves, they darkened his reputation. He would regain the throne if he could, but damned if he would let Stonebreaker make him look like a monster.

"I do not wish to see three countries ruined," Cobalt said.

Firestoke met his gaze. "Yet you threaten us—surrender or fight. We will not submit to these demands. This will be true no matter how many threats you make."

"We have given you our terms," Varqelle told Firestoke. "Take them to your king. We will await his response."

"I already know his response," Firestoke said. "He will never surrender Harsdown. That is why he sent me here."

"Then it is decided." Varqelle's voice rumbled. "And you are fools."

Firestoke rose to his feet. "We will defeat you again, Lord Varqelle."

Cobalt's father stood as well. "You would do well to remember that the man you address will soon be your king."

Firestoke faced him across the table. "You will never rule in Aronsdale. Not as long as I live."

"I wager that will not be long," Varqelle said.

"You threaten my life?" Firestoke asked, his tone hard.

A muscle jerked in Varqelle's cheek. "You are here only on our tolerance."

Stonebreaker was watching the confrontation with an avid interest that sickened Cobalt. The Chamberlight king glanced at Varqelle, who met his gaze. Then Varqelle beckoned the guards posted at the door. "If you would escort Lord Firestoke to a place of custody."

Damnation! Cobalt knew exactly what such "custody" meant. They would kill the envoy as a message to King Jarid. The situation was spinning out of control. Even if the Houses of Chamberlight and Dawnfield had already declared hostilities, murdering such an honored emissary would inflame an already volatile situation.

Cobalt stood up. "No."

Everyone turned to him.

"You would proceed in another manner?" Varqelle asked.

"Yes." *How?* Cobalt thought fast. He had to get Firestoke safely out of the country, but in a way his father wouldn't see as a betrayal.

The answer came to him with sudden, blinding clarity. By freeing his father and setting up this situation, he had forced the House of Dawnfield into a corner. They knew what Stonebreaker's armies could do to them. They would be desperate. It gave him the perfect chance to take what they would never otherwise give. He suddenly knew how he could attain his goal—Harsdown—without destruction.

Both triumph and foreboding filled Cobalt. "I have a proposal for your king," he told Firestoke. "I would have his answer without delay." They had to let the envoy return to Aronsdale if Cobalt wanted him to carry the proposal.

Firestoke went very still. "Yes?"

Cobalt regarded him with an unwavering gaze. "I propose that I marry Muller Dawnfield's daughter, the current heir to the Jaguar Throne."

5
The Jaguar Groom

In the silence that followed Cobalt's words, he thought he could hear his own pulse. His insane proposal made perfect sense. If he married Melody Dawnfield, she became Melody Dawnfield Escar. Their child would inherit the Jaguar Throne. It would return the title to the House of Escar without shedding one drop of blood.

Varqelle stared at Cobalt as if his son had grown a second head. For once Stonebreaker seemed at a loss for a comeback.

Brant Firestoke narrowed his gaze at Cobalt. Then he said, "I will carry your proposal to King Jarid."

Stonebreaker slowly rose to his feet. "So you have come around after all," he told Cobalt.

After all? Cobalt could have socked him. Stonebreaker

wanted it to sound as if he had suggested the marriage and his grandson had resisted until now.

Cobalt crossed his arms. "I hope you won't continue your attempts to talk me out of this, Grandfather. My decision is made."

A muscle twitched in Stonebreaker's cheek. He didn't like his own duplicitous methods turned against him. Well, he could live with it. Either that, or he could start a verbal war right here and weaken their position.

Stonebreaker turned to Firestoke. "My men will escort you to the border. We await King Jarid's response."

Relief washed over Cobalt, though he schooled his face to keep it hidden. He had no wish to marry a Dawnfield, especially not a woman who reputedly looked like a man, but it would achieve their ends. The proposal probably wouldn't satisfy his father; it would put his grandson on the throne, not him. But Varqelle surely saw the advantage of protecting Harsdown—his country, his people, and his home. Although the idea wasn't perfect, it just might work.

If Dawnfield agreed.

The creak of stable doors awoke Mel. She lifted her head from her pillow and peered into the darkness. Predawn light sifted through the window nearest her bed. The stamp of hooves and the snort of horses came from outside.

Mel got up and went to the window. A short distance behind the house, men were dismounting from horses. They wore the livery of King Jarid at Castle Suncroft. Her father was out there as well, a robe over his sleep shirt and trousers as he spoke in a hushed voice with the visitors.

She laid her hand against the diamond shapes engraved in the window frame. Closing her eyes, she imagined green leaves and lush grass. A spell grew within her, and she probed her father's mood. The diamond was a weak shape, just two dimensions with only four sides, so her spell picked up only a vague sense. Something dismayed him—

Her?

Mel opened her eyes. She could think of nothing she could have done to trouble her father, at least beyond the normal state of affairs. She went to her bed and moved the sleeping kitten off her robe. As she pulled on the velvet dressing gown, she left her room and padded barefoot down the hall.

It was cool outside. Mel walked through the gardens behind the house and approached the stables, where her father was talking to the messengers, and stable hands were seeing to their horses. In the flurry of all that activity, no one noticed Mel.

"It is worse than her riding with my cavalry," her father told one visitor, a craggy man with a sunburned face. Muller was clenching a scroll with the seal of Castle Suncroft.

"King Jarid won't force her to accept the decision," the man said. "It is her choice."

"What choice?" Mel asked behind them.

Muller spun around. When Mel saw his look of pain, she realized what had happened and a chill went through her. "It has begun, then? Varqelle has invaded?"

"How much did you hear?" Muller asked.

She pushed her hand through her tangled hair. "That you believe a choice I have to make could be worse than riding with your army."

He spoke with difficulty. "Mel—"

"Tell me." She felt as if she were about to fall.

"Stonebreaker has a proposal that will avoid this war."

Such news should have overjoyed him. Why did he look as if he were attending a funeral? "What is it?"

He didn't answer. When the moment stretched out too long, Mel said, "Father? What do they propose?"

He spoke in a dull voice. "That you and Prince Cobalt wed."

Mel waited for him to laugh. It was a horrendous joke, one she would never have imagined from him.

He didn't smile.

Finally she found her voice. "This is a terrible jest."

He looked as if he had aged ten years. "It is no jest."

"No." She couldn't accept that.

"It is the perfect solution." Bitterness edged Muller's voice. "Brilliant. The Misted Cliffs win. Chamberlight wins. Escar wins. Everyone wins." Grimly he added, "Except us."

"No! Father, no."

"Gods forgive me, Mel, but I could never see you marry that man no matter how much it would mean for our people."

Mel folded her arms and shivered in the chill autumn morning. "Cobalt the Dark is crazy."

"They are all crazy," Muller said, "if they think I would give you to such a monster."

"I am betrothed to Aron."

Her father lifted the scroll he held. "This includes a letter signed by both King Jarid and his son Aron. It releases you from your betrothal if you decide to accept the Chamberlight proposal."

Her mind whirled. "And if I don't agree?"

"The Misted Cliffs will invade." His fist gripped the scroll. "They swear they will not stop until the House of Dawnfield is destroyed in both Aronsdale and Harsdown."

Mel felt ill. "They could succeed."

"It is a devil's offer!" her father said.

"What devil?" a sleepy voice asked.

Mel spun around just as her mother ambled up to them,

dressed in her robe and silk pajamas, her hair tousled. The queen smiled drowsily. "You are all up early." As she looked from Mel to Muller, her smile faded. "What happened?"

Muller told her, briefly, without comment. He needed none. His pale face said it all.

"This is ludicrous." Chime stared at him. "They believe we would sacrifice our daughter so they can steal the throne they lost through their own belligerence?"

The world seemed to tilt around Mel. "If I tell them no, many of our people could lose their lives, lands, and homes."

Her father lifted his chin. "We can defeat any army the Misted Cliffs sends against us."

"Can we?" Mel felt as if a band were tightening around her torso, cutting off her breath. "They are so strong."

"We will find a way," Muller said. His hollow expression belied the confidence he was trying to project.

"At what cost?" Mel whispered.

"Ah, saints." Chime held out her arms, and Mel went to her mother. Chime held her, and Mel hugged her hard, unable to stop shaking.

"What can I do?" Mel said.

Her father clasped her shoulder, but his hand shook. No matter what he or her mother said, what reassurance could they give? Mel couldn't say yes, but she didn't dare say no. Her mother murmured her name over and over. Chime's voice caught, and Mel felt the wetness of her mother's tears against her hair and cheek.

Every instinct urged Mel to run from this proposal. She wanted to go to Aron, her betrothed. If only they were already married. Although they weren't in love, she had always been fond of him. Her feelings surely could have grown into more, given time. She couldn't bear to think of losing him for a prince of night and terror. But if she said no, how many of her people would die beneath his sword and the ferocity of Escar vengeance?

Mel's voice cracked. "I have no choice."

Her parents both held her, the three of them forming a grief-stricken knot in the yard. The messengers and stable hands waited in silence, no one intruding. Tears slid down Mel's face. She had known a good life here with a loving family and friends. Now that would end. In the rest of Harsdown, the sun was rising, but for her family, it was sunset.

Cobalt gazed into his wedge-shaped bedroom. Here in the narrow end, the entrance curved in an elegant horseshoe arch. Curtains hung along the wall to his left, and oil lamps lined the other wall, though none were lit. The only light trickled from a single lamp on the wall outside. His bed stood across the room at the wide end of the wedge, its covers bunched up or thrown on the floor. Every night he went to sleep in a perfectly made bed and every morning he awoke with it torn to pieces. He tossed and turned throughout the night. And he was too big. His bed had to be tailor-made for his body; otherwise, his feet hung off the end.

"Goodbye," he said. It felt odd to speak; he rarely did it even around people. But today it seemed appropriate. This was an ending to the first half of his life. It called for something dramatic. A spoken word seemed to fit that requirement, though he supposed most people would find his conclusion amusing. Or perhaps not. Cobalt Escar and amusing weren't concepts found in the same thought for most people.

"Brooding on your soon-to-be-lost freedom?" a familiar voice asked.

Cobalt turned around. Matthew stood behind him in the

circular chamber in the center of his suite, here at the top of the tower where he lived in the Castle of Clouds. He smiled. It even felt natural. Matthew was one of the few people who actually seemed to like him. "My greetings of the morning."

Matthew bowed. "Is it all right that I'm here?"

"Yes. Of course."

"Thank you." Matthew was wearing rough trousers and a homespun shirt. Cobalt knew he had finer clothes; after so many years with the Escar household, Matthew had a high status among the staff and was in charge of the stables. But he seemed to prefer simple garments and a simple life.

"It is good to see you," Cobalt said. "But unusual, eh?" Matthew was usually working in the stables at this early hour.

"It is hard to believe you will soon leave for Harsdown."

Cobalt crossed his arms. "I would prefer not to believe it. But it seems I must do this. I'm the idiot who suggested it."

Matthew's mouth curved upward. "Perhaps your bride will be comely and sweet."

"Or she might have two heads."

The older man laughed, a mellow sound. "Ah, well, I hope not." His voice quieted. "It was a good idea."

Cobalt was just glad he wouldn't lead his men into defeat. He had no doubt he could act as Varqelle's general, and he wanted the chance to prove himself to his father. He had thought this driving need to seek challenges would calm after he freed Varqelle; instead it had grown stronger. But they couldn't have won this damn war. His unplanned plan to conquer Harsdown without combat had worked out perfectly— except for one thing. He had to get married.

He squinted at Matthew. "Rumor says Melody Dawnfield looks like a man."

Matthew chuckled. "Perhaps she is a pretty man."

Cobalt scowled at him. "Very funny."

"You need a wife," Matthew admonished. "It shouldn't have taken such extremes to make you propose."

"I don't want a wife. Especially not this one. She is also said to be a sorceress. Saints, Matthew, what if she turns me into some vile creature?" Cobalt knew the "mage" powers probably didn't exist, but he had no doubt his bride could find some way to bedevil him with arcane rituals.

Matthew wiggled his fingers. "Poof. You are a roach."

Cobalt glowered at him. "Did you come here this morning to torment me?"

"Actually, no." Matthew cleared his throat. "I request that you take me on your journey to Harsdown."

Cobalt had intended to ask, but he hadn't been certain Matthew would come. Stonebreaker wanted Matthew to take extra care of the stables in preparation for the bride. "Are you sure you can leave your work here?"

"Yes, certainly." Matthew hesitated. "Your Highness…"

Cobalt groaned. "Whenever you say 'Your Highness,' I know I am in trouble."

"No trouble. Not for you, anyway."

"Surely *you* aren't in trouble." That would be a first.

"Not now." Matthew spoke awkwardly. "I was one of the people who helped your mother leave Harsdown all those years ago. Back then, I worked in the stables of your father's castle."

Ah. Cobalt had long suspected as much, though his mother had never told anyone, not even him. No guarantees existed that Varqelle wouldn't someday return, and she had always acted to protect those servants who had risked their lives and his wrath by helping her leave Harsdown.

"Has my father said anything to you?" he asked Matthew.

"I don't think he remembers me. But I fear he will." Matthew grimaced. "The more I avoid his presence, the better."

"I will arrange it." Cobalt put his hand on the older man's shoulder. "I will let no one bring harm to you."

"My thanks." Matthew started to say more but then stopped.

"Yes?" Cobalt asked.

"Forgive my presumption," Matthew began.

Cobalt snorted. "Since when has my forgiveness or lack thereof stopped you from presuming?"

"It is just— I couldn't help but notice you have somewhat confused responses to your sire."

Cobalt glowered. "I am never confused." It wasn't true and they both knew it. He had nothing to say because Matthew was right. Cobalt's reaction toward Varqelle had always been too convoluted for him to untangle, and he felt no more able to talk about it now than he had any of the other times Matthew had tried to draw him out over the years. He might need a lifetime to figure out his emotions in this, but at least now he had the chance.

He hoped he hadn't made a mistake in this attempt at a truce with the House of Dawnfield. A part of him wanted to fight. He had pledged his fealty to Varqelle, and he would keep that word. He finally had his father, after thirty-three years, and he didn't want to lose him.

If this marriage didn't work, they would still go to war.

Mel and Shimmerlake had been friends for as long as Mel could remember. They had played together as toddlers, run through the orchards as children, snuck out at night to swim in the lake, commiserated on the embarrassing names their parents had inflicted on them, and shared their secrets. Now Shim was helping her prepare to leave home, and Mel feared she would never see her friend again.

Shim arranged Mel's silk dress. It fell in blue drapes around her body, layered and soft, with gold under-panels that glimmered. By tradition, a royal bride wore the color of her mage power. In making the cat spell, Mel had shown she could access the power of a blue. They didn't know what sub-level yet; different shades of blue corresponded to variations of power.

"You look gorgeous," Shim stated.

Mel grimaced. "I look like an idiot."

They were in Mel's bedroom. The sunbask walls glowed in the sunshine that poured through the windows. Light and air; that had been her life until now. Mel couldn't believe it would end, with marriage to someone named "The Dark" and "Midnight" no less. She hoped he didn't look as monstrous as his reputation claimed.

Shim turned her toward the mirror on one wall. "Look."

Mel did so. A stranger stared back at her. Shim had brushed Mel's hair into a yellow fall of curls that spilled over her shoulders and arms to her waist. Her friend had even twined blue flowers into it, skybells, which grew only in the lowlands. A pendant hung around Mel's neck, a twenty-sided sapphire in a gold claw. Mel didn't know yet the number of sides she could draw on as a mage, but her mother could use a faceted ball with up to twenty sides, so Skylark considered it a good guess for Mel, also. Mel thought it was overly optimistic, but she didn't have the heart to tell her mentor.

Mel bit her lip. After today, she would have no one to help her learn magecraft. Cobalt Escar had made it clear no one could accompany her to his home. What reasonable prince refused his bride even one lady-in-waiting or companion? Mel had intended to ask Shim and one or more of the housemaids to come with her, and one of the red or orange mages who studied with Skylark. But Cobalt the Dank and Dismal forbade it. She hoped his carriage broke an axle on the way here and fell over a ridge.

"I look silly." She frowned at her reflection. "That isn't me."

"No, it isn't." Shim put her hands on her ample hips. "But most brides don't stomp to their wedding in riding boots, wool leggings, and an old tunic."

"I ought to," Mel muttered. "Maybe it would scare him away."

A clatter came from beyond her window. Mel went to peer out. At least thirty riders in dark livery were headed to the stables behind the house. They were leading more horses, probably spares so they could travel faster without overworking their mounts.

"Ho!" Mel said. "He's here!"

"Are you sure?" Shim joined her. "Black livery? How unsuitable. It doesn't match your gown."

"Oh, Shim. Who the hell cares if it matches my gown?"

"He should have worn sky blue."

"That livery has blue lining," Mel offered.

"Cobalt blue," Shim said darkly.

"I don't see any carriage," Mel said. Her groom had sent word he would arrive in one. Perhaps this wasn't him after all.

The riders gathered in front of the stables, their horses stepping and snorting, stirring up dirt. Stable hands were running out to meet them.

A carriage rolled into view.

It was black, all of it, with the Escar jaguar emblazoned on its side, visible only by the narrow blue border that set it off from the rest of the black surface. Black horses pulled the carriage. The reins, bridles, and uniform of the driver were black. Even the carriage wheels were black.

"If that is supposed to scare me," Mel said, "it doesn't." Never mind that her voice shook.

Shim laid a hand on Mel's shoulder. "You'll be fine."

"He's in there, Shim. I'm sure of it."

"Do you think he is as grotesque as they say?"

Mel frowned at her. "As who says?"

"Everyone."

"Everyone who?"

"If you are asking, do I know anyone who has actually seen him, the answer is no. But, Mel, rumors like that don't start out of nothing."

"Thanks, Shim," she muttered. The longer the carriage sat there, the more her pulse sped up.

A Dawnfield groom came over and reached up to the carriage door. Before he touched it, though, the door swung outward, creaking on its hinges. A large, muscular man with a shaggy mane of gray hair jumped out. He wore gray riding clothes of a fine cut, though without the elegance that Mel was used to seeing on her father. Then again, probably no other man alive had Muller Dawnfield's style.

"He's big," Shim said.

Mel studied him. It was true, he was taller than most men, with a bulkier physique, but he wasn't as huge as she had heard. Although he wasn't handsome, he had regular features and a pleasant mien. In fact, if she hadn't known better, she would have described his expression as kind.

"He isn't monstrous," Mel said, relieved.

"He doesn't look so bad." Shim smiled at her. "If that's him, then perhaps you will be all right."

"Wait." Mel caught a flicker of motion behind the man. "Someone else is still in the carriage."

"Can you see him?" Shim asked.

"Not yet. He's coming—"

The second man stepped out into the yard.

"Saints almighty," Shim whispered. "You're dead, Mel."

6
The Skybell Bride

He was the tallest man Mel had ever seen. He towered over everyone in the yard. His broad shoulders, heavily muscled frame, and long legs made her think of a powerful charger. His hair fell to his shoulders, thick and black. His dark clothes had no adornment save one: his cape bore the jaguar crest of Escar, which only a king or prince of that House could wear. His face would have been handsome if it had held even a hint of compassion, kindness, anything to make him seem like a man rather than stone. But no trace of humanity eased those hard features. Nothing. Combined with his monstrous size, it made him look inhuman.

Her groom had arrived.

Cobalt longed for the nightmare to end.

He hadn't wanted to leave his horses with stable hands in

hostile territory. He had no wish to be on this land of his enemy. Everyone looked as if they believed he would curse them with demonic spells. He just wanted this over with, so he could load his unwelcome wife into his carriage and return to the Castle of Clouds, where she could live in another tower and he would never have to deal with her.

Her home bewildered him. It was beautiful, built from an astonishing golden wood that almost seemed to glow, but it was a *farmhouse*. He supposed a royal family didn't have to live in a castle. This was foolish, though. If someone attacked, this place had no wall, battlements, moat, chasms, cliffs, or other means to protect it. Just trees. Many trees. He had ridden past row after row of pear and apple trees. Yes, Muller Dawnfield had a regiment of the army here, but even so. Cobalt would have chosen to live in Castle Escar in the Blue Peaks of the Escar Mountains.

They held the wedding in a large parlor. Arched windows let in copious sunlight, and rugs warmed the parquetry floor. Cobalt stood with Matthew on one side of the hearth, Cobalt in black, Matthew in gray. One of Stonebreaker's top officers, General Cragland, stood on Cobalt's other side, crisp in his military white and blue surcoat, trousers, and blue boots. Protocol required his presence, but he also served as an unspoken reminder to the Dawnfields of the alternative to this marriage.

Muller and Chime stood on the other side of the hearth with Sphere-General Fieldson. The royal couple left Cobalt feeling as dark and as dour as his name. The king was resplendent in gold trousers, a white and gold vest, and a snowy shirt with gold embroidery. His queen shimmered in green and gold silk, with her yellow hair swept up on her head and threaded with emeralds. They looked utterly beautiful and utterly exhausted. Dark rings showed under their eyes. Neither smiled. Cobalt didn't blame them. He wouldn't have wanted to marry his daughter off to someone like him, either.

Ten rows of high-backed chairs filled the room, with an aisle in the center. People occupied all the chairs, and more guests sat on banquettes in the back or against the side walls. Cobalt recognized no one but Lord Brant Firestoke, who represented King Jarid. Firestoke had brought the documents for the treaty established by this marriage. Earlier today Muller, Chime, and Cobalt had signed all of them except those that Cobalt and his bride would complete after this ceremony.

By mutual agreement, on Stonebreaker's advice, neither Jarid nor Varqelle had attended. Too many hostilities lay between them from the war. Given that each would have liked to kill the other, their presence here seemed a less than spectacular idea.

Dancer had planned to come, but Stonebreaker convinced her it would be unwise to travel into hostile territory, where she would be a target for abduction or assassination. All the royals were, though Stonebreaker hadn't mentioned the risk with his grandson. Obviously, Cobalt had to go to his own wedding. As a sign of good faith, Stonebreaker had suggested Cobalt go to fetch his bride rather than demanding she come to him. That his grandfather advised it had almost made Cobalt stay home, but he had to admit the idea had merit. He didn't want his antipathy toward his grandfather to prod him into bad decisions. So he went.

Stonebreaker, however, did stay home. If it wasn't safe for Jarid Dawnfield to travel to the Misted Cliffs, it obviously wasn't safe for the king of the Misted Cliffs to enter Dawnfield territory. But it meant *no* member of Cobalt's family attended his wedding. He didn't want to believe his grandfather had set it up that way, but he had known Stonebreaker too long to be naive. Cobalt refused to let anyone see how much it hurt. Nothing bothered him. He was stone that no one could break.

Now he waited for his bride to appear. She was taking a lot of time. Why? She needed only come in here and repeat the blasted vows, and then they could be done. He doubted she had any desire to prolong this business, either.

People shifted in their seats. Conversation trickled among them, but no one spoke loudly. The Bishop of Orbs stood a few paces away, by a display case with figurines and vases. He was going over the scroll he would read for the ceremony. His long robes, white with indigo embroidery, were patterned with designs of spheres. In a back corner of the room, four musicians were warming up, a man with a harp, a woman with a violin, another woman with a star-harp, and a man with per-cussive instruments.

A stir came from the doorway at the back, and a young woman entered. Cobalt stiffened. Was this his bride? Relief washed over him. She didn't look like a man, after all. She was above average height and had a sturdy build. Her brown hair gleamed with auburn highlights. She wore a simple dress, attractive without being showy, blue and yellow, with a snug bodice and a skirt that swirled around her legs. She was no great beauty, but tolerable enough. He could have done a lot worse.

She barely glanced at him when she entered. He couldn't tell if she wasn't interested or if she was avoiding his gaze. Instead of coming down the aisle, she hurried to the musi-cians and conferred with them. They all stilled their instru-ments and nodded.

Cobalt waited, wondering if and when the girl would acknowledge him. She didn't; she left the room and closed the double doors behind her.

Sweat ran down Cobalt's neck and soaked into his collar. It was humid here in the lowlands and hotter than the cliffs of his home, hotter even than the lowlands of his country. He glanced at Muller, and the king inclined his head. Cobalt returned the nod. Maybe that girl hadn't been the bride. She didn't look much like either Muller or Chime, who both had yellow hair and blue eyes. It was hard to know, though. Children didn't always have the same color hair or eyes as their parents.

The quartet started to play. The sparkling song reminded him of the River of Diamonds above the Castle of Clouds. That water was cold and icy, though, whereas this dulcet melody had warmth. On another day, he might have enjoyed the music.

A housemaid opened both doors at the back, and everyone turned to look. The girl with auburn hair came in again, and this time she did walk down the aisle. She was holding a bouquet of blue flowers. Cobalt flushed, then stood straighter and watched her. She wouldn't meet his gaze. She didn't come over to him, either. Instead she went to stand by the king and queen. They nodded to her, but neither showed what looked like parental attention. Cobalt was confused. She had come down the aisle, but she wasn't acting like a bride. Not that he knew how one normally acted.

A stir came from the back of the room. Cobalt looked—

And froze.

Another girl stood framed in the doorway. He couldn't absorb her presence. The colors! He lived in a colorless world. The castle, clouds, cliffs all were white. His mother tended to pale colors or white. The Diamond Palace was white.

Chamberlight livery was white and blue like ice and shadows. Pale, blanched. He spent most of his time around soldiers, who never wore much color. His own life was dark. Black.

The girl in the doorway overwhelmed him. Her dress was dyed such a vivid blue, he could barely take it in. Gold shimmered in the drapes of the gown. It clung to her, outlining her body. She had incredible curves, full and buxom, with a small waist and a height that suggested long legs.

Then he realized one of her gold drapes wasn't a drape. It was her *hair*. It flowed over her shoulders, arms, and torso to her waist. Blue flowers adorned it, and she held a bouquet with more of them. As his mind adjusted to her colors, he finally took in her face. An angel's face. No one could be so pretty. The curve of her cheek, the small nose, those large eyes as blue as the flowers in her hair—no, it wasn't possible. He couldn't absorb it all. This creature couldn't be his bride.

Matthew spoke in a voice only Cobalt could overhear. "I would say she doesn't look like a man."

Cobalt couldn't answer. He couldn't move. He thought perhaps he might die right now, because surely if he touched that impossible creature it would kill him. Nothing as dark as the Midnight Prince could survive such light.

She walked down the aisle, and she wouldn't look at him, either. He finally recovered enough to glance at Muller and Chime. It told him all he needed to know about this apparition approaching him. Only parents would look so anguished at the wedding of their daughter to Cobalt Escar.

The girl came to the hearth and stood next to him. She didn't raise her head, she just stared at the empty fireplace. Cobalt gazed at her shimmering hair and thought he would never be able to feel it. Saints only knew how he might damage it. He had a tendency to break fragile things, not through any wish of his own, but because he had too much strength and too little sense of how to use it sparingly. He didn't want her to break, and she might if he touched her.

The bishop came over and bowed to Muller and Chime. Then he turned to the bride and groom. Melody glanced quickly at the older man and nodded, though still she avoided Cobalt's gaze. His anger stirred, but he pushed it away. None of this was her fault.

The bishop unrolled his scroll and the musicians stopped playing. Then the bishop read the ceremony. He kept it short and simple, which relieved Cobalt. When the older man finished, he turned to Cobalt. "Do you have a token to give your bride?"

Cobalt stared at him blankly. "Token?"

"A ring?" he asked. "Bracelet? Heirloom?"

"No," Cobalt said. No one had told him he was supposed to give her something.

The bishop flushed. But he continued with the ceremony, his voice awkward. "Cobalt Chamberlight Escar, do you declare for this woman, as her husband?"

"Yes," Cobalt said. At least he knew that part.

"Melody Headwind Dawnfield," the bishop said. "Do you declare for this man, as his wife?"

She spoke softly. "Yes."

"It is done." Although the bishop kept an appropriately dignified demeanor, his posture relaxed slightly. He rolled up his scroll. "You may kiss her now."

Kiss her? In front of everyone? He never touched anyone in front of other people. He looked at Melody's bowed head. He couldn't kiss her here, in enemy territory. Saints above, her parents were watching.

With no warning, she looked up at him with her vivid blue

eyes. So much color! He couldn't move. Fighting a battle or climbing a mountain was easier than this.

After a moment, Melody looked away. Cobalt released the breath he had been holding.

The bishop cleared his throat. "Well." He spoke awkwardly. "You are now wife and husband."

Then it was done. Cobalt was consort of the heir to the Jaguar Throne. It should have been his father's throne, not that of the yellow-haired man who was now his father-in-law, but this would have to do. Only time would reveal if his ill-conceived marriage could stop a war.

7
The Starlight Engagement

Mel sat on a banquette in the hearth room. When everyone else had filed into the dining room for the buffet, she had stolen away to her bedroom seeking the comfort of Fog. Now she sat here with the kitten curled in her lap while her guests ate and carried on stilted conversations in another part of the house. She wondered what her large husband was doing. He really was as big as the tales claimed. She hoped the rumors of his cruelty weren't as accurate.

She laid her hand on circles carved into the wooden arms of the banquette. When she concentrated, gold light glistened around her. The sparkles cloaked her body with one of the best golden spells she had ever managed, and Fog began to purr loudly. The spell didn't help her, though. Maybe it was the color; orange spells soothed pain and yellow soothed emotions. Gold was somewhere between the two. Mel strained to shift the hue. She felt as if she were trying to train with an improperly balanced sword or sew with a needle that was too thick. Gradually, though, the spell brightened into yellow, as if sunshine had come inside the house even here, where it couldn't reach from the window. The spell was like velvet brushing across scar tissue; she knew it was there, offering comfort, but it couldn't smooth away the rough edges of her mood.

A sigh escaped Mel. A yellow spell couldn't heal, it could only warm her mood. Right now she wasn't even certain what she felt aside from confusion. She let the spell fade until no color remained in the air.

Footsteps sounded by the door, and Mel looked up as Brant Firestoke entered the room, elegant in his white silk shirt and gray velvet finery. His silver hair gleamed.

"A good evening to you, Lord Firestoke," she said.

"And to you, Your Highness." He bowed. "May I sit with you?"

"Yes, please." She patted the cushioned bench. Fog growled and started to stand up, a prelude to jumping to the floor. He paused when Mel scratched his ears, then settled back into her lap with a wary look at Brant. Apparently the lord met with the kitten's grudging approval.

Brant sat next to her. "I wish this day could have been a time of joy for you."

"Perhaps it will all work out." She doubted it, but she didn't want to say that. She tried not to think of Aron, her former betrothed.

"Perhaps." He didn't look as if he believed it, either.

"Can you tell me more about Prince Cobalt or his family?" she asked. "You're the only one of us who has met them all."

He grimaced. "They damn near executed me."

"Saints, Brant, why?"

"I didn't say what they wanted to hear."

"Then why this wedding?"

"Prince Cobalt suggested it as they were about to toss me in their dungeon."

It made a twisted sort of sense. "Do you think they planned it that way to ensure you would carry his proposal?"

"I suppose." He hesitated. "My impressions are probably nothing more than an old man's uncertainties."

"You've a mind as keen as a knife, Brant."

Amusement flickered in his eyes. "Your father didn't think so at your age."

She had heard tales about her father's lack of enthusiasm in his youth for his role as a Dawnfield heir. It made her smile. "I'd like to hear what you think."

"What I think is that Cobalt came up with this marriage idea to stop them from killing me." Brant rubbed his chin. "He had a rather odd exchange with his grandfather."

"Odd, how?"

"Stonebreaker spoke as if Cobalt had already rejected the idea of marriage. Cobalt acted as if Stonebreaker was the one who rejected it." He shook his head. "I don't think either of them had considered it prior to that moment."

Mel knew little about Stonebreaker; he was the only leader in the settled lands she hadn't met. He would interact only with the Dawnfield men and apparently let no men speak with his daughter. "Why would they pretend otherwise?"

Brant shrugged. "Perhaps because it is a good idea and both wanted credit."

"You don't sound convinced."

"I will tell you more, but only in confidence."

"You have it." He knew her word was good.

Brant spoke slowly, seeming to think through his words. "Stonebreaker is off kilter somehow. I don't trust him. And he is intensely jealous of his grandson."

"Cobalt is..." She searched for a word without negative connotations. "An impressive man."

"He's dangerous, Mel. So are his grandfather and father. Especially his father. Varqelle wants the throne." Brant laid his hand on her forearm. "Your marriage is all that holds him in check."

"You think he will try to separate me and Cobalt?"

His gaze never wavered. "Or have you killed."

Her hand tensed on Fog, and the kitten mewed in protest. "Brant, don't say that."

"I'm sorry. But it's true. You must be careful."

Mel loosened her hold, and Fog jumped down, then ran under the banquette. She looked back up at Brant. "I will remember what you've told me."

They left the farmhouse at sunset. Cobalt's new in-laws asked him to stay the night, and he knew they wanted more time to say goodbye to their daughter, but he couldn't bear to wait, even if it meant traveling in the dark. He was exposed here. Unprotected. It wasn't just that he was in hostile territory. Had that been the only reason, he would have stayed one last night. But his emotions were at risk. The warmth in this house came from more than lowland humidity. The people created it. He had no context to understand his bride's family, and it left him anxious to escape. How these gentle people could bring him harm, he had no idea, but he had to leave.

His bride hugged her parents on the veranda of the house. They were all crying. Cobalt waited by the open door of the carriage, so uncomfortable that he wondered if something was wrong with him. The thirty men in his honor guard surrounded his carriage, all of them on horseback, including Matthew. Cobalt had already gone over strategies with General Cragland and his men for protecting the carriage during the trip back to the Misted Cliffs. He had nothing to do now but watch his bride weep with her parents.

Mel finally came over, carrying a wicker basket on her arm. She looked up at him, her face wet with tears, and he wanted to crawl under the carriage and hide from those vivid eyes. She was too alive for him; he was dead inside, though he hadn't realized it until now. She stepped up into the carriage, then turned and waved to her parents, also to the girl who had stood up for her in the wedding and was on the porch now with Chime and Muller.

When his bride had gone into the carriage, Cobalt started to follow. He paused with one leg up, though, the hairs on his neck prickling. Looking over his shoulder, he saw Muller Dawnfield standing behind him.

Cobalt stepped back down from the carriage. "Yes?"

Muller spoke in a quiet voice. "Treat her well. Or you will answer to me."

Cobalt almost didn't respond, as with threats from his grandfather. But no, he should answer. Muller had reason to speak in such a manner. So he said, "Yes."

"Good." Muller's face was creased with lines of strain. "Be well, Your Highness."

Be well? People never said such to him, especially not anyone with good reason to hate him. He didn't know how to answer, so he just nodded. Then he swung up into the carriage. Within moments they were on their way.

Melody—no, they called her Mel—sat across from him in

the seat that faced backward. She held the basket in her lap. He stretched out his legs and his feet hit her bench, but he managed to avoid tearing the silk drapes of her gown. So bright, that blue and gold. Belatedly, he wondered if he should have given her time to put on travel clothes. He had worn his to the wedding, but women seemed to change their clothes a great deal. He was glad that she hadn't though; it felt good to see her in that dress.

Her face was turning pink. "Are you going to stare at me for the entire trip?"

Cobalt jerked. She had spoken; he should answer.

"No," he said.

"Oh." Her blush deepened.

They sat for a time as the carriage rumbled along. The ride was reasonably smooth compared to some journeys Cobalt had taken. This was a popular thoroughfare and well tended. The driver had lit his lanterns, but shadows were filling the carriage as the evening deepened.

"Would you like me to make some light?" Mel asked.

Cobalt tapped the lamp in its claw on the wall. "I can light this. But it is smoky. I tend to leave it out."

A silence followed his words. Then she said, "That was incredible."

Cobalt blinked. "The lamp?"

"No. You. That was three sentences. I haven't heard you say that much before."

He felt a flush spread in his face. His anger stirred, but then it subsided, just as it had during the wedding. Usually when the anger came, it stayed. But not with her. She obviously wasn't mocking him. She sounded relieved. Sweet, even. Had he been that closed since meeting her?

"Do you want me to light the lamp?" he asked.

"No. This is fine."

"Are you cold?"

"No. I'm fine. Really."

Cobalt scratched his ear. He didn't know what to do with this wife he had acquired. His body knew, though; he recalled well how her dress had fit her curves. "Come sit here."

Her voice wavered. "Next to you?"

He slid over and laid his hand on the seat. "You will fit."

She clutched her basket and stared at him with eyes large in her face. Her dress rustled as she stood. She had to stoop to keep from banging the top of the carriage. Cobalt knew that problem; he had it in most places. She was small and probably rarely had to bend her head, but this ceiling was low.

She almost fell on top of him as the carriage lurched. Cobalt caught her arm and helped her sit down. When she inhaled sharply, he let go, afraid he might bruise her the way Stonebreaker so often bruised Dancer.

"Are you all right?" he asked.

"Y-yes."

Only moonlight came through the window, but even in that dim glow her hair glimmered. He picked up a length and pressed it against his cheek. "So odd."

She sat like a statue. "Odd?"

"Your hair is like silk." He carefully arranged the lock back over her arm. "Even softer."

"Have you never felt long hair before?"

"My own." It only went to his collar, though, and was much coarser than hers. He thought of the courtesans he had known. "A few other women. Not like you."

"Oh."

He touched the basket on her lap. "Is that food?"

"Saints, no. It's Fog."

He squinted at the basket. "It doesn't look foggy."

To his unmitigated surprise, she laughed. "Fog is my kitten."

Cobalt barely heard her answer. Her laugh riveted him. It sparkled. It was music. And *he* had caused it. That had never happened to him. It was astonishing.

After a moment, he recovered enough to respond. "Your kitten is quiet."

"He's sleeping."

"Ah."

Mel said nothing else, and Cobalt had exhausted his supply of conversation ideas. She sat by his side, her back erect, her hands gripping the handle of her basket.

Eventually, her head nodded forward and she slumped. At first he thought she was hurt. When he bent toward her, he realized she had fallen asleep. Moving with care, so he didn't wake her, he put his arm around her shoulders and settled her against him. It was pleasant. He wished they could have spent their wedding night at the Castle of Clouds. They needed their own place; he couldn't have stayed their first night together in her childhood home. Unfortunately, they had only this carriage and he hardly intended to do anything here. He hadn't expected he would want her so much. This could have been a dismal wedding night, but oddly enough, he felt content.

He was growing drowsy. He took Mel's basket with its misty kitten and set it on the floor. Wedging himself into the corner where the seat met the side of the carriage, he slid his leg behind his slumbering wife, his knee bent since the carriage wasn't wide enough for him to stretch out. He braced the boot of his other leg against the floor and shifted Mel so she was sleeping against him, between his legs, her head on his chest.

Then he closed his eyes and went to sleep.

* * *

A jostle awoke Mel. Her neck ached from sleeping in an odd position and it took her a moment to orient to her surroundings. Cobalt was reclining against one side of the carriage, asleep, with her lying against his chest. One of his boots was braced on the floor; the other leg was behind her. He had his arms around her, muscular arms, strong and solid, as a bride might desire from her groom. In his sleep he held her more naturally than when he had touched her hair earlier, with that exaggerated care. His strength made her tingle as if she were afraid, but it wasn't unpleasant. If she hadn't been so groggy, she might have jerked back from him, but she was only half awake, and he seemed less imposing when he was asleep.

His vest rubbed her cheek. She had thought earlier today that it was unadorned, but now she felt embroidery. The thread was dark, hard to see on the black. She traced the designs on his chest, circles and hexagons in interlocked chains. Running her finger around them, she envisioned fields of grass. The shapes began to glow a rich green. As the mood spell intensified, she focused on Cobalt, but she couldn't reach him. She felt as if she were straining to draw more power than a two-dimensional form could give. Perhaps she needed more experience or a higher order shape. She questioned how much either of those would help, though. His emotions were distant, out of reach. Mental armor protected them.

Mel let the spell fade. She lay in his arms, acutely self-conscious, and wondered about him. Such a strange man. Would she spend the rest of her life in conversations of one or two words, perhaps a few sentences now and then? His coldness toward her family at the wedding troubled her. He had shown almost no reaction to any of them, not even when her mother entreated him to stay one last evening rather than venture into the darkness.

However, Mel felt no hostility from him, either. He might hide it behind the impenetrable armor that defended his mind, but if that were true, he could be hiding gentler feelings, too.

The carriage jolted and Mel's elbow hit the paneling behind them. As Cobalt stirred, the carriage lurched to one side. She would have fallen to the floor if he hadn't tightened his arms around her. Outside, someone shouted.

"What?" Cobalt set her upright, then sat up and rapped on a trap door in the roof. He didn't even have to stand to touch the top of the carriage.

"Matthew!" he called.

The trap door opened and starlight filtered into the coach. A man peered down at them, the gray-haired fellow who had first come out of the carriage when Cobalt's party arrived at her parents' farm, and who had stood up with Cobalt at the wedding. No trace of gentleness showed in his expression now.

"There are at least thirty of them," Matthew said.

Cobalt swore. "My sword."

Matthew withdrew from sight.

"Thirty?" Mel asked. "Are they attacking?"

Matthew reappeared and lowered a sword belt to Cobalt. As the prince buckled it around his hips, the carriage lurched to an abrupt stop. Mel's foot hit the basket and a distressed mewl came from within.

Cobalt turned to her. "Stay here. My men and I will be protecting the carriage."

"Do you know what is happening?" Mel asked.

He didn't answer. Instead, he opened the door and jumped

out into the night. Beyond him, a melee of men on horseback surged in the starlight. The clang of metal hitting metal rang out. Mel heard him call out orders to his officers, and then he slammed the carriage door.

Fog wailed, and Mel leaned down to the basket. "Shush. Don't draw attention." She comforted the frightened kitten, then closed the basket and hid it under the protection of the seat.

Outside, a man cried out, but it cut off abruptly. Mel felt the blood drain from her face. She knew where Cobalt's men had packed her belongings on the carriage, in the back. She stood on the seat and pushed open the trap door. Although small, the opening was large enough. Grabbing its edges, she hoisted herself up. Her gown caught and then tore as she clambered out onto the top of the carriage.

For a moment, she clung to the smoothed wood. They were in a narrow valley with woods on either side. She couldn't see clearly, but the stars gave enough light to show men fighting on both sides of the carriage, here and farther out. Cobalt had brought thirty, but there were at least twice that number now. She crawled to where her bags and packages were lashed to bars on the back of the carriage. She knew where she had put everything, but nothing seemed to be where she remembered. She fumbled through the packages, searching, searching—it had to be here—there! She undid her sword from its wrappings and fastened the belt around her hips. A metal stud on the leather ripped her wedding dress more.

Mel edged back to the trap door and lowered herself into the carriage. Fog was crying and scratching inside his carrier. Crouching by the basket, she cracked it open enough to pet the terrified kitten. "Shhh," she whispered. "Please, Fog." It did no good; the kitten kept crying.

The door suddenly jerked open, leaving a large figure silhouetted against the starlit sky. He wore rough clothes under crude leather armor, and he held a long sword. Lunging inside, he grabbed her arm.

"No!" Mel tried to pull away.

He yanked her out of the carriage. Mel fell to the ground and her legs tangled in the cursed wedding dress. Several men in Chamberlight armor lay sprawled on the ground, unmoving. She scrambled to her feet, unmindful of the tearing silk.

"Stop!" she shouted.

"No Escar will sit on the throne again." He shoved her back against the wheel. "Neither your husband nor your child."

Mel grabbed the hilt of her sheathed sword. She was aware of others fighting near the carriage, but no one was close enough to help.

"You should never have married him," the man said. His blade glinted in the starlight as he swung at her.

Mel whipped out her blade and parried his blow. Their swords rang, adding to the clangs and grunts of the fighting around them.

"What the hell!" He stepped back. "You're *armed.*"

"You don't want to fight a Dawnfield heir." Her anger was flaring like a stoked flame. This was no practice match with blunted swords, but a combat for her life.

He didn't answer, he just came at her again, with more force this time. Mel countered the blow, her swing fast and sharp. She had to rely on speed, because she sure as hell didn't have the strength to match him. She had no time to be afraid; she reacted with single-minded concentration, her senses heightened and focused. He was stronger but less well-trained, probably a farmer rather than a solider. When he drove her against the carriage, she ducked and came at him from the side, catching him with a wound along his arm. She had never deliberately drawn blood before, but rather than shock, she felt a fierce triumph.

When he caught her blade with his, she staggered from his force; when she evaded him, he couldn't keep up with her speed. They went back and forth past the wheels of the carriage. As Mel tired, she slowed down and desperation intruded on the fire of her will. She knew, without doubt, that if she lagged now, she would die. Her opponent was breathing heavily, also slowing, but he retained his strength. She barely managed to parry his next thrust, and when his blade hit her sword, she stumbled into the wheel.

No! Anger surged in Mel and added strength to her arms. Clutching the hilt of her sword with both hands, she thrust upward. He blocked her strike, but her blade caught his sword and knocked it out of his hand, smashing it into the door of the carriage.

For one instant, the man stood with his mouth open, staring at her. Suddenly he arched. His face crumpled and his grunt ended in an odd gurgle. As his legs folded, he collapsed, but he didn't hit the ground; he hung about two handspans in the air. A huge figure stood behind him. Cobalt. He had run his sword through the man's chest and was holding him up. Then he yanked his sword out of the body, and the man sprawled in front of Mel, very, very dead.

"Saints almighty," she whispered, her heart pounding.

Cobalt lunged over the body and grabbed her arm. "Are you all right?"

"Yes." She couldn't pull away; his grip was so tight it hurt her arm.

"What are you doing with a sword?" he demanded.

She stared at him. "Defending myself."

"He could have killed you!" His arm was shaking, not from fear, but from whatever blood lust had gripped him in battle and still had him in its thrall. "I told you to stay in the carriage."

"Damn it, I didn't have a choice!"

"You will not use that language with me!" He dropped her arm and jerked his own up high, the fist drawn back, his elbow lifted.

Mel knew a blow from that height, from a man this strong, would break her bones. She was still holding her sword, but she couldn't strike her own husband. She tried to back up—and hit the carriage wheel.

Cobalt groaned and grabbed his raised arm with his other hand, his palm smacking against his wrist. He lowered both arms and crossed them over his torso. "I won't hit you. I swear, Mel. I won't."

Someone was approaching them, more a shadow than a person. As he neared, he resolved into Matthew. "I think that's the last of them."

Cobalt turned to him. "You will go with my wife in the carriage. I will ride Admiral."

Matthew looked at Cobalt holding his arm. "Cobalt, listen—"

"No." He spoke in a low voice. "Do you remember how you used to hide me in the stables?"

"Those days are gone," Matthew said, his gaze intense. *"Gone."*

Cobalt didn't seem to hear him. He motioned at Mel. "I task you now with her protection—" His voice cracked. "Just don't tell me where you hide her."

Matthew grasped him by the shoulders, something Mel could never have imagined anyone doing to the Midnight Prince. "Have you ever struck a woman? Or a child? *Ever?*"

"No," Cobalt whispered.

"Nor will you."

Cobalt pushed off his hands. "I am him, Matthew. I am his blood, his grandson, his spawn. Ride in the carriage with her." Then he strode away, toward a cluster of men who were tending another man on the ground.

Mel was starting to tremble. She sagged against the carriage door, above the body crumpled at her feet, the hilt of her sword clutched in one hand, her arms folded across her stomach. Bile rose in her throat.

Matthew came over to her. "I'm sorry."

She raised her head. "Who are you?"

"His stable hand."

She wanted to laugh, then cry. This man was obviously far more than a stable hand to Cobalt.

"Can I help?" Matthew asked.

She doubted anyone could help now. "He frightens me."

"Aye. He does everyone."

"Doesn't he feel it?"

"Too much," he murmured. "He feels far too much. If he didn't, his wounds wouldn't be so deep."

Mel was clenching her sword so hard, she couldn't release the hilt. As she pulled herself up straight, Matthew slid his hand under her elbow in support.

"No." Mel pulled away. "Don't touch me." She climbed into the carriage and sat down on the bench where she and Cobalt had slept. Her legs shook, but she couldn't let a reaction set in; she had to keep going until she reached a place of safety where she could release her frayed control. Except she had no place of safety anywhere.

Matthew followed her in and swung the door closed. He sat on the bench across from her. With dogged resolve, she picked up a layer of her dress and cleaned the blood off her sword. Then she sheathed the blade at her hip.

Fog began crying, frantic and disconsolate. Mel pulled the basket out from under the seat. Before she even finished opening it, the kitten scrambled out and burrowed into her lap. She tried to pet him, but her arm had no strength and she could only rest her hand on the trembling animal. Matthew watched them with a strange look, as if the sight filled him with grief.

Mel didn't know how long they stayed at the site of the battle. It could have been moments or hours. Voices called outside and several times men cried out in pain. She tried to build a blue spell of healing, but she couldn't summon the strength for anything at all.

"I've never seen a woman fight with a sword," Matthew finally said.

"They should learn," Mel answered dully.

"Your Highness—"

"I do not feel high, Matthew. Please do not call me that tonight."

"I'm sorry." The starlight coming in the window turned his gray eyes black.

"They killed any attackers who survived, didn't they?" she asked.

His voice sounded carefully neutral. "I don't think any survived the fight."

Mel didn't dispute him. She didn't believe him, either, but regardless of the truth, she doubted any were left alive. It was one more part of this terrible night.

The carriage lurched and rolled forward. Their journey to the Misted Cliffs had resumed.

8
Borderland Glade

Cobalt rode in a trance. They had rested the horses and then continued through the night. Now the sky was lightening. In the distance, the Misted Cliffs rose up from the borderlands in a barrier that blocked the world. A blurred barrier. He could have put on his glasses, but he didn't want people to see him wearing them. Even hazy, though, those magnificent cliffs looked as if they could be a great wall erected for the saints themselves.

In truth, Cobalt found it hard to believe saints existed. They were spirits from the ancient legends, and they took their essence from colors of the rainbow, which supposedly corresponded to the "spells" of a mage. Azure saints glazed the sky, dawn saints added their blush to the sunrise, verdant saints breathed new crops into life, and on and on with the foolish tales. What of blood and the fire of rage? Those existed only in hells never touched by any spirit of life. And in him.

Last night, only one of their attackers had broken through the defenses Cobalt had set up around the carriage. Only one. But that was all it had taken. Had Mel not known how to defend herself, she would be dead now. Her blood would be on his head.

The carriage rolled ahead of him, carrying his bride. If any saints did exist, they had surely cursed this young woman. He found it hard to believe that the slender, fragile beauty he had married had turned into the swordswoman of last night, but her fire wouldn't protect her from his darkness. She would spend the rest of her life with a monster who could shatter her as easily as a china dish falling onto a stone floor.

As easily as Stonebreaker had shattered his queen.

No. *No.* His grandmother had died from a fall. Everyone told him so. He couldn't believe otherwise.

The carriage rolled to a stop ahead of him. As Cobalt approached, the door opened and Matthew jumped out. The older man rubbed his eyes, then shielded them with his hand as he looked around at the empty, flat countryside. The sun had just risen behind them. Ahead, the wall of cliffs stretched from north to south as far as they could see.

Mel stepped out of the carriage. Her wedding dress, that vibrant creation of silk, hung in torn layers with dried blood crusted on the hems. Cobalt's stomach tightened. Beauty had finally come into his life, and he had left it ripped and trampled.

He reined Admiral to a stop and dismounted. Matthew gently pried the reins from Cobalt's hand.

"I'll take care of him," Matthew said.

Cobalt nodded stiffly, aware of Mel watching. Without the

excuse of tending his horse, he had no reason to avoid her. At least Matthew hadn't given him any warning looks to suggest his bride would run away from him.

Cobalt went to her. Dark circles showed under her eyes, but she spoke in an even, melodic voice. "Good morning."

"How are you?" he asked.

"Fine." She smiled ruefully. "Your Matthew is a saint. Fog ran all over him in the carriage, but Matthew never complained."

"Ah." Her smile mesmerized him. "Matthew is kind."

"Yes. He is." She hesitated. "If we have time, I would like to clean up."

"Yes. Of course." She seemed even more delicate close up. After last night, though, he knew better. Anyone who wielded a sword so well would have toned muscles and more strength than some youths. She unsettled him, because she very definitely curved like a woman. How would those curves feel under his hands? He wanted to find out. He had the right; she was his wife. After last night, though, she would probably shrink from his touch.

An alarming thought came to him. Perhaps she would pull her sword when he came to her. He wasn't certain if the idea appalled or aroused him. She was certainly a woman like no other. Then again, he knew almost no others.

"Your Highness?" she asked.

Cobalt realized he had just been standing here, staring at her. He mentally shook himself. "I will have someone accompany you while you perform your ablutions."

"No!"

"No?"

"My, uh, ablutions are private." Then she said, "If you had let me bring a maid, she could have accompanied me."

"A maid?" He vaguely recalled mention of such, but of

course he had said no. Stonebreaker allowed no women at the Castle of Clouds except Dancer, and now Mel. Cobalt's mother had plenty of ladies-in-waiting and female servants at the Diamond Palace, but Grandfather had left no doubt; if she insisted on living away from him, she could damn well do without the comforts associated with her station. He had obviously expected his daughter to come home rather than look after herself.

Dancer had stayed at the Castle of Clouds.

"We have a staff at the castle," Cobalt said. Male servants helped Dancer when appropriate, but that left a great deal for the queen to do herself.

Spots of red appeared on Mel's cheeks. "No one here can help."

He suddenly realized what she wanted. To bathe. His pulse jumped. "I will go with you."

Her blush deepened. She nodded awkwardly, and he thought she wanted to protest. She didn't, though. Who else could go with her? Certainly not one of his men. He would punch any of them who tried to watch her bathe.

While she retrieved some clothes from one of her valises, he set men to guard the carriage and to check the surrounding area, including a ridge about a hundred paces away. A river wound across the otherwise dry land, providing a place where his men could water their horses. It disappeared into the ridge. Not much thrived in these borderlands, but trees grew along the banks of the river and a small forest covered the hill.

As soon as Cobalt and his men established that the area was safe, Mel headed for the trees. Cobalt followed and caught up as she entered the woods. He could have reached her sooner, with his stride so much longer than hers, but she seemed more comfortable without him looming about. He also liked being behind her, watching the sway of her hips while she walked.

Mel neither looked at him nor spoke as they went through the forest. Birds fluttered among the leaves and added splashes of color to the morning.

"Your cat would like this," he said. "Lots of birds to eat."

Mel looked up with a start. Then she laughed, that same lovely sound she had made yesterday. "I imagine he would, when he's old enough. He's just had mush in the carriage."

Her laugh so surprised him that he stopped. She kept going a few steps, then halted and came back to him. "What is wrong?"

"Nothing." He felt foolish. She didn't know he wasn't used to hearing people laugh. "Come. We shouldn't tarry too long."

"All right." She scratched her chin, but started off again.

No path wound through the trees, so they made their way by pushing aside scrubby bushes with pink flowers and thorns. Cobalt doubted anyone came here much. They were far out in the dry lands between Harsdown and the Misted Cliffs. Not many people lived in this region, which had few resources. This was the only river he had seen all morning.

They climbed the ridge and discovered a hollow between it and a second ridge. The river fell in a waterfall over a ledge and filled a small pool overhung with trees.

Cobalt looked around. "This looks like a good place. You should have privacy here."

"Yes." She stood a few paces away, her face red.

After several moments of standing there, Cobalt said, "Didn't you want to bathe?"

"Yes." She pressed the knuckles of one hand against her cheek. "Are you going to stay?"

"Someone must." He walked over to her. "We are married. It is all right."

"I know." She didn't move.

Cobalt offered her his hand. She started to take it, then looked down and froze. He followed her gaze.

Dried blood crusted his fingernails.

"Hell," Cobalt muttered, quickly dropping his hand. He wasn't doing this well.

Her exhalation was almost inaudible. She sank to the ground and lowered her head, holding the clothes she had brought in her lap. Cobalt knelt next to her, at a loss for what to do. He wanted to say, *I'm sorry*. But he couldn't. Never apologize. Never admit vulnerability. Never acknowledge a mistake. Show no weakness. Except that was his grandfather in his mind, not him; he *couldn't* let it be him. But he couldn't say the words. He had killed men last night, ten, maybe eleven. He had done what had to be done, and even in that he had almost failed. Mel could have died. Filled with adrenaline and battle fury, he had raised his fist. On her wedding night. He wouldn't have struck her, but that moment was seared into his mind. And he couldn't even say *I'm sorry*. No wonder people thought he was a monster.

Cobalt sat down and put his arms around her, with his legs on either side of her body. She sat rigid in his embrace. Then her shoulders began to shake. He drew her closer and she slumped against him, her cheek on his chest.

And she cried.

Her sobs were quiet. He could barely hear them, but he felt her crying. He kept her in his arms, awkwardly smoothing her hair, his head bent over hers. He didn't know what else to do.

Her shaking gradually slowed. A bit later it stopped. She sat in his arms, leaning against him, her head bowed, her eyes closed, her gold lashes long on her tear-stained cheeks. Cobalt wondered how a woman could look so much like an angel and yet fight like a warrior. He realized he was rocking her back and forth. Confused, he slowed down and then stopped moving.

Mel lifted her head to look at him. He still had his head bowed over hers, and her face was only a finger span away from his. She regarded him with large, moist eyes, but she didn't flinch or recoil. He did then what he had wanted to do since the Bishop of Orbs first offered him the opportunity. He kissed his wife.

She could have jerked away. He wouldn't have blamed her after everything that had happened. Instead she sighed and relaxed against him. Her lips were warm. She tasted of light and strength, tart and sweet. He rubbed his hand down her back, over her hair. His tongue rasped across her lips until finally she relented and parted them so he could kiss her more deeply, with his tongue. That she had no idea how to return such a kiss only made him want her more.

Mel eventually pulled her head away, not much, just enough to see his face.

"Sweet Mel," Cobalt murmured.

"I'm sorry." Her voice trembled. "I didn't mean to fall apart."

"Don't." *Sorry.* Unbidden, a memory came to him: He was a boy cowering on the cold stone floor in the Diamond Palace while the king disciplined him with fists and a leather belt. He had crouched there, too small and skinny to fight back, shaking and crying, saying he was sorry over and over again, though he hadn't known what he had done wrong—other than just *existing* and being so much less than a king deserved for his heir.

"You never have to apologize to me," he said.

She traced a circle embroidered on his vest. The sunlight

played tricks on his sight and made the circle glow green. Then he saw it reflected on her fingers and realized the green light was real.

Cobalt jerked and pushed away her hand. "What are you doing?"

Her eyes were luminous with tears. "What hells have you lived?" she murmured, "that you need such heavy armor to protect your emotions?"

"What did you do to me?" Thoroughly alarmed, Cobalt rubbed his hand over his vest. It had stopped glowing.

"It was a mood spell."

"You cursed my mood?" He had expected something more dire. His mood was usually bad anyway.

"Well, no. I can't curse anyone." She leaned her head back on his chest. "I can make light or warmth. A little. I can sense someone's mood, vaguely, though my interpretation isn't always accurate. Sometimes I can soothe a person or help heal a minor injury."

Cobalt found it hard to credit, but it was clear she believed her words. And he had seen the green light. "I heard you are a mage." It made him feel both uneasy and foolish to say the words.

"Not a very practiced one, I'm afraid."

"It is hard to believe the tales of Aronsdale sorceresses."

She wrinkled her nose. "I'm afraid to ask what you've heard."

He didn't want to relate tales of harridans inflicting blights on unsuspecting travelers. He didn't believe them anyway, even less after meeting Mel and her mother. He had always told himself that this business of magecraft was no more than a sham, but a part of him wondered if it could be possible. Behind all the lurid tales, he had also heard that mages were healers. He couldn't admit any of that, however. All this talking made him feel exposed. Either she was a mage or she wasn't. Time would reveal the truth.

After his silence went on for a while, Mel sighed and closed her eyes. Cobalt liked sitting here, holding her, surrounding her with his legs. He brushed his hand over her shoulder and pulled down the edge of her dress. "Do you still want to bathe?"

"I—I think so." She didn't move, though.

He bared her shoulder. "I can help."

"Ah. Oh." She swallowed.

He brushed the tangles of her hair off her face. "If you wish me to leave, I will."

She did look up at him then. She touched him tentatively on the cheek. "Will you swim with me?"

"Yes." *Oh, yes.*

She smiled then, one of the few times she had done so specifically for him. The expression trembled and vanished as fast as it had come, but while it lasted, it was wonderful. Astonishing that a simple flash of teeth could be so arresting.

He slowly pulled down the top of her gown. She averted her eyes, but she didn't pull away. The skin of her shoulders was pale and soft. And unmarked. She had no scars from fights or a leather strap. He touched her arm where it met her shoulder, wondering at her perfect skin. Then he pulled the silk more and uncovered her breasts. Beautiful breasts, large and erect. No, she definitely did not look like a man. He filled his hand with one of them and she drew in a sharp breath.

"Do you want me to stop?" he asked.

Mel shook her head, her eyes averted. He stroked her, first one breast, then the other. He was on the verge of laying her on the ground when she eased out of his arms. Before he could pull her back, she stood up. The dress fell down past her waist and draped around her hips, leaving her upper body bare. She reminded him of the ancient statues he had seen of the goddesses his ancestors had worshiped, except that instead of marble, she was golden and warm. *Alive.*

"Saints almighty," Cobalt muttered. He wanted to look and look at her body, and then pull her down under his own.

Mel froze like a deer mesmerized by a lamp—except he was the one who riveted her in place. He rose to his feet, towering over her, and reached for his wife, hungry, no longer thinking clearly. Mel shied away. She wouldn't meet his gaze, but she tugged down the gown and let it fall to the ground. He wanted to look at her more, but she splayed her hand to cover the triangle of hair between her thighs. Then she crossed to the pool and eased into it. It was deep enough for her to submerge up to her shoulders, leaving her body no more than a blur under the water.

He almost groaned. Why couldn't she just lie down with him? In truth, he knew the answer. She was nervous. His impatience would scare her away. He didn't know how to approach her, though. The only talk he ever heard about women was the crude jokes among his men, and that hardly seemed useful now.

Well, she had asked him to swim, which he wouldn't do in his clothes. Cobalt took off his cape and dropped it next to her silks. He unbuttoned and removed his vest and then his shirt. The sun was warm on the bare skin of his torso. Mel watched, her eyes large. He had never been self-conscious about his body before, but now he wondered if she found him desirable.

He pulled off his boots while he was standing up, which

was no small feat of balance. Then he unfastened his trousers and removed them as well, along with his undergarments. Her eyes widened and she swam backward, staring at him. He hoped his arousal didn't frighten her. He couldn't do anything about it without her help. Actually, he could, but he didn't want to. From the way she watched him, he wasn't sure if she would swim closer when he came into the water or scramble out and run away.

Cobalt eased into the pool, and she backed all the way to the other side. He walked out to the middle, where the water came most of the way up his chest.

"It's warm," he said.

"F-freezing." Either her voice was shaking or her teeth were chattering, he wasn't certain which.

"Here." He held out his hand and his arm floated on the water. "I can help."

She pushed off the edge of the pool and drifted toward him. He caught her easily, sliding his arm around her waist. Her body felt soft and hard at the same time, her skin like velvet and her muscles firm under that provocative layer of softness. Her breasts pressed against his chest. He didn't know how much longer he could hold back from taking her, hard and fast. He didn't want to damage her and she was so small, but it was becoming difficult to control himself.

He pulled Mel against him and bent his head next to hers. As he bit at her neck, his breath quickened.

She set her palms against his shoulders. "Wait."

"Don't say no," he murmured.

"I—I'm afraid."

He teased her earlobe with his teeth. "Put your legs around my waist."

She wrapped her long legs around him and he groaned. He

knew he should take the time to figure out what she needed, because he had never done this with a woman who had no experience and he didn't want to ruin her first time. If it *was* her first time. In all of the negotiations, it had never occurred to him to ask, though it should have. He would worry about that later; right now he didn't want to think.

The top of her head brushed his chin. "Tell me what to do," she whispered, as if afraid to say it louder.

Love me. He held her with his left arm and slid his right hand down to hold her behind. It fit neatly into his palm. When she moved in his arms, rubbing against him, he lost his final shreds of control. His hips jerked as his seed spurted against her stomach in the water, and his mind blanked with pleasure and relief. He stopped thinking altogether.

Coherency returned slowly. His breath stirred her hair.

"Cobalt," she gasped. "I can't breathe."

Bloody hell. He loosened his hold and she gulped in air.

"Better?" he asked.

"Much better." She inhaled deeply. "Did something just happen?"

He gave an uneven laugh. "Oh, yes."

"Ah."

He nuzzled her hair. "Are you broken?"

"Broken?" She sounded perplexed. "Well, no."

His pulse surged. He hadn't hurt her. He hadn't caused harm. He hadn't violated her or ruined the trust she had offered when she asked him to "swim" with her. It relieved him so much that it took a moment to remember he hadn't done anything else for her, either.

"Ach," Cobalt muttered. He was a coarse rogue if ever there was one, thinking only of his own pleasure.

"Ach?" Mel smiled. "Does that have a translation?"

With her hair damp and tousled, and her blue eyes wide, she was so appealing that he wanted to stay here forever. When they left this hollow, they would have to face reality, the deaths of the men last night, Stonebreaker and Varqelle, and all the harsh uncertainties that went with his life. But right now he had just Mel, his astonishing, unexpected wife, and he could forget the rest for a while.

Something odd was happening to his face, as if his features were arranging themselves into new expressions. Gentle ones. He kept one arm around her waist and lifted his other to touch her cheek. "Ach means we need more time."

"We do?"

"Yes." Still holding her, with her legs around his waist, he walked to the edge of the pool where they had left their clothes. He lifted her up and sat her on the rocky shelf. Water cascaded off her body and sparkled in the sunlight. As Cobalt climbed out next to her, she crossed her arms over her breasts, hiding herself.

"Don't," he murmured. He spread his clothes on the rocks and nudged her down until she lay on top of them, on her back. She stared up at him, still nervous, but she seemed curious, too. Encouraged, he tugged on her arms until she let him pull them down. Then he lay on his side next to her, his head propped up on one hand, and just looked. Her face turned red. So pretty. Even her blushes were pretty. Drops of water beaded on her nipples and ran down her breasts.

He lowered his head and took her nipple into his mouth. Mel exhaled, stroking his hair while he suckled. When he slid his hand between her thighs, he found another surprise; she was ready for him. He hadn't expected that. Here he was, finished, and she was waiting. He rolled against her, half lying on her body, and moved up so he could put his lips against her ear. "I need more time."

"Time?" She sounded confused.

"Umm..." Cobalt wished they could stay here all day.

When Mel moved her pelvis against his hand, he stroked her, using his fingers to help satisfy a need in her he didn't think she even understood. He also found the answer to his question about her experience; she was a virgin. It didn't surprise him. She had been betrothed to the crown prince of Aronsdale. The women of that country might be freer in many ways, but when it came to ensuring the royal line remained true, Aronsdale princes would be just as obsessive as any others. He was probably the only heir in centuries, in any of the settled lands, who had forgotten to verify that his bride was untouched. Well, hell. It was an intrusive question. He was glad he hadn't asked.

He took his time with her, enjoying the process of exciting her almost as much as he had for himself. The uncertain motions of her hips became more urgent, more demanding. She rocked against his hand, her eyes closed, breathing fast. Suddenly she stiffened and cried out. She stayed that way for several seconds, her hips pushed up off the ground, against his hand. Then her entire body went limp. It was more erotic than any deliberate seduction any courtesan had ever tried on him.

"Ah..." Her voice trailed off. She had her arms around him, though he didn't remember when she had put them there. She stroked his back the way she had petted her kitten earlier. It made him want to laugh, which was a response rare enough that he didn't know what to do with it.

He slid his hand over her breasts and kissed her ear. "Better?"

"Much...better." She sounded embarrassed. But happy. "I didn't know it could be that way."

"I could tell."

"Does that bother you, that I don't know anything?"

Bother him? She was an angel. A miracle.

"No," he said. Cobalt raised his head to look at her. Her face was flushed, this time from exertion, and her hair was even more mussed than before. So sensual. Here he was, ready again, and now she was finished. They would have to learn to time themselves better. Such sweet lessons those would be. Maybe this marriage idea hadn't been such a bad one after all.

She touched his lips. "You say so little. What are you thinking?"

That I want to stay right here, forever, with you.

"We should go back," he said. If they were gone too long, his men would look for them, which could be embarrassing.

"All right." She sat up slowly and gave him an apologetic look. "I got your clothes wet."

He smiled and it didn't even crack his face. "They'll be fine."

Mel stared at him with the oddest expression.

"Really." He felt his shirt. It was damp, but it would dry quickly. She was still staring, though. He spoke uncomfortably. "What?"

She touched his lips. "You have an incredible smile. It lights up your whole face. You should use it more often."

I rarely have reason. Perhaps that would change. He knew he was deluding himself, that when they reached his home, he would have to deal with the same miserable life he had owned before he married her. Maybe with her it could be just a little different, enough that he might smile every now and then.

"But, Mel." He stood up, drawing her with him. "It would ruin my reputation."

She gave a startled laugh. She seemed less...wary? Less something. It was a good thing.

Mel gathered up her fresh clothes, a blue tunic with gold trim and blue leggings, and began to dress. His clothes were damp where they had soaked up water from her body, but it didn't bother him as he put them on. It made him think of the drops rolling down her breasts, pooling in her navel, dampening her hair. It didn't help that her tunic and leggings clung to her, an inescapable reminder of the body underneath. This wasn't going to be easy. She made it difficult to concentrate. Such pleasant distraction, though.

"What do you think when you stare like that?" Mel asked.

Stare indeed. "I'm wondering how long it will take us to reach the Cloud." The ride up to the castle was a long one.

She smiled uncertainly, as if she thought he was making fun of her. Then she headed back into the woods. Cobalt didn't know why his answer bothered her, or even if it really did, but she said nothing when he caught up with her. A few paces ahead of them, a man was leaning against a tree, sharpening a dagger.

"Matthew." Cobalt walked over to him. "What are you doing here?"

Matthew glanced up. "Keeping watch."

Like a bodyguard. Cobalt had spent most of his life with such protection. He didn't know who they were supposed to have protected him from, given that the only person who ever hurt him had been the king, whom none of his bodyguards would have dared to defy. Only Matthew had sheltered him during those days. Today, Matthew undoubtedly had posted himself for a far milder reason: to keep the other men from looking in on the newlyweds. Matthew seemed pleased, though why, Cobalt didn't know. This stop had delayed them over an hour. He had no objections, but then, he had reasons no one else shared.

As they all walked together, Cobalt thought of Mel and felt that strangeness happen to his face again, the gentling. She didn't see, fortunately; she was looking up ahead, through the trees. His fear that he would hurt her was abating. Perhaps it would be safe for him to ride with her after all. He wanted to hold her in his arms for the rest of the day.

The forest soon thinned out enough to show the open land up ahead. His honor guard waited out there and throughout the woods, pacing and probably impatient to get moving. His good mood faded. They had fewer men than before. They couldn't carry the bodies, so they had buried the six who had died last night. The task of telling their families would be his.

"Your men seem restless," Mel said.

"Yes." Cobalt was walking with Mel to one side and Matthew to the other. The sun filtered through the trees. "Would you like to ride with me on Admiral?"

She smiled. "I would like that."

For some reason, Matthew scowled at him.

Cobalt let Mel pull ahead until he and Matthew were a good ten paces behind her. Then he spoke in a low voice. "What?"

"This is hardly a time for her to ride a horse," Matthew said.

"Why not? I'm sure she knows how."

"I was thinking of her comfort."

"Admiral is a good horse."

The older man made an exasperated noise. "And you are a dense dolt." Then he added, "Your Highness."

"Explain," Cobalt said. He certainly was dense, because he had no idea what Matthew was getting at.

"She is a, uh, young bride." Matthew's face reddened. "The two of you go off together. You come back, both with wet hair and she has on different clothes. It would not be a stretch to imagine that for an inexperienced young woman, well, that is—riding a horse right now might be painful."

"Oh." Cobalt felt like an idiot. He thought of her question: *Did something just happen?* If he had managed better control and initiated her in the proper manner, Matthew might have reason for his concerns. As it was, the point was moot. He could hardly tell Matthew that, though. So he said only, "She will be all right."

The older man scowled. "You are impossible," he muttered. He strode away before Cobalt could respond.

When Cobalt reached the carriage, his men were mounted and ready to go. Matthew stood holding Admiral's reins, with Mel at his side. Rather than saddling the horse, he had strapped a blanket across Admiral's back. Cobalt took the reins, avoiding Matthew's gaze. As soon as he mounted, he reached down for Mel's hand. He pulled her up easily and she straddled Admiral in front of him.

Cobalt put his arms around her, and for a moment, he just sat with his head bent over hers. Her hair smelled damp, a trace of the soapy fragrance from yesterday lingering. He was aware of everyone watching them. He wondered what his men thought, if they envied him, if they considered him insensitive, like Matthew, or if they even cared. He pressed his lips against Mel's head and snapped the reins. Admiral started off at an easy pace across the land.

So they left their fragile refuge. Their interlude had ended.

Up ahead, the Misted Cliffs loomed in the sky.

9

The Airlight
Room

Mel thought Admiral must surely descend from the mounts ridden by the ancient wind saints of Aronsdale. He was magnificent. Like his rider. Cobalt sat easily with his arms around Mel. Her face warmed when she thought of her husband. She doubted she would forget those moments when he had undressed this morning. Such long legs, broad shoulders, narrow hips, all those planes of muscle, hard and lean. She blushed. Did he know what a fine figure he cut? He didn't seem to care. Perhaps her reaction was only that of an untutored woman seeing a man that way for the first time, but she didn't think so. She couldn't imagine that he had any match.

Although he was a strange man, he wasn't unkind. She had seen that this morning. He had more to him than the darkness of his reputation. She recalled Matthew's words: *He feels far too much. If he didn't, his wounds wouldn't be so deep.* What was it like to be the son of a warlord who had lost his throne? Whatever stories Cobalt may have heard, it hadn't stopped him from seeking recompense for Varqelle. But not vengeance. If that had been his intent, he would never have offered this marriage and the treaty they had all signed.

Mel wanted to understand him. The survival of three countries could depend on how well she judged his intentions and those of his father. Hell, her own survival probably depended on it. How Stonebreaker came into all this, she didn't know, but Brant Firestoke's warnings remained in her thoughts.

She closed her hand around the twenty-sided sphere that hung around her neck. If only she could draw on such a high-level shape, she might pick up more from the moods of her husband and the other people around her. She focused on the sphere, imagining emeralds and jade, sparkling green stones, tens, hundreds, thousands. But no spell formed. Frustrated, she tried harder, increasing her concentration.

Pain jabbed her temples.

"Ah!" She let go of the pendant with a jerk.

"Are you all right?" Cobalt asked.

Mel took a calming breath. Remembering how uneasy he had been about mages, she said only, "I'm fine. Just a little tired."

They continued on in silence.

The Misted Cliffs hadn't seemed far away this morning, but it took all day to reach them. They rose up, taller and taller, until they dominated the sky, a great wall that sheered out of the lowlands as if the world had split in two here, half of it dropped down and the other half standing like a barrier fit for the saints or the stars.

As they rode, the sun crossed the sky, never directly above them even at its highest point. They rested the horses and then continued on. Their party reached the base of the cliffs in late afternoon, as the sun sunk out of view and shadows stretched across the borderlands. They stopped to transfer Mel's belongings from the carriage to the spare horses, which included the mounts of the six men who had died. Cobalt directed his men with confidence. He didn't need to demand or bark; they responded to his taciturn self-assurance with a respect that had obviously been earned over time. The warriors were silent as they worked with the animals. Every now and then a man would bend his head in the traditional gesture of honor for a fallen soldier.

As Cobalt rode up to the carriage, Matthew came forward with Fog's basket. He handed it up to Mel and she smiled.

"My thanks for looking after him," she said. "Did he behave himself?"

Matthew pretended to grimace, but it didn't hide his good mood. "Ran me ragged, he did, scampering all around the carriage. Ate my soup and drank my water." His expression softened. "He's been a busy young fellow. I think he needs a good rest."

She lifted the top of the basket. Fog blinked at her, half asleep. "Good kitty," she crooned, petting his fur with long strokes. He butted his head against her arm.

"You should do that with me," Cobalt said behind her.

She smiled as she scratched behind Fog's ears. "Are you a sweet, cuddly kitten, Husband?"

His answering snort sounded like a laugh.

After she gave Fog some mush from leftover grain and meat, she closed up his basket, and Matthew fastened it to the travel packs on one of the horses. The carriage driver started up again, heading south along the cliffs. Four of the honor guard went with him and the others remained with Cobalt.

Mel watched the carriage recede. "Where is he going?"

"To a southern pass." Cobalt guided Admiral toward the cliffs at a slow walk. "They will go on to the Diamond Palace."

"Aren't we going there?"

"No."

"But—then where?"

"My home."

"Your home isn't the Diamond Palace?"

"No."

Mel tried again. "We're going into the cliffs?"

"Yes."

"Will you tell me where?" she growled. "Or must I extract the answer as if I were pulling a broken tooth from your mouth?"

"Ach, I hope not." He sounded alarmed. "I had my back teeth removed when I was young. It was exceedingly painful. I should never like to repeat the experience."

"I'm sorry to hear that." She was impressed, though. That was four full sentences.

"We are going to the Castle of Clouds," he said. "It is closer than the palace. I am concerned about the attack. The sooner we reach safety, the better."

Mel shuddered at the memory. "Yes."

"My mother and I usually live there," he added.

"Your mother." Panic touched Mel.

"She might appreciate another woman to talk to."

"Might?"

"I don't know," he admitted.

"Don't other women live at the castle?"

"No."

"None?" She didn't want to believe that.

"None."

"Surely servants."

"No."

"Don't the men have wives?"

"Some do."

"But they don't live with their husbands?"

"My grandfather has never allowed it."

This sounded strange. "But why?"

"I don't know." His voice had lost its vibrancy.

She had a feeling he did know, but didn't want to say. "Your mother must be lonely."

His silence stretched out. Then he said, "Yes."

Why would his grandfather deny her companionship? It sounded bleak. "Are your friends there?"

"I have no friends."

Mel couldn't tell if he really meant it. She had thought he was having fun with her this morning when he said they were going to "the Cloud," but now she realized he had meant the castle. Surely, though, he couldn't be serious about having no friends.

"Are you teasing me?" she asked.

"No."

If he truly believed he had no friends, he led an even more parched life than she had thought. "There is Matthew."

"My stable hand?"

"Does he really work in your stable?"

"Since before I was born."

"He acts like your friend." She thought of the disparity in their ages. "Or a mentor."

"He is my stable hand."

Mel gave up. She had friendships with many of the young

people who worked in the stables at her home, and she had done chores there herself, at her parent's insistence. But the Misted Cliffs had a more stratified society. Suggesting to the crown prince that his only friend was his stable hand might be an insult. Or perhaps he thought he had no friends because he didn't recognize friendship.

They rode through a natural archway in the cliffs and up a path that wound back into the great wall. In some places, the trail was a crevice open to the sky; in others, it became a tunnel, jagged and uneven. Their honor guard ranged ahead and behind them.

After a while, Cobalt said, "You are quiet."

"I was wondering."

"About what?"

"You."

"What about me?"

She decided to have another go at solving her puzzle of a husband. "Do you have other members of your staff like Matthew?"

"Other stable hands?"

"Men you talk to as you do with him. As if his companionship pleases you." She recalled how Matthew had stood up with him during the wedding. "As if you trust him."

His voice hardened. "I trust no one."

Surely he had someone in his life. "Were there…women?"

"Women?"

"Um, concubines."

"No."

"Oh." She didn't believe him. He had seemed too experienced at the pool this morning. "Then who?"

"Who what?"

"Who taught you so well?"

"You ask many questions." Now he sounded embarrassed.

"Were you married?" He was thirty-three, after all.

"No."

"A mistress?"

"No!" He made a frustrated noise. "I have known several courtesans. Now stop asking me these questions."

"You mean prostitutes?"

"I do not wish to have this conversation."

Mel let it go. His answers bewildered her. Surely he hadn't spent his life with no companionship except soldiers, prostitutes, and servants he wasn't allowed to acknowledge as friends.

They rode quietly after that, with only the clatter of hooves to break the silence. The shadows deepened and several riders lit torches. Their mounts went slowly, both for safety and to conserve strength. Sometimes they walked the horses. Mel was sore and stiff, but she had always liked to ride and she enjoyed this solemn procession despite the strangeness of going at night. One time Fog woke up and cried. She fed him and played with him until he let her coax him back into his big basket. Then they set off again, and Mel rode with Cobalt. Every now and then, a night bird cawed or a small animal scuttled into the shadows, but even those intermittent noises seemed muted.

She drowsed for a while, held by Cobalt. When she awoke, they were climbing a steep portion of the trail. Late-night constellations shone in the sky. She could see the borderlands to the east, over a natural wall of rock. They had gone high into the cliffs and the rest of the world had become distant and removed. Wind gusted through the open chasm beyond the trail. With a sigh, she stretched her arms.

"You're awake," Cobalt said.

"Hmm." She wasn't sure. "Aren't you tired?" He had slept only a few hours last night and none tonight, as far as she could tell.

"I am fine." He moved her hair aside and brought his lips to her ear. "Look."

Mel almost said, *At what.*

Then she saw.

They were coming out at the top of a cliff. Dawn had tinted the sky red in the east. A castle rose before them in a wonderland of towers. Their onion tops evoked the palaces of the southern countries rather than the turrets of Aronsdale. Bridges arched among them and their spires were silhouetted against the paling sky.

"Ah, saints," she said. "It's lovely."

He blew against the sensitive ridges of her ear. "Yes."

A wall about four stories high circled the keep. Sentries walked along its crenellated top, disappearing behind merlons carved in elongated onion shapes and then reappearing again. They must have already seen the party, for a large gate was opening in the wall. The honor guard escorted them past the wall, twenty men with Cobalt and Mel in their midst. Inside, pages were running across an odd courtyard, a wide strip of ground that curved around the bases of three towers. Other towers rose behind them and to the sides.

"I've never seen a castle like this," Mel said.

He kissed her ear, which was distracting, especially with his body pressed against hers. She felt warm in places he wasn't even touching.

"This is my home," he said.

"Then what is the Diamond Palace?"

"A place in the western lowlands. Grandfather lives there." He dismounted with unexpected agility, given how long they had been riding, and gave the reins to a groom. Then he reached up for Mel. She hesitated to trust him, but she knew she had no good reason to believe he would drop her, and she was tired enough to accept help.

Mel maneuvered her leg over Admiral so she was sitting sideways. Then she slid into Cobalt's arms, putting hers around his neck. As he eased her to the ground, her palms slid down his chest. He wrapped her in his cloak, enveloping her in wool that warded off the predawn chill. Then he held her close, his head bent over hers as Mel hugged him around his waist. It was hard to believe this man was her husband. He was a stranger, yet not a stranger. His embrace could have menaced; the top of her head only came to the middle of his chest and she felt the immense power in his arms—he could break a person's spine with this hold.

Mel didn't feel threatened, though. She leaned into him. "Tired…"

"Don't go to sleep," he murmured.

With a sigh, she straightened and drew her head back, out of his cloak. The sun hadn't risen, but it was light enough to see. People filled the courtyard and stable boys were leading away the horses.

As she and Cobalt stepped apart, a commotion came from a horseshoe arch in a tower to their left. The people coming out of it seemed to be headed this way, but she couldn't see much with so many others in the way. Mel felt too worn down to meet anyone new. She had no moorings and little sense of what they expected of her here. She had to depend on Cobalt, whom she had known only two days.

The newcomers drew nearer, and the courtyard cleared around them. Ten men in blue and silver livery surrounded a man with thick hair. Mel's breath caught. The center man's resemblance to Cobalt was unmistakable. They were both tall, though this man didn't have Cobalt's extraordinary height. He did have the same mane of dark hair, his streaked with gray. His face had that same aristocratic cast, the dark eyes, strong nose and chin, and high cheekbones. Both men had a hardness to them, as if they had been annealed in the same forge until nothing soft remained.

Mel stayed back while Cobalt greeted the newcomer. Her husband gave him a deference he had shown no one else.

The man inclined his head and spoke in a rumbling voice. "I am glad to see you returned safely, my son."

My son. This, then, was the notorious Varqelle.

"I almost didn't return," Cobalt said.

His father's gaze was like a hawk's. "What happened?"

As Cobalt recounted the ambush, Mel lost the contentment she had managed to gain during their ride here. She hadn't realized how severe their situation had been two nights ago. Cobalt estimated the number of their attackers at forty. He and his men had killed eighteen and the rest had fled. Mel remembered how Cobalt had reached out to her yesterday morning, with blood on his hand. Nausea rose within her.

"They were men of Harsdown?" Varqelle asked.

"Probably not," Cobalt said. "They dressed like farmers, but I think they were borderlands outlaws."

"Mercenaries," Varqelle said.

"Yes."

"Hired by whom?"

Mel recalled the man who had yanked her out of the carriage. He had attacked because she had married Cobalt, not because she was a Dawnfield. "Someone who doesn't like the House of Escar," she said behind Cobalt.

Everyone turned to her. When no one spoke, Mel flushed.

"Who are you?" Varqelle said.

Cobalt spoke. "Father, may I present my wife, Melody Dawnfield Escar."

"Your *wife?*" Varqelle stared at her. "This does not look like a man, Cobalt."

A man? Mel flushed. What the blazes did that mean?

"She fights like a man," Cobalt said.

"But doesn't look like one," Varqelle murmured.

Mel's face flamed, not only because they spoke as if she wasn't there, but also from the way Varqelle watched her, as if she were prey.

Falling back on the safety of protocol, she bowed as a royal woman in Aronsdale would to a member of another royal family, with one arm at her side and the other holding the cloth of her tunic. Customs varied among the realms, but the ways of the Misted Cliffs were closer to those of Aronsdale than to those of the eastern lands of Jazid and Taka Mal. "I am honored by your presence, Your Majesty." She gave Varqelle the title for a king, though her own father sat on the Jaguar Throne.

Varqelle glanced at his son. "She speaks well."

Cobalt squinted at him. "She speaks a lot."

"Women do that," Varqelle said.

Mel wished they would speak *to* her instead of about her. With Cobalt, she doubted the slight was deliberate, but Varqelle was another story. Nor could she forget: This was the man who had almost brought Aronsdale to its knees eighteen years ago. Had he succeeded, he would have killed her uncle Jarid and her father as well, possibly her mother, too, or taken Chime as a prize. Mel could think of nothing positive to say to him, so she said nothing.

Thinking of her cousins made Mel remember Aron, and

her heart seemed to lurch. She had put him out of her mind, knowing she must, but now memories flooded back. He was full of life and mischief, with his brown hair sticking up over one ear. They had known most of their lives that they would marry. He had written her poetry. Now all of that was gone. Instead, she had lain with the son of the man who had tried to kill Aron's father. Even worse, she had enjoyed it. Guilt washed over her and she wanted to sink into the flagstones.

Mel looked away, past the guards, horses, and grooms to the open area beyond the entrance in the great wall. Men were cranking the gate closed, turning huge wheels wound with ropes as thick as her arm. The massive portal rumbled into place and cut off her view of freedom.

From a distance, the bridge looked like frozen lace carved in ice. It arched between two towers. When she and Cobalt reached the span, Mel realized it was white marble flecked with silver. Its walls came up to mid-torso on her. Holes shaped like heptagons were carved into them, and her mage power stirred.

The wind pulled at her braid and tossed Cobalt's hair around his head and collar. By the time they reached the top of the span, midway between the towers, Mel was chilled through her tunic. The courtyard was five stories below. A cloud had drifted under the bridge and obscured the view. She thought of Fog. Matthew had promised to see the kitten safely put in Cobalt's suite, fed, and closed in so he wouldn't run away. She hoped Fog was all right. Mel had so little else left of home.

At the end of the bridge, Cobalt opened a door and they entered a chamber tiled in circles and squares. This entire castle was full of shapes. Everywhere. The Misted Cliffs had no mages, but they favored tessellated mosaics similar to those in Aronsdale, interlocked geometric shapes that mesmerized. It had oversensitized Mel's mage talents until a low-level mood spell surrounded her. Dark emotions saturated this tower.

"Who lives here?" Mel asked.

"On this level, no one." Cobalt wouldn't look at her. "My grandfather lives on the top floor when he visits."

"Oh." The mood she felt didn't speak well of Stonebreaker. She wondered if the emotions came from Cobalt.

They followed halls tiled in blue and white mosaics, crossed another bridge in the clouds, and entered another tower. Her spell stirred again; the moods here were warm, especially toward Cobalt. He took her to a large room hung with translucent drapes that shimmied in the breezes coming through many open windows. He disappeared through a door behind the drapes, and Mel waited, feeling vulnerable. Alone. This tower might be better for Cobalt, but she sensed no welcome for herself.

He pulled aside the drapes. "Come."

Mel followed him through another horseshoe arch. In the study beyond, a slight woman with black hair was sitting at a desk. Silks draped her body in pale yellow layers, and goldrimmed spectacles lay on the table next to her. She had exquisite skin, almost translucent, but her dark eyes seemed too large for her face. Gray streaked her hair and fine lines showed around her eyes. Her features were delicate, including a rosy mouth, straight nose, and the high curve of her cheeks.

Cobalt drew Mel over to the woman. "Mother, may I present my wife, Melody Dawnfield Escar." He turned to Mel. "My mother, Her Majesty, Dancer Chamberlight Escar."

Mel bowed deeply to the queen. Compared to Dancer, she felt clumsy and crude.

The queen spoke softly. "So you are Melody."

Mel straightened up. She saw no welcome in her mother-in-law's gaze. She wanted to create a better mood spell, but she had no shape to touch and she feared to relax her concentration. Everything in this fortress seemed saturated with warnings, unspoken and unwritten, like shadows that would swallow her and leave no trace that she had existed.

She said only, "A good morn, Your Majesty."

"Have the staff treated you well?" Dancer asked.

"Yes, ma'am." Mel hadn't actually met any of them yet. At home, they would have gathered in the front parlor to greet a new member of the household, but here everyone seemed to take their cue from Cobalt, and she had a feeling he had no clue how to introduce his new wife to the staff. Since she had nothing to add about them, she said, "It is beautiful here."

"Yes," Dancer murmured. "Let us hope it stays that way." She took her son's hand and touched the end of his finger. He still had a trace of blood under the nails. Dancer tried to scrape it off one finger, then gave up and set his hand back by his side. He didn't pull away, but neither did he explain.

Dancer put on her spectacles and studied Mel. "Bring no bloodshed into my home."

"Mother." Cobalt frowned at her. "The only thing my wife has brought into our home is herself." Then he added, "And her cat."

"An animal?" Dancer took off her glasses. "I hope it does not get underfoot. I can't guarantee one of the men won't step on it and break its neck."

Mel blanched. No wonder Cobalt was so strange, with this charming family of his.

"For saints' sake," Cobalt said. "No one is going to step on her cat." He put his hand on Mel's shoulder. "Perhaps we should see to your things in my suite."

His servants were taking care of her belongings, but right now Mel would have agreed to anything to escape the queen. She bowed to Dancer. "My pleasure at your company, Your Majesty."

"Is it?" Dancer asked.

Mel flushed. She had no answer to that, either.

They left as they had come, through the rippling drapes that veiled the room.

Mel sat on the cushioned bench of a window seat in the Airlight Room of Cobalt's suite. She held Fog in her lap and petted the kitten while she gazed out the window in dispirited silence. Cobalt lived at the top of the East Tower, which afforded a spectacular view of the borderlands far below the cliffs. The land stretched out for many leagues until, at the distant horizon, it blended into the Tallwalk Mountains.

The room was an expanse of white stone with no furniture. Breezes wafted through the open windows and rustled the gauzy drapes. Cobalt had fewer of the curtain-walls than Mel had seen in other rooms, but these were enough to give the room an airy feel, as if she were among clouds even inside the castle.

A scrape came from behind the hangings and a blurred figure appeared across the room behind the hanging cloths. Then Cobalt pushed aside a drape. He was dressed in black, as always, and he cut a stark contrast against the white marble and diaphanous curtains.

He came to stand by her at the window. With his hands behind his back, he looked out at the borderlands. "Would you like to eat supper up here tonight?"

From what Mel had overheard among the staff, the family ate on the ground floor of the Storm Tower where Stonebreaker stayed during his visits. Right now, it was only Cobalt, his parents, and her. "Won't we be expected downstairs?"

"Not tonight," he said.

She thought of her reception here. "Maybe never."

He shifted his gaze to her. "Why do you say that?"

"Your family doesn't like me."

He leaned against the wall and folded his arms, watching her now instead of the view. "They don't much like me, either."

Mel couldn't imagine what sort of life he had, that he could speak that way with such casual disregard. "Your mother does. She doesn't think I'm good enough for you."

"Ah, well." He shrugged. "My mother thinks you married me only to stop me from attacking your country, that you have no love for this place, and that you wish you were home instead of here. She thinks I should have married a woman who loves me."

"Oh." Mel reddened. She could hardly deny any of it.

"That is why she distrusts you," Cobalt said.

"She's afraid I'm going to hurt her, too."

His forehead furrowed. "Why do you say such a thing?"

"All the shapes." She traced the pentagons carved into the stone frame of the window. "They're everywhere. It sensitizes my mind to spells."

His face seemed to shutter. "Mage spells."

"Yes."

"Perhaps you should unpack," he said.

"Cobalt, don't."

"Don't what?"

"Shut me out."

He just looked at her. She wasn't certain he even knew what she meant.

She bent her head over Fog. Here in his home, Cobalt had receded from her. She touched a pentagon and concentrated on a green spell. It was a weak one, fed only by a five-sided, two-dimensional shape, and it told her very little, only that Cobalt was guarding his emotions from her. Especially from her.

She didn't see how she would bear to live in this ice castle for the rest of her life.

Cobalt didn't know what to do.

Mel sat by the window petting her absurd cat, which was small enough to fit in his palm. Although it batted at her hand, she didn't play with it today. The sunlight made her hair shine and brought a glow to her cheeks—but not to her eyes. They were full of tears.

He had done this to her and he had no idea how to fix it. His father wanted her gone. His mother objected to her. None of the staff trusted her. He thought Matthew liked her, but the stable master lived in the clock tower by the stables and didn't often come into the castle. If everyone here followed Stonebreaker's dictates, then the only person who would even speak to Mel, aside from her husband, was Dancer, and his mother had made her opinion on that excruciatingly clear. Mel had good reason to bend her head over her cat and cry.

She was sitting sideways on the seat, her back pressed against the window frame, with the window on her right. She had stretched her legs across the short bench, and her feet hit the opposite side. It wasn't a large seat; she took up most of it. When he sat on the edge next to her knees, it left no room at all. His leg pressed her thigh, penning her against the window. Her hand jerked and the cat mewled in protest. Cobalt hadn't meant to corner her, but he couldn't make himself less large. He scratched Fog's ears the way he had seen her do. Perhaps if he could make her cat like him, she might like him, too.

"Mel, listen," he said.

She managed a misty smile. "Are you going to talk?"

"Yes." He gave Fog one last scratch, then laid his hand on his thigh. "Tonight I must meet with Varqelle and discuss the treaty I signed with your father."

"What will your father say, do you think?"

"That he hates it," Cobalt admitted.

"Oh."

"You should stay in my suite," he said. "Don't go anywhere without me for these first days, until people know you better."

"Do you think someone will hurt me?"

"I don't know." Cobalt wished he had better things to tell her. He lifted his hand, intending to touch her cheek, but he stopped when she flinched. He felt as if someone had socked him in the stomach. Did she think he would hit her? If he could have taken back that moment when he had raised his fist after the battle, he would have done so a hundred times. But nothing could change it. He couldn't even swear it would never happen again. He had never struck a woman or a child, but he had brawled with many a man. Outside a tavern one night, years ago, a thief had tried to rob him. Cobalt had sought only to defend himself. He hadn't intended to kill the man.

They had buried the thief the next morning.

He looked at his nails. He had cleaned away the blood, but he could never clean the stain from his soul.

Mel touched his fingertip. "Does it bother you?"

He knew she meant the killing. "Yes."

Her voice trembled. "I—I couldn't tell if it did."

Don't fear me. He wanted to say it, but he couldn't form the words. They would be false. She had good reason to fear him.

"I am not a good man, Mel. I never will be." He met her gaze. "But I can vow this—I will always protect you."

"Goodness and gentleness aren't the same." Tears gathered in her eyes. "They have much in common, but you can have one without the other. A man's life may harden him. It may make him harsh. But that doesn't mean he is evil."

He couldn't face her words. They skirted dangerous territory. He touched a tear as it ran down her face. "Don't cry, Mel."

"Don't you ever cry?" she asked. "Does anything soft remain behind all that armor?"

"It was never there."

"Cobalt—" Another tear rolled down her cheek.

He was breaking inside. "Does my home sadden you so much?"

"I don't cry for your home."

"Then for what?"

"You," she whispered.

He wanted to run from her. "Don't."

She squeezed his hand. "Go talk with your father. I will be here when you're done."

His heart stuttered. His empty suite was empty no longer. But he feared she wouldn't stay.

10
The General

Dancer lived on the top floor of the West Tower and Cobalt at the top of the East Tower. It hadn't surprised Cobalt that Varqelle chose the South. The compass towers at the corners of the castle were the largest of its eleven, except for the Storm Tower in the center where Grandfather sometimes lived.

Cobalt strode through dusky corridors in the Sphere Tower. He held a long metal tube capped at each end. Torches on the walls sputtered and cast oversize, misshapen shadows of his body against the stone walls.

At the end of the hall, he pushed open a door. Wind blasted him. He crossed the bridge between the Sphere and South Tower with no light except from the stars and a crescent moon. Inside the South Tower, he followed the hallway that circled its girth until he reached the stairs. Those took him to his father's suite, which occupied the top level. The ceiling was open to the onion dome and its graceful curves arched over Cobalt's head. In the past, this room had been partitioned by gauzy drapes, but Varqelle had had them removed. It was all open space now, airy and full of light during the day.

Varqelle's study was to Cobalt's left, with a desk and wingchair. The canopied bed stood on a dais far across the room. A table with several chairs occupied the center of the tower. Cobalt and Mel weren't the only ones who had dined alone; platters from Varqelle's dinner remained on the table. Now the king sat at a darkwood table by a window, relaxed in an armchair, gazing at the night. A crystal flask of red wine and two goblets waited on the table.

Cobalt crossed the room. When he was several paces from Varqelle, he paused. "Father?"

Varqelle glanced up at him. "Ah!" He motioned to a chair across the table. "Come. Sit. Have some wine."

Cobalt settled in the wingchair and stretched out his legs under the table. They reached all the way to the other side. He set his tube on the table between them, then filled the goblets with wine and offered one to his father.

Varqelle accepted the drink. "Did you settle her in?"

Cobalt knew he meant Mel. "Yes."

His father sipped his wine. "Enjoy her now, while you can."

Cobalt took his goblet. "While I can?"

Varqelle's face seemed shadowed. "Before she betrays you."

Why did Dancer leave you? Cobalt hardly knew Varqelle, but he could already see how much he and his father had in common. Varqelle didn't seem a monster. Hardened, Mel might say. Perhaps she would say worse; Varqelle had tried to conquer her people. But Cobalt didn't see why Dancer had fled.

How did she think this man could have been worse than Stone-breaker? He couldn't ask outright, but perhaps he could probe.

"Mel would not take my child from me," Cobalt said.

"I didn't believe your mother would, either."

"Did you ever think of having another?"

"Another child?" Varqelle seemed startled. "Of course not."

Cobalt spoke with care. "One might acknowledge a child born in less than auspicious circumstances."

His father took another swallow of wine. "If you mean, did I take comfort elsewhere, I certainly didn't spend all those years alone. But even if I had other children, which I don't to my knowledge, I couldn't recognize them. You are my heir, son. I would have it no other way."

His words warmed Cobalt. "Nor I."

"I am pleased."

"I would have my child know you, too."

Varqelle inclined his head. "I would like that."

"Or my children," Cobalt added.

His father blinked. "You can have only one."

"King Jarid is royal. He has several." Cobalt had thought it odd, too, but now he wondered. "The stars did not clatter out of the sky."

Varqelle snorted. "Mad King Jarid."

Although Cobalt had heard rumors about the eccentricities of the Aronsdale king, he also knew many considered Jarid a good ruler, if somewhat taciturn. Cobalt didn't know him, but he found it hard to credit the stories of Jarid being a mage.

His father leaned forward. "If your wife takes your child home to her father, we will fetch him back. Whatever it takes."

Whatever it takes. As he had done to free Varqelle from the

Citadel of Rumors. "Did you ever consider coming here to reclaim me, after Mother left?"

Varqelle regarded him steadily. "Every day of my life."

Cobalt wished his father had succeeded. But he had no way to know if his life would have been better with Varqelle. "I would have welcomed the chance to know you sooner."

"I also." Varqelle spoke quietly. "I tried to send men here secretly, to take you back. But your grandfather guarded you too well."

Cobalt stiffened. "You would have had them kidnap me?"

"Does that horrify you so much?"

Cobalt didn't know what to think. To be ripped away from Dancer—he would never have wanted that, as a child. But to escape Stonebreaker would have been a gift. "Just me? Or Mother and me?"

"I tried both. And just you." Varqelle exhaled. "Neither worked." He set down his goblet. "So I tried another method."

"Conquest." The word had a dark appeal.

"I had intended to take Aronsdale first," Varqelle said. "I thought I had the best chance of defeating their military. Then Shazire. By that time, I might have had an army strong enough to face the Misted Cliffs." His gaze took on a fierce intensity that called to the restless energy within Cobalt. "Eventually I would have had all the settled lands."

A heady thought, that, sweeping across the land at the head of a force that would conquer the world. "A powerful vision."

Varqelle sat back. "Yes, well, it failed."

"Not completely." Cobalt thought of the tube before them on the table. It contained his copy of the treaty. He knew he should take it out. He and his father had much to discuss. But this matter of heirs was unfinished.

"I have thought lately on how a father might be to his son," Cobalt said. He had no one to base his approach on except Stonebreaker, and he would die rather than use the Chamberlight king as a model. He intended to discuss it with Matthew, when he found a good time, but the subject seemed appropriate now.

"You must be strong with him," Varqelle said.

"So Grandfather says."

"Your grandfather raised you, didn't he?"

"With Mother, yes."

"I would never have chosen it that way." Varqelle paused. "But he seems to have done well."

Cobalt felt ill. "He had a heavy hand."

"It didn't defeat you." His father nodded with respect. "You have become a fine man. I am pleased."

Cobalt felt cold, then flushed. The father approved of the son. He hadn't expected this, hadn't even imagined it could be possible. He had spent decades laboring under the weight of his grandfather's censure, until it became a way of life, a necessity to deal with but never escape. Although he had hoped his father might be different, it had been too far outside his experiences to imagine Varqelle might look on him with high regard. Cobalt would do anything, descend from the cliffs and spread his father's rule across every settled land, from the western coast through the Misted Cliffs, Harsdown and Aronsdale, through Blueshire, Jazid, Taka Mal, and Shazire, anything at all, to keep that approval.

He had no idea how to express any of that. So instead he said, "I descend from a strong line."

"The House of Escar goes back a millennium. It has known greatness." Varqelle leaned forward. "It will again."

Cobalt's pulse quickened. "Yes."

His father's eyes glinted. "Together, you and I can make it happen."

"We are already." But the more Cobalt thought of their peace treaty, the less satisfied he felt. It had been necessary, yes; what point in ruling a broken land? He wanted Harsdown whole. But it didn't appease the hunger within him, the drive to push outward, sword in hand, his men at his back, challenges ahead of him.

Varqelle touched the tube as if probing a disappointment. "The treaty?"

"Yes." Cobalt opened it and pulled out a scroll. A red string tied the parchment. He undid the string and unrolled the scroll in front of his father. "The agreement stipulates that neither the Misted Cliffs nor the House of Escar will raise an army against Harsdown or Aronsdale. Nor will the House of Dawnfield attack Escar or Chamberlight. The marriage will put my heir on the Jaguar Throne."

"Your son."

Cobalt cleared his throat. "Actually, it says 'heir.'"

Varqelle scowled. "That is why these mage countries are so perverse. Their women do too much."

Cobalt had no problem with that stipulation of the treaty. Had he been able, he would have made his mother heir to the Sapphire Throne of the Misted Cliffs. He thought of Mel, who had rescued herself during the assault on the carriage. He had ultimately killed her attacker, but if she hadn't defended herself, she wouldn't have survived.

"The Dawnfields breed strong children," Cobalt said.

"They certainly don't look strong." Varqelle scanned the parchment. "This all seems in order."

"It is a good agreement," Cobalt said. "We maintain peace

and your House inherits the thrones of both Harsdown and the Misted Cliffs."

"So it does." Varqelle looked up at him. In a shadowed voice, he said, "Why stop at Harsdown and the Misted Cliffs?"

Cobalt's pulse surged. *Why stop?*

He had prepared an army. Catching bandits and mercenaries who preyed on farmers wasn't enough. After the engagement at the Citadel of Rumors, he had grieved for the deaths. But they had achieved a worthy goal—the rescue of the true Harsdown king. For the first time in his life, Cobalt had operated to a greater purpose. He had freed his father to reestablish the House of Escar, and he had thought that would be enough, but it hadn't eased the edgy hunger that drove him every day, always challenging, always striving, always pushing.

Cobalt said only, "The treaty is signed."

"So it is." Varqelle's gaze never wavered. "You have the makings of a great general, Cobalt. Would you let a marriage weaken you?"

Cobalt didn't realize his fist had clenched on the table until his nails bit into his palm. It wasn't from the rage that too often took control of him, though. He had subconsciously been gripping the hilt of a sword, prepared to do battle, not with Varqelle, but with...he didn't know.

"We gave our word," Cobalt said.

Varqelle rolled up the treaty and tied it with the string. "You and I are of a kind." He regarded Cobalt steadily. "Remember that."

Cobalt felt the truth in those words. The restive spirit he had hoped would calm after he rescued Varqelle had instead intensified—and found an answering spirit within his father. Cobalt felt hungry and fierce, filled with a fire that nothing seemed to quench. For the first time, in his father, he had met someone who sparked an answering fire.

He returned the scroll to its tube. "I will remember."

Mel was walking through the round chamber at the center of Cobalt's suite, holding Fog, when she heard a tap. It sounded like it was in the hallway stretching from this chamber to the corridor that circled the outer wall of the tower. Almost instinctively, she thought of the straight hall as the radius of a circle and the hall that ran around the tower as its perimeter. As soon as she envisioned the circle, gold light filled the chamber all around her. It wasn't only the lights from the lamps in the wall sconces; this illumination came from a well deep within her. The spell happened without her even trying to make one. Fog nuzzled her arm and purred loudly.

In the past month, her mage abilities had come to life more than in all her previous eighteen years. She wasn't sure why, but perhaps it related to the fact that she had matured late physically, too.

The tap came again.

Mel's spell slipped away and the gold radiance faded until only torchlight remained. She went down the hallway to the outer wall of the suite. The main entrance was a horseshoe arch eight feet tall, bordered by marble columns tiled halfway up with blue and white mosaics in sphere designs. She remembered Cobalt's warning about not leaving this suite tonight. Fog wriggled, seeking freedom from her hold, and gave an annoyed mewl. Mel was so tense, she hardly noticed when he dug his claws into her sleeve.

"Who is it?" she asked.

A man answered. "Matthew, Your Highness."

Relief trickled over her. Matthew she liked. Still cautious, though, she only opened the door a crack. "Yes?"

Matthew stood outside, his arms full of scrolls. He bowed to her. "I am sorry to disturb you, Your Highness. Her Majesty finished with these and Prince Cobalt wished to read them."

Mel hesitated. She didn't know which would cause more offense, if she refused to let Matthew complete a task Dancer had given him or if she let him enter Cobalt's suite when she was here alone. She couldn't ask him to bring a female servant. She had seen no women on the staff here. It was bizarre. The men even did the cooking and cleaning. Mel could believe Dancer might have sent Matthew to vex her new daughter-in-law, but she found it hard to believe Matthew would offer to bring in the scrolls if he shouldn't be here. She didn't know him well, so she could be wrong, but he struck her as the type who would have let her know if this could get her into trouble.

Mel moved aside. "Come in."

"Thank you." Matthew entered and Mel closed the door, then followed him down the hallway. Fog struggled in her arms, and she let him jump down. When Matthew reached the center chamber, he turned to her with a kindly expression on his weathered face. Fog ran around him once, batted at his foot, and then tore off into another room.

Mel smiled. "I think he likes you."

Matthew laughed good-naturedly. "He has good taste."

"Do you know where to put the scrolls?" Each room in the suite was a wedge in the circular tower, six in all, with entrances on their narrow ends that opened into this chamber.

He indicated an entrance to his right. "The library."

Mel went to the horseshoe arch. She had yet to explore many of the rooms here. A single lamp illuminated the library, gilding the shelves of varnished darkwood that lined the walls from floor to ceiling. Scrolls and books filled them, with gilt titles on the spines of the tomes and gold ribbons tying the parchments. To her left, a desk was pushed into the corner where the curving outer wall met the straight wall. Windows in the curving section let in starlight. A large globe on a stand was set in the right corner, with its continents painted in gold, the seas in blue and green, and the lettering in black. Globes were rare in Harsdown, but she expected they were more common here, in the only country with a coast where visiting ships brought news of other lands. A telescope stood next to the window. At least Mel thought it was a telescope. She had never seen one before.

"It is a nice room," she said.

Matthew sighed. "One could wish he spent more time here."

"Does he read much?"

"He likes history." Matthew entered and set the scrolls on the desk. "It is an interest he and Dancer share."

Mel thought of her icy mother-in-law. "She was reading when I met her."

"She has much interest in the history of her people, especially the women." He spoke in a confidential tone. "I think she would like to write her own treatise. She feels the histories of the Misted Cliffs ignore the contributions of women."

That didn't surprise Mel, given what she had seen so far. "It seems like a good idea. Does Cobalt read about women, too?"

Matthew chuckled. "Ah, no, I don't think so. He reads about wars. All the battles and strategies."

"Military history."

"It fascinates him."

She could well imagine. "Well, I will let him know you brought his scrolls."

He bowed. "Thank you, Your Highness."

After Matthew left, Mel wandered back to the library and looked at the materials he had brought. Fog dashed out of a hiding place under a nearby table and jumped up on a chair, and from there to the desk. He batted curiously at the scrolls, and Mel nudged him away, lest he harm the parchments. They were inked in beautiful calligraphy with colorful borders, apparently modern copies of works several centuries old. It took her a while to decipher the antiquated language, but she could tell they were histories of campaigns from the days when Shazire had been part of the Misted Cliffs instead of a separate country. Eventually she retied the scrolls. Her husband, it seemed, had many facets she had yet to learn.

Fog stalked around the desk, looking for something else to bedevil, since she had denied him the scrolls. He swiped at a paperweight shaped like a blue cube, and it skittered off the desk, then clattered to the floor. He jumped down and pounced on it with all the ferocity a kitten could muster.

"Oh, Fog, honestly." Mel bent down and rescued the paperweight. "You're going to get us into trouble if you reduce my new husband's library to shambles."

Fog seemed unconcerned. He ran off to explore one of the bookshelves, which had just enough space for him to crawl under the bottom shelf.

The cube fit easily into Mel's palm, and she gazed at it thoughtfully. She didn't know if her failure with her pendant had come about because she didn't have the strength to use such a high-level form or because she lacked experience. Skylark wouldn't have given her the pendant if she didn't believe Mel could use the shape. Perhaps she needed to build her strength with spells much as she built her muscles when she practiced with a sword. A six-sided cube might offer a good test of her developing skills.

Mel took a deep breath to settle herself. She concentrated on the cube, imagining strawberries, and roses with their red petals drifting on the wind. Her temples throbbed, but the pain wasn't unbearable—and red light glowed around her hand. Excited, she carried the cube to the windowsill, where an unlit candle stood. Outside, the night shed cold starlight across the ghostly towers of the castle.

"Everything is chilly here," Mel murmured. She held her hand with the cube above the candle, and her spell expanded until its red glow enveloped the wick. She focused harder, intensifying the spell. Unlike when she used circles or other two-dimensional shapes, she didn't have to strain with this cube to find the power she wanted.

The wick burst into flame.

"Ha!" Mel grinned. Bringing the fire had felt almost effortless with the strength of a cube behind her spell, and she had controlled it much better than her last fire spell, the mistake in the orchard back home.

The red light soon dimmed, but the candle stayed lit. She returned to the desk and set down the cube. Although she was tired, and her head ached, she also felt invigorated, full of unused power. After a hesitation, she folded her hand around her pendant. This time she imagined oranges, sweet and succulent. Pain sparked in her temples and she struggled to keep her focus—

Suddenly orange light flared all around her. She hadn't realized her sword arm was sore until the ache receded now. The library was warm with orange radiance.

"Incredible," Mel murmured.

The pain in her head spiked and her spell slipped, then

crumpled. As the light winked out, Mel groaned and let go of the pendant. Standing before the desk, she pressed her fingertips into her temples and rubbed hard.

A plaintive mewl came from the floor, followed by a body rubbing her ankles. Mel looked down as she lowered her arms. Recognizing the kitten's tone, she couldn't help but smile. "I just fed you, you foggy scamp."

Fog jumped up to the desk and sat there, posed with his feet together and his tail curled around his body, as regal as a statue. Laughing, Mel scooped him up in her arms. "You're beautiful," she crooned, rubbing her cheek against his fur. "My head hurts like the blazes, though."

Fog settled into her arms and purred.

"Time for sleep, eh?" Tomorrow she would practice again, both her mage skills and with her sword. After the attack on the carriage, she couldn't risk letting down her guard.

What unsettled her most about the fight, though, were those few moments when she had felt exhilarated rather than terrified.

Cobalt's suite was quiet when he returned. Unlike his father's tower, this one had solid interior walls. A lamp glowed in the center chamber and its light trickled into his bedroom, but the other rooms were dark. Standing within the horseshoe arch, he couldn't tell if Mel was in his bed or not. If she made a mound, it was too small to see from here.

He thought about his father's words. Did she weaken him? Had he lost sight of greater goals because of her? No, he was the one who had suggested this marriage. She couldn't have ensnared his heart and weakened his resolve before he even met her.

Cobalt walked to his bed. As he neared, he saw a low ridge

on one side. It didn't look big enough to be a person. He sat next to the ridge and lifted the blue quilt. Mel was underneath, on her side, her cheek against the pillow, her eyes closed. Fog was curled in the crook of her arm.

He scratched Fog behind the ears. "Cat," he admonished. "You may not replace me here."

Fog mewed drowsily.

Cobalt slid his palm under its body and lifted it carefully out of the bed. It blinked sleepy eyes at him. The animal felt fragile and soft, and he didn't want to hurt it. He brought it closer to his face so he could see it better.

"You are small," he said.

The kitten butted its nose against his wrist.

Cobalt smiled. "Yes, well, in this bedroom, she is mine." He looked around for someplace to put it, but he saw only the floor. The stone would be too cold and hard. He opened the drawer of the nightstand and pulled out the shaving things he had put there, except for the towel he used to wipe his face. His razor and soap wouldn't mind a cold floor. He set them by the bed, then put the kitten in the drawer on top of the towel. It looked up at him and mewed.

"I know she is warmer," Cobalt said. "But I need to be warm, too."

The kitten sat for a moment considering him. Then it yawned, wide and large, showing him its small fangs. It turned around a few times on the towel and settled down, curled into a ball. Then it closed its eyes and appeared to go to sleep. Cobalt didn't know enough about cats to guess if it really was sleeping or just ignoring him, but it seemed content.

He turned back to Mel. She hadn't stirred at all. He undressed and left his clothes in a heap on top of the razor and soap. Then he went around to the other side of the bed and slid in behind her. She was wearing a filmy nightdress. He moved his hands over the cloth, tugging here and there, but he couldn't see how to get it off.

"What...?" Mel stirred, warm and drowsy, and turned onto her back.

Cobalt fumbled with the ties at the neck of her gown. He couldn't undo them, but the ribbon broke in his hand and her gown opened. He slid his hand over her breast. Propped up on one elbow, with one hand braced on a pillow and his other stroking her nipples, he gazed at her face. Angel face. He lowered his head and kissed her.

Mel went very still. Her lips were warm, inviting him, but she didn't respond the way she had at the pool. He lifted his head, puzzled. Her eyes seemed too large and she had no smile for him tonight.

Don't be afraid of me. He wanted her to desire him. Was this what his father meant by a woman weakening him, this need that made him feel as vulnerable as the cat in the drawer? Unlike Fog, he couldn't just turn around a few times and go to sleep.

After several moments of him looking at her and her looking at him, Cobalt realized she wasn't going to scream or beat him off. He tugged at her nightgown. "Can you make it go away?" he asked. "It tears when I try."

Mel hesitated. Then she wriggled out of the gown, her body moving sensuously against him until he wanted to groan. He didn't, though. He made no sound at all. When she had the gown partway over her head, he pulled it off and tossed it over the side of the bed. She lay beneath him, gazing up with luminous eyes. Eager for her, he lowered himself on her lovely body.

* * *

Mel awoke in darkness. Someone was fumbling with her nightgown. She opened her eyes, groggy and confused. Cobalt had pinned her on her back and was looming over her. His hands moved on her body, grasping and large. He pressed his lips against hers while he mauled her breast. He was too heavy—she couldn't breathe—he was going to crush her.

Cobalt lifted his head and his hand stilled on her breast. Mel stared at him, her heart beating hard. She could breathe now, though. After a moment, as her pulse calmed, she exhaled. She remembered the first time they had lain together. His power could be as erotic as it was overwhelming, but he was different now, darker, less patient. Or perhaps he had been that way before and she hadn't noticed.

Cobalt tugged at her gown. "Can you make it go away? It tears when I try."

Did she want to refuse him? He was her husband, and a fine figure of a man—if she could just stop being afraid of him. She did want him, she realized. She struggled out of her gown, which tangled with her limbs. Before she finished, he pulled it away and threw it somewhere. Then he stretched out on top of her, his weight pressing her into the mattress. She had to turn her cheek against his shoulder to breathe. It was too much. He was huge, his head above hers, his biceps hard against her, his hands grasping her breasts until she felt suffocated.

"Mel." He whispered her name. "Sweet angel."

"Can you lift up?" She slid her arms around him in a tentative embrace. "You're heavy."

He pushed up on his elbows, easing his weight off her. Then he grinned, his teeth a flash of white in the darkness, and leaned down his head to rub his nose against hers.

Mel gave him a shaky smile. "What is that?"

"Like Fog. He did it when I put him in the drawer."

"The drawer?"

"Hmm." Cobalt caressed her breast. Then he kissed her again. He pressed his hips against her, spreading her legs apart while he pushed her lips open with his tongue.

Slow down! Mel struggled under him, but it only seemed to make him more insistent. His hands kneaded her too hard, enough to leave bruises.

Mel pulled away her head. "Stop!"

Cobalt froze. "Stop?"

"You're hurting me."

Even in the dark, the alarm on his face showed. "Tell me what hurts. I will stop."

"It's just—your hands. And I— It's hard to breathe."

He slid off and lay against her side. His hand slowed on her breast, stroking only, no longer kneading.

"Better?" he asked.

She blushed. "Yes."

"You are small," he said, more to himself than to her. "Like Fog. I will have to be more careful."

"Don't put me in a drawer," she said, managing a laugh.

His face softened into his most incredible expression, that smile he so rarely showed. "You wouldn't fit in the nightstand, Mel. You aren't *that* small."

She touched his lips. "You are beautiful to look at and to touch, my husband, but too much of anything, even such a desirable man, can be overwhelming."

His grin flashed. "So I am desirable."

"Hmm…" She kissed him tentatively, and he responded with that fierce intensity of his, but more controlled this time, enough that she didn't feel overwhelmed. Knowing she provoked this response from such a powerful man aroused her in a way that sweet words or suave expertise could never have done. His strength, his urgency, his muscles hard against her body: it was unlike anything she had imagined. He touched her everywhere. Although he would never be a gentle lover, his hands weren't as rough as before. Her breasts ached, but without his weight pressing her so hard, she no longer felt as if she were suffocating. She ran her palms over his back and buttocks, and her breath quickened.

"You're beautiful," she whispered.

For a moment his hands stopped. Then he groaned and rolled on top of her, holding himself up on his elbows so she could breathe. He pushed his hips between her thighs and she tensed when he tried to enter. She was too tight, too small, he was pushing too hard, she couldn't take him—

Mel cried out as her barrier gave and Cobalt thrust inside, hard and deep.

"Mel?" He paused, breathing heavily.

She didn't want him to stop, not now. "It's—all right."

He moved with great thrusts, all that power and ardor concentrated on her. His hands gripped her waist. Sensations flooded her and she responded with a passion she hadn't known she possessed. The pleasure he had given her at the pool was nothing compared to this. She arched against him, and the world broke into pieces.

Mel didn't know how long they built together, their rhythm increasing. Then Cobalt thrust so hard, he shoved her deep into his mattress. Contractions of pleasure rippled inside of her and swept away her thoughts.

Gradually Cobalt slowed to a stop and sank onto her. It was

hard to breathe again, but that no longer seemed to matter. She could have floated away on the clouds, sated and content.

After a while, he pushed up on his elbows and looked down at her with intense dark eyes. "You are mine."

She touched his mouth. "Your queen. Someday."

His gaze seemed to burn. "I will make you an empress."

A thorn pricked her contentment. "The Houses of Escar and Chamberlight have a treaty with the House of Dawnfield."

"Yes," Cobalt said.

A chill went through her. "Then why call me empress?"

"I gave my word I wouldn't invade Harsdown or Aronsdale." Then he said, "I never promised I wouldn't conquer Jazid, Shazire, or Taka Mal."

11
Fists

Mel ran across the bridge between the East and North towers. The clank of metal and the thump of swords on wooden shields came from below. She stopped at the high point of the arch and leaned over the rail, breathing hard. Cobalt and Varqelle were working with the Chamberlight warriors in one of the few straight portions of the courtyard. A wooden fence marked off the practice area, along with a row of risers for anyone who wanted to watch. A few grooms sat there and some of the castle staff. The physician had set up a station near the risers where he could treat injuries. The swordsmen worked with blunted metal weapons, in pairs, parrying back and forth or trying various moves. Farther down the yard, the archers were training. Their arrows thwacked into the targets with unsettling precision. In Harsdown, she would have practiced with them, but here none of the soldiers would even look at her, let alone train with her.

Cobalt's words from last night echoed in her memory. *I never promised I wouldn't conquer Jazid, Shazire, or Taka Mal.* Nothing Mel had said or asked since then would convince him to reveal his plans. Would he and his father attack countries that had lived in peace for many generations? Yes, Jazid and Taka Mal had once attacked the Misted Cliffs without provocation. And yes, Shazire and the western edges of Harsdown had once been part of the Misted Cliffs. But that had been over two centuries ago.

Mel had to face the truth. With a Chamberlight army and Cobalt as his general, Varqelle could conquer Shazire, which had a relatively small military. If he added the Shazire army to his, they might take Jazid and Taka Mal, as well. Blueshire would fall without a blow; that tiny realm didn't even have a real army, only a glorified honor guard. Varqelle would hold every country surrounding Aronsdale and Harsdown. What good would a treaty do then?

Taking hold of the pendant around her neck, she tried to call forth a green spell. She imagined the orchards at home during the height of their foliage, with acre after acre of leafy green trees. Her head didn't hurt at first, but as she strained for green, a higher-order spell, the ache rekindled in her temples. Still nothing. She had to stop—

Wait! A shimmering bubble of green light spread out from her body, covering a greater area than any spell she had created before. She turned her focus toward the practice yard below. She knew she was too far away to feel much, but she tried anyway. Her spell thinned as it grew, like a soap bubble blown from a child's ring toy. Incredibly, moods came to her then, diffuse and hard to differentiate—except for one. She recognized Cobalt's intensity, fierce and sharp even when he was only practicing. She also felt his determination.

He wanted more.

More *what?* When Mel tried to probe further, her headache flared. With a groan, she lost the spell and sagged against the railing, weak and dizzy.

Gradually her head cleared. She inhaled deeply and stood up straight. She had to warn her parents and King Jarid. But what message should she send? She knew nothing definite, only Cobalt's vow, made in the aftermath of a passion that had nearly incinerated them both. She wanted to think he hadn't meant it, but she had seen that ferocity in his eyes when he called her an empress. It would know no appeasement except by the sword.

If she couldn't send a message, she would take it herself. But she was trapped here. Cobalt hadn't even let her bring Tangle.

Mel took off again. She ran through the horseshoe arch at the end of the bridge and entered the fourth floor of the North Tower. Drapes rippled in wind that gusted through the open windows. She raced across the room and down the spiral stairs, her soft boots thudding on stone, her tunic fluttering. At the bottom, she shoved open a door into streaming sunlight. The courtyard twisted among the towers, and the clang of swords echoed off the walls.

It took Mel only moments to reach the stables. She hefted open the door of the center building. The air inside was quiet, and sunlight filtered through cracks in the planked walls. Dust motes drifted in the shafts of light. She walked to a stall with its upper half-door open. The horse inside stood in a bar of sunlight from a high window. His black coat glistened over the lines of his incredible muscles.

He wasn't as fast as a charger, but he was the largest horse Mel had ever seen. The most powerful. Magnificent. Like his rider.

"A good morn to you, Admiral," she said.

"Take care," a man warned. "He tolerates very few people."

Mel turned with a start. Matthew was standing a few steps away. "Good morning. I was looking for you."

He bowed deeply. "I am at your service."

Relief washed over her at his welcome. He didn't walk away or ignore her. Impulsively she said, "Matthew, have I caused offense here? No one else will speak with me."

He didn't look surprised. "It isn't you, Your Highness. King Stonebreaker has forbidden the men here to speak with women of the royal family."

"Whatever for?"

"Your protection."

She put her fists on her hips. "Surely I am not in danger of their saying, perhaps, 'Greetings of the morning.'"

"They must obey their king."

"But there are no other women here. Who does he expect Dancer to speak with?"

He answered with care. "Her Highness is always welcome at the Diamond Palace. She has many ladies-in-waiting there."

The more Mel learned of the Chamberlight king, the less she wanted to meet him. If he had intended to force Dancer's return to the palace, though, it hadn't worked.

"You talk to me," she said.

"I am attached to the House of Escar."

"Won't King Stonebreaker still disapprove?"

Matthew rubbed his ear. "His Majesty has not forbidden me to speak with Her Highness or with you."

Mel suspected that had more to do with Stonebreaker being

unaware of Dancer's interpretation of his decree than his intent. "I am glad."

"May I help you with something here?" he asked.

"I was hoping to find a horse I could ride."

His weathered face crinkled with his smile. "I have some gentle mares you might like."

Gentle mares, indeed. He was misguided if he thought all females were gentle, and that went for humans as well as horses. "I prefer an animal with spirit."

"Spirit?"

"Perhaps one of the horses used by the soldiers."

"You cannot take such a risk." Matthew blanched. "If you come to harm, Prince Cobalt will haul me over hot coals."

"What harm?" Mel tilted her head toward Admiral. "I could ride him."

"Saints above! Your husband would kill me."

Mel could imagine. She relented and said, "We brought a gray up from the lowlands, the one with blue and white cords braided into his bridle." Softly she added, "The man who rode him fought well. His memory will be honored."

Matthew inclined his head with respect. "He did, indeed."

"Does the gray belong to his family?"

"Nay, lady. To the House of Chamberlight. He is one of the mounts provided by the king for the men quartered here."

"May I ride him?"

"He is a warrior's mount, Your Highness."

"Good." She waited.

"Saints," Matthew muttered. He raked his hand through his hair. "You are sure you won't take a mare?"

"Very sure."

"Well. So." He shook his head as if he were seeing the downfall of the civilized world. "Come with me."

As Mel followed him out of the stable, she heard him mutter under his breath. It sounded like, "Aye, Cobalt has his hands full." She held back her smile.

They found the gray in another stable. Mel offered him bits of a small apple from the kitchens and the horse pushed his nose into her hand. While he chewed, she looked him over. He had a healthy coat. She found no scars from poorly treated saddle sores. His legs were strong with no swelling, and his hooves had no cuts or pebbles. His excellent condition, and that of his stall, told her a great deal about Matthew, all of it good.

"What is his name?" she asked.

Matthew had watched intently while she examined the gray. "Karl called him Smoke."

"Karl?"

"His last rider."

Mel nodded, subdued. Karl lay in a grave in the borderlands. She laid her hand against the horse's neck. "May I ride him?"

She expected Matthew to urge her again about the gentle mare. Instead he said, "Aye, I think so." He showed her Smoke's gear and watched while she saddled the horse and prepared for their ride. Then she pulled over a stool and swung up on his back. Smoke stepped restlessly and whinnied.

"Good beauty," Mel murmured, patting his neck. She guided him out of the stable.

Matthew walked with them. "You've a good touch."

Mel inclined her head in thanks. "Where can I ride here?" From what she had seen on the journey up, the area was mostly gorges and cliffs.

"The trails are out there." Matthew indicated several gates in the wall behind the stables. They were smaller than the main entrance, but looked just as thick.

Mel walked Smoke toward the wall, past the stables, getting a feel for how he moved, the way he lifted his head, how he reacted to her touch. Matthew released heavy bars on one gate and cranked it open. As Mel rode past, she raised her hand and he smiled at her.

She came out into a flat area. The mountains rose beyond, gray and mottled with stubby bushes. Streamers of cloud banded the sky. Cliff-terns wheeled above the castle, and their eerie cries echoed across the peaks. Birds with iridescent green chests darted from cracks in the wall. The air had a pure quality with none of the dust or pollen common in the lowlands. It invigorated her.

Several trails led from the clearing into the mountains. Mel chose the largest. Smoke seemed to know the way, and she slowed down as they climbed higher. The trail wound around boulders and switch-backed up cliffs with spectacular views of plunging gorges. The River of Diamonds poured over a high ledge brilliant with green ferns and fell a long way into a series of pools Mel could barely make out from so high. For the first time since she had left her home, she began to relax.

She spent the morning exploring the region around the castle and getting acquainted with Smoke. He was solid beneath her, spirited but responsive to a firm hand. She headed back around noon, tired but gratified. Smoke was a good horse. They would do well together.

A stable hand opened the gate for her and scowled as she rode past. Mel had an impression he would have liked to leave her outside. Except for Matthew, none of the staff seemed to like her much.

As she entered the courtyard, Matthew came striding over. Mel reined in Smoke and dismounted. "What is wrong?" she asked.

"Where have you been?" His face was pale.

"Riding. You knew that."

"You've been gone for hours! Cobalt is angry."

Mel frowned. "He doesn't control my time."

Matthew reached for the reins. "Better you discuss that with him."

Mel gently pulled away the reins and walked Smoke toward his stable. "I can tend my own mount."

He went with her. "I'm sure you can." Dryly he added, "But so can I. And I'm afraid *only* you can tend to His Highness."

Well, perhaps he had a point. With reluctance, she handed Matthew the reins.

Mel wasn't certain where to find Cobalt. She heard no one in the training yard now. She climbed the North Tower to its fourth floor. The open room was the same as when she had crossed it earlier this morning, empty, just gossamer drapes, no people. She wouldn't have been surprised to see a cloud drift in the window.

She returned to the East Tower and found Cobalt's suite empty except for Fog, who was visiting the library. Mel scooped up the kitten and cuddled him until he squirmed out of her grasp and jumped to the floor. She laughed as he chased a wooden ball he had found somewhere. It was as big as his head.

"What have you there?" she asked.

"It's a billiard ball," a dry voice said behind her.

Mel spun around. Cobalt was standing in the entrance of the library, leaning against the door frame with his arms crossed. He obviously intended to present a stern demeanor, but it had a very different effect on her. The way he folded his arms made his biceps bulge and reminded her of the previous night. Her face heated and her body tingled.

"My greetings," she murmured.

He scowled at her. "Where have you been?"

"Riding."

"Smoke is no animal for a woman."

"Why not?"

He seemed at a loss for words. It made her wonder if no one ever disagreed with him. She had a feeling he had assumed she would quake.

"What do you mean, 'why not'?" Cobalt finally growled.

She walked over to him and set her palm against his chest, above his crossed arms. "He is a good horse. I like him. He likes me. It pleases me to ride him."

"Matthew says you ride well." Now he looked flustered. Or aroused. Maybe both.

"Of course I ride well." Mel could feel the muscles of his chest through his shirt. She moved her hand in a circle and murmured, "Very well."

"Saints, woman." Cobalt pulled her against him. With one arm around her waist, he bent his head and tried to kiss her. He was too tall to manage with them standing, so he lifted her up with her feet dangling. Her tunic bunched up in his hands.

Mel laughed as she slipped. "Cobalt, stop!"

He made a frustrated noise and set her down on her feet. "Wife, you play with dangerous weapons."

"Are you?" she asked, intrigued.

His face actually reddened. "Maybe my father is right."

"About what?"

"You distract me." He glowered. "Weaken my resolve."

"Your resolve to do what?" Her voice cooled. "Will you be the weapon he uses to subjugate all the settled lands?"

"Do not speak ill of him."

"I speak ill of no one. It was a question."

He folded his arms again. "You ask many questions. You do many things. I don't recall giving permission for any of it."

"I don't recall asking for permission."

Cobalt sighed and lowered his arms. "No, I don't imagine you would." He put his hand under her chin and tilted her face up to him. "Would you ride at my side, like the warrior queens of your past?"

"Why a warrior?" Mel pulled her head away. "We have peace now. I would have it stay that way."

"Why?"

"It is better than killing."

He leaned toward her. "Battles are triumph. Not killing."

"Unless you lose them."

"Until a man dies, his battles are never lost." The name Varqelle remained unspoken between them.

Mel felt as if walls were closing on her. "He demands too much of you."

His gaze darkened. "He demands nothing. I freely give."

She laid her hand against his chest, this time to hold him off rather than draw him near. "Honor the spirit of the treaty you proposed."

"I do." He folded his hand around her fingers. "You like that horse?"

"Smoke?" The change of subject caught her off guard. "Yes, I do."

He pulled her hard against his body, still gripping her hands in one fist, his other arm tight around her waist. "Then ride at my side, wife. Not against me."

"Do not ask me that." Mel didn't know how to deal with this force of nature she had married. He watched her with his sensuous dark gaze, compelling and indomitable, and she knew she could no more stop him than she could halt the ferocity of a blizzard or the thunder in the sky.

Cobalt paused outside his mother's suite. The drape before him rustled as air gusted in the windows. He pushed it aside and went to knock on the door within the elegant horseshoe arch.

"Come," Dancer called.

He laid his palm against the door and bent his head. Perhaps he should leave. Come another time.

The door opened, and he lifted his head. Dancer stood there in her silk tunic and trousers, wearing her spectacles. "Cobalt?" She smiled. "What are you doing?"

"I came to talk with you."

She moved aside so he could enter her study. "You seem troubled. Is it your bride?"

"No." He walked into the familiar room, but today it all looked different. He turned to Dancer as she closed the door. "He is not a monster."

"Who?"

"My father."

She stiffened. "I will not speak of Varqelle."

Cobalt paced away, toward her desk. Her history scrolls lay open, weighted down by small statues of ice-dragons. "You deserted your husband and denied me my father." He swung around to her. "You let Stonebreaker raise me." His anger threatened to flare, but he kept control. "Why? You've always told me it was for my protection. Against *what?* I have met this supposed devil and he is no demon."

"I told you the truth." She took off her spectacles. "I have also told you that I will say no more."

"Did he hurt you?" Cobalt knew he skirted the edges of de-

cent questions. He was neither deaf nor dense. He had heard
the rumors of his father's appetites in the bedroom. He had
no wish to know what cruelty might have gone into his con-
ception. But if that was why his mother had fled his father,
how could she look him in the eye and claim it had been to
protect him? She had given them both a lifetime of hell.

Dancer spoke stiffly. "This is not a conversation I will have
with my son."

"You betrayed us both."

She came over to him. "I did not."

"Prove it!" His fists clenched at his sides. "How could you
subject us both to that monster you call a father?"

Her voice snapped with anger. "You will not speak of the
king in that way."

"Why? He deserves it." He was breaking the unwritten
rule they always kept. Never acknowledge the truth about
Stonebreaker. But everything had changed with Mel and his
father here, and his world was shifting in ways he didn't yet
understand. Today he couldn't keep the long-suppressed rage
out of his voice. "The day will come when no man or woman
dares to raise a hand against me."

"Ah, Cobalt." She seemed full of grief. *So sorry.* But she
would never say the word. Never admit that vulnerability.

"Tell me why you left him!" Cobalt demanded.

"I have said all I have to say."

His fury threatened to incinerate him and leave only cin-
ders. He had to go before he lost control. He walked away, to
the door, but when he went to turn the knob, his hand was
still clenched. He stood and stared at his fist. He was so full
of the rage, he felt as if he would burst if he even moved.

Dancer spoke behind him. "Don't leave like this."

Cobalt slowly relaxed his hand. Then he opened the door.

He walked into that airy room of gauze and beauty and nightmares, the room where he had so often sought refuge. He would run to Dancer, and she would hide him, but in the end Stonebreaker always found them. Cobalt walked past the doorway of the closet where his grandfather had locked him as punishment for fleeing a king's rage. He had spent hours there in the dark, terrified no one would ever let him out. The door was closed now, the closet used to store ladders and paint.

He strode across the room, whipping aside the drapes. It wasn't until he was descending the spiral stairs of the tower that he stopped. He sagged against the wall and a sound escaped his throat, a half gasp, half sob. He slammed his fists against the stone. His rage welled up and exploded out of him. He hit the wall again, again and again, gouging his skin on the rough bricks, expending his fury until his hands were bloody and battered, his skin torn to shreds. He wasn't his grandfather. He could never break the stone. His bones would shatter first. If the king of the Misted Cliffs had been here now, Cobalt would have turned his fists against him and brought on his own execution for attacking, even killing the reigning sovereign.

Finally his rage wore itself out. He sank down on a step and put his head in his bleeding hands. He grieved for what he would never have, for the friends he had never known, for the normal life he had glimpsed, however briefly, with his bride's family. He had taken Mel and run from that place, unable to face the love that they all shared without apology or subterfuge.

Cobalt made his decision. Together he and Varqelle would create a world where no one could ever again harm him or anyone he loved. He would do this—no matter what price they had to pay.

12
The Tiled Pool

Mel went to the highest room of the Zephyr, a small tower west of the central Storm Tower. Its top floor had no furniture, no partitions, nothing but hanging gauze and windows open to the night. She sat on the floor with her back against the wall, drew up her knees, rested her elbows on them, and put her head in her hands, the heels of her palms braced against her forehead. Moonlight flowed through the windows and silvered the room. It was so *quiet* here at the Castle of Clouds. She could hear only the keening of wind outside the tower.

They had been such fools. Of course Cobalt wouldn't break the treaty he had signed with Harsdown and Aronsdale. When they combined forces, those two countries had the strongest army in the settled lands, one controlled by the House of

Dawnfield. Cobalt would keep his promise not to attack—for as long as he honored the treaty, so too did it bind the House of Dawnfield. They had vowed they wouldn't fight the House of Chamberlight. Her marriage was a sham, a brilliant ploy to neutralize the only military force that had a chance of defeating the Chamberlight army.

Mel lifted her head. She had to warn her father. But how? She realized now that if she took Smoke and fled, as she had originally intended, it would negate the treaty. Another Escar woman would have deserted her husband. She doubted any army could stand against a force led by an enraged Cobalt. And he would come for her. She had seen the possessive fire in his eyes this afternoon.

Her body had betrayed her. Mel wanted his touch even now, as she dreaded his plans. This was no untried youth writing pretty sonnets. She hated herself for setting Aron aside in her thoughts, but Cobalt stoked a fire within her that could consume her heart, even her soul.

She had to take action. But she had no recourse here, no allies, nothing. Cobalt had called her a mage queen. Although he didn't believe his own words, they had truth. She had done little beyond inconsequential spells, but she descended from warrior mages. She had always assumed she would learn her skills over the years and use them for the good of the realms she and Aron would rule, he as king of Aronsdale and she as queen of Harsdown. She had imagined her days spent in scholarly pursuits, especially mathematics. No longer did she have those choices. She had to learn her abilities *now* and in ways she had never expected. Ways of violence.

Mel focused on the chamber around her, a squat cylinder, three dimensions instead of two, small for the top floor of a tower but huge compared to shapes she had used in the past.

Power surged within her, erratic and unfocused. She couldn't focus any spell. It might be the imperfect shape; the open windows and drapes marred its form. Probably had more to do with her lack of skill.

Concentrate. What did she want? Green spells were within her ability. They revealed moods, and a skilled adept might send as well as receive them. She needed to relay her warning to her mother or father, to communicate her fear of what Varqelle and Cobalt intended. She had neither the power nor the gift for such a spell, and if she pushed too hard she could burn out what talent she did possess, but she could think of no other way.

Mel tried to imagine the fields and orchards of home, but those memories had dimmed. So she envisioned emeralds, cold and hard, brilliant. It was the highest level of green.

Power surged within her.

A door scraped open. Mel opened her eyes into a green haze. The mist filled the Zephyr Chamber. A woman was crossing the room in the shimmering light. Dancer. Her silks fluttered around her body and took an emerald tinge, as if she were a jewel herself. Mel felt her mood clearly; Dancer had seen the light from the windows and had come to investigate. Shock emanated off her: Until this moment, she hadn't truly believed mages existed.

The queen stopped before Mel. Her mouth moved, but Mel heard nothing.

"Again?" Mel asked—and froze. Her words resonated with a volume and fullness nothing like her normal voice.

"Witch." Dancer had fear in her eyes and her mood. "You will destroy us all."

"I am no witch." Mel's words rolled through the room in defiance of her denial.

"You have turned my son against me." Dancer lifted her chin and clenched one fist at her side, but her voice shook. "Will you drive him to his death in battle to satisfy your thirst for more lands than are your due?"

"I would have him stay home," Mel said. "Raise a family, come to the hearth at night, work in the orchards." She spoke with pain. "Can you see him living such a life? The thirst for conquest comes from him, Dancer, not me, and your husband feeds it because he knows of no other way to exist."

"No!" She stepped toward Mel, then stopped when light flared around them. "Cobalt is not like his father!"

Mel heard the anguish in her cry. She wished she could help Dancer, but she could barely help herself. "Whether he pays for his father's sins or becomes his father's image, neither will change his nature. He was born a conqueror."

"He must not," Dancer said.

Mel rose to her feet. The mood spell was pouring into her and she felt as if she would go up like a torch with more power than she could control. Her voice echoed. "Varqelle gives Cobalt the paternal regard he has craved his entire life, and neither you nor I can stop your son from hurtling toward his destiny."

"You know nothing," Dancer said. "You would see him die, false Harsdown queen."

Mel could have called Dancer the false queen, but she knew better. Dancer was every bit her heredity. "The throne will return to the House of Escar with the birth of my child."

"That is too late." Bitterness edged Dancer's voice. "Varqelle wants it for himself. Do you believe he will be satisfied to see Cobalt as your consort? I think not."

"We have a treaty." Mel spoke as much to convince herself as Dancer. The resonance faded from her voice.

Dancer's voice quieted. "What will that treaty mean when your lands are surrounded by the empire my son has conquered for his father?" She spoke with the sound of tears she was too proud to shed. "No more will we see peace in our lands."

Then Dancer turned and walked away, leaving Mel alone with her fading spell and her fears.

Cobalt's suite was empty when Mel returned. She felt worn out, numb from straining for a spell out of her reach. She hadn't even thought she could use a shape with a level as high as a cylinder. Apparently so; nothing would have happened if it had been beyond her ability. She desperately wished for Skylark, the mage mistress, but she had no one to help her here. She had to find her own way.

She went to the library. Usually it eased her mind, with its tomes, scrolls, and the globe of the world on its stand, but today it all seemed so frail. Historically, conquerors in these settled lands had killed scholars and burned libraries. It was easier to control a people if their intellectuals didn't agitate against the new regime. Scholarship was such a fragile part of human endeavor. Now when it was too late to continue as before, she realized the gift her parents had given her with such a good education.

A rattle came from one shelf and a purple billiard ball rolled out from under it. Fog ran out after the ball, slipping and sliding on the parquetry floor.

"Ah, Foggy," Mel murmured. "He doesn't want you to play with those." She picked up the ball—

Light flared around Mel. Pain seared her hand and she dropped the ball with a cry.

Her vision cleared slowly. Her hand throbbed, and a burn covered the palm where she had touched the ball.

"What the——?" She looked around. Fog had run under the desk and was crouched in the shadows watching her with large gold eyes. The ball had rolled against the doorstop. It was no longer purple; the paint had been scorched, leaving it black.

Mel crouched down and tapped the ball. An echo of power vibrated through her fingers. It wasn't the ball. It was *her*. She hadn't properly concluded her spell in the Zephyr Tower, so her power had discharged when she touched the ball.

Chills went up Mel's back. A sphere was the highest mage form. This was a solid ball rather than a hollow sphere, but that made no difference. The shape was the same. King Jarid in Aronsdale was the only mage who could use a sphere in its pure form. Mel's father was also a sphere mage, but his spells never worked with ideal forms, and they came out flawed when he used flawed shapes. Given the power of a sphere, Muller could do great damage with such a spell; as a result he almost never used his abilities.

Mel found it hard to believe she had called forth power from such a shape. It couldn't be true. She was a Dawnfield, yes, but neither she nor Skylark had expected such a degree of ability.

"What is this?" a voice asked.

Mel looked up. Cobalt was standing by the bookshelf. She rose to her feet, holding the blackened ball. "How long have you been there?"

"Long enough to see you nearly burn down my library."

His voice was so tightly controlled, she wondered it didn't snap. His knuckles were a mess, torn and ragged, crusted with blood.

"Saints, Cobalt, what happened?"

"Nothing."

"But your hands——"

"It is nothing." Cobalt came over and took the ball out of her grip. He grasped her palm and turned it from side to side. "This is a bad burn."

As dizzy as she felt from the overuse of her abilities, Mel knew she wasn't yet done. She took the ball from him and cupped it in her burned hand, then put his hands over it and covered them all with her uninjured palm.

"What are you doing?" he asked sharply.

Mel concentrated, only half believing she could manage with a sphere. Outside, the blue sky vibrated until it entered her mind and filled her body.

The ball glowed with blue light.

Cobalt yanked away his hand. "What are you doing?"

Mel was too drained to answer. The ball continued to glow in her palm. She took Cobalt's hands and once again folded them around the ball, covering them with her own. His fingers tightened into claws but this time he held on, his face creased with strain.

The spell drained her. It trickled away like sand running through her fingers, and the glow around the ball faded. Her legs buckled and she collapsed like a rag doll.

Cobalt caught her as she fell. He knelt down, easing her to the floor. Then he held her against him, her head on his chest. "What did you do?" His voice held an echo of Dancer's fear.

"Too tired…" She lifted their hands—and saw only smooth, unmarked skin on both his and her own. No injury remained for either of them.

"It isn't possible," Cobalt whispered.

"Apparently it…is."

Then she passed out.

* * *

It was dark when Mel awoke. She was lying in Cobalt's bed with the covers pulled all the way up to her eyes. He had taken off her tunic and leggings, leaving only her camisole and lace trunks. Fog was curled on her pillow, apparently having forgiven her for the dramatics in the library.

Mel rolled onto her back. She felt as if a horse had stamped on her head. She needed a glass of water, but she wasn't certain she could stand up. The pain in her temples surged when she looked around the room, which was empty except for herself. Had she been at home, someone would have tended her, a maid or her mother. Here she was on her own.

Mel sat up and groaned. She pressed the heels of her hands against her throbbing temples. When the worst of her dizziness passed, she swung her legs over the edge of the bed, out from under the rumpled covers. Fog mewed as she jostled the pillow. She tried to stand, then sat down heavily as her head swam.

"You can do it," she muttered. She took a breath to steady herself and then slowly stood up. Her vision blurred and her mind reeled. She very much wanted to sit down. But she steeled herself and stayed on her feet. The cold air raised goose bumps on her bare skin.

When her head cleared a bit, Mel left the bedroom. The circular chamber in the center of the suite was empty, too. Although most of the castle was colorless, as white as the clouds, the colors here glowed richly in the golden light shed by the lamps. Six horseshoe arches opened into the chamber from the six wedge-rooms that made up Cobalt's suite. Stained glass filled the curved portion of the arches, each with a luminous design of blue, white, and gold spheres. She walked around the chamber and peered into the bathing room, study, parlor, library, and Airlight room. No Cobalt.

For a while, Mel leaned against the marble column of the entrance to the bathing room. When she felt steadier, she went inside and eased into the shallow end of the pool. The water came to just above her breasts. Its warmth soothed her, enough that she slid down and dunked her head. She traced the mosaics on the bottom of the pool, green, blue, and silver designs of polygons, circles, crosses, stars, all in chains and curving patterns.

Blue light filled the pool.

Saints! Mel broke the surface and gulped in air. Her headache had vanished. Then a spark of pain returned. She had to be careful with this strange loop of power; if she made spells that helped her heal from straining her talents, she could end up straining her talents again.

She floated across the pool to a slanting section and lay on her back, half out of the water. Her underclothes clung to her body, wet and almost transparent.

After a while, Mel had an odd sense, as if hairs on her body were standing up. She opened her eyes. Cobalt was leaning against a nearby column with his arms crossed, his clothes dark against the pale blue, green, and silver mosaics. He was staring at her with a hunger so raw, her pulse stuttered.

Mel pushed up on her elbows. Her skin felt sensitized and her body tingled. No man had ever looked at her that way before; it both aroused and alarmed her. She wanted to hide herself, but she wanted even more for him to come to her and expend that powerful hunger. Letting her head fall back, she arched her back and stretched her legs.

"Saints, woman," Cobalt said. He stalked over to her, his boots striking the tiles. At the pool, he knelt in the shallow water, fully dressed, with his knees between her thighs. He rubbed her breast through the lace. Then he clenched a handful of the cloth and jerked. The camisole ripped off her body. He threw the wet rag onto the floor and then tore the lace trunks away from her hips. She was breathing harder now, either from lust or fear. Or both.

Cobalt lowered himself on top of her. He didn't remove his clothes, not even his boots, he just opened his trousers. Nor did he tease or seduce—he just entered her hard and fast. She was ready for him, even more than she had realized. Lying here thinking about him had been enough. She was sore from last night, and she gasped at his thrust, but when she groaned, it wasn't from pain. She lifted her hips, answering his urgency with her own. His onslaught drove her. She needed *more*. Even the scrape of his trousers on her thighs aroused her. He thrust harder, his head above hers, and she cried out. Cobalt went rigid and his muscles corded against her body as if they were made of iron rather than human sinew.

The spasms inside Mel seemed as if they would last forever. She stopped thinking altogether and let the sensations sweep her along. Gripping Cobalt's biceps, she pressed her body into him.

Gradually Mel became aware again, as her tremors subsided. Cobalt lay on top of her, his breaths coming more slowly now. He moved inside her again for a few moments, as if he didn't want to stop even after he had finished. Then he sighed and settled his weight on her body. They lay still, and his hair tickled her ear.

A few minutes passed. Then Cobalt said, "I seem to be wet."

Mel smiled drowsily. "I guess so."

He lifted his head and looked down at their bodies half in the water. "I was a bit impatient."

"A bit."

"Are you hurt?"

"Ah, no," Mel murmured.

His gaze darkened with pleasure. "You *are* a sorceress. So angelic in appearance, but a she-devil in my bed."

Her lips curved upward. "We are hardly anywhere near as comfortable as in a bed." The tiles were hard and wet, though she hadn't noticed until now.

He rose onto his knees. Water dripped off his shirt, but he paid no attention, he just sat back and gazed at her. Mel let him look. She was too sated to move.

"Do you put tantalize spells on me?" he asked.

"Do I what?"

He pushed back his damp hair. "Spells to make me want you."

"Of course not." Her voice turned husky. "You must be putting spells on me. I am a proper woman of a venerable line. Yet you make me into someone wild and uncontrolled."

His lips twitched upward. "I like you that way."

"Umm." Her fatigue was returning. Too many spells and too much love. She sat up, but she could only slump forward.

Cobalt pulled her against his chest. His muscles ridged through his wet shirt. "My mind tells me to ward off your magecraft. My instincts want me to embrace you."

She sighed drowsily. "Ward off? Silly Cobalt."

"I am never silly," he stated.

She smiled as her eyes closed. "I can't do anything but make warmth and comfort with my spells."

"Very warm." His voice deepened. "You should go to bed. Rest."

Rest, indeed. "That means you can't come with me."

"I need to make sure you are all right." Cobalt stood up and lifted her, one arm under her knees and the other around her back. He settled her head against his shoulder and carried her out of the room, dripping water the whole way. Even with her eyes closed, she knew he was going to his bedroom. Mel suspected he wasn't going to stay out of bed, either. She doubted either of them would sleep much the rest of the night.

He dried her off with an extra blanket set out on the end of the bed, taking his time as he rubbed it over her body, especially her breasts and thighs. When he finished, he laid her on his bed, then undressed and threw his soaked clothes on the ground. As he stretched out next to her, he spoke in a low voice, dark and ominous and full of a sensual promise. "I will lay the world at your feet."

Mel didn't answer. She let herself think of nothing and feel only his hands on her body and his lips on her breasts. She didn't want to know his dreams, for if he tempted her long enough with his warlord's spell, he might seduce her into anything, even loving him—and if she fell that far and that hard, she could someday find herself riding into battle with him against the people of all the settled lands, even her own.

13

Chamberlights

Mel found the main library in the Sphere Tower. It took up the entire base of the structure. Books and scrolls filled the shelves there. Stained-glass windows glowed with sunlight high on the walls, patterned in circles, hexagons, and diamonds. Colored light slanted over the mellow wood tables. An elderly soldier was cleaning the globe on a stand across the room, a larger sphere than the one in Cobalt's library. Mel felt odd when she concentrated on it. Light-headed. Strained. No spells stirred. It made her uneasy. What if her spells never came back? She couldn't let herself believe that might happen. After having achieved so much, she couldn't bear to have it all vanish. It would be worse than losing her sight.

The soldier scowled as she entered the library. Then he went back to work, pointedly ignoring her. He seemed to be the only librarian. She hesitated, then took a deep breath and walked over. She stopped before him, uncertain how to proceed. He rubbed his cloth on the bronze stand that held the globe, his concentration on his work, but she felt certain he knew she was there.

Mel spoke awkwardly. "Greetings of the morning, Good sir."

He kept polishing the same section of metal.

She tried again. "You have a beautiful library. I don't want to disrupt your procedures. Please let me know if I can do anything for you, or if you have any preferences for how I treat the materials here."

His polishing slowed, but he didn't look at her. After another moment, Mel bit her lip. But just as she was about to turn, he looked up at her and spoke gruffly. "If it be pleasing you, Your Highness, I'd ask you be gentle with the books. That is all."

Mel smiled at him, her relief warming her expression. "I will indeed, kind sir."

At her smile, his cheeks turned red. He even seemed on the verge of smiling himself. Mel wasn't certain why people reacted that way when she smiled, but she was glad to see his unfriendly demeanor soften.

After taking her leave of the librarian, she browsed the library—and found a treasure. An entire set of shelves was devoted to geometry. She eagerly gathered up an armful of books and scrolls and carried them to a table. Soon she was engrossed in proofs about the diagonals in polygons.

"You are doing mathematics," a woman said.

Mel looked up with a start. Dancer was standing only a few paces away. She held two large scrolls, one with a title penned on the outside: *Historical Perspectives on Agriculture in the Western Cliffs.*

"Oh, yes," Mel said. She motioned at her books. "These are wonderful. I've never seen most of them."

Dancer seemed perplexed. "You like to read?"

"Very much."

"Ah." The queen lost some of her cool reserve. "That is good. Always good." She inclined her head. "I will leave you to your studies." Then she went away with her scrolls.

Mel watched her leave, bemused. She hadn't expected Dancer to value education, though now that she thought about it, she wasn't sure why not. Perhaps she and Dancer had a great deal to unlearn about each other.

Varqelle stood with Cobalt on a balcony of the South Tower. They gazed out to the east, toward Harsdown. Without his glasses, Cobalt couldn't see the borderlands well, but the night was too dark to make out much even with them. He could distinguish the constellations if he squinted. That gave him a headache, though. It was why he liked his telescope; it turned the night sky into a sparkling wonderland he had no trouble seeing. He couldn't view many stars at once with such a powerful lens, but he liked it anyway.

His father was discussing matters with far less appeal than star patterns. "The messenger from the Diamond Palace arrived this morning," Varqelle continued. "Stonebreaker will be here tomorrow."

Cobalt suppressed his hatred. He had to hold it in check, because they needed Stonebreaker. Only the Chamberlight king could provide them with an army. When his grandfather had tried to make him responsible for invading Harsdown, Cobalt had challenged him. And won. Cobalt wouldn't have hesitated to ride against Harsdown if he had thought they could succeed. Both his father and Stonebreaker wanted the

Jaguar Throne at any cost, but Cobalt had no desire to destroy his goal in the process of achieving it. He preferred his solution. Although neither he nor his father would ever sit on the Jaguar Throne, he had brought it back to their House without bringing ruin to their country or people. And now they had other options, for neither Harsdown nor Aronsdale could move against the Misted Cliffs. Tomorrow he would face Grandfather again, and this time he would give Stonebreaker what he wanted: conquest. But it would be on Cobalt's terms.

"You are quiet," Varqelle said. "Do you not wish to see your grandfather?"

Cobalt gritted his teeth, then realized what he was doing and stopped. "I never wish to see him."

"You do not like him," Varqelle said.

"No."

"Why?"

Silence.

"He kept me apart from you and your mother," Varqelle said. "I have no great love for him, either."

"He is—" Cobalt could think of no tactful way to voice his true opinions of the king, so he said only, "Harsh."

"A man needs to take a firm hand even with his family," Varqelle said. "Strength gives rise to strength."

The thought made Cobalt ill. He would sooner throw himself off a cliff than harm his child. He wanted his son or daughter to have the security neither he nor Dancer had known. He wished for his family what Mel had with hers.

"Is that what you would have me do with my son?" Cobalt asked coldly. "Beat the 'strength' into him?"

"Of course not. I do not approve of beating children." Varqelle paused. "But neither would I have you spare the switch. A child who never knows discipline becomes weak in character."

Cobalt's fist clenched on the balcony rail. "And you would take this 'firm' hand with your wife?"

Varqelle scrutinized him. "This Dawnfield woman preys on your mind."

"She does not prey." If anything, he was the predator. Yet she had bewitched him with her spells. He thought of her constantly. Nothing would free his mind from her.

"You must control her," Varqelle said.

Anger sparked in Cobalt. "Is that what you did with Mother?"

"Apparently not enough."

This was a side of his father he didn't want to see. "Or too much."

Varqelle frowned. "It is not your affair."

"I would have you tell me."

"Why?"

"It would explain her fear of you."

His father answered with scorn. "She fears strength."

Cobalt crossed his arms, so tight with submerged rage that his words grated. "Perhaps she fears being punched in the stomach, the back, the arms, and the legs until she can't bloody damn *walk*."

Varqelle stared at him. "What lies has she told you about me?"

"Nothing." Cobalt wished he could blur his memories as easily as his vision blurred. "That was what I watched Stonebreaker do to her."

"I cannot believe such."

Cobalt gripped the railing. "That you can't believe it doesn't change its truth." He had no stone wall to hit and he didn't want to lose control in front of Varqelle, but his father was treading on dangerous ground.

"I would never countenance such behavior," Varqelle said.

"That is the truth." He suddenly went still. "Saints, Cobalt, did he hit you?"

"No longer. I am stronger than him." Cobalt was clenching the railing so hard, his knuckles hurt. "Now."

His father swore. "It was unforgivable for Dancer to bring you here. That my son should have endured such is a crime she can never undo."

Cobalt gave him an incredulous look. "What about her? She endured the same."

"She deserted her husband. That has consequences."

"She deserves to be loved."

Bitterness edged Varqelle's voice. "She is incapable of it."

"She loves me."

"Then why did she bring you here?"

Why, indeed? That question had tormented Cobalt his entire life. He knew he should let it go. This bond he and his father were forming could all too easily break. Their connection was unlike anything he had known and he would do almost anything to protect it. But Varqelle and Dancer had molded his life. He *had* to understand. His need drove him when prudence cautioned he remain silent.

"Why does Mother fear you?" Cobalt said.

"She poisons your mind against me."

"She says nothing of you."

Some tension eased from Varqelle's stance. "As is right."

"Maybe you didn't beat her like Stonebreaker, but you hurt her." Cobalt couldn't stop. "And you did other things. At night."

Varqelle's voice turned chill. "I will not discuss this with my son."

Why? You are what I have to emulate. Cobalt had thirsted his entire life for his grandfather's approval, but he had never wanted to become *like* Stonebreaker. With Varqelle, he lost his moorings. He and his father were so alike. He saw much to admire in Varqelle but also much that angered him. No easy answers were here.

Moonlight silvered the planes of Varqelle's face. "Know this, Cobalt. Power burns within you. If Stonebreaker was cruel, if he tried to break your spirit, he succeeded only in forging you into a greater man. History will record your campaigns, my son. You will be remembered as the greatest general ever known."

Cobalt stared at him. With Varqelle he could go from anger to stunned disbelief in a matter of moments. No one had ever spoken of him with such pride. That Varqelle would do so swept away Cobalt's simmering rage and filled him with a longing he could barely define. He knew only that he never wanted to lose his father's esteem.

"I will be remembered as your son," Cobalt said.

Varqelle inclined his head, accepting the offered respect. But then his gaze darkened. "Do not let a woman ruin what you can become. Allow her to weaken your will and she will destroy you."

Destroy? No. Perhaps Varqelle would call his driving need for Mel a weakness, but she made Cobalt feel invincible. Nothing could stop him. Knowing his father saw so much within him changed everything. They would join forces, he and Varqelle. It might be an alliance made in hell, but it would have no equal.

The king of the Misted Cliffs arrived late in the day, as shadows stretched across the land. He brought several hundred soldiers and they poured into the courtyard. Grooms, stable boys, and the castle staff ran to accommodate them.

Mel stood on a balcony in the Storm Tower and watched the commotion. Cobalt already had over fifty men here. With the cavalry Stonebreaker was bringing, their numbers swelled to more than four hundred. Everywhere she looked, warriors dismounted, called, strode, and gathered. They would lodge in towers, in tents set up in the courtyard, and in the open areas outside the wall. Stonebreaker actually had thousands of men, and rumors floating about the castle said the rest of them were assembling at the base of the cliffs, down in the borderlands. The Chamberlight king hadn't brought a retinue. He had come with his damn army.

He expects to fight. The thought haunted Mel. No one would mount an operation this large just to meet his grandson's bride. Stonebreaker might say he intended to show honor, but Mel didn't believe it. This was either an unsubtle threat or the prelude to an invasion. Or both.

Leather creaked behind Mel. She turned to see Varqelle silhouetted in the archway. She bowed to him. "Good evening, Your Majesty."

A chuckle came from the silhouette. "I'm hardly majestic, even at the top of a tower."

"Matthew?" Mel winced. "My apologies. I thought you were Varqelle." Now that she looked more closely, the difference was obvious. Matthew had a similar height, but kinder features and a huskier build. His hair was completely gray.

He came onto the balcony. "I'm sorry to disturb you. But I must prepare for King Stonebreaker's arrival."

"I will go. I should be downstairs anyway." She would have preferred to stay away, but she couldn't hide from Stonebreaker forever. Sooner or later she had to face him.

The Storm Tower contained many rooms, including the suite at the top where Stonebreaker stayed. Clerks worked in the mid level on the day-to-day business of the castle. Other floors had halls where Cobalt or Stonebreaker could meet with the staff that ran the castle. The chef and his staff had a huge kitchen below the ground level.

Mel descended to the bottom floor and stood in the shadows of an archway that opened onto the courtyard. In the hubbub outside, no one acknowledged her. The few people who glanced her way quickly averted their gazes. Their behavior didn't surprise her. She didn't even know the names of the soldiers quartered here. They kept apart, never speaking to her, especially as rumors of her magecraft spread. People made discreet snapping gestures with their hands when she walked by, signs to protect themselves against whatever evils they imagined within her. At home, her family and friends would have rejoiced to see her power growing, but here people avoided her as if she carried a plague.

She spotted Varqelle outside talking to several officers. Neither Cobalt nor Stonebreaker was anywhere in view. She had never met the Chamberlight king, but she had seen portraits here of him. Cobalt might have already escorted him to a place of welcome. Given his antipathy toward his grandfather, though, she questioned if Cobalt would even come down to the courtyard. His sense of duty was strong, however, and she thought his enmity for the king masked his desire for Stonebreaker's good opinion.

"He has many men," a woman said.

Mel almost jumped. Looking across the archway, she saw Dancer standing in the shadows. Mel had expected her mother-in-law to denounce her as a witch after what happened in the tower, but Dancer had remained silent these past few days, watching, judging, appraising. Although Mel wasn't certain what to make of it, she could see that Dancer genuinely loved Cobalt. The mother was evaluating her son's wife.

Mel spoke carefully. "I've heard over five thousand more of his men are gathering down in the borderlands."

"These are for show," Dancer said. "An exhibition of Chamberlight strength. For you." Dryly she added, "My father has never been a subtle man."

A dark figure formed in the shadows behind the queen—and resolved into Cobalt. He came up beside his mother. "It is time to greet him." His words had a hollow sound.

"Where is he?" Mel asked.

"With the last wave of men," Cobalt said. "The sentries spotted him."

Mel couldn't read him now. He was like a shuttered window. He and Dancer stood side by side as if they gained strength from each other against a threat.

"Why would he come last?" Mel asked.

Dancer folded her arms as if she were cold. "For a better entrance."

Cobalt laid his palm on his mother's arm, an unmistakable offer of protection. "Come. We will meet him at the gate."

"Very well." She caught her lower lip with her teeth.

Cobalt turned his stark gaze on Mel. "You can wait here. If you wish."

Mel felt as if cool fingers walked across her shoulders. Of course she should greet the king. But watching them, she wanted to retreat to Cobalt's suite until Stonebreaker left. No matter how she felt, though, it would be wrong to hide.

"I will go with you," she said.

Dancer gave her an odd look. If Mel hadn't known better, she would have thought it was approval. Cobalt inclined his head to Mel, and she caught the flicker of fear in his gaze. Never before had she seen that emotion from him, and she had questioned whether he was capable of it. Even now, he masked it well. But she had come to read him better these past few days. He feared his grandfather.

Dancer arranged the silk folds of her tunic as if they were armor. Then she stepped out into the slanting rays of the late afternoon. One of the arrivals, a warrior in Chamberlight armor and chain mail, glanced at her. He did a double take, then knelt before her and bowed his head.

"Please rise," she said. Behind her, Cobalt was stepping out of the tower.

As the man stood, Cobalt joined his mother. The soldier blanched and went down on one knee again, with a sharper drop of his head. Nor was he the only one. Several others had seen them as well. All of Stonebreaker's men who could see Dancer and Cobalt knelt. Their expression of fealty spread like a wave across the narrow strip of courtyard that curved around the base of the Storm Tower. Everywhere, they knelt in honor of the Chamberlight heirs.

Cobalt spoke, a short phrase Mel didn't catch, and the men closest to him rose to their feet. The rest followed suit, and the wave spread in reverse now as the men stood. Cobalt turned and extended his hand to Mel. Taking a deep breath, she went to stand with him and Dancer. The soldiers watched with no welcome in their gazes. A bead of sweat ran down her temple. Had she not been with Dancer and Cobalt, she wasn't certain she would have made it through this crowd without incident.

They walked across the odd, curving courtyard toward the main gate. Men on horses continued to ride through it, and others walked inside, leading chargers or pack animals loaded with feed. The men followed a custom she had never seen back home, bowing to Dancer and Cobalt from horseback. Dancer inclined her head, but Cobalt showed no trace of a response. His face was like carved stone.

A formation of six horses around a seventh appeared. Mel's breath caught. The Chamberlight king sat astride the central mount, his head raised high. Stonebreaker. Cobalt resembled him even more than he did Varqelle. They both had the same broad-shouldered, long-legged build, the same pride in their carriage, the same powerful physique. But Cobalt was more. He had even more height, greater musculature, stronger features. He and Stonebreaker were two powerhouses, but the heir surpassed the sovereign.

Next to Cobalt, Stonebreaker would always seem second, even though in authority and status he was first. Mel recalled Brant Firestoke's comment, that Stonebreaker was jealous of his grandson. Although she could see why, she would have expected the king to be proud rather than resentful. What better indication of his ascendancy than to see it reflected in such an exceptional heir? The more she learned about the Chamberlight dynasty, the more uncomfortable they made her.

Stonebreaker and his personal honor guard entered the courtyard at a regal pace. The king wore the leather and metal armor and chain mail, with a massive sword at his hip. The wind blew back his silvered hair, and he held a helmet under one arm.

Mel spoke in a low voice. "He is impressive."

Neither Cobalt nor Dancer answered.

Mel wasn't certain of protocols. Although her parents tended to avoid ceremony, the royal court in Aronsdale was formal. She knew the expected behavior there, but she was less certain here. She had read what she could find about the

Misted Cliffs and the Chamberlight dynasty after she accepted Cobalt's proposal. Most of it applied specifically to the court at the Diamond Palace; she recalled nothing about greeting the king in a lovely but strange citadel on top of a cliff. It was probably best to follow Cobalt and Dancer, or deal as she would in the Diamond Palace. If she felt uncertain, she could fall back on the customs at Castle Suncroft. Different countries had different ways, but Aronsdale, Harsdown, and the Misted Cliffs weren't that dissimilar.

The king reined in his horse and surveyed the yard. When he settled his gaze on Dancer and Cobalt, they each bowed to him. Mel followed suit, copying their motions. Stonebreaker inclined his head much in the way they had done with the riders who bowed to them. High up on his stallion, with his armor and helmet glittering, he seemed the epitome of majestic splendor.

As the king dismounted, Cobalt walked over to him. Mel hung back with Dancer. The two men greeted each other and stood together, surrounded by the bustle and flow of soldiers, guards, and servants like columns of rock in a turbulent river. Dressed in black, Cobalt seemed shadowed compared to Stonebreaker. Mel wondered if he deliberately played down his own qualities in his grandfather's presence. If Stonebreaker did envy him, such an approach would be a way to appease the king's displeasure.

Stonebreaker and Cobalt seemed respectful of each other. It took her a moment to pinpoint what was missing; neither man showed any sign he was glad to see the other. In her family, they would have been hugging, talking, laughing. She had seen the reserve in how Cobalt and his mother interacted, but this coldness went beyond that.

Mel touched the pendant around her neck. She concentrated on a spell. Her power did respond today, but it stirred only weakly. She couldn't control the green light that formed around her hand. Dancer glanced at her sharply, and Mel lowered her arm, letting the spell go. She didn't want the Chamberlight king to think she was trying to curse him or some such nonsense. Nor was she certain she wanted to know more; her brief spell had been enough to reveal the darkness Cobalt felt toward his grandfather.

Stonebreaker and Cobalt came toward them, but the men in the Chamberlight honor guard stayed back. The king looked Mel over without a smile, then turned away as if she were of no consequence. He stopped in front of Dancer and nodded. "You look well today, my dear."

Dancer returned his nod with formal, icy perfection. "Thank you, Father."

Cobalt drew Mel forward. "Grandfather, may I present my wife, Melody Dawnfield Escar."

Mel bowed to the king with one hand holding the silk layers of her tunic, the greeting of an heir to a sovereign of higher rank among her people, and among Cobalt's as well, from what she had read. When she straightened, Stonebreaker was looking the other way, at the men setting up tents in the courtyard. He spoke to Cobalt. "We won't be able to lodge everyone here."

A muscle twitched in Cobalt's cheek, and for a moment Mel thought he would speak in anger. She tried to catch his eye, to tell him the slight didn't matter, but he wouldn't look at her.

"You have brought many men," Cobalt said. The rebuke *too many* remained implicit.

"If you are unable to deal with them," Stonebreaker said, "I can take care of the matter."

Cobalt stiffened. "I regret that your advisers were unable to plan ahead of time."

Mel stared at him. He had practically suggested the king's advisers were incompetent.

"Ah, well," Stonebreaker said, as if making allowances for his grandson's ineptitude. "I am sure you did your best."

Cobalt's fist clenched at his side.

Dancer spoke quickly. "We have a feast planned tonight, Father, to honor you."

"I imagine so." The king finally turned to Mel. "Perhaps you will fetch everyone drink to slake our thirst. We have traveled a long way."

Mel had no idea how to respond, especially after his bizarre exchange with Cobalt. She wasn't a servant. Even if that had been the case, what did he expect, that she would provide wine for the hundreds of men arriving here?

Cobalt spoke. "We have refreshment inside." He sounded as if he were gritting his teeth.

"That will have to do." Stonebreaker offered his arm to Dancer. "Come, Daughter. I should like to catch up on news."

Dancer answered stiffly. "Of course." She set her palm on his arm and they started for the Storm Tower.

Mel looked up at Cobalt, at a loss for how to respond to all this. His gaze had darkened. He presented his arm and she set her palm on it the way Dancer had done with Stonebreaker. They followed the king and his daughter, and Mel was aware of Stonebreaker's guards coming behind them. She vowed she would learn their names, rank, even their favorite food, *anything* to make them people rather than more unnamed soldiers.

Inside the Storm Tower, a large hall took up the entire bottom floor. Youths from the kitchen staff were setting platters of food on a large table in the center. Ice sculptures graced the table, one carved to resemble the Diamond Palace and the other like the Castle of Clouds. Servers were escorting guests into the hall, highly ranked officers from among the men Stonebreaker had brought and in the company already quartered here.

Varqelle entered through another archway, accompanied by Cobalt's honor guard. They escorted him through the bustle of soldiers and servers, and everyone they passed stepped aside, bowing to the Escar king.

When they reached Stonebreaker, Varqelle inclined his head to the Chamberlight king, one sovereign to another. "You honor us with your visit, Your Majesty." The rigid set of his shoulders belied the courtesy of his greeting.

Stonebreaker returned the nod. "You look well. I hope my home agrees with you."

The Escar king answered with stiff formality. "It does you honor." The courteous words didn't hide his discomfort with the man who had kept him from his wife for thirty-three years.

Varqelle glanced at Cobalt and his face relaxed into a smile. "My greetings, son."

Cobalt bowed deeply, showing a son's respect for his father. He could have bowed that way to his grandfather, too, had he so chosen. Varqelle clapped him on the shoulder, and incredibly, Cobalt smiled. Mel realized it was the first time anyone had greeted her husband with good wishes today. Stonebreaker's men had knelt to him, yes, but out of duty, not because they were happy to see him. It was no wonder Cobalt had taken to his father; Varqelle might be evil in her eyes, but he was the only one here aside from Dancer who treated Cobalt like a human being.

When Varqelle turned to Mel, his expression hardened. She met his gaze, knowing hers held just as much distrust. He would use Cobalt to gain his ends, and Cobalt would do what-

ever his father wanted, because Varqelle gave him the accep-
tance that the rest of the world had denied him his entire life.
Stonebreaker was a fool if he had let envy poison his relationship with his grandson. He might covet Cobalt's power, but
in trying to destroy his grandson's spirit, he would only turn
that power against himself and his reign.

The royal party went to a dais at one end of the hall where
a smaller table stood, long and narrow. Stonebreaker led the
way, flanked by two men in his honor guard. Varqelle and
Dancer came next, followed by Mel and Cobalt. It was the
first time Mel had seen Cobalt's parents walking side by side.
Neither looked at the other. Varqelle didn't offer his arm for
Dancer's hand and Dancer made no attempt to take his elbow.

High-backed chairs stood along one side of the table, each
a work of art, made from darkwood and set with blue and
white silk cushions. The central chair was a white marble
throne inlaid with sapphires and diamonds. The table was
also darkwood. A circular mosaic inlaid its center, displaying
the insignia of the House of Chamberlight, a blue sphere on
a white background.

Stonebreaker went to stand in front of the throne. He nodded to his family, and they took their places in front of the
chairs that flanked him, Dancer and Varqelle to his left, Mel
and Cobalt on the right. The six officers in Stonebreaker's
honor guard went to chairs at the ends of the table, three to
the left and three to the right.

They all faced the hall. Below them, about fifty guests stood
at the larger table. Stonebreaker lifted his chin and surveyed
his men. Then he raised his hand. Immediately, kitchen servers filed up to the dais with platters for the high table and a
frozen sculpture of the mythical ice-dragon said to live in the
highest reaches of the Misted Cliffs. They set out crystal gob-

lets shaped like orchids and flasks of red wine imported from the lowlands. Mel would have preferred apple juice, but they had none. Although a few of the trees grew up here, they were scraggly and bore little fruit. She had no desire to eat, knowing this feast honored the commander who had gathered one of the largest armies ever seen in the settled lands—and poised it on the border of her country, Harsdown.

The royal family remained standing while the table was set. After the servers withdrew, Stonebreaker settled into his throne. At Cobalt's nudge on her elbow, Mel joined the Chamberlight family in taking their seats. Stonebreaker's honor guards sat next. Only then did the rest of their guests settle into their chairs at the big table. Mel was relieved they all knew what they were doing, because she had no idea. Had she been expected to assign seating, she wouldn't have known who to put where or when to do it. No one had told her about this meal despite her inquiring in the kitchens both yesterday and earlier today about preparations for the king's arrival. The castle had a staff of over twenty, plus the stable hands and soldiers, yet she felt completely isolated.

Her introduction to Stonebreaker only made it worse, and she had little doubt it was intentional on his part. Cobalt's protective attitude toward his mother and his strange verbal battle with his grandfather caused her to wonder how much he, too, was a victim of Stonebreaker's control. Mel couldn't imagine how she would survive up here. Saints, she missed her family.

No emotion showed on Cobalt's face, but something flickered in his eyes when he looked at her, an apology maybe. Or perhaps she only wished to see it. She didn't try a mood spell. Hers always created light and that would draw unwanted attention, possibly even endanger her life if Stonebreaker's men feared she would harm the Chamberlight king.

Supper was excruciating. With eleven of them sitting along one side of the table it was difficult to talk to one another. Stonebreaker asked Dancer for news about the castle and listened with patience while she spoke. His officers said nothing. Had Mel been at home and her family invited her father's officers to dinner, they all would have been talking and laughing around the table. Now she didn't even know if she could talk to anyone. She had lost track of all the decrees Stonebreaker had for the behavior of his family.

The officer to Mel's left was a tall man with hair the color of bronze and a colonel's ebony ring on his finger. He dined with gusto, but he never broke protocol by eating with his hands or spilling food. The same couldn't be said of the soldiers at the table below. Mel was glad she wasn't the one who would clean up after the feast. Though perhaps she shouldn't be so certain, given the way Stonebreaker had treated her this afternoon. Pah. She shouldn't let him bother her this way.

Mel spoke cordially to the colonel. "Is the food to your liking, sir?"

The man froze. Then he slowly set down his knife and looked at her. "Yes, Your Highness. It is excellent."

"I am glad you are enjoying it, Colonel…" She let his title hang as a question. She didn't expect an answer; when she had tried this technique with Cobalt's men, they only bowed and went about their work, refusing to talk to her.

This fellow, however, smiled amiably. "Leo Tumbler, ma'am."

Leo Tumbler. Finally! She had a name for someone. She smiled and said, "My pleasure at your acquaintance, Leo Tumbler." She heard Stonebreaker speak to Cobalt, the first time it had happened during the meal, but she didn't catch the words.

Tumbler flushed when she smiled. Then he beamed at her. "The honor is mine, ma'am."

A hand touched Mel's arm. "Your roast grows cold," Cobalt said.

Startled, she turned to him, and he shook his head slightly, warning her to silence. Her anger sparked. Beyond him, she saw Stonebreaker cutting his venison. Although the king didn't seem to be paying attention, she had no doubt he was listening. She gritted her teeth. *You want Cobalt and me to argue, don't you.* Stonebreaker knew how isolated she and Dancer were here; he had set it up that way. Of course she wanted to talk to someone. So Stonebreaker manipulated Cobalt into stopping her. It could leave her and her new husband ripe for a spat.

Mel gave Cobalt her sweetest smile, the one her friends at home had always said made her look angelic. "Why, thank you, love. It is kind of you to notice."

Cobalt gaped at her. Suddenly his grin flashed—and lit up his entire face. It vanished immediately, but the sight was enough to warm Mel through ten dinners. Stonebreaker stabbed his fork into his meat, too hard, and the shaft bent.

Mel couldn't imagine raising a child in this family. If Stonebreaker was always like this, he would make the child doubt her worth. Or his. Varqelle would teach a boy his unforgiving view of life and probably despise a girl. She had no idea how Dancer would respond. If only she could raise her child with her parents. The likelihood Cobalt would ever agree to such, though, was about as great as that of the Misted Cliffs toppling into the borderlands. The shame of it was, Cobalt could probably be a good father if he had the chance to find that side of himself. But in this place, she didn't see how that would ever happen.

With the Chamberlight army gathering, they had room only for thoughts of war.

14
The Sphere Tower

Cobalt disappeared with Varqelle and Stonebreaker after dinner. Left on her own, with no one who wished to talk to her, Mel wandered through the castle. She stood on a bridge between two towers and gazed at the night sky. She thought of the telescope in Cobalt's library. Perhaps sometime he would come out here with her and look at the stars. It was hard to imagine him taking the time for such a dreamy pastime, though.

Eventually she returned to Cobalt's suite. He was in the parlor, practicing at the billiards table. She had never heard of the game before coming here; it was an import brought by a merchant ship from the west. Legends claimed that in the past, the Misted Cliffs had boasted a thriving sea trade. These days, only a few merchants came from across the Blue

Ocean, and only a few Chamberlight vessels traveled the world. Ships that ventured out often disappeared or somehow became lost and ended up back on the shores of the Misted Cliffs.

Mel stood in the doorway. Cobalt was using a polished stick to make balls hit each other and roll into pockets on the edges of the table.

"I'm sorry about the purple ball I burnt," she said.

He jerked the stick and missed the shot. But as he looked up at her, his face relaxed. He set his stick on the table and came over. Then he put his arms around her waist. "Thank you."

She blinked. "For ruining your game?"

He laughed, that full, rumbling sound he so rarely let out. "No. For tonight. Dinner."

"Oh." She had no idea what she had done. "Conversation seemed a bit strained." To put it mildly.

"It usually is with my family." Cobalt led her to a small sofa against one wall and drew her to sit with him on its gold and crimson cushions.

Mel took his hands. "I would love for you to visit mine."

His grip tensed on her fingers. "What?"

"Come stay with my family."

"I cannot."

"But why?" She lifted his hands and pressed her cheek against his knuckles. "I would like them to know you."

"Your family hates me."

"No." She wasn't actually certain he was so far from the truth, but they needed more of a chance to know him. "You were there less than one day."

He put his arm around her shoulders. "I have much to do here. I cannot traipse around the countryside."

"This is a cold, cruel place. It is bad for us."

He shuttered his expression. "It is the best home I have ever known."

Mel wanted to weep for him, if this was the best he had known. "Life can be full of laughter and light. Let me show you another way."

His gaze darkened. "You would sap my strength."

"Oh, bah." She thumped her palm against his chest. "Your strength is just fine. You should quit worrying about it."

He bent his head over hers and brushed his lips over her hair. "My father thinks you weaken me with such talk."

"Saints forbid I should weaken you by suggesting you have a right to a happy, contented life."

"Happy and contented by whose standards?"

"Anyone's."

"No. Yours." Cobalt shook his head. "Perhaps my father is right. But I cannot see the world as he does."

It wasn't exactly a declaration that he would visit, but it wasn't an outright refusal, either. "Does that mean you will consider my invitation?"

He paused. "Perhaps."

"I miss my family."

"You've been here less than a month."

It had felt like years. "Come visit. You will like them." Inspiration came to her. "Bring Dancer."

Silence.

"Cobalt?"

He drew back and regarded her with his forehead furrowed. "You would like my mother to visit your family?"

"Yes."

"It would be odd."

"Why? Families do it all the time."

"Not us."

"It could make her happy."

"She is happy here."

"She has no friends." It was heartbreaking if they considered this happiness. "No companions aside from you."

He spoke awkwardly. "She doesn't even have me."

"What happened?"

"I got angry at her."

"You didn't seem angry with each other this afternoon."

"That was a truce, because of Grandfather's arrival. Unspoken, but we both knew. We face him together." A muscle twitched in his cheek. "But I got angry with her because of him."

"What happened?"

"She let him bring me up."

This sounded like an anger several decades in the making. "Surely she had a reason."

"She will not tell it."

Mel touched his cheek. "Go to her. Make it better."

"I don't know how."

"Invite her to Harsdown."

He made an exasperated noise. "What makes you think she wants to go?"

It was a good question. Mel didn't have a good answer, because she suspected Dancer would rather walk in a swamp than visit her daughter-in-law's family. "She would go if you asked." Another idea came to her. "Bring Matthew." Dancer seemed to like him, too.

Cobalt regarded her doubtfully. "I don't know."

"Just for a visit." Even if Cobalt didn't like it enough to stay, at least she would have tried. "Think on this, too. Suppose your mother and my family get along? If anything ever happened to you, Dancer would have people she could stay with, people who would treat her well." Guessing at truths he only alluded to but never spoke, she added, "People who would protect her from anyone who would cause her pain."

He sighed. "You fight a fierce and difficult battle with your words."

I fight it for us—and for the settled lands. Maybe nothing could ever calm his tormented spirit, but the demons that drove him would never stop as long as he stayed here, influenced by Varqelle and Stonebreaker. He had never known any alternative. She could show him one. He might not want it, but she had to try. He deserved a chance to find his own peace.

Mel had learned enough of her husband to realize he would say no more for a while, until he thought on the matter. She wondered, though, if anything could ever be enough to satisfy his hunger for validation from his family, or if he would bring the world to its knees in his drive to make his grandfather acknowledge him as a man of worth.

Cobalt walked with Matthew to the West Tower. "The men seem less suspicious of Mel now."

"She conducts herself well," Matthew said.

"I wish they appreciated it more."

Matthew hesitated. "Well, Your Highness…"

Cobalt recognized his tone. Wary now, he said, "Yes?"

"You must not get angry."

Cobalt scowled at him. "About what?"

"Some of them believe she has enchanted you."

"She has," Cobalt said dryly.

"They thought so more at first. They are less certain now. She is kind to everyone, even though they never speak to her." Matthew chuckled. "And when she smiles that way, like an angel, it melts the hardest heart." His smile shifted into a frown for Cobalt. "But she is obviously lonely. You must find companions for your wife. Female companions."

Even if Stonebreaker would have allowed it, Cobalt couldn't imagine more women at the keep. "They would talk all the time."

"So?"

"It doesn't bother you?"

"Of course not. Their voices are music."

Cobalt snorted. "Hardly." In truth, he liked to listen to Mel. But he had no idea what it would be like with more women here. He hadn't been around enough to have an opinion on the subject. As long as Dancer refused to live at the Diamond Palace, Stonebreaker wasn't likely to allow her companions. Cobalt could have brought them anyway, as he had done with Mel. But right now he didn't want to challenge his grandfather, lest Stonebreaker change his mind about giving him command of the Chamberlight army. In planning campaigns with Varqelle, Cobalt found a satisfaction in his work that his life had never given him before. He was *made* for this—and his father understood.

He knew now that nothing would appease the fire that drove him. Except conquest.

Dancer didn't smile when she opened the door. She simply stood aside so Cobalt could enter her study. He went to her desk, uncertain of himself. Today she was reading a tome about the tiny country of Blueshire and taking notes with a quill on a parchment. He steeled himself and turned to face her.

Dancer remained by the open doorway. "It is late. Have your say and be done."

"Mother." He took a deep breath. "I would not be at odds with you."

Some of her ice seemed to thaw. "Yet we are."

"It troubles me."

"I also." She came over to him. "I wish I could undo the nightmares you endured in your youth. I cannot. But you are the one light in my life. I do not wish to be at odds with you."

"I worry for you, staying here."

She shuddered, though the room was warm. "I will not return to the Diamond Palace."

"Perhaps a place of sun and laughter would be better."

"I know of no such place."

Neither do I. But he had glimpsed it when he went to fetch his bride. It had hurt to be at that house among the apple trees, and he didn't know why. When he thought of Dancer there, though, he felt a deep relief.

"I am sending Mel to her family for a while," he said.

"I think it is for the best. She disrupts our lives." Dancer sounded uncertain, though. Cobalt had noticed that his mother was having trouble disliking his wife, hard as Dancer might try to be hostile.

"She has invited you to go with her," Cobalt said.

"What?" Dancer stared at him. "No!"

"Why not?" It was the same question Mel had asked him.

"It is a trick. They would never accept me there. I am the wife of the man who invaded their country and the mother of the man who took their daughter."

"Nevertheless, Mel has invited you." He rubbed his chin. "My wife is rather formidable. If she insists they accept you, I believe they will do so."

"Your wife is a witch."

"Well yes, that, too."

She blinked. "It doesn't bother you?"

"It terrifies me." But he smiled.

Dancer studied him. "You are odd tonight."

"How?"

"I don't know. Calmer." She thought for a moment. "You seem happy lately."

"I don't know." He wasn't sure how "happy" differed from his normal state. He did know, however, that with Mel he felt strong. Happy? Perhaps.

"I cannot imagine going back to Harsdown," Dancer said.

"I would like you to."

"Why? Do you not want me here?"

"I worry for your safety when I am not here."

She didn't look surprised, but her shoulders tensed. "Where are you going?"

He couldn't tell her about his counsels with her husband and father. Nothing was certain. He spoke carefully. "I may ride with Grandfather's army. I haven't decided yet." Then he added, "I would have for you a place where you may have other women as friends. Where you may walk among flowering trees. Hear laughter. See happy children. Have a pet."

She seemed bewildered. "A pet?"

"If you want." Stonebreaker had never allowed Cobalt the hound he had longed for as a boy, and eventually Cobalt had stopped thinking about it. Now he shared his suite with a scrap of gray fur that chased spiders but ran away from anything larger and alive. Oddly enough, it wasn't unpleasant.

"I don't want a pet," Dancer said.

"You might enjoy traveling."

She didn't look convinced. "It's been so long since I've been outside of the Misted Cliffs. Decades."

"Think of it as adventure," Cobalt suggested.

"I don't like adventure."

"As fun."

"It doesn't sound like fun."

Exasperated, he said, "At least consider it, Mother."

She twisted her hand in her pale tunic. "Very well. I will think on it."

Well, it was a start. He hoped she would go. It would be good for her. And perhaps she could deal with Mel better than he could—for he had no idea how he was going to tell his wife that she was going home without him.

Mel stood in the highest chamber of the Sphere Tower, under its dome, which curved in a hollow globe, except where it opened to cap the chamber. She imagined the globe completed. She couldn't hold it the way she would hold a ball, but she knew her mother could make spells without touching the shape, if she was close enough to it. Mel concentrated now on doing the same.

Power surged within her, erratic but more settled than the last time she had tried a spell this large, that night Dancer had found her in the Zephyr Tower. Mel still didn't know what Varqelle intended, but she wanted her parents warned that the House of Chamberlight was gathering its army.

Green light filled the dome above her, and she raised her hands. She couldn't have touched the light even if she could have reached that high, but it helped her focus. She thought of home, of her father writing at his desk in his calligraphic script, of her mother preparing to meet with the Glassblowers' Guild. She thought of Shim, of Bricklayer, of her other friends, of Skylark and her tutors. Memories filled her like wine in a goblet. She could almost *feel* her home.

Her parents were both mages, Muller the stronger of the two but Chime the more adept. Mel focused on her mother, an emerald mage who responded strongly to green spells, and on her father, an indigo sphere mage. She sent her mood to them, her concern about the Chamberlight army amassing at the base of the cliffs. She reached across the borderlands, hills, glades, rivers, and woods and poured her fear into her spell.

Mel had no idea if she contacted either of them. She opened her eyes into a haze of green light that filled the chamber and spilled out the windows into the night. Her arms felt too heavy to hold up, and she let them drop back to her sides. She had never tried a spell this strong nor pushed it so hard. Nausea roiled over her. Her vision blurred and needles seemed to bore into her temples.

With a cry, she collapsed to the floor.

Someone was shaking her. She pushed at his hand, but she couldn't dislodge the iron grip. She tried to roll away and he pulled her back. He continued to shake her. Hard. It hurt. Her spine knocked against the stone floor.

Mel opened her eyes. King Stonebreaker was kneeling at her side, his hands clenched on her shoulders as he strove to wake her up. When she looked at him, he finally stopped knocking her back and forth. She would have bruises where he had banged her against the floor.

"Are you awake?" he demanded.

"Yes." Groggy and confused, Mel slowly sat up. Didn't he realize he could hurt a person that way?

"Why are you sleeping here?" Stonebreaker's scorn was almost palpable. "Is your husband's suite that distasteful to you?"

"No…" Mel wasn't certain herself what had happened. She couldn't have been unconscious long; the Hunter constellation still showed in the sky, through one window. Her dazed thoughts wandered. Legend claimed that if a captain sailed his ship west, the Hunter would take him to other lands. But in the distant past, an immensely powerful mage had spelled this small continent so that ships had trouble leaving or finding it. As the ages passed, it became more and more difficult. Someday all other lands would be lost to her people. Mel found the tales hard to believe, but she had no better explanation for why fewer ships came every generation.

"Are you mute?" Stonebreaker asked. "Why were you lying on the floor? You looked dead."

Mel struggled to gather her thoughts. "I grew dizzy and fainted." She didn't know why she had passed out, but she thought it had something to do with pushing her abilities too hard. By collapsing, her body had forced her to stop.

"Are you ill?" Stonebreaker asked.

"No…just overwhelmed." She rubbed her eyes. "How did you know I was here?"

"I saw the green light in the windows." He sat back with one leg bent and his forearm resting on his knee. "But I see no way you could make such a light."

"I was practicing a spell." She couldn't pretend nothing had happened. If the people here believed she was trying to hide her skills, it would only make them distrust her more.

"A spell." His voice hardened. "Then it is true what they say. You are a witch."

"No. Just a mage." She rubbed her temples. Her head had never hurt this much. "I only do warmth and comfort spells."

"Warmth and comfort, eh?" Stonebreaker cocked his head. "And what sort of enchantment would those involve? Perhaps an incantation to ward off my grandson."

Mel had no intention of giving him that satisfaction. "It was a mood spell. I sought to divine if he loved me." She smiled angelically at Stonebreaker. "He is such a magnificent man, Your Majesty. You must be so proud of him."

The king scowled. "You drank too much wine tonight." He let his gaze travel over her body in a way that made her face burn. Then he wet his lips. "You are a lovely young woman. Cobalt must seem too old to you."

She wanted to slap him. "He's perfect."

He leaned forward. "So you are up here in the night making spells to discover if he has passion for you."

That wasn't exactly what she had said. "Love."

"I would think you would find a better answer if you spent the night in his suite rather than up here."

Well, yes. The verbal sparring was tiring Mel. Her temples ached and her mind felt fuzzy. If she kept pushing her abilities, she could burn them out. Too much, and she could injure or even kill herself.

"Well," she said. "I should go join him."

"You should stay here, witch woman." Stonebreaker grasped her arm. "He will never notice your absence." His fingers dug into her skin hard enough to bruise.

"Your Majesty." Mel tried to pull away. It hurt where he gripped her.

Stonebreaker yanked her toward him so their faces were only a handspan apart. "I told you to stay here." He clenched both of her upper arms until his grip felt like a vise. Then he looked down the front of her tunic. "Why would you waste yourself on him?"

"Stop!" Mel tried to pry her arms free. "It hurts."

"I am your king." He shook her hard. "You will not put others before me."

"S-stop!" Mel managed to pull one arm away.

Stonebreaker slapped her across the face. Mel gasped as her

head snapped to the side. She couldn't believe this. And what decent man looked at his grandson's wife as if he were undressing her?

"Stop lying," he said. "Tell me what deviltry you were up to in here." He lifted her up and then knocked her back down on the floor, on her back. "I will have an answer!"

"D-don't." Her cheek throbbed where he had hit her and her head spun. She rolled away from him, but instead of letting her go, he raised his fist—in a motion identical to the way Cobalt had threatened her that night their carriage was attacked. Cobalt had held back the blow, but she had no doubt Stonebreaker fully intended to beat her.

"You *bastard*." A dark figure yanked Stonebreaker away from Mel. "Let her go!"

The king jumped to his feet and spun around. Cobalt stood in the moonlight flowing through the windows, his face contorted almost beyond recognition by fury.

"Don't *touch* her." Cobalt ground out the words.

"You will not speak to me in this manner." The king's voice was low and angry.

Mel struggled to her feet and stepped toward Cobalt. Her head ached and she swayed, barely able to stand. Her thoughts whirled.

Stonebreaker put out his hand to catch her, and Mel stumbled away from him in the same instant Cobalt grabbed for her. She was already falling when he caught her. He pulled her to his side, away from Stonebreaker, the muscles in his arm tensed against her waist. Still sensitized by her mood spell from before, she felt Cobalt's rage like grit against her skin. A fisted anger throbbed within Stonebreaker, clenched and ugly.

"Touch her again," Cobalt said, "and I will tear you apart."

Mel stared at him. He had just threatened the king with bodily harm, even death. Stonebreaker could have him tried for treason and executed.

His grandfather regarded him with no trace of remorse. "Do not threaten me, boy."

"Leave my wife alone."

"You should ask your wife why she lies here on the floor at night, alone and seductively dressed."

Cobalt answered in a voice so tight, Mel thought he would snap. "Good night, Grandfather."

"Leave me," Stonebreaker said, his eyes glinting. "Sleep well. If you can." He made it into a curse.

Cobalt kept his arm around Mel as he turned away. His tendons ridged like steel cords against her torso. He reached across his body with his other hand and held it out to her. When she took it, he gripped her fingers, helping support her, but she thought also to calm himself. She could only imagine the effort of will it took for him to walk away. That he managed it told her more about his self-control than anything he could have said. It probably also saved him from being thrown into the dungeon for attempted regicide.

They left Stonebreaker in the tower. She had no doubt he intended to search for a source of the green light. She and Cobalt descended the spiral stairs, holding on to each other.

Mel started to tremble about halfway down the tower. Once her tremors started, they wouldn't stop. She pulled away from Cobalt and sat down heavily on the step. Crossing her arms over her stomach, she leaned forward with her head bent. Shudders racked her body.

"He had no right," Cobalt said, his voice dark and low.

Mel looked up. He stood several steps below her, breathing as if he had been running. His fists were clenched at his sides.

"Cobalt—"

"No." Anger suffused his face. "No!"

With no warning, he slammed his fist into the wall. He jerked back his arm and hit the bricks again—and again and again, with a force that could have shattered Stonebreaker had he expended it against his grandfather instead of an unyielding wall. Any harder and he could break his own hands. The bricks were old and ragged, and half of one cracked from his blows, then disintegrated the next time he hit it. The uneven blocks ripped his skin until blood smeared his knuckles. Jagged bits of mortar and stone crumbled to the steps and dust swirled in the air. Mel pressed back against the stairs, afraid to make a sound. She didn't believe he would turn his fists against her, but she had never seen him lose control before. He pounded the wall as if he wanted to destroy the castle itself.

Gradually his rage abated and his blows slowed. Finally he pressed his palms against the bloodied stone and rested his forehead on the wall, his chest heaving from exertion.

"Cobalt?" Mel whispered.

He made a choked sound. Then he pushed away from the wall and turned to her. "I won't hurt you. I swear." Blood dripped off his torn knuckles and splattered on the cracked step by her foot.

"Your hands," she said, shaking.

"It doesn't matter." He knelt next to her. "Are you all right?"

"Yes." She lifted his hand and blood trickled across her fingers. Even now, when she was stunned from his rage, from Stonebreaker's behavior, and from her struggle with her magecraft earlier tonight, she still automatically folded her other hand around her sapphire pendant and tried to form a blue spell of healing. A terrible pain lanced through her head and she gasped, dropping the pendant. No hint of a spell formed. Nausea swept over her, then dismay. Was it possible she had burned out her mage abilities? This aftermath was much worse than the last time. She couldn't heal even herself right now, let alone Cobalt.

"I'm sorry," she whispered. "I can't help."

He searched her face as if trying to find an answer. "You were alone up there."

"Cobalt, I swear, I wasn't doing anything wrong."

He put his bloodied fingers against her lips. "I know. But why were you alone?"

Mel couldn't tell him why. But she could tell him another truth. "I feel so out of place here. I needed some time for myself, to practice my craft. When people see me doing spells, they think I am some sort of demon. Cobalt, I'm not evil—"

"You are a gift," he said, his gaze never leaving her face. "I don't understand your spells. And yes, they disquiet me. But I know you intend only good, not evil." He sat on the step next to her. "I never wanted you to witness any of that. Not Grandfather. And not—not me."

"He has hurt you." Mel had no doubt about it. Saints only knew what Stonebreaker had done to Cobalt and Dancer.

"It is over," Cobalt said.

Mel knew it wasn't, not if he bloodied himself this way. "You need to escape this place."

His gaze darkened. "I will kill him if he hurts you again."

She knew Cobalt was capable of it. What then? Would his people execute him for murdering the king? She doubted it. He would be king then. It would be a nightmare. Would they revolt? They all feared him and he had control of the army. No matter what happened, he would hate himself. It would poison everything he did. He had it within him to become a great leader, but she didn't think it would happen if he didn't get away from here and heal. She couldn't bear to see his promise destroyed in the flames of his rage.

"Don't talk that way," she said.

"I have decided," he said. "My mother will go to your family with you."

Relief flooded Mel, so sudden and welcome that it made her light-headed. "It is a wonderful idea. You will like my family, too."

He didn't answer.

"Cobalt?" Her unease stirred. He had said *with you.* Not *with us.* "You are coming, aren't you?"

"I will escort you with the army."

Mel froze. "You are bringing them into Harsdown?"

"An honor guard wasn't enough to protect you the last time. Now it will be both you and my mother."

"You cannot bring an army to my family's home!"

He wouldn't meet her gaze. "We won't stay there."

"Cobalt, look at me."

He turned to her. "I will escort you home. Then I will take the army to Shazire."

"No! Don't do this."

With unexpected gentleness, he smoothed her hair back from her face. "I will give you the world, Mel."

Her voice caught. "I don't want the world."

He spoke quietly. "But I do."

She didn't know how to make this nightmare stop. "You could be happy with my family."

He smiled with sadness. "I might wish that were true. But it is not."

She grasped his forearms. "Shazire has never done you harm."

"It is part of the Misted Cliffs!"

"That was over two hundred years ago."

"Then we have been apart too long."

Her pulse stuttered. "The western edge of Harsdown was also part of the Misted Cliffs."

He cupped her face in his hands. "I won't go back on my word to you. We will not attack Harsdown."

"Then why?" She grasped his wrists and moved his palms away from her face. "*Why* must you take back Shazire?"

"Why must a lion stalk its prey? Why must lightning stab the earth during a storm?" Cobalt pulled away his arms. "I am not a man to tend orchards. I never will be." He regarded her steadily. "And neither are you such a woman."

"No," she whispered.

"A fire burns in you."

"You are wrong."

"Someday an empire will kneel to you."

"I don't want people to kneel to me." All she wanted was a happy life with him and their child. Most of all, she feared he would seduce her with his dark promises of glory and power.

His gaze burned. "I will become invincible. No one will ever hurt you, my mother, or any child you bear me."

She knew then that Stonebreaker truly had been a fool. The small boy he had so easily terrorized had grown into an indomitable man, one haunted by the demons of his childhood.

Now the rest of humanity would pay the price.

15
The Living Sea

In the end, Dancer agreed to come. Mel suspected it had nothing to do with meeting her son's in-laws. She feared remaining at the keep without Cobalt—for Stonebreaker was to stay there. Varqelle insisted the Chamberlight king not risk his life with the army, and though Stonebreaker protested, in the end he reluctantly agreed to abide by his son-in-law's wishes. Mel didn't believe his reluctance for one moment. The king of the Misted Cliffs wanted as little blame as possible for this campaign he was supporting. He desired the result, that his grandson would restore the size and wealth of his realms, but not the responsibility.

Today Mel wore a gray tunic and leggings, with soft boots. She left the castle by a small door behind the stables and crossed the yard outside where she often rode Smoke. To the west, cliffs towered over the castle; to the east, the rugged land crumpled in folds and ridges, then dropped down to the borderlands. She walked slowly, lost in thought, her pendant heavy around her neck. Several stable boys were training horses in the yard. Most of them paid her no heed, but Jumper waved. She smiled and waved back at the towheaded child. He often helped her tend Smoke. Sometimes he forgot he wasn't supposed to talk to her and told her jokes about his favorites among the horses.

Mel wandered a trail that climbed into the mountains. Eventually she reached a ledge near the top of the waterfall created by the River of Diamonds. Water thundered over the rocks and down, down, down to the Lake of Ice far below. She sat cross-legged on the ledge and folded her hand around her pendant. Then she imagined red roses, flushed cheeks, bright red ribbons on a festival pole, red, crimson, scarlet, the simplest mage color.

Nothing.

She envisioned rubies sparkling on red velvet.

Nothing.

She thought of cherries and apples, rosy and round, and red leaves on the trees in autumn.

Nothing.

Moisture filled her eyes. It had been this way ever since that night she had collapsed after trying to warn her parents about the Chamberlight invasion. No spells. She couldn't manage even the simplest, a little warmth, a little light. That night in the Sphere Tower, had she incinerated the essence that infused her as a mage? She closed her eyes and squeezed back the tears. Although she had always valued her magecraft, she had never before realized how much she based her sense of herself on her ability to perform spells. She had never heard of a mage losing her power this way, nor did she have any idea how to heal herself. She didn't even know if it was possible. Without her abilities, she felt shorn and reduced.

"It's a lovely view, Your Highness," a voice said.

Mel opened her eyes. Colonel Leo Tumbler stood about five paces away, where the end of the ledge met the path coming up from the castle. His yellow hair curled on his forehead and his demeanor was friendly. Ever since she had spoken to him at the dinner on the afternoon of Stonebreaker's arrival, he had been courteous to her. He seemed unfazed by the rumors of her purportedly evil magics. Mel knew Cobalt had asked him to watch over her, but she didn't understand why her taciturn husband trusted him. Leo Tumbler was among Stonebreaker's top officers. Cobalt would reveal nothing of his reasons or even admit Tumbler was guarding her.

"Greetings of the morning," she said.

"May I join you?" Tumbler asked.

Mel indicated the ledge. "I've no chair to offer, but you are welcome to sit here if you would like." Dryly she added, "Though I thought bodyguards were supposed to stand."

Tumbler smiled slightly. "Ah, well." He didn't deny being her bodyguard.

He came closer, to within about three paces, but he did remain standing, his gaze flicking around the area. Mel rose to her feet so he wouldn't loom over her. "Leo, I was wondering if you would mind my asking you a question."

He regarded her curiously. "Yes, Your Highness?"

"Have you ridden with the Chamberlight army for long?"

"For years."

"Always with Stonebreaker?"

His face became guarded. "Always with the House of Chamberlight."

His evasive answer only made her more curious. "Cobalt is a Chamberlight by blood."

"So he is."

"Did you ever know Cobalt before?"

His expression was carefully neutral. "Ever since we were boys together at the Diamond Palace."

Interesting. Apparently they had a long history. "He must be glad to see you."

"I am always glad to see my prince."

So. This was beginning to make sense. "It must be useful for Cobalt to have someone he knows well in Stonebreaker's army." Like a spy.

He almost smiled that time. "It is an honor to serve the royal House."

Based on what she had seen of the Chamberlight king, she doubted he would have brought Tumbler here if he had realized Cobalt trusted the colonel. Her respect for Tumbler's courage increased even more. King Stonebreaker imprisoned suspected spies and executed those convicted of the crime.

"Are you impatient to ride to Harsdown?" Mel asked. "It's been so many weeks since you all arrived." The staff at the castle had been sending stores down to the main body of the military force gathered at the base of the cliffs, and they were organizing which servants would go as support for the army.

"It would be foolish to leave before we are ready," Tumbler said. Then he released a long breath. "But, aye, Your Highness, I grow restless."

Mel couldn't say the same. She had tried every argument she knew to change Cobalt's mind, with no success. Soon his forces would move inexorably into Harsdown—and beyond.

* * *

The Chamberlight army headed out on a morning late in the winter when all moisture had frozen out of the air and the sky arched overhead in an icy blue dome. Mel rode Smoke. An honor guard of six officers surrounded her, including Leo Tumbler. She wore a sturdy tunic and leggings, all light blue, with leather armor. Her sword hung on its sheath on her belt.

Mel avoided Cobalt. She couldn't bear to ride with him. She couldn't talk to him. She couldn't look at him. Dancer rode a dappled mare alongside her son up ahead, separated from Mel by about fifty riders in the column of mounted warriors. The cavalry and troops were happy to be moving out. Their spirits were high. Mel's could go no lower.

The army consisted of six thousand men, about one thousand more than the combined forces of Aronsdale and Harsdown, three times the size of the Shazire army. Two thousand were cavalry and the rest marched as troops. They brought food and other supplies, and many horses, including packhorses and chargers for battle, and carts drawn by plow horses. The army flowed from the base of the Misted Cliffs across the borderlands, a great ocean of people rolling inexorably toward Harsdown.

Mel's honor guard formed a hexagon around her. Had she still been able to act as a mage, she could have filled the hexagon with spells to encourage and support the soldiers, just as her ancestors had done before her. She died a bit more each time she thought of her lost abilities. This army would go into battle without mages—and because of that, more men would die. Maybe Cobalt. She didn't want to fear for his survival, but nothing could stop the pain that came when she realized his life could end. She was falling in love with her warlord husband and no amount of self-reproach could stop it from happening.

Magnificent in his armor and plumed helmet, Varqelle rode at the head of the great column, flanked by six standard-bearers. Three sat on white stallions and carried the banner of the House of Chamberlight, the blue sphere on a white background. The reins of their horses were strips of blue leather braided together, and silver tassels hung from the bridles. The other three rode black stallions and carried Escar banners with the black jaguar on a dark blue field. Cobalt and Dancer rode behind Varqelle, surrounded by another honor guard. In his dark armor and chain mail, Cobalt made an imposing figure next to his mother, who wore a riding tunic and leggings with no armor to shield her slight form.

Whatever Cobalt claimed, everyone could see the hostile message this sent, that the Chamberlight army entered Harsdown with that country's deposed king and queen. Mel knew her father might have spies in the Misted Cliffs, but Stonebreaker was obsessive about secrecy. A good chance existed that Muller hadn't known this army was preparing to ride on Harsdown. When her father learned of the march, he would mobilize his forces. Was this an act of war? If the Chamberlight army attacked, Aronsdale would come to the defense of Harsdown, but by the time they arrived, thousands of people could have died.

Mel didn't trust Varqelle to honor the treaty established by her marriage to his son. She wasn't even certain about Cobalt anymore. He hungered for a campaign of conquest, and it wasn't only his desire for his father's approval. It was *him*. Whatever drove Varqelle burned even hotter within Cobalt.

He gave his word. Whenever Mel began to brood, she reminded herself of Cobalt's promise to honor the treaty. She had to believe him; otherwise, she was riding against her own family.

The cavalry crossed the borderlands throughout the morning. Mel had brought Fog in a large basket strapped to her saddlebags. He liked to ride that way, lulled to sleep by the rocking motion. Horse-drawn carts rolled past, heaped with provisions: dried meat and fruits, grains, piles of gourds, feed for the horses, barrels of water and ale, and mounds of other foodstuffs. Women from the Diamond Palace guided the carts, cooks who would prepare the food and other servants who would tend to the needs of the army.

A cluster of young warriors rode by and glanced at Mel, their dark eyes curious. She had already realized the people of the Misted Cliffs considered her yellow hair exotic. The youths looked back at her after they had passed, and one smiled shyly. Colonel Tumbler scowled at him, and the boy flushed and quickly rode on, soon swallowed up in the surging mass of humanity.

After several hours, they stopped to rest the horses and let the foot soldiers catch up. Mel fed the kitten and played with him until the army set off again. At this pace, it would take more than a day to reach the woods where she had lain with Cobalt for the first time. She didn't want to remember, but she couldn't stop herself. Even now she wanted him, and she despised herself for that weakness.

As the hours passed, clouds gradually spread across the sky. By afternoon, the day had darkened. A fog bank appeared in the south, and a few drops of rain pelted Mel's face. The soldiers continued to ride, and the fog swelled on the horizon, stretching from east to west, dark and dense.

Then Mel realized it wasn't fog.

It was another army.

Mel spurred Smoke forward. Her guards came with her, Leo Tumbler at her side. They passed armored men with swords at their hips or strapped across their backs. A few wore their helmets, angular affairs that covered most of the face, with slits for eyes, but most had lashed the helmets to their gear. Their mounts raised clouds of dust.

Mel slowed as she neared Cobalt. Her guards fell back, leaving her room to join her husband. Dancer was riding on his other side. She turned a cool gaze to Mel, but said nothing. Nor did she make any attempt to ride with Varqelle. She seemed to prefer even Mel's company to that of her estranged husband.

Cobalt glanced at Mel. "Do you recognize them?"

She knew he meant the other army. "They're too far away." They both had a good guess about who it was, though. "You gave your word not to attack my people."

He spoke tightly. "As did they, for my people."

Her pulse beat hard. "What will you do?"

He answered in a careful voice. "I will not violate the treaty first."

First. If he believed her father's army was attacking his, she had no doubt he would respond in kind. She had never been sure she believed in the saints of nature and color revered by her people, but now she silently petitioned every one she could think of to keep everyone calm, both Cobalt's men and those who rode from the south to meet them.

The two forces drew nearer throughout the afternoon, and the "fog" resolved into columns of warriors. After several hours, the armies reached a long, narrow valley that stretched from east to west, separating the two forces. There they halted. Men poured in throughout the evening, thousands of riders, archers, foot soldiers, grooms, and support. Cobalt's people gathered on the northern crest of the valley and the other army gathered on its southern crest. They filled the land as far as Mel could see in either direction.

Mel recognized the banners carried by the standard-bearers for the other army—the violet and white pennant of the House of Dawnfield. Her family. Then her breath caught. Her father was with them, seated on his white charger, tall and imposing. Gone was the well-dressed country gentleman; this man wore armor with a burnished breastplate and plumed helmet. His shield gleamed even in the overcast day. He had become a war leader, a stranger to her.

Somehow Mel managed to speak calmly, though her heartbeat felt as if it had doubled. "I would speak with him."

"Yes." Cobalt didn't have to ask who. He prodded Admiral forward and they rode to where Varqelle sat on his mount, flanked by the Escar and Chamberlight standard-bearers. His gaze was hard and his attention fixed on his counterpart across the valley, the man who had taken his throne.

Cobalt drew alongside Varqelle. Mel stayed on the other side of her husband, keeping him between her and his father. Varqelle didn't look at them; he continued to watch the other army.

"They are many," he said.

"About six thousand, I would estimate." Cobalt studied the Dawnfield forces as they continued to amass along the ridge across the valley. Neither army was setting up tents or looking after the many needs of a force that size as it settled in for the night. Foot soldiers stood at attention and cavalrymen gathered in geometric formations, ready to fight.

"They must have had warning," Cobalt said.

Varqelle scowled. "How? No one left the keep. In the borderlands, you can see for leagues. We watched. No one came to or left the army."

"Even so," Cobalt said. "Someone told them."

Mel's pulse hammered. Had her warning succeeded? If so, it had been worth burning out her mage talent.

"Well, it seems we must negotiate," Varqelle muttered.

Cobalt cocked an eyebrow at him. "As was always the plan."

When Varqelle didn't answer, a chill went up Mel's back. She hated to think what might have happened if her father hadn't been prepared to meet this force. Cobalt had sworn to her that he would honor the treaty, but his father had not. The Chamberlight army followed Cobalt, for he was the crown prince of the Misted Cliffs, but they knew he acted as general for his sire, who had once ruled this land. She wasn't certain they—or Cobalt—would have refused Varqelle if he had ordered them to fight against Harsdown.

Cobalt laid his hand on Mel's arm. "Will you talk with your father?"

She nodded, aware of Varqelle's hard gaze. "Do I have your word that you ask only for safe passage through Harsdown? No combat?"

"Yes."

Mel looked from him to his father. Two men with predator's eyes. "Both of your words?"

Varqelle's mouth twisted. She knew he thought she had gone too far. It didn't matter. She wouldn't negotiate for them without his guarantee.

Varqelle glanced at Cobalt, and his son met his gaze. After a moment, Varqelle said, "You have my word." He looked as if he had eaten a sour fruit.

Mel exhaled, but she strove to hide her relief. The less Varqelle could read from her, the better. She urged Smoke into a trot, and he made his way down the slope of the valley. He seemed to flow beneath her, strong and sure, though his hooves tore up the wild grasses. He gathered speed as the slope leveled out. When they reached the creek at the bottom, he jumped it without hesitation, his leap so fluid she barely felt a change in his pace. Within moments, they were climbing the southern slope.

Mel slowed as she neared her father. As she approached, he came forward with Sphere-General Fieldson and Hexahedron-Lieutenant Jason Windcrier. Officers in the Dawnfield army had ranks based on the geometric hierarchy of spells. They weren't mages, but the custom originated in the mages who had ridden with the military in past eras. The shapes subdivided each rank, with triangle as lowest and sphere as highest. A square-lieutenant held a higher rank than a triangle-lieutenant; however, he still had a lower rank than a triangle-captain because all captains outranked all lieutenants. No one ranked above a sphere-general. Fieldson was the only one in either Harsdown or Aronsdale, and was another reason Muller had a strong military.

Seeing her father, Mel wanted to jump off Smoke and run to him. But she held back, determined to retain her dignity. As they came up alongside each other, he pulled off his helmet and held it under his arm. She saw the moisture in his eyes. Neither of them would cry, not here with so many people watching, but it was all she could do to hold back her tears, for both her joy in seeing him and her grief in the circumstances.

His voice caught. "Greetings, Daughter."

"It is good to see you, Papa." She heard the tremor in her words.

"Are you all right?" he asked.

"Yes. Fine." She scowled. "My husband is sending me home. For my safety."

A startled smile flashed on his face and he seemed to drop ten years. "You are coming home?"

"Aye, Papa." Mel took a deep breath. "My husband, Cobalt of the House of Chamberlight, does ask if you honor the treaty our countries have signed."

"If *I* honor it?" His voice hardened. "He is the one who brought an army."

"He gave me his word. He wishes only safe passage through Harsdown."

"For what purpose?"

"They go to Shazire."

Muller spoke grimly. "Why?"

"Ah, gods, Father," she said, miserable. "Why do you think? My husband is his father's son."

Muller gazed out at the Chamberlight army blanketing the countryside. "We cannot stand by while he invades Shazire."

"If you fight them, you void the treaty. It goes both ways. When the House of Chamberlight swore never to attack the House of Dawnfield, we swore never to attack them."

He made an incredulous noise. "They expect us to let them through so they can subjugate another country?"

"It is part of the Misted Cliffs."

His face paled. "So was part of Harsdown."

"Cobalt swears they will leave here in peace. But if you try to stop them, they will call it a violation of the treaty and attack Harsdown." Her hands clenched the reins. "Varqelle seeks the Jaguar Throne. He will not hesitate to kill for it." She left unspoken what they both knew—that the man he wanted to kill was her father.

Muller was shaking his head. "The treaty was meant to give peace among our countries."

"And it does." Mel felt heavy. Tired. "But it said nothing of Blueshire, Shazire, Jazid, or Taka Mal."

Muller looked ill. He faced a horrendous choice: sacrifice the well-being of his own country, possibly his throne and his life, to defend other lands; or keep his people safe and stand by while Cobalt brought those other lands to their knees.

Muller blew out a gust of air. "I must think."

"I understand." Mel hesitated. "I would ask one thing of you."

"Yes?"

"The Escar queen rides with us. She is my companion." That was probably pushing their relationship too far, but it would have to do. "She has no wish to see her estranged husband wage war and she desires no part in his campaign. I would ask that you accept her into our home as you accept me."

Muller stared at her. "Hell and damnation, Mel."

"She has nowhere else to go." Then Mel added, "And Father—as long as she is with us, in *our* territory, it is an added incentive for her son's good faith. He wishes her safe."

Muller studied her face. "As he does with you?"

Mel knew what he was asking; were she and Cobalt estranged or did they live as husband and wife.

Mel had to tell him the truth. "As with me."

"You *accept* this man?"

"The good in him."

Her father snorted. "I have yet to see it."

Mel doubted he would have the chance. The world would know Cobalt by his campaigns. No one would see the man she knew, the Cobalt who dreamed of stars and gazed through a telescope, who had taught her to hit wooden balls with a stick, and who was so awkward and yet so gentle with her kitten. The world would know only Cobalt the Dark. Or perhaps Cobalt the Great, if his campaigns succeeded; victors invariably rewrote history in their own favor.

"It exists," she said quietly. "His mother has had some difficult years. I would like her to know life can be better than what she has seen."

"You are kind," he said. "Also terribly naive."

"Will you take her?"

He sighed. "All right, Mel. We will take her."

Her shoulders relaxed. "Thank you."

"For the other," he said. "Tell your husband I will have an answer for him in the morning."

"I will."

"Mel—"

"Yes?"

He raised his head to look out at the Chamberlight forces. Then he turned back to her. "If we had not been prepared, what would have happened with this army?"

She told him the truth. "Were it just Cobalt, I think nothing. But he and his father are of different minds."

"His father." His fingers gripped his helmet. "He almost destroyed my homeland eighteen years ago."

"But not this time."

"We had warning." His expression softened. "From a mage."

She averted her gaze. "A mage no longer." The words cut like a blade.

"Spells that powerful can injure."

She looked up at him. "They can destroy."

"Injuries heal."

Her voice broke. "How?"

"I don't know." He spoke gently. "I pray they will."

"It may never happen."

He inclined his head with respect. Sadness showed in his eyes. "If it turns out that way, your sacrifice will be honored by an entire country."

"Papa——" He couldn't stop the pain of losing her abilities, but his words helped ease her sadness. A tear ran down her face. "Thank you."

He touched her cheek. "Be well."

She folded her hand around his arm. "You also."

He set his palm over her hand. They separated then, he returning to his army and she to hers.

In the morning, Sphere-General Fieldson delivered Muller's reply to Cobalt: The Dawnfield forces would give them passage to the southern border of Harsdown. Mel grieved for what she knew that decision had cost her father.

As the army prepared to ride, Cobalt took Mel to a secluded copse of sunbask trees. She wanted to say so much, to argue, cajole, plead, insist he change his mind. But it was useless. She had already tried every approach she knew.

He enfolded her in his arms and held her under the swaying branches, her cheek against his chest.

"Don't be a hero," she whispered.

Cobalt drew back and put his hand under her chin, tilting her head up so he could see her face. "Why do you say that?"

She laid her palm against his chest. "I want you to come home to me. Alive."

He searched her face. "Why? You have every reason to hate me."

"I don't hate you."

"No?"

Softly, with pain, she said, "No, saints forgive me."

He released a long breath. Then he lowered his head and kissed her. Mel leaned into him, her arms around his waist, and she wanted him even now. When he raised his head, his eyes had a luminous quality, sadness and light.

They spent too long among the trees, and Leo Tumbler came to fetch them. After they returned to camp, Cobalt and Dancer said their farewells. Dancer didn't cry, but tears glistened in her eyes. Cobalt looked as if he felt the same. Yet they didn't embrace. Mel had never seen any member of his family unrestrained enough to show affection.

Then Mel and Dancer rode across the valley, accompanied by Mel's honor guard. As they approached her father's army, he rode forward with a hexagon of his cavalrymen, who exchanged places with the Chamberlight men. Leo Tumbler and his men bowed to Dancer and Mel from horseback, and Leo raised his hand in farewell. Dancer nodded, regal on her silver horse. Although the queen held her head high, Mel saw her white-knuckled grip on the reins.

Muller bowed to Dancer. "Welcome, Your Majesty."

"Thank you, Your Majesty." Her face was pale and she swallowed as she looked around at the slopes crowded with the Dawnfield army.

Muller put more warmth into his voice. "My daughter has spoken for you. You are welcome in our home."

She gave Mel an odd look, as if she would decipher what lay beneath her daughter-in-law's innocent exterior. Mel hoped Dancer didn't always feel this constrained among her people, that in time they might build some trust.

Within an hour, the Dawnfield and Chamberlight armies were moving out, headed south. They left hills and meadows trampled in their wake, and Muller's forces escorted their unwelcome visitors around settled areas. They crossed Harsdown with the two largest military forces in the settled lands, a sea of men and horses that stretched as far as Mel could see.

In the evening, Mel's father separated a contingent of his most trusted officers from the main body of his forces. He sent them west—with Mel and Dancer. They left the sea of warriors and rode for the Dawnfield orchards.

Mel brooded. She abhorred being sent home while so many others went to risk their lives—including her husband.

16
The Citadel Within

Chime was waiting on the veranda in back of the farm-house, dressed in a tunic and trousers, green silk with shimmering gold layers. Jason Windcrier stood with her, dusty and tousled. He had ridden ahead to warn the household that Mel and Dancer were coming. Brant Firestoke was at Chime's side, tall and imposing in gray, with his silver hair swept back from his forehead.

Dancer and Mel rode with their guards around the house to the stables. Grooms ran out to meet them. Chime came down from the porch with her tunic fluttering in the breeze, flanked by Jason and Brant. Her face was drawn but she walked with poise despite her obvious fatigue.

Mel dismounted from Smoke and let a stable girl take the reins. A sandy-haired youth offered his hand to Dancer and she accepted his help with a regal nod. When she was safely on the ground, she turned to face Chime. Her gaze had the same shuttered quality Mel had seen so many times in Cobalt. At first, Mel had thought it meant Cobalt felt no emotions. She had soon come to realize he was guarding them because he was afraid of being hurt. So, too, would Dancer guard herself as she met the woman who had taken her title as the queen of Harsdown.

Seeing her mother, Mel felt as if she were coming out of a thunderstorm that had drenched her in darkness. She wanted to run and hug Chime, but she held back in front of Dancer, she wasn't sure why. Perhaps it was the painful reserve Cobalt's family had with one another. But Chime had a familiar gentle expression, the special one for her daughter. Mel could restrain herself no longer. She went into her mother's arms and Chime held her close, her head against Mel's head.

"Welcome home," Chime murmured. "I am so very, very glad to see you."

"Me, too." Her answer was muffled against her mother's hair. Everything was catching up to Mel, the long ride, her months at the Castle of Clouds, a time of wonder and misery, the magic of learning to know Cobalt, her dread of his plans, her pleasure in his touch and the sight of him, and her fear of Stonebreaker. She squeezed her eyes closed and held her mother.

After a few minutes, they drew apart. Self-conscious, Mel turned to Dancer. The queen had stayed back, but she didn't seem offended.

Mel spoke. "May I present my mother, Chime Headwind Dawnfield." To her mother, she said, "Dancer Chamberlight Escar." She deliberately avoided titles. Who would she call queen? No matter what she said, it would offend someone. So she said nothing.

Dancer and Chime nodded to each other, two women of influence, both of them forged by difficult lives, Dancer's heavy with the demands of heredity and pain, and Chime's with her responsibilities as a mage as well as a queen.

"I hope you will dine with us," Chime said.

"I appreciate your hospitality," Dancer said.

So polite. Mel doubted either of them wanted to spend the evening together. What would they talk about? *I wonder when we'll know if they've crushed Shazire.* The armies wouldn't reach the border for many days.

"Would you like to freshen up?" Chime asked. "I've a girl who can help you."

Dancer put her palm against her cheek as if she wasn't certain what to do. It was such a simple thing Chime offered, a chance to recuperate with help from someone—except for Dancer it was a luxury, one deliberately denied, given only when she left her refuge and went to a place she hated, the Diamond Palace.

"I thank you," Dancer said with brittle formality.

Chime lifted her hand in a gesture of invitation, and Dancer joined her as they walked to the house. Jason and the other officers went into the stables to check their horses.

Brant fell into step with Mel, following the two queens. "How are you?"

"One moment I feel like mourning," Mel said. "The next I miss him terribly."

He didn't have to ask who. "Do you grieve for Shazire? Or him?"

A good question. "Both. For Shazire's losses. And for what Cobalt could have been if his life had been less harsh."

"Is he such a monster, then?"

"No. He's not." How to describe him? It would be like trying to explain lightning or thunder. "He could be a great
leader."

Brant studied her face. "And his father?"

Mel thought for a moment. "Varqelle is not the horrendous
man I expected, but neither is he good. He has neither Cobalt's compassion nor his kindness. For all his power, Varqelle
lacks wisdom about people. He considers gentler emotions a
weakness." She struggled to express what she had trouble de-
fining for herself. "Somehow that makes him weaker than
Cobalt, not stronger. He and Stonebreaker criticize Cobalt,
yet Cobalt is more than either of them. I think they know,
even if they don't understand. Varqelle admires Cobalt and
Stonebreaker fears him."

"It is not Cobalt who will rule in Shazire and Blueshire if
his army conquers them."

If. If Cobalt didn't die in the process. Mel shuddered. "Do
you think my father will break the treaty to defend Shazire and
Blueshire?"

"I have no doubt he has asked himself that question every
hour since he made his decision." He continued without
hesitation. "He will keep his word. He has always done what
he believed right and stood by his decisions."

"He never had to make one this terrible."

"No," Brant said softly. "He never did."

Mel sighed, saddened by everything. "You remind me of
Matthew."

"Who is that?"

"A good friend." He was her only one at the castle, though
at least the staff no longer seemed to resent her.

Brant inclined his head. "I am honored."

She slanted him a look. "He's in charge of the stables."

He didn't even blink at the comparison. "From what I saw of your horse, it is well cared for."

"Yes. It is." Brant was so very different from Cobalt's family. She couldn't imagine Stonebreaker or Varqelle accepting such a comparison. "I wish we could stay here."

He watched Dancer and Chime ahead of them. "You may end up living in Shazire."

It was a sobering thought. Mel had no idea how this would end. Dancer and Cobalt had survived and remained free after Varqelle failed to conquer Aronsdale, but only because they no longer lived in Harsdown. Otherwise, Jarid would probably have sent them into exile. If Cobalt lost this campaign against Shazire, Mel doubted that Prince Zerod, the emir of that country, would let him live. Cobalt had sent her and Dancer here to ensure that if he failed, his wife and mother would be safe, not only from Zerod, but from Stonebreaker, as well.

Mel would have rather risked her life in the upcoming war than have come here to safety. If she could no longer act as a mage, she could do little to help the army. But she couldn't bear to stay here while Cobalt courted death.

They took supper together, Mel and Chime, Dancer, Brant, Jason, and the other five officers from the honor guard. Dancer said little and avoided looking at Chime.

When Brant and the officers became involved in a discussion of vintage wines Muller imported from Taka Mal, Mel's interest wandered. She picked up the bronzewood ring that had held the cloth she used to clean her hands. It glistened in the candlelight. The wood seemed to glow with rosy light. In fact, it *was* glowing—

With a start, Mel dropped the ring. It clinked on the table and the glow faded.

"Mel," her mother admonished.

She glanced up. Only Chime had noticed; everyone else was talking or paying attention to their food. Mel's pulse raced. *A spell!* It was a small one, yes, but real. She hadn't lost all her abilities. Elation surged within her, followed by an absurd urge to cry.

Mel wasn't embarrassed that her mother had seen her fumble the spell. She wanted to jump up and yell. Barring that, she beamed at Chime, evoking a perplexed look from her mother. Mel said nothing. If she explained about the injury, Chime would want to know how it happened. The answer would reveal to Dancer that Mel had warned Harsdown about the invasion. If she didn't answer, it might look odd. She could tell her mother later—though it might be a long time before she had the chance.

After dinner, they relaxed around the table and drank wine mulled with spices and apples. Brant spoke to Dancer. "Do you have any hobbies, Your Majesty?"

Mel approved of the title he used. Technically, Dancer was a Highness, as a Chamberlight princess. Given the circumstances, though, Mel was glad he had chosen to forget she was no longer a queen.

Dancer seemed bewildered. "Hobbies?"

"I play chess," Brant said.

"I know the game."

"Perhaps we might try a game later," he offered.

Dancer regarded him warily. "Perhaps."

Chime smiled. "I enjoy working in the orchards, when I have a chance."

"We have men who tend the crops," Dancer said. It could

have sounded like a slight, as if she looked down on Chime for doing such work, but Dancer spoke with no disdain. She seemed more baffled than anything else.

"Her Majesty is an expert in the history of the Misted Cliffs," Mel said.

"History?" Chime's interest perked up. "I've always enjoyed the subject. A lot is there to be learned."

For the first time since they had arrived, Dancer smiled. "It intrigues me how much our lives have changed over the centuries. The past was a simpler time." She sounded wistful. "Or perhaps it only seems that way now, when our lives have too many complications to bear."

A silence fell around the table. Mel didn't think Dancer realized what she had said. With her life, the former queen had no reason to think people might live without complications that seemed unbearable.

Chime spoke gently. "You are welcome to visit our library. Our scrolls and books are at your disposal."

"Thank you." Dancer had a strange expression, as if she expected that any moment someone would yank the rug out from under her chair.

Later that night, after everyone had retired, Mel walked down the hallway carrying a candle. Its mellow light reflected off the sunbask walls, but the house was otherwise dark, the lamps on its walls doused. She carried her basket over one arm with Fog sleeping inside.

"You're getting heavy," she murmured. "Not such a baby anymore." She hoped Fog would sleep well for the next few hours. If she left him outside her mother's door and the kitten woke up alone, he would be frightened inside his basket. Mel had decided to slip it inside her mother's room and crack open the lid. That way, Fog could climb out, but he wouldn't end up wandering and lost in a house he probably didn't remember. Knowing Fog, he would jump on the bed and sleep under the covers next to Chime.

Mel had come to a decision as soon as she had realized her magecraft was returning. No matter how much anyone else might disagree with her—especially her husband or father—she couldn't shirk the responsibilities conferred by her power.

Up ahead, the door of the library opened. Dancer stepped into the hallway, holding open the door with her back, a lamp in one hand and her attention absorbed by a gilt-edged book in her other hand. She looked vulnerable with her velvet robe over a pale nightdress and her unbound hair hanging down to her waist. Startled, Mel stopped. At that instant, the queen glanced up and froze, as if she expected attack.

"My greetings of the evening," Mel said. She could make out the title of the book, a historical treatise on agriculture.

Dancer hesitated. "I hope I didn't disturb you."

"Not at all."

The queen nodded stiffly. "Well. Good evening."

Mel returned the nod, feeling self-conscious. "Did you enjoy the library?"

"Very much. It is a splendid collection." Although impeccably courteous, her tone had a finality that left little doubt she had no wish to converse. She walked past Mel, in the direction of her room. "Good night."

"Good night." Mel watched Dancer, helpless to do anything, though she didn't know *what* she thought she needed to do.

The queen paused and turned back. "Thank you."

Mel wasn't certain why Dancer was thanking her. Whatever the reason, she was glad her mother-in-law's attitude had softened. "You are welcome."

Dancer inclined her head. Then she continued on her way.

When she turned the corner, Mel resumed her errand. She felt somehow lighter, as if sunlight had slanted through a window, though it was night.

A half-moon lit the yard behind the house. Mel lifted a wood panel at the back of the stable, taking care to make as little noise as possible. When the wood creaked, the crickets went silent. She hadn't even noticed them until they stopped their racket. That was why the Castle of Clouds had seemed unnaturally silent; it had few of the night sounds she knew from these fertile valleys. No crickets.

After a moment, they started up again, like a host of miniature saws cutting wood in the night. Mel ducked into the stable. She padded across a dirt floor strewn with fragrant straw, and the smell of hay tickled her nose. A horse snorted in one of the stalls.

In her youth, Mel had worked in these stables. Her mother had decreed she wouldn't grow up "spoiled." Prior to her betrothal to Muller, Chime had lived as a commoner. Mages had always been rare, and a royal heir in Aronsdale was expected to marry the most powerful female mage who would accept his suit, which meant Dawnfield men often wed the daughters of farmers, merchants, or shopkeepers. Some said it was the reason their line remained so robust. Mel didn't see why that mattered, but she knew enough about livestock to realize inbreeding could have a harmful effect on offspring.

In any case, Chime had worked on her family's farm in her youth and she was determined her daughter would do the same. So Mel had mucked out stalls and fertilized crops along with all the stable boys and stable girls. Now others were tasked with those onerous chores, but Mel had never lost her love of the horses.

She went to Smoke's stall and leaned across the open half-door. He pushed his nose against her hand, searching for the apple she often brought him. She offered him a succulent fruit she had taken from the kitchen. While Smoke crunched it, she rested her hand on a carved ball that decorated the half-door.

Blue light glowed around the ball.

Saints! Mel moved her hand and the light faded. Elated, she grasped the ball again and focused, using extra care. Blue light flickered. Had she wanted to make a brief spell, she could have managed. Tears welled in her eyes. "Well, Smoke. That is my second spell tonight. It seems I am still a mage after all."

He nuzzled her hand, searching for sweets, unconcerned about the momentous event. Mel laughed and scratched his neck. "Sorry. No more."

It didn't take long to prepare him for their ride. The supplies she had hidden earlier this evening were in the back of the stable where she had left them. She changed into the armor she had taken from the storeroom and strapped on her sword belt. The familiar weight of the blade reassured her. When she fastened the travel bags across Smoke's flanks, he stepped with restless energy. Like her, he wanted to be off and moving.

The front doors of the stable creaked more loudly than her private entrance. Mel held her breath as she walked Smoke into the yard. No calls came from the house, and no lights glowed on. Even the reading lamp in Dancer's bedroom was dark. Mel knew by heart the schedule for the sentries who protected the house; she had only a few moments before they would come by here. She mounted and guided Smoke past the house in a wide circle to minimize the chance of waking anyone. When she reached the orchards, she urged him down a row of trees, slow enough for safety but fast enough to get them away as quickly as possible.

She couldn't stay here, coddled and safe. She had no wish to fight Shazire, and she couldn't stop Cobalt, but if she could use her mage powers to ease the ruin brought on by battle, she was honor-bound to try.

As soon as she and Smoke reached the dirt road, Mel gave the horse his head and he broke into a gallop. She finally began to breathe more naturally. He was a good horse, fast and strong. Mel would be long gone by the time her mother found her letter in the morning.

Cobalt paced the ridge above the fields where his men had camped for the night. Neither he nor Muller Dawnfield wanted his forces below those of the other army, so they both ended up camping on separate regions of the grassy plains. This was rich land, so different from the rocky cliffs of his home. He felt saturated. It was like eating too much sweet food; it seemed a good thing, but afterward you felt queasy. Too much, and your body became sluggish and heavy. A part of him wanted to return home, and the other wanted to gorge on this lush countryside.

The sky had just barely begun to lighten, and dawn was more than an hour off. A few fires burned as cooks prepared the morning meal. Fragrant traces of smoke drifted around him, a richer smell than produced by the hard woods of his home.

Cobalt climbed to the top of the ridge and looked back across the hills they had crossed yesterday. He had thought eleven thousand people would strip the land bare, but the scattered woods were still standing. A creek meandered at the foot of the ridge, its path muddied and shifted. In the predawn light, he could see little of the damage done by the army, just the natural beauty of the land. No one stirred in the hills, though yesterday they had swarmed with people, horses, livestock, and carts.

Almost no one. A rider was crossing a distant bluff. Cobalt squinted. His vision wasn't usually bad enough to make his spectacles necessary, but this early-morning light bothered him. He took his glasses from a pouch inside his shirt and put them on. The rider resolved into a man in armor, which meant he could be from either the Dawnfield or Chamberlight forces. The fellow had probably traveled a good distance, since the armies had passed no settlements in this region. Given the time, well before sunrise, he must have left at a very early hour, indeed.

By the time the rider reached the base of the ridge, Cobalt had deduced that he came from Muller's army. His helmet resembled the head of a bobcat found only in these southern hills. Cobalt's men had the Chamberlight sphere emblazoned on their breastplates, whereas this man had a blank one fashioned from leather. The Chamberlight men used more metal in their armor, which offered better protection but less agility. This fellow's chain mail also had a less solid look. Nor was he large. He was probably a fast fighter without much strength.

Cobalt was standing under an outcropping that jutted up from the ridge. It was a deliberate choice; in the open, he would be silhouetted against the paling sky, giving away his position. The rider climbed the ridge more to the east, where a mounted sentry from the Chamberlight army intercepted him. Cobalt watched as the riders conferred. Then they headed over the ridge and down the other side. He expected them to veer eastward, toward the Dawnfield army, but instead they went through the Chamberlight camp. In fact, they were headed toward his own tent. Puzzled, Cobalt jogged down the ridge.

The sentry and the Dawnfield man arrived at Cobalt's tent first. Cobalt slowed to a walk, watching them. The two riders dismounted, and the sentry spoke with Matthew, whom Cobalt had left on guard. The Dawnfield man waited back a few paces. His chin showed under the bottom of his helmet, well formed but too delicate for a grown man. He was a boy. Probably he had wanted to join Muller's army and they had turned him away because of his youth. Although Cobalt approved of determination, he didn't see why the sentry had brought the boy here. A few of Muller's men had deserted their army and asked to join Varqelle's forces; they had served him eighteen years ago, and they returned now to swear their loyalty. Although it was a smaller number than his father had hoped for, it had gratified Varqelle. They were older men, however. This boy probably hadn't been alive during the last war. Cobalt frowned. He had doubts about a soldier who changed sides so easily.

"I will inform you when he returns," Matthew was saying in his deepest voice.

Cobalt smiled. Matthew had often used that voice during Cobalt's youth, when the young prince had misbehaved. It could rumble with just as much authority as the highest general in the land.

The sentry seemed unduly agitated. "It wouldn't be wise to wait, sir."

"You have no choice," Matthew said.

Cobalt walked up to them. "What is the problem?"

They all turned with a start. The sentry took a step backward as he saluted, his hand snapping to his shoulder in the Chamberlight tradition. "Sir!" He was staring at Cobalt oddly.

Cobalt suddenly realized he was wearing his spectacles. Embarrassed, he took them off and put them in his pocket. "You have a message for me?"

The sentry indicated the boy. "You've a visitor." He swallowed and took another step back.

Cobalt wondered at the sentry's behavior. He knew he unsettled people, but this seemed extreme. The fellow had never acted with such trepidation before. Cobalt frowned at the Dawnfield youth. "Remove your helmet. Let me get a look at you."

The boy inclined his head in an oddly regal gesture. He pulled off his helmet—and masses of gold hair spilled free.

Bloody hell. Cobalt swore in several languages. Decked out in armor and mail, his wife regarded him with an unwavering gaze, her chin lifted. Then she gave him that devastating and deceptively angelic smile of hers.

"Good morning," she said.

Cobalt glowered at her. "Not anymore." He jerked his hand toward his tent. "In there."

Mel nodded to the sentry who had escorted her. "Thank you, sir." She walked forward and gave Matthew a courteous nod. "It is good to see you." Then she entered the tent. Cobalt didn't miss that she neglected to nod to him. Well, hell. How was he supposed to greet her? Now he had to worry about sending her home, and saints knew, he dreaded that conversation.

He yanked aside the flap and stalked inside. Mel was standing across the tent by the brazier holding her helmet under her arm. Her hair tumbled about her body in golden waves, and the hilt of her sword glinted in the ruddy light. Her House took its name from ancient tales of a warrior goddess who came down from the stars in the dawn sky. Right now,

Mel could have been an incarnation of that goddess. She took his breath away. She would also drive him to drink. He had no idea how to deal with this wife of his, who carried the blood of warrior queens in her veins.

"You must return to your mother," he stated.

"I must stay here," Mel answered calmly.

Cobalt crossed his arms. "I do not see your mother riding with your father's army."

She scowled at him. "That is because someone has to rule Harsdown while my father makes sure your marauders do not pillage our lands."

"We do not maraud," he growled.

Mel walked over to him. Her head came up to his chest and she was probably less than half his weight. She was also thoroughly intimidating.

"I will not leave," she said.

"Why not?" Cobalt lowered his arms. "You wish to fight Shazire?"

"Saints, no. I wish I could stop you. But I cannot." She turned her palm up as if showing him what she had to offer. "As a mage, I am sworn to do no harm. If you must do this, I must do what I can to ease the harm."

"You would fight against me?"

"You are my husband. I would not go against you." In a low voice, she added, "Though I feel I am betraying my own people because of it."

"I would not have you betray anyone," Cobalt said. "The solution is for you to go home."

"I cannot."

"You are one person," Cobalt said, bewildered. "What could you possibly do?"

"I am a mage. I can help an army." She spoke as if she were

forcing out the words. "I also know Shazire. My parents felt I should learn about the neighbors of the country I will rule. Shazire has little chance against this mammoth army you bring against them. Nor do they have strong allies. Aronsdale is probably the only country they could have relied on for help, and we are bound by our treaty with you to withhold such support."

The tendons in Cobalt's neck tightened. "Are you saying you will use your mage abilities to help them defeat us?"

"No." She made no effort to hide her regret. "I could never achieve such a miracle. You have three times the men, resources, and armaments they can bring to muster. I cannot change that with a few spells. But I know the House of Zerod. They have great pride. They will never surrender. Even now, they will be scrambling to prepare, sending envoys to other countries asking for help, even to the borderlands to hire mercenaries. But it will be too little too late."

The clicks, buzzes, rustles, and hums of the night receded until Cobalt heard only Mel. "Then what are you suggesting?"

She spoke quietly. "I can help you win your campaign with as little loss of life and destruction as possible."

Cobalt was certain he had heard wrong. "You will help me conquer Shazire?" With her at his side, he truly would be invincible.

Her voice turned cold. "I have no wish to help you conquer anyone." She laid her hand on the hilt of her sword and the ball at its tip glowed blue. "I have come to minimize the harm."

Cobalt was beginning to see. "You can heal, yes? You will help my physicians."

"That is part of it. I can also bolster confidence and health among your men. My mood spells can gauge the morale of armies you fight, even their plans if I can get close enough to them. I can save lives when men fall." She was clenching her the hilt of her sword. "I will help you win your campaign as fast and as cleanly as possible, my husband, because it is the only way I can see—the only realistic way—to minimize the harm you will do."

It was what he had wanted, to have her support, but it sobered him that it came because she saw him as a destroyer and was desperate to help those she expected him to hurt.

"Mel, listen." He drew her to sit with him on his pallet. She remained cross-legged, stiff and distant though they were only handspans apart. He had tried to make her see before, but he found it hard to speak so much. He would try again, and yet again, until she would know his visions as he knew them.

"I have no wish to harm," he said. "I too hope for as few deaths as possible. Shazire is a beautiful country and I would keep it that way. But it is *our* country. The House of Escar will rule. Someday we will take Jazid and Taka Mal. When I am king of the Misted Cliffs, it will unite the Escar Empire. Then you will inherit the Jaguar Throne. Mel! It could be the greatest empire ever known among these settled lands, one that will endure for ages." He took her hands. "This is my dream. I would bring our peoples together."

"It is a powerful dream. But is it real?" She tensed her fingers around his. "You conquer. How does that make you different from a tyrant?"

"I am no tyrant."

"Why not?"

"A tyrant oppresses. Destroys. Kills."

"You will kill and destroy to defeat Shazire."

Why could she not see? "People die in battle."

"How is it not oppressing people when you force them to

deny their leaders and accept you?" she demanded. "How is it not destructive to trample their lands, to kill their sons and fathers and brothers, all so you can take the throne?"

"Jazid and Taka Mal did exactly that when they tore apart the Misted Cliffs." He flexed his fingers, easing her viselike grip. "I do not claim it will be easy or gentle. That does not mean it isn't a vision worth the price of its realization."

"It is a brutal price." She opened his hands and showed him his palms. "Soon you will cover these in blood. Will you do the same to anyone who defies you? Where is the line between an 'acceptable' price and tyranny?" In a quieter voice, she said, "And if you succeed? Where does that leave Aronsdale? Surrounded on every side by your empire."

He hesitated. "I might hope, through you and our child, that someday Aronsdale would join us. Perhaps the tie could be strengthened through a marriage."

"I don't think that could ever happen."

Cobalt didn't know how to make her see. In the light from the brazier, her face had a gilded quality, as if she had stepped out of a legend like an antique goddess. He wanted to lay an empire at her feet, but she wouldn't accept it. He put his arm around her waist and drew her against his body, his legs on either side of her.

"Mel—"

"No!" She set her palms against his chest. "You cannot seduce me into this."

"Be my empress."

"Why would I wish this?"

It seemed obvious to him. He was offering her immense power. He wanted to give her so much and she didn't want it. What did a husband give his wife, then? He had little to offer, but this was something he could do and do well. So he tried again. "If you fear for the future, then sit at my side and do what you think is right for the peoples of the lands that become ours."

"Cobalt…"

He waited, but she said no more. At least she wasn't refusing. "You say that a lot. Just my name. It sounds very fine, but I think when you say it, you have other purposes in mind than to enchant me with the sound." He trailed his fingers across her mouth. "Do you truly think I am evil?"

Her lips parted. "No."

Ah, saints. What could he do when her mouth invited him that way? He bent his head and kissed her, making her lips part even more for his tongue. At first she stiffened, and he thought she would shove him away. She kept her hands up, exerting pressure to hold him at bay, but she kissed him back with a hunger that fed his own.

"Mel." He reached for the fastenings of her armor.

She pushed back from him. "Stop it."

"Why?"

"You seduce me."

"Good."

"It is not good."

"I am your husband."

"Cobalt."

Exasperated, he said, "There it is, my name again."

She hesitated. "You asked if I thought you were evil."

"You have already changed your mind?"

"Listen," she said. "You simmer like a fire. Soon you will flare like a blaze."

"Why does this upset you?"

"What will history remember you for?" She splayed her fingers on his rough shirt. "You have so much goodness within you. But the capacity for evil is there, too. You live on the edge between your own darkness and light. What will drive you across these lands? Will you become a tyrant?"

Cobalt knew he had problems with his rage. "Anger alone does not make a tyrant."

"What if a person angers you? A village? A country? What will you do when there is no one to stop you?" She shook her head. "You say a price must be paid to achieve your visions. Who decides what price? When does it stop?"

He couldn't fight her with words. But this differed from his verbal battles with his grandfather. He needed to answer Mel fairly, and that made it much harder.

"If ever I go too far," he said, "pull me back."

She paled. "You have no idea the task you put to me."

"I can think of no one better for it."

"Do not ask me to be the conscience of a conqueror."

"I cannot stop being what I am, Mel. If you would call me a conqueror, then so be it." He lowered her onto the pallet and lay next to her, half at her side and half on top of her body, propped up on one elbow so he could look at her. "Be my wife. My adviser. My queen. The mother of my heir."

"Stop." She set her palm against his cheek. "When you do this, when you touch me, I can't think straight."

Cobalt caught her hands and brought them down to the pallet, one on either side of her head. He pinned her there. "I do not wish to think right now."

"I will not do this with you. Not now." But her voice had that husky quality it took on when they lay together.

He kissed her forehead, nose, lips. "Your body and your voice say otherwise."

"It does not matter."

He might take over the world, but it seemed he could not conquer his wife. "Do you truly see such evil in me?"

"No!" Her eyes were doing what he dreaded, filling with tears. "I see the man who can best the most accomplished swordsman among his men one moment and hold a purring kitten the next. I've seen your kindness to your mother, your men, your staff. I've known the Cobalt who can be gentle to a scared bride one day and bring alive her passion the next. I've seen the way your face lights up when you laugh, those rare, rare times you laugh." A tear leaked out of the corner of her eye and ran down her temple. "I've seen the good in you."

He had no name for the sensations welling within him. He released one of her hands and touched her tear. "Why do you cry?"

"Because I cannot leave you."

His heart felt strange. Breakable. "Why?"

"I can't—"

His voice caught. "Why, Mel?"

A tear escaped her other eye. "Because I am falling in love with you."

The armor around his heart cracked then, and she stormed the citadel he had built to protect his emotions.

"Do not cry," he whispered.

"Cobalt—"

He put his finger over her lips. "If I could live ten centuries, still my life would be meaningless without what you have just said."

"I don't want you to live ten centuries." Her voice caught. "Just one lifetime. With me. Without all this conquest and ambition."

"I cannot be other than what I am." He kissed her, more

softly now. "I do not know if I am capable of loving a woman. But when I am with you——" He wrestled with the words. "I know I am the most powerful man alive, that I could live forever, that I would make the stars fall to the ground at your feet. And I know that if I ever lose you, I will die a thousand times over."

She touched his lips. "I cannot leave you."

"And this makes you weep?"

"Ah, Cobalt." She pulled her other hand out of his grip and put her arms around him. "Just love me."

He touched her sword and smiled. "You are armed, my lady. I fear I take my life into my hands."

She laughed then, and her blue eyes filled with tears.

In the hour of dawn, he made love to his wife. He died in the circle of her embrace and came alive again, and his life would never be the same, for he had let this woman topple his defenses and in doing so he had given her the power to hurt him. Why that terrible deed created such joy within him, he would never understand.

17
Blueshire

On the thirty-second day of their march, in early spring, the two armies reached the southern border of Harsdown, which it shared with the tiny country of Blueshire. The Dawnfield army stopped, massed on the border, while the Chamberlight forces crossed into Blueshire. Mel sat with her father high on a ridge and watched the elite of the Chamberlight cavalry riding below. Muller was holding the reins in a grip tight enough that his horse picked up his tension and stepped agitatedly beneath him.

"I wish you would reconsider," Muller said, again.

"Would you?" Mel asked. "In my place?"

He let out a tired breath. "No. I wouldn't."

"Will you stay here?" Mel asked. The border between Blueshire and Harsdown wasn't a long one, extending only along the southeastern edge of Harsdown. Shazire curved around Blueshire and bordered the southwestern edge of Harsdown.

Muller answered grimly. "As long as your husband's army is marching, we will stay here to protect Harsdown." He watched her as if his heart were breaking. "Be careful, Mel. Come back to your mother and me. Live to make us grandparents."

Her smile trembled. "Even if the father of my child is conqueror of the world?"

"Even so." His voice caught. "Be well, Daughter."

"And you." She wanted to hug him, but she felt constrained with all the warriors riding by them. Although none looked up at the ridge, they all knew she was here with the king of Harsdown, the man who had taken Varqelle's throne.

Blueshire was so small, the Chamberlight army could have crossed it in one or two days. It took only two hours to reach Oldcastle, the city that served as the seat of the government. While the Chamberlight forces spread out in the hills surrounding Oldcastle, Varqelle entered the town with two hundred cavalry, including Mel and Cobalt. People watched from houses and shop windows, but whenever Mel looked up at them, they pulled their shutters closed against her gaze. No one ventured into the streets.

The Blueshire army waited in the town square—all fifty of them, twenty men on horses and thirty on foot. Baker Lightstone, their king, sat astride a white horse at the head of his tiny cavalry. He was more of a mayor than a king, but he had the royal title and a lineage that went back two centuries. Blueshire had also been part of the Misted Cliffs and had broken off into a separate country at the same time as Shazire. Lightstone was an elderly man, neither tall nor husky, and Mel knew he walked with a limp because one of his legs was slightly shorter than the other. She had always liked him. He and his daughter were chess experts, and his wife played the harp beautifully. Mel had spent enjoyable evenings at his country estate. She hated coming here this way, with an occupying force.

Lightstone waited with his wife on her gray mare to his right and his daughter on her chestnut to his left. Varqelle walked his dark stallion up to the Blueshire king, flanked by Cobalt and Colonel Tumbler. The rest of the Chamberlight column filed around the plaza and encircled the Blueshire army. Mel stayed with the cavalry, but close enough that she could hear Varqelle.

"You are Baker Lightstone of Blueshire?" Varqelle asked.

Lightstone lifted his chin. "I am."

Varqelle spoke without fanfare. "Your House no longer holds sway here."

Lightstone answered tightly. "You come for Chamberlight?"

A muscle twitched in Varqelle's cheek. Mel doubted he appreciated that his victories would be possible only because the man who had kept him from his family for so long now gave him an army. In the end, it didn't matter. Varqelle would take the throne here. She doubted he had much interest in Blueshire; it just happened to be a splinter on the way to Shazire.

"I come as the House of Escar," Varqelle said.

Lightstone glanced around the plaza at the two hundred men who had confined his "army." Then he looked out at the hills that rose beyond Oldcastle and the mass of humanity that blanketed them, six thousand strong.

Lightstone's shoulders slumped. He turned to Varqelle. "Will you accept our surrender?"

Relief poured over Mel. If Lightstone had chosen to fight

the invasion, it would have been a slaughter. But he was a man of proud heritage. Had it been only his life in question, she had no doubt he would have defied Varqelle no matter how futile the attempt. But his fifty men were loyal and would follow whatever decision he made. It didn't surprise her that he chose the one most likely to preserve their lives.

Varqelle said, "I accept your surrender."

Cobalt walked with his father through the dusk. The lurid sunset had faded into a crimson line on the horizon. Tents and fires dotted the hills outside of Oldcastle, but an open strip of land here offered a buffer zone between the city and the army.

"I left a company of our men to guard Oldcastle," Cobalt said. "Plus the fifty men in the Blueshire military."

Varqelle frowned at him. "You left the opposing army in charge of their own city? Whatever for?"

His father's challenge was oddly refreshing. Stonebreaker would have made an oblique insult to Cobalt's intelligence, then gone behind his back and undermined his authority with the men until they doubted his decision. Varqelle did none of that; he just came out with his objections and expected Cobalt to support his decisions or change them. He did it constantly, until all the talking made Cobalt's head hurt, but dealing with him was easy after Stonebreaker. Varqelle listened when he spoke and actually made effort seem worthwhile.

"The Blueshire soldiers aren't going to fight us," Cobalt said. "They swore allegiance to you today. They aren't really an army, anyway; they're more of a police force. The people here trust them. We are more likely to hold Blueshire if we don't trample their people the way we are trampling their hills."

Varqelle snorted. "We would hold Blueshire with our thumbs tied behind our backs."

"Well, yes. But this way, its people will resent us less." Cobalt cocked his head. "I found out a lot, talking to the soldiers. Many families here have histories from when Blueshire was part of the Misted Cliffs. Although the people like being independent, they also seem to miss the security and affluence they had when they were part of such a powerful country."

"You worry too much about how they feel." Varqelle waved his hand toward the outskirts of the city. "Why do you need so many soldiers to guard this little town?"

Cobalt indicated the Chamberlight warriors encamped all across the hills. "The guards will keep the rest of our warriors from getting out of hand."

Varqelle lifted his finger in front of Cobalt as if he were teaching a schoolboy. "Our men need a release and the town has good taverns. Women, too."

"All the more reason to make sure our forces behave."

"I fail to see why."

Cobalt scowled at him. "Because we are civilized people. Not a horde of plundering barbarians."

"Tomorrow we march on Shazire. The men will have little chance to release all this pent-up energy before then."

"What pent-up energy? They have been marching for twenty days. They need sleep."

Varqelle crossed his arms. "And I suppose you would have me let King Lightstone and his family go into exile?"

"Yes."

"Cobalt, you sorely bedevil me."

"Why?" Cobalt knew, but he intended to stick with his recommendation anyway.

"You even have to ask?" Varqelle lowered his arms. "Jarid

Dawnfield was a fool to let me live. Mind you, I am glad to be alive and gratified I have such a magnificent son who would free me from that hellhole." He glowered at Cobalt. "Would you have King Lightstone someday go free and come after you?"

Cobalt couldn't help but smile. "With his fifty men?"

"It is not amusing."

"Where would Lightstone get this army to attack me?"

"Jazid. Taka Mal."

"How would that be any different from our situation now?" Their intention to engage Jazid and Taka Mal would be the same regardless of whether Lightstone asked those countries for help.

"It changes their stance from defense to offense."

Cobalt shrugged. "Either way, they have the same armies."

"There is also Aronsdale."

"We have the treaty with them."

Varqelle snorted. "Do not assume they will honor this treaty just because you married one of their women. If the House of Dawnfield joins with Taka Mal and Jazid, we will be hard pressed to overcome them."

"I have studied the history of these lands." It had always fascinated Cobalt. "Jazid and Taka Mal have never allied with Aronsdale. They have trade relations, yes, but they are otherwise cool in their dealings. The cultures are too different. My marriage to Mel will make them even more suspicious of the House of Dawnfield. An alliance is possible, but unlikely. Jazid and Taka Mal have much stronger ties with Shazire, yet our scouts report nothing about their forces moving to defend that country."

"They haven't had time," Varqelle said.

"This is true," Cobalt admitted. Yet Muller Dawnfield had

known, and with time enough to gather both Harsdown and Aronsdale forces. He suspected Mel had had something to do with that, though she would never admit it. He couldn't fault her for defending her family and her country. Although he would never tell his father, it had relieved him to find Harsdown so well defended. Treaty or no, he wasn't naive enough to believe Varqelle would overlook an opportunity to reclaim the Jaguar Throne.

"Jazid won't ignore us," Varqelle said. "Neither will Taka Mal."

"Eventually we will have to deal with them." Cobalt spoke thoughtfully. "How we conduct this campaign matters. It will affect how other countries respond to us. Send Lightstone and his family into exile. Show humane treatment. Not barbarism."

"Perhaps," Varqelle grumbled. "I still don't like it."

They were walking along the edge of camp, near a campfire, and its light delineated the planes of Varqelle's face. For Cobalt, it was like looking into a mirror thirty years down the line. He found it hard to believe his father was sixty-three; Varqelle was as fit as men half his age and had almost no gray in his hair.

"Eighteen years in the Barrens," Cobalt mused. "It is a long time."

Varqelle grimaced. "I don't know which was worse, the imprisonment or the boredom."

"They treated you ill?" It hadn't seemed that way, but Varqelle hadn't talked about it much.

"Not really. I just had nothing to do." Varqelle looked around the camp with the same edgy need to move that Cobalt often saw in Admiral, his horse—and in himself.

"We are much alike," Cobalt said.

Varqelle didn't respond, and Cobalt thought his father must deem him presumptuous for such a comment. Just as Cobalt was about to withdraw the statement, Varqelle said, "Very little in my life has mattered enough to me that I would die for it. Only two things." He gazed at the campfires scattered over the hills like blossoms of flame in the night. "One is the Jaguar Throne."

"It will return to the House of Escar," Cobalt said. "In one generation."

"But not in mine."

Cobalt had no good answer. He could do a great deal for his father, and would gladly, but he couldn't put him on the throne. He had done his best and it felt like a failure. If he couldn't give his father Harsdown, he would bring him an empire.

"What is the second thing?" Cobalt asked.

Varqelle spoke quietly. "My son."

Cobalt felt again that disquieting sensation that had come over him when Mel spoke of love. It was terrifying and magnificent at the same time. "I am honored."

Varqelle stopped and laid his hand on Cobalt's shoulder. "A man, a king, and a father could not ask for a better son."

Cobalt tried to answer, but the words failed him. He tried again and his voice came out low and intense. "I, too, for you."

Varqelle smiled, an unusual expression on his ascetic face. "Well." He lowered his hand. "Now we must see to your having an heir, eh?"

Cobalt thought of Mel and felt warm. "Yes."

As they began walking again, his father spoke musingly. "I would never have imagined my grandchild would be half Dawnfield."

"It is a good line."

Varqelle snorted. "Pretty, anyway."

Cobalt supposed it would be asking too much for his wife and his father to deal well with each other. But he wondered about Dancer. "You and Mother have not done so poorly, living at the keep together."

"By avoiding each other."

"Father—"

"Cobalt, no." Varqelle shook his head. "She robbed me of all those years with you. And for what? Were you better off with her father? I think not."

Cobalt was beginning to accept that he might never learn Dancer's reasons. But he knew his mother. If she said she had acted on his behalf, she believed it. He either had to let go of his anger or turn away from her. He could never repudiate her, nor had he ever doubted she loved him, so he would have to find a way to live with never knowing the rest.

"Wives can be confusing," Cobalt said.

"Yours is rather disobedient," Varqelle said sourly.

Cobalt laughed. "That she is."

"You think it is funny?"

"I think it is maddening."

"You should deal with her more firmly."

Cobalt winced. "I would rather face an oncoming horde from Taka Mal, Jazid, and Shazire combined."

Varqelle waved his hand. "Take a switch to her."

Cobalt's good mood vanished. "No."

"She will get more unruly."

This was an aspect of his father he didn't want to see. "I am no Stonebreaker." He rubbed his knuckles, recalling the bloodstains they left in the towers of his home. "Nor a breaker of women and children."

"I do not countenance brutality." Varqelle shook his head with a firm, unyielding motion. "But Cobalt, you must make your wife behave. Break her as you would an unruly horse."

"I never break a horse." Cobalt thought of Admiral. "Destroy the spirit and you lose what you love."

"Such women are incapable of love." Varqelle's voice hardened. "Judge by their actions, not their false words."

Cobalt wished he could soften his father's view. "Have you no sympathy for Mother?"

"Why would I have sympathy for a woman who hated me from the day we wed?"

"Sometimes a woman needs time."

"An eternity wouldn't have melted her." Varqelle's voice lost some of its edge. "The only woman who ever gave me any warmth was a girl I got from Jazid."

So his father had kept a concubine. It didn't surprise Cobalt. Stonebreaker had several, and Varqelle didn't seem the type of man to spend all those years alone. "Did you bring her to Escar after Mother left?"

"Before. She consoled me for your mother's cold heart."

Cobalt's sympathy vanished. He scowled at his father. "Perhaps your mistress was the reason your wife lacked warmth."

"You want a miracle reunion. It will never happen." Varqelle's answer held no anger, only sadness. "You must stop hoping."

"The three most important people in my life all hate one another. I cannot help but hope it will change."

"Then see to your wife. She is the one you can most affect." Varqelle's eyes glinted. "You spend a great deal of time with her at night. Make it mean something."

"Mean something?" Cobalt asked, perplexed. It meant a great deal, all of it very private.

"No reason exists why punishing her should not give you pleasure."

Cobalt felt as if Varqelle had punched him deep in the stomach. His rage stirred, and it took a great effort not to raise his fist. "I do not wish to have this conversation."

"Ah, Cobalt, I do not mean to offend you." Varqelle paused. "Just think on what I have said. Do not let her pretty words blind you."

Everything Mel did blinded him. She remained in his thoughts always. She terrified him, yet he would do anything, anything at all to hear her tell him that she loved him. Was this weakness? Should he rethink the way he dealt with her? The thought of her coming to harm was unbearable.

"Was there never any love between you and Mother?" he asked.

Regret showed on Varqelle's face. "I'm sorry I cannot give you the answer you want."

Sorry. Just like that, his father said, *I'm sorry.* Never in a millennium would Stonebreaker have apologized for anything.

Varqelle smiled. "It is true, though, that the one time she sought me of her own volition was the night you were conceived."

Cobalt's face flamed. "I don't believe I should hear this."

"Ah, well, perhaps not." Varqelle chuckled. "You were born as you lived, impatient and demanding to conquer the world. You couldn't even wait the full nine months."

"I was born early?" Dancer had never told him.

"About a month."

"Was I sickly?"

"Not at all. You were always big and robust."

"Perhaps Mother mistimed the dates."

"I don't think so. She slipped and fell. That was why she went into labor early. But she and you were both fine."

"Well, I am glad to be born." It was one of the few times in his life when Cobalt genuinely felt he could mean those words.

Varqelle clapped him on the shoulder. "Indeed."

They continued on together, father and son, discussing plans for their future.

King Lightstone and his family left in the early morning. Mel rode out to meet them with a scroll in her hand. Lightstone, his wife, and their daughter, Sky, were mounted and ready to ride, accompanied by an honor guard of twenty Chamberlight and twenty Lightstone men. Varqelle sat on his horse a distance away with a company of his men, observing, and Cobalt was speaking with Lightstone.

Mel rode through the honor guard, aware of everyone watching her. She reined to a stop alongside Sky. The Blueshire princess regarded her with red-rimmed eyes.

"I am sorry," Mel said. She and Sky had known each other all their lives, not well, but with friendship.

Sky indicated Cobalt. "Are you the one who convinced him to let us live?"

Mel told the truth. "It was his decision. But I spoke in support of it."

Sky nodded and they sat awkwardly. There seemed no more to say. Whatever friendship they might once have shared had no place here.

"Be well," Mel finally said.

"I would wish the same for you." Sky glanced at Cobalt, then at Mel. "If such is possible."

Mel had no answer for that. After she and Sky bid each

other an awkward farewell, Mel rode to where Cobalt conferred with Sky's parents. They all fell silent as Mel bowed to King Lightstone. Then Cobalt backed up his horse, giving her privacy with the king and queen.

"Your Majesty." Mel offered him the scroll. "This is a letter on your behalf to my cousin, King Jarid in Aronsdale."

Lightstone accepted the scroll and inclined his head in a formal gesture of thanks. "Perhaps someday we will meet again." His voice cooled. "Though you are no longer Dawnfield."

What could she say? She had married the Escar prince whose army had overrun Blueshire. Nothing would change that.

Cobalt's men would ensure the Blueshire party reached the Harsdown forces at the border. From there, her father would have them escorted to Aronsdale. Mel had no doubt her parents would offer to take them in, but given her marriage to Cobalt, she doubted the Lightstone king would accept.

The queen spoke quietly. "Goodbye, Mel. I hope you fare well."

Mel nodded to her. "You also."

They left then. An hour later, the Chamberlight army was on the move as well, headed for Shazire.

18
Flame Caller

Mel had always thought Shazire beautiful. She had loved to visit as a child. Never in any of her imaginings would she have expected to ride through its lovely countryside as part of an invasion. The army flooded the hills and meadows and churned the wildflowers into pulp. They forded rivers and left behind swamps. Six thousand strong, they marched southward.

Scouts who had ranged ahead of the main force for days came back and reported to Cobalt; the Shazire army was amassing in the Azure Fields north of Alzire, the capital city. Estimates put their numbers at roughly two thousand, with four hundred spearmen from Jazid.

Mel rode with her hexagon guard. They surrounded her but kept enough distance to give her privacy. The Chamberlight cavalry proceeded in columns, and pages led additional mounts. Carts rolled forward, carrying men, women, and supplies. The foot soldiers traveled more slowly but had to rest less often than the horsemen. Several officers from the Castle of Clouds rode past Mel and one raised his hand in greeting. She nodded to them, gratified that their attitude toward her was beginning to thaw.

Toward midday, Colonel Tumbler pulled his horse alongside hers. He bowed and smiled with reserve, his two crooked front teeth giving him a boyish look.

"My greetings," Mel said.

"I wondered if you required anything," he said. "Food or water? You are so stoic, never complaining."

"Thank you." They were practically the first kind words anyone had said to her during this march. Although the people here still didn't speak to her much, she suspected it was more now because she was Cobalt's wife than because of any decree from Stonebreaker. "I appreciate your concern. But I'm fine."

"Let me know if you need anything."

Mel smiled. "I will."

At her smile, Tumbler blushed. He nodded formally, then let his horse fall back into formation, as was appropriate. But he stayed close enough that she could easily call on him if she had any request.

His gesture touched Mel. Nor was his the only one. It was just a nod here, a wave there, but they no longer seemed hostile. It lifted her spirits, which were otherwise dark.

The antiqued sunlight of late afternoon was slanting across the land when Mel saw Cobalt riding back along the lines. He sat tall on Admiral, long-legged and broad-shouldered, his armor glinting. He held his helmet under his arm, and the wind tossed back his hair from his strong-featured face. His aura of power caught Mel and left her breathless. She had no doubt that this man, Cobalt the Dark, the Midnight Prince, would someday be known as Cobalt the Great—if he didn't burn himself out in the flame of his ambition.

He rode over to her. "Did you forget to eat?"

Mel blinked. "No. Why do you ask?"

"Because," he said smugly, "you were looking as if you wanted to devour me."

She glowered at him. "You have an avid imagination."

He grinned and continued to ride at her side, looking around, conducting an informal inspection of his cavalry, at ease on his mount. Men saluted as they passed and Cobalt nodded in acknowledgment.

"Have you had any message from the emir?" Mel asked. She knew it was a futile hope. Prince Zerod, who ruled Shazire, would never surrender, not if he faced an army ten times the size of his own. One of the greatest tensions among the people of Shazire was that they had a culture steeped in the traditions of the Misted Cliffs, but their rulers now came from the eastern lands, Jazid and Taka Mal, creating a clash of cultures that had never sat easily on the populace.

"A letter arrived this morning," Cobalt said.

Her pulse leaped. Was she wrong? Perhaps Zerod would surrender. "What does he say?"

"It was very wordy, formal, and polite," Cobalt said dryly. "Stripped of all that, it said, 'Get the hell out of my country.'"

Ah, well. It had been a foolish hope.

He glanced at her. "You are wearing armor and a sword."

"So are you."

He crossed his arms, his reins tight in one hand. "I would not have you fight tomorrow, when we engage Zerod's army."

Her voice cooled. "I have absolutely no desire to kill people."

"Nor I."

"Don't you?"

"No. Of course not." He unfolded his arms and motioned at the land around them. "I desire this. And more."

She shook her head. "What will you do, Cobalt, when there are no more lands to conquer?"

"I will keep these lands." He indicated his father, who was riding ahead of them. "For him."

Mel knew she could never win where Varqelle was concerned. Cobalt's bond with him was forged in a furnace of shared goals and personality, and annealed by Varqelle's longing for a son and Cobalt's need for a father. Nothing she could say would stop Varqelle from despising her, and if she spoke against him, it would only estrange her from Cobalt.

"Why does your face cloud so?" Cobalt asked.

"I wish your father and I got along better."

"So do I."

"Do you think it will ever change?"

He thought for a while. "I do not think he likes women."

There's an understatement. "He loathes me."

"He believes women should be submissive. Especially pretty ones." His lips quirked upward. "You are never the former and always the latter."

She tilted her head. "You've changed."

"I have?"

"You smile sometimes. And you use full sentences."

He spoke with mock solemnity. "I must be more careful about that."

"Cobalt."

He laughed. "There it is. My name again."

She grunted at him.

"Mel, listen to me."

"Yes?"

His smile faded. "You must promise you will stay away from the fighting tomorrow."

"I do not wish to fight." She had no desire to see battle. But she couldn't give him her word when she didn't know yet what she would be able to do as a mage. She just didn't know.

"You must promise," Cobalt told her.

She said nothing.

"Wake up," Cobalt said.

Mel groaned. "It can't be dawn yet."

"It isn't." He kissed her ear. "You need to dress."

She turned on her back and opened her eyes. He was propped up on his elbow, looking down at her. One of his shirts dangled from his raised hand.

"I do?" she asked, groggy.

"You do." He pulled her up until she was sitting. Then he tugged his shirt over her head and down around her knees. She regarded him with bleary eyes. No light yet showed around the cracks between the entrance flap and the front of the tent.

"It must be almost an hour before dawn," she mumbled.

"I know. I have to go." Cobalt drew her to her feet.

Mel swayed. "Too sleepy."

"Here." He led her over to where they had hammered a post into the ground to hold up his tent. "Sit here."

Mel yawned. "I need one of those metal balls your men use in the catapults."

"The catapults?" He put her back to the pole and pushed her down so she was sitting against it. "Why?"

"Cobalt, what are you doing?" Mel tried to get up.

He hugged her as if he were embracing her, but he was also pulling her arms behind the pole. Before she could react, he had wrapped a rope around her wrists.

"What—stop!" Mel tried to yank her arms free, but he held her pinned in his arms and quickly bound her wrists together.

"No!" Mel struggled against him. "Let me go!"

He did finally let go, though he stayed kneeling in front of her. He spoke firmly. "I would die before I would let you near a battle. You must stay here."

She jerked on the ropes that kept her arms behind her back. "You bastard."

"I assure you my birth was quite legitimate."

Mel swore at him with the choicest words she had picked up from her father's officers during training.

Cobalt winced. "Your language is extraordinary."

"What if Shazire warriors break through here?" she demanded. It was unlikely; they were far from the Azure Fields. But it wasn't impossible. "What then?"

He rose to his feet. "Matthew will be here to see that you are protected and give you meals."

She couldn't believe he was going to leave her half naked and bound to a pole. "You have to untie me."

"No." He picked up his clothes from where he had laid them out the night before. "I do not."

Mel wrestled with her bonds. When she couldn't loosen the ropes, she tried to pull the pole out of the ground. That didn't work, either. While she struggled, Cobalt dressed, donned his armor, strapped on his sword, and picked up his shield and helmet. He lifted the tent flap, and his body made a dark silhouette against a sky just barely lightened by dawn.

"I will see you when I return from the Azure Fields," he said.

Mel turned her head and refused to acknowledge him. It was several moments before she heard him leave. The flap crinkled as it fell back in place.

"Are you all right?" a man asked.

Mel jerked and nearly choked. A man with broad shoulders and long legs stood in the entrance, dark against the paling sky. It wasn't Cobalt—she couldn't defend herself—

"Matthew!" She sagged against the pole. "You scared me."

He came over and crouched next to her. "I am sorry."

"Will you untie me?"

"You know I cannot do that."

She scowled at him. "You are perfectly capable of doing it."

"I won't disobey Prince Cobalt's orders." At least he had the decency to look uncomfortable.

She twisted her hands behind her back, trying to work them free. All she succeeded in doing was scraping her wrists. "I can't believe he did this."

"I've never seen him treat a woman in such a manner," he admitted. "But then, I've never seen him so intense about anyone, either."

"You mean tying them up? You're right. He's intensely crazy."

"He's in love."

"He has a damn fool way of showing it."

"What would you have him do?" Matthew asked. "Let you go into combat?"

"Yes."

"*That* is crazy."

"He goes, and I have to agonize over his safety."

"That is different."

"Like hell it is."

"You know," Matthew said, "you not only fight like a man, you swear like one, too."

"Yes, well, Cobalt doesn't tie his men to poles." She wrenched at her bonds. "He listens too much to his father."

Matthew's voice quieted. "I would take care how you speak to him of his father."

"I know." Mel leaned her head back against the pole. It was too irregular in its cut to provide a good shape for a spell. "I need to calm down."

"This would be good."

She sent him an annoyed look. However, a plan was coming to her. She lifted her head and put on a wistful expression. "I guess I'm afraid."

His gaze softened. "I won't leave your side."

"I wish Fog were here."

"He would be comforting."

"My people have a custom—well, it's rather silly. But it does offer comfort."

He squinted at her. "What custom?"

"When we are afraid, we hold a favorite object and sing."

Matthew blanched. "You want to sing?"

Mel glared at him. "I don't have that bad of a voice." Then she remembered she was being conciliatory. "But I wouldn't sing this early in the morning. It would be calming, though, to have something to hold."

He looked uncertain. "What sort of thing?"

"Have you ever seen Cobalt's billiard balls?"

"Indeed." He smiled dryly. "In his youth, I often had to take them away when his mother wanted him to study."

"I should like one of those to hold."

"We have none here."

"Oh." She let her disappointment show.

"I might find you some seeds."

"They would trickle through my fingers."

He thought for a moment. "The balls for the catapults are the right size."

She gave him her most angelic smile. "Would it be all right if I had one to hold?"

He seemed to melt in front of her. "Aye, I could manage that." He stood up. "It won't take long."

"Thank you," Mel murmured.

After he left, she let her chin sag forward to her chest. She intended to stay awake until he returned. Her head felt so heavy, though. Her eyes closed …

"Princess Melody?" Someone's knees popped. "Wake up."

Mel cracked open her eyes to find Matthew crouched beside her. Princess Melody, indeed. He showed her a metal ball, blue-gray with an iridescent sheen. Then he reached back and slid the ball into her hands. "There you be."

She smiled beatifically. "You are a lovely man."

He blushed. "Are you hungry?"

"Not now. I'd like to sleep some more."

"I'll be right outside, then." He stood up. "Call for me if you need anything."

"I will."

As soon as Matthew left, Mel concentrated on the ball. She didn't try any high-level colors. Her abilities had only begun to heal, and with such a powerful shape, she wasn't certain she could control blue and green spells. So she thought of red. She had too little precision to risk a spell with the ropes; she might hurt her wrists. Instead, she chose a point across the tent. It was still a risk, but if she didn't try, people could die who didn't have to, all because Cobalt had tied her to a pole. She concentrated on the cloth. Focus…

The point glowed red. She built the spell—a spell of heat—

Flames erupted out of the point.

"Matthew!" Mel shouted. "Fire!"

He swept aside the flap and strode into the tent, which was already burning. He knelt behind her, and the ropes snapped as he cut them with his knife. As soon as her arms fell free, he jumped up and hauled her to her feet. An entire side of the tent was in flames.

Matthew pushed her toward the entrance. "Run!"

She grabbed his arm. "Not without you."

"This is Cobalt's tent! I have to—"

"No you don't!" She dragged him forward.

They broke into a run as flames caught the peaked roof. Just as they burst out of the tent into an overcast day, a man heaved a bucket of water on the fire. A line of people was forming, made up of the men and women who tended camp while the soldiers were in combat. It stretched to a creek about a hundred paces away. Mel and Matthew joined them and helped pass buckets up the line. Cobalt's shirt flapped around Mel's knees and she had to roll up the sleeves to her elbows. She moved forward each time the first person in line ran back to the creek with an empty bucket. The people all worked together with a practiced efficiency that told Mel a great deal about how well Cobalt trained his army, not only the warriors, but everyone.

The fire was out in a matter of minutes. Mel stood with Matthew in front of the remains, breathing in gulps, her hair straggling around her and ashes on her arms. The flames had burned one side of the tent and about half the roof. She blanched when she saw the scorched pole where she had been tied. What if Matthew had left his post for some reason? No, she wouldn't dwell on what-ifs. That hadn't happened—and now she was free.

"Saints," Matthew muttered. "That could have been you." He turned to her. "How did it start?"

"It was across from where I was sitting," she said. "It was hard to see." Which was true.

Matthew grimaced. "I think maybe no more poles, eh?"

Mel exhaled with relief. "Yes. No more."

They spent the next hour cleaning up the remains and setting up a new tent. Her belongings were intact, though they smelled of smoke. She pulled leggings and a sturdy tunic on over Cobalt's shirt and put on boots. She fashioned a sling for her metal ball out of a scarf and hung it from her belt. Although she had found her armor and sword where Cobalt had hidden them under a pile of rugs, she ignored them. Matthew was keeping an eye on her. The entire time, she worried about Cobalt. His men would have engaged Zerod's army by now.

When they finished with the tent, Mel went to see Smoke. Matthew followed at a discreet distance, but close enough to stop her if she tried to get on her horse. Smoke didn't need anything; one of the grooms had already seen to his care. But she spent time pampering him. When Smoke was blocking her torso from Matthew's view, she folded her hand around the ball in her sling and gazed over Smoke's back at a distant cart heaped with blankets and folded tents. Then she concentrated. Yellow. Her favorite silk tunic. Her mother's hair. Wild suncups.

Yellow light glowed around the cart.

"What is that?" someone asked.

Mel intensified the light. A new voice called, "Look!"

Matthew glanced at the cart, then frowned and walked toward it. While that occupied his attention, Mel grabbed her saddle from the nearby gear, threw it onto Smoke, cinched it, and scrambled up on the horse. Leaning over his neck, she urged him toward her tent. As soon as they reached it, she jumped off, snapped up the bottom edge—and yanked out the sword she had just happened to leave at the edge of the tent.

"Hey!" Matthew shouted.

Damn. She didn't have time to get her armor. She grabbed her sword belt and swung back on Smoke. Then she took off, one hand gripping the belt. Matthew would follow, but he had to get his horse. Smoke was fast. Very fast. And she was a good rider. Better than good. He wouldn't catch her, nor would anyone he called on for help.

Smoke galloped through the camp, urged on by Mel. Her hair streamed behind her. A cook looked up from his pot, and a blacksmith paused in repairing a sword. A camp follower walked out of an officer's tent and stood watching her. Smoke headed south, his long stride eating up the distance.

They soon left the camp behind.

19

The Azure Fields

Mel heard the battle before she saw it. It came to her first as a distant rumble. She had followed the route taken by the army, through demolished meadows, until she saw a line of low hills. Her sword hung at her side, but she had told Cobalt the truth; she didn't want to use it. Unless they had no choice, mages kept out of sight during battle. Usually one or more polygon formations of warriors protected them, but she had no one at all.

As she galloped onward, hills rose out of the countryside and the rumble swelled until it separated into individual sounds, a cacophony of yells and cries, the twang of arrows, the pounding of hooves, the groan of catapults, the clang of metal on metal, and a hundred other sounds she couldn't identify. It swelled into a roar.

By the time she reached the first line of hills, sweat was dripping down her neck. She kept to the quilt-work of forest that patched the land, though at times she had to ride in the open to reach the next woods. She guided Smoke away from the soldiers who were serving as pickets, the men who kept watch. With such a large area to monitor, they were stationed at wide intervals, under cover, and she managed to avoid them. In the last hills, she rode into a clump of trees. The woods ended at the crest of a ridge where she stopped. A slope rolled down in front of her. She looked out into the plain beyond—

It was bedlam.

Thousands of men surged across the Azure Fields, on foot and on horseback. In some places, scattered soldiers fought, parrying with swords; in others, their numbers were so thick it was hard to make out individuals. It was a collection of battles. One would flare, then die down as men retreated and regrouped. A line of Shazire archers stepped forward and fired a volley of arrows into the advancing Chamberlight troops. Then they stepped back and their cavalry thundered past, cutting and striking Chamberlight foot soldiers from above. To the west, other warriors all fought on foot. A man lost his sword and scrambled out of the fighting; two others fought hand to hand; another swung his blade against the neck of his opponent—

Mel groaned and leaned over Smoke, afraid she would retch. She had never seen a man beheaded before and she prayed she never would again.

It was a while before she could swallow the bile in her throat and heave in a shaky breath. Then she raised her head and searched the fields below, looking for Varqelle. The battle was too large to find one person. She had overheard some of the war councils Cobalt held with his top officers; they considered Varqelle too valuable to risk and wanted him to stay out of the combat. She also knew how much Varqelle loathed the idea. He was a warrior king, not a statesman.

She continued scanning the field—and froze. Cobalt was at the top of a knoll, on foot, surrounded by his men. His sword cut through the air, silver and crimson. And in that moment, she understood without a shred of doubt why he felt driven to keep her as far from combat as possible, for she died a million deaths every moment she saw him with his life in danger.

Mel tried to steel herself. She had to put aside her emotions and do what she had come to do, for as long as she could manage, until someone stopped or killed her. She slid her hand around the ball in the sling that hung from her belt.

Mage power built within her like the embers of a fire stoked into life. Blue sky stretched overhead, and seemed to fill her, luminous and full. Blue light glowed around her body. The battles blurred in her vision, hazed with the radiance. When her head began to throb, she eased her concentration; when the pain receded, she focused again. She didn't force the spell. If she pushed too hard with such powerful colors and shapes, she wasn't certain she would survive.

"Mel?" The voice seemed far away. "What are you doing?"

She slowly turned her head. Matthew was sitting on his horse a short distance away, his body limned in blue light. He held his reins tightly.

"Don't interfere." Her words echoed.

"You are a sorceress." His face had paled. "You started that fire in the tent and made the gold light at camp."

"I am a mage," Mel said. "You knew that."

"I thought it was a glorified title for a woman who healed with herbs."

"I know little about herbs."

"What are you going to do?" Matthew asked.

"Shazire will fall." A shudder went through her. "Will this battle rage for days until all who fight for Zerod are dead? Until the exquisite capital of Alzire is razed to the ground? Until this land and its people are beyond repair?"

"You think you can stop it?"

"No——" Her voice cracked with the pain of knowing how little she could do. "But I can soften it. I will do everything I can to sway Shazire to surrender. I will help Cobalt win with as little bloodshed as possible, strengthen his men in mind and body, in morale and prowess, and I pray, in their capacity for mercy. I will do this, Matthew. Do not try to stop me."

He looked down at the battle. In profile, his features were even stronger, the straight nose, high cheekbones, and firm chin. It was the profile of a king.

"Cobalt tasked me with guarding you." He turned back to her. "I will remain here and do so for as long as you work."

Mel released the breath she had been holding. "Thank you."

"Wait here," he added. "I will return soon."

Mel blinked. She wasn't certain why he was leaving when he had just sworn to stay, but she trusted him. "All right."

After Matthew rode back into the woods, Mel refocused on her spell. Blue light inundated her mind. Although she watched the battle, her concentration turned inward.

A short time later, branches crackled behind her. She looked back to see Matthew riding with two sentries. They stared at Mel. One began to speak, then stopped, his face ashen. The other leaned forward as if he would kick his mount into a gallop. The horse neighed and shook its head. But then the sentry straightened again and drew in an audible breath. Matthew had chosen well; both men stayed.

As the three guards took up formation around her, Mel said, "Can you make a triangle? The shape will strengthen my spells."

They nodded tensely and moved into place, each a vertex of the shape. A triangle was a low-level shape and gave little power, but that also meant she could easily fill it with a spell. A blue spell. Physical strength. She poured it into the three guards. She added green swirling along the diagonals of the triangle. A mood spell. She sent them confidence.

When her triangle spells were complete, Mel returned her focus to the battle. Had the Dawnfield army been below, they would have fought in polygon formations, creating shapes for their mages. If the enemy formed such shapes, it worked against them, for Mel could just as easily pour dismay and weakness into her spells. Such tricks came at a high price, however, for they also affected her; when she gave others strength or confidence, her own increased, and if she demoralized or impaired them, so she also affected herself. It was why mages sought light rather than darkness.

Historically, armies without mages had never fought in polygon formations, especially against a military force backed by the Dawnfields, the only House with good access to mages and the knowledge to train them. To form a polygon on the battlefield was to invite a mage to fill it with a spell. Neither the Chamberlight nor Shazire forces presented Mel with formations she could use. No matter. Every one of Cobalt's men, from the youngest to the most experienced, had one thing in common on the breastplate of his armor.

The Chamberlight sphere.

The Misted Cliffs was the country farthest from Aronsdale. Its people either didn't believe mages existed or else didn't understand how spells worked. When they thought of mages, they associated them with tales of witches and arcane signs rather than geometrical shapes. That was especially true with spheres. The ability to use such a shape, particularly a flawed representation of one, was almost unheard of even in Aronsdale. But Mel was a sphere mage—the child of another sphere mage who could use only flawed shapes.

The design on the breastplates wasn't a circle; the raised curve evoked a shape in three dimensions rather than two. Nor was it a true sphere; it couldn't be on armor. But the intent was obvious. It clearly represented the highest shape.

Mel reached out with her power.

Her spell diffused across the battle with no moorings. She affected no one. She could create it using the catapult ball, but she had no way to direct the spell. Envisioning the breastplates of Chamberlight warriors had no effect. Pain sparked in her temples, and it took a conscious effort to stop herself from pushing too hard.

The spell caught.

It felt like the mental equivalent of silk snagging on a sharp edge. Her spell hooked the breastplate of a warrior, then ripped and began to slip. She strengthened her focus and the spell held. She filled the round depression on the inside of the breastplate with blue power.

Mel reached again, searching—and caught another sphere. Then another. As she poured her power into the Chamberlight spheres, her spell built and spread. The more spheres she filled, the easier it became to find others. She sent Cobalt's men health, confidence, acuity, renewal. She gave them strength and prayed they used it wisely. Subdue without massacring. Shazire couldn't win, but in the fiery rage of battle, it was easy to forget, to destroy. To slaughter.

When Mel could offer succor to a fallen warrior, she gave

it freely for Chamberlight and Shazire alike. She couldn't stop them from dying or mend fatal wounds, she could only speed healing that would happen anyway. She tried to help the dying, and she wept when she failed.

Show mercy.

The day passed, and the combat wore on beneath an overcast sky heavy with dark clouds. Mel either sat on Smoke or stood by the horse, all the time maintaining her spells, green and blue, as she watched the armies fight. She felt it all, the blows, wounds, deaths, and grim emotions. She could hardly see for the light that surrounded her and the tears in her eyes. Her strength drained away until she floated in a sea of exhaustion.

And she watched Cobalt.

Mel had known men feared her husband's prowess as a warrior. She had watched him train at the castle. She had even seen him kill, the night they were attacked in the carriage. But she had never seen him fight, truly fight.

He terrified her.

Cobalt cut a swath through his challengers. No one could stand against that huge sword or a warrior of such uncommon height and strength. Sometime during the day, he regained his mount, not Admiral but a black charger with great speed. The Shazire warriors fought with bravery and would face almost anyone, but Mel saw men run in panic when the Midnight Prince bore down on them.

As the day darkened, a ripple went through her awareness of the battle. She turned her head, her body heavy with the spells that saturated the air. A rider was galloping across the field, his sword high. He looked as if he had been fighting hard and long, his armor dented and his shield cracked. With her awareness so sensitized, she could even tell that the hilt of his sword was fashioned into a true Chamberlight sphere, one of the few on the battlefield. It grabbed her spell like a great claw.

Varqelle.

Do not slaughter. Mel pleaded with her spell, but even with a true sphere enhancing it, she couldn't reach him. His battle fury was too intense. He was Cobalt, but with a cruel edge, one honed first through the loss of his family and then his years of captivity. Of all the officers in the battlefield, only Varqelle and Cobalt had led engagements beyond this one, and only Varqelle had previously led an army to war. His presence rallied the men. He was the king who would make this land his, and he could no more stay out of the battle than could Cobalt.

Mel's power flagged. She had held her spells for too long. Varqelle's charge had started their collapse but her own exhaustion sent them spiraling down. She slumped against Smoke and bent her head. As the blue and green light faded around her, Smoke whinnied and blew out air.

"Mel?" Matthew laid his hand on her arm.

She straightened up and gazed dully at him. No other of Cobalt's men would dare touch her or call her by her first name. Did he even realize he took for granted privileges allowed no one else? Dancer had brought him to the Castle of Clouds thirty-four years ago and he had been a part of her life and Cobalt's since then.

"Are you all right?" he asked.

She answered in a low voice. "Who is your father?"

"What?"

"Your father."

He lowered his hand from her arm. "A blacksmith. Why?"

"At Castle Escar?"

"Yes. I was born there."

"And your mother?"

Puzzlement creased his forehead. "A seamstress."

"For who?" But she already knew.

"Varqelle's father."

"You are sixty-four." Her voice was almost a whisper.

"Mel, what is this about?"

"*You* are the eldest."

"What are you talking about?"

"Don't you see it?"

"See what?"

She pointed to where Varqelle was leading a charge on the Azure Field. The horses built up speed as they approached the enemy line, led by the king. The conqueror. "It should have been you on the throne."

He gripped her arm. "What strange spell do you weave now?"

"It is no spell." She pulled away her arm. "Is your mother still alive? Your father?"

His posture had become rigid. "They both died years ago."

No one remained who could reveal the truth. "The blood is in you, Matthew. You are an Escar." Varqelle's half brother, if she was right, born on the side of the sheets that left him with nothing, even though he was the firstborn son.

Emotions sped across his face: fury, dismay, shock. But not surprise. "You go too far."

Too far? She thought no one had gone far enough for him. "You deserve so much more in life."

"I am happy with my life, Mel."

"I know." Whatever drove Varqelle and Cobalt wasn't in Matthew. She wished it were otherwise for Cobalt, but even having been raised by Matthew rather than by Varqelle, Cobalt reflected his father more.

She could see them in the fields below, Varqelle and Cobalt, together now, on horseback, no longer fighting. The battle had begun to wane. It could have been so much worse; it hadn't spread beyond the Azure Fields, and Mel thought that less than five hundred men had died on either side. From the remnants of her mood spell, she felt Zerod's will fading. If he surrendered now, Cobalt would accept it. And if Cobalt accepted it, so would Varqelle. It would end. Today would see no massacre.

Then catastrophe hit.

20
The Mortal Spell

For Cobalt, it was an apex in his life. He sat on his charger at his father's side, his blood fired, his head high, his body powerful, and he knew they had been destined for this. He had never fought so well as today. His men had isolated the Shazire forces into controllable pockets of resistance. Prince Zerod had to surrender; his army was no longer a coherent force. The Jaguar King would triumph. Even better, they would manage as Mel had asked, with a minimum of bloodshed and death.

The fighting had stopped around the hillock where Cobalt and Varqelle were now. They rode up it together, each looking out for the other while their men stayed on guard below. From this vantage, they could survey the remains of the battles.

A flurry of motion erupted to Cobalt's left. His men were

fighting again—a mammoth of a warrior had engaged them. Tall and immensely broad-shouldered, the man wore Shazire armor and rode a mount as large as Cobalt's horse. He wielded a massive sword. He cut his way through the defenders with ease, and his horse lunged up the hillock. He was the largest man Cobalt had seen this day, possibly the most formidable he had ever faced.

As the Shazire man bore down on him, Cobalt lifted his shield. They were on a slope, a difficult place for the horses, but he was above and the other man below, which could give him an advantage. Then the giant was upon him, and their blades rang together. The man's mouth pulled back in a snarl under his helmet. Cobalt blocked his next thrust, but the blow vibrated along the sword through his arm to his shoulder. Such power!

For the first time, Cobalt faced someone of his own strength. He shouted a war cry as his blade sliced through the air. The other man deflected the blow, and the impact nearly unseated Cobalt. Filled with battle lust, he saw only the giant before him. Their horses slipped as they fought and churned the ground with their hooves as they struggled for purchase.

The Shazire man turned.

For one instant, the man left himself open, his left side only partially covered by his shield. Cobalt went for the vulnerable spot and slashed him across the ribs. It wasn't a fatal wound, but it would slow him. But even as Cobalt struck, the Shazire man was lunging to the right—

At Varqelle.

With sudden, chilling clarity, Cobalt knew his mistake. He had never been the target. This warrior didn't want the general, he wanted the king. By leaving himself open, the man had distracted Cobalt for that one second he needed to go after Varqelle. His and the king's blades clanged as they came together. Caught unaware for that single instant, Varqelle countered a moment too late and didn't recover fast enough to stop the second blow from his attacker.

The Shazire warrior buried his sword in Varqelle's chest.

Everything around Cobalt stopped: the battle, the shouting, the setting sun, all of it. He saw only his father's shocked eyes through his helmet.

An agonized cry tore out of Cobalt's throat. Time snapped back and the Shazire warrior yanked his blade out of Varqelle's chest. Cobalt's vision turned red. His fury exploded as he bore down on the Shazire man, who in attacking Varqelle had left himself open to Cobalt. His had been a suicide lunge, for he must have known even he couldn't take on both Cobalt and Varqelle. The giant tried to counter Cobalt's thrust, but he had no chance. Cobalt drove his blade into the man's torso with so much force, it went through his body and lifted him off his mount. He swung his sword with the Shazire warrior still on it and literally threw the giant. The man fell through the air, ripped and bloodied, and hit the ground hard.

More Chamberlight men were moving in to defend the hillock. Cobalt jumped down from his charger and dropped to his knees near the fallen giant. The man was dead, his body broken. Cobalt scrambled to Varqelle, who lay on his back staring at the darkening sky.

"Don't die." He grabbed his father's hands. "You mustn't die!"

"Cobalt—?" Varqelle's eyes clouded.

"I'm here."

"You must…keep fighting."

Cobalt looked up as men gathered around them. "Get him to the physicians. Now!"

Several men knelt around the king, and another was guiding a cart up to them. Most of the fighting had moved elsewhere or stopped, but it made no difference whether a thousand warriors or only one had attacked the hillock. It had taken only one thrust to topple the king.

Cobalt had seen mortal wounds before—and he recognized his father's. He had no name for the pain within him. Grief, shock, rage: none were enough. He clenched his father's hand as the men lifted him into the cart. "I will avenge you."

Then they took Varqelle away.

Cobalt grabbed the reins of his horse from the man who had caught them. He swung back on the charger and spoke to the cavalry officers around him.

"Kill them." Cobalt ground out the words. "Every last Shazire man on this cursed field." Grimly he added, "And when we're done here, we will burn Alzire to the ground."

"No." Mel cried out as Varqelle fell from his horse.

Cobalt's fury swept through her like fire. She couldn't stop watching, though she wanted to hide her eyes. When he killed the giant who had struck down his father, a brutal echo of the blow vibrated through her fading spell. She groaned and felt as if a part of her had died as well.

It ended in seconds, and Cobalt jumped down from his horse. He knelt by his father, leaning over Varqelle's body.

"He's alive!" Matthew said.

Mel wasn't certain. Although the vitality she had sensed in Varqelle was gone, she couldn't tell much else with so many fragments of her spells swirling and fading. But nothing could mute Cobalt's fury. His rage immobilized her. He mounted his horse again and his resolve shattered the night.

There would be no mercy.

"Saints, no." Mel wanted to shout her protest. The overcast day was nearly dark now, but nothing would stop Cobalt. He would drive his men to fight by torchlight if he had to, but drive them he would, for Shazire had ripped away the father he had waited a lifetime to know, the man who had made him believe he mattered.

Matthew grabbed her arm. "We have to leave."

"No!" She pulled away from him.

His voice snapped with authority. "You *must* go. This is going to get a lot worse. If anything happens to you, it will kill him." He reached for her again—and Mel drew her sword.

She held the blade up between them. "I mean it, Matthew. I will not leave."

"What are you going to do?" he demanded. "Go down there and stop them? It's going to be a bloodbath, Mel. You've done what you can. You must *leave*."

She gripped the hilt of her sword with both hands and held it upright before her body. The blade glinted in the fading daylight. She had worn out her high-level spells; she had to go to a lower level or she would kill herself and achieve nothing.

What was lowest? Red. Simplest? Light.

She pulled the ball out of her sling and clenched her sword again, this time with the ball pressed between her palm and the hilt. A red spell was so simple. Simple—and useless. How would light stop the carnage?

Mel made the spell anyway. Driven by the sphere, the power swept through her like fire. Red light ran up the blade, deepening until the metal seemed to burn. Matthew took a fast step backward and the horses of the sentries shied away.

Mel gripped the ball and focused. The light flared in brightness. She concentrated harder—and it leaped into the sky. Across the Azure Fields, heads turned toward her and the fighters paused. It was only light, nothing more, and it could do nothing to stop anyone, but it stretched in a column up to the darkening sky.

She had no armor. She could barely do more than maintain the spell. She was defenseless. If she went down on that field, it could be her death.

Mel took a ragged breath. She left Smoke with one of the sentries and started walking down the hill. She held the sword high in front of her body, the blade pointing up, and a pillar of red light stretched from it up to the sky. It surrounded her in a brilliant red glow and cast shadows from every rock, every tree, every person around her.

None of her three guards spoke. Incredibly, neither did they leave. Matthew walked beside her, far enough away that the light didn't envelop him. The two sentries rode behind them, bringing Smoke and Matthew's horse.

Mel continued down the hill.

By the time she reached the field, the fighting at the base of the slope had stopped. Men from both armies were watching her, standing with swords at their sides or bows in hand. The cavalrymen sat on their horses. She saw them through the light, as if she burned without heat. The lull spread as more warriors turned to look. Mel kept going, terrified, walking through the middle of the battle with no protection other than red light.

Far across the field, a hillock jutted upward like the clawed hand of a stone giant. Varqelle had fallen there. Mel walked toward the knoll, and crossing that distance seemed to take forever. By the time she reached the mound, no one was moving on the Azure Fields. No one approached her. Matthew and the sentries stopped at the bottom of the hill, leaving her to go on alone. She never paused. She never looked around. She just climbed. And concentrated. As she ascended, her spell grew until it encompassed the entire hill. The blaze from her sword reached into the darkening sky as if it would pierce the clouds.

Finally she reached the top. She raised the blade above her head, holding it in one hand with her arm extended at its full length over her head. The radiant sword blazed across the land and Mel stood there, bathed in its fiery light.

Someone moved at the base of the hill. A tall man. He climbed up to her and stopped at her side. Of all the people on the fields, only he stepped close to the light.

Cobalt.

"No more," Mel said. She meant the words only for him, but her spell amplified them and they resonated across the Azure Fields. Her hair tumbled around her body, and tears streamed down her face.

"No more killing!" She shouted the words and her grief fed the spell. Her voice rolled like thunder across the fields, the armies, the thousands of warriors.

Cobalt regarded her with an expression unlike anything she had ever seen from him before, a satisfaction so intense, it burned as fiercely as her light. He spoke in a voice only she could hear.

"You are a goddess."

"Let them surrender." This time she kept her voice low enough that only he would hear.

He turned to the field. "Zerod!" Caught in her spell, his shout thundered and echoed many times before it died away.

Mel stood with her sword high, blazing. She felt as if she were on fire, though the light generated no heat. She had pushed herself too far, even with this simplest of spells. She had to rest. But she couldn't, not yet.

Cobalt stood at her side, his feet planted wide, his body

bathed in the light. Everyone else throughout the Azure Fields remained where they were, staring at them.

Movement came from the east. A group of warriors was riding across the fields. As they drew nearer, Mel recognized them as a Shazire honor guard.

Zerod rode in their center.

The Shazire ruler sat astride a magnificent stallion with a tasseled bridle and ornate saddle. He was a stocky man of middle age, with black hair and eyes, a hooked nose, and heavy eyebrows streaked with gray. He had married the daughter and only child of the previous ruler, and in Shazire that meant he would always have the title of prince, though he ruled here.

Zerod and his men halted at the bottom of the knoll. The ruddy light cast his face into sharp relief. Mel swung her sword down, the weapon streaming radiance, and drove the blade deep into the ground. The light flared as if it would consume her and Cobalt. She could see the two of them reflected in the metal shields of Zerod's men, their images distorted, blurred and red. Cobalt towered behind her, fierce in the darkness, and she blazed, her hair wild around her body.

"Surrender," she told Zerod. She was pleading with him, but it came out with the same resonance as before. "Surrender or they will massacre your army and raze Alzire to the ground."

Without taking his gaze off her, Zerod dismounted from his stallion. His honor guard followed suit. He walked up the hill and his men came with him, resplendent in their bronzed armor. When Zerod was several paces from Cobalt, he stopped.

Then the prince of Shazire went down on one knee.

Zerod bent his head and set one arm across his raised knee. His men knelt, as well, in a semicircle around him. Zerod removed his belt with its sheathed sword and laid it on the ground, and his guards did the same with their weapons.

Cobalt spoke. "Rise."

They all stood, quiet, somber. Zerod spoke in his Shazire dialect, which clipped consonants and drew out vowels, giving his voice a richness unlike the colder speech of the north. "The House of Zerod surrenders to the House of Escar."

Cobalt spoke in a shadowed voice. "Escar accepts."

The relief that hit Mel was so intense, it hurt. They would see no slaughter, no carnage, no sacking of the capital, neither tonight nor tomorrow. She let the light fade then, until the red glow covered only her body. She wanted to collapse, but she didn't dare, not now. She could do nothing less than stand next to her husband. Cobalt the Dark.

If Varqelle died, Cobalt would rule Shazire, Blueshire, and soon the Misted Cliffs as well, given his grandfather's advanced age. He would reign over the largest empire ever united in all the settled lands.

Cobalt rode Admiral without a saddle, and Mel sat in front of him. Admiral might not have as much speed as the charger Cobalt had taken into battle, but with his great strength, he easily carried his two riders. Mel sagged against Cobalt's chest, limp in his arms. Her red light had vanished, and they crossed the Azure Fields in darkness, Matthew riding on one side and Leo Tumbler on the other. People with torches moved on the fields, tending the injured or lifting them into carts so they could be taken to the physician's station. Some were picking up weapons or catching horses that had lost their riders. Others were trudging off the battlefield.

The torchlight seemed paltry to Cobalt after Mel's light. He would never, if he lived a century, forget that moment when she stood on the hill with her sword thrust in defiance at the sky, her body radiant in a column of flame. Except it had been light, not fire, no matter how dramatic it appeared. He had stood within it and felt only the barest hint of heat. Nothing would have stopped anyone from killing her. And Mel had *known*. She had walked into the middle of combat with no more than red light as her defense. His witch of a wife had pulled off a monumental bluff. He would never gamble with her at cards, but he would admire her bravery from now until forever.

None of that changed what had precipitated it all, however, neither his raging grief nor her desperate attempt to pull him back to sanity before he laid waste to Shazire.

His father.

His men led him to the medical station where they were bringing the wounded, between two rows of hills in a grove of trees. Admiral walked with care past the men on pallets. Those who could raise their arms saluted Cobalt. He nodded in return, subdued in their presence.

Mel braced her hands against his arms.

"What is it?" Cobalt asked.

She answered in a low voice. "I can help…later."

He thought of the scorched billiard ball, her burned hand, his ragged knuckles. She had healed them both. He found it hard to understand why he had ever feared her abilities as a mage. She was a miracle.

A question came to him, one that had the power to shake his world. "Can you heal my father?"

Silence.

"Mel?"

"I—I don't know." Softly she added, "I can help injuries heal, but I cannot mend what would not mend on its own."

"Please." It was a word he rarely used.

"Cobalt—"

"I know you and he do not like one another." Although he meant to be calm, his voice shook. "But he is my father."

"I swear, Cobalt, I would do no less for him than anyone else."

"Will you not try, then?"

"But if I fail?"

He bent his head over hers. "We all must fail sometimes."

"I just—"

"Please," he whispered.

Her voice broke. "I will try."

Cobalt pressed his lips against the back of her head, more grateful than he knew how to say. He had seen how badly the Shazire man gored his father. He wanted to shout at Varqelle for refusing to stay out of the battle. His father, like his wife, had his own mind and nothing would dissuade him from his decisions. Now Varqelle lay here, in this place of moans and pain, dying.

Ahead, a tent stood hunched between two trees. As Admiral approached, an army physician stepped out of the entrance. Cobalt dismounted and put up his arms for Mel, though usually she frowned at him and got off his horse without help. It told him how tired she was tonight that she slid into his arms without protest and let him lower her to the ground.

Matthew came over and extended his hand for the reins. Grateful, Cobalt handed them to him. *Friend.* Mel had called Matthew his friend. He put his hand on Matthew's shoulder and the horseman nodded, sympathy in his eyes.

Cobalt and Mel headed to the tent. She swayed, and her slow pace warned she wouldn't be on her feet much longer. But when he offered his arm, she shook her head and continued on her own.

The physician moved aside so they could enter. Although Cobalt bent his head, it still scraped the rough cloth of the entrance. Braziers shaped like jaguars were set in corners of the tent, and their coals shed ruddy light. Varqelle lay on a pallet between two of them, just as he had once slept in a bed with posts carved in totems of the great animal. Jaguar. His namesake. In the ancient language spoken in Harsdown a thousand years ago, "escar" meant the great mythical cat that prowled the high mountains.

Cobalt knelt next to his father. Varqelle regarded him with black eyes so very much like those that Cobalt saw when he looked into a mirror. The bandages wrapped around Varqelle's chest were soaked with blood.

"Father." The one word felt as if it ripped Cobalt.

"Remember me," Varqelle whispered.

Cobalt put his hand on his father's arm. "You will be here to remind me."

Varqelle exhaled, his breath strained, but he didn't answer.

Mel went to the other side of the pallet and sat cross-legged by the king. With her tangled hair falling over her body and her haunted eyes, she resembled images Cobalt had seen of the saint of souls that shepherded the spirits of the deceased across the ocean of death.

Varqelle turned his head to his daughter-in-law. "They have told me what you did at the battle."

"She can help to heal you," Cobalt said.

Mel looked as if she tried to smile but her lips wouldn't hold the curve. She took a catapult ball out of a sling on her belt and cradled it in her hands.

"Why...help me?" Varqelle asked her.

"You are my husband's father." Her voice caught. "He loves you."

A strange expression came over Varqelle's face. He rolled his head back to Cobalt. "Is it true?"

Cobalt set his hand over his father's. "It is true."

Varqelle squeezed his hand and closed his eyes. "I...am fortunate."

Mel bent over the ball. A blue glow appeared around her hands and deepened as it surrounded her body. Then it enveloped Varqelle. This was nothing like the harmless red light she had created on the battlefield. Cobalt felt power swelling around her. It saturated the tent.

Mel looked across to him, her eyes filled with moisture. Then, ever so slightly, she shook her head.

No. Cobalt wanted to shout the word.

She bent her head again and the glow intensified. A tear dropped onto her ball.

"Father?" Cobalt asked.

Varqelle's grip eased on Cobalt's fingers. "The wound is mortal, son. But...the pain goes..."

Cobalt could barely speak. The words felt thick in his throat, full of the tears he couldn't shed. "You will ride with me again."

Varqelle looked at Mel. "I know of no other woman who would ride all night...to stand by her husband in battle. With a sword of fire." He struggled with the words. "It was honorable."

"Aye." Cobalt could say no more. His eyes felt strange.

Varqelle squeezed Cobalt's fingers. "Remember that...I love you." Then his hand went limp, and the blue glow faded from his body.

For the last time, Varqelle Escar's eyes closed.

The wave of grief that had been roiling in Cobalt surged up and swept over him in an unbearable flood. He made no sound. He wanted to shout to the skies until the clouds froze and shattered, but he couldn't move.

"Father," he rasped.

Mel was sitting with the ball in her lap. In a nightmare of slow motion, her body crumpled and she fell to the side. Cobalt jumped to his feet, but he couldn't reach her before she sprawled next to his father's body. In that killing moment he knew the truth. She had drained herself to stop him from crushing Shazire. She had nothing left to give—and he had insisted she help the man who had attacked her people eighteen years ago and would have killed her family. He truly was the monster of his reputation.

"Mel." Her name caught in his throat.

Cobalt lifted her body. He put his palm against her cheek and found it ice cold. He shook her arm but she didn't stir. Her head rolled against his chest. He bent his head to hers and felt no breath from her mouth against his cheek. He found no pulse in her wrist or neck. He knelt with her limp body in his arms, and he knew then that nothing would ever matter again, that this night, at this moment, the world had ended—for he had lost them both, his father and his wife.

The Midnight Prince threw back his head and shouted. The cry was huge and agonized, and it wrenched out of him. The anguish rose from his throat and cracked open the night as his heart tore apart with grief.

21
The House of Zerod

Cobalt saw no one. He was dimly aware of leaving the tent and striding into the night, but he paid no heed to where he went. No one tried to stop him. He had no idea how he looked, but warriors who had fought on the Azure Fields without flinching backed out of his way now. He went blindly through the trees while inside he died a thousand times. He made no sound; he was screaming in silence.

They had come into his life, Mel and his father, and changed him, made him alive, made him believe he could love, that he was *worth* loving. Now they were gone and he knew the truth: Stonebreaker had always been right, he was nothing, worthless. He could topple a hundred countries and it would never be enough to prove his grandfather wrong. Perhaps he could have survived the death of his father, though he would have grieved forever, but without Mel he had nothing.

Sometime later he came to his senses enough to comprehend that he was crouched by a creek. Darkness surrounded him, and he could barely see the water running past his feet. He rubbed the heel of his hand over his cheek and it came away wet. Mel. Melody. She was a melody of light and love and laughter. He had extinguished that light.

"Forgive me," he rasped.

The ruddy light of a torch cut through the darkness. Then Matthew spoke. "Cobalt?"

"I sent her home to her mother." Cobalt choked out the words. "She came back. I told her to stay out of the battle. She said no. Saints, Matthew, I tied her to a damn pole and still she came back. Now I've killed her."

Matthew knelt next to him. "You shouldn't blame yourself."

"Yes. I should." The words cut like broken glass. "I don't know how to be anything else but what I am. And that ended her life."

"I gave her the catapult ball," Matthew said. "Blame me if you must blame someone."

"No. I would have asked her to heal him no matter what. I didn't know spells could kill. I didn't *know*. She feared I would hate her if she didn't try." Blinded by grief, he had wanted his miraculous sorceress to save his father, and because of that he had lost them both.

"Come." Matthew spoke kindly, though he sounded as if he were breaking. "Come back to camp with me."

"I must—must make arrangements." Cobalt stood up with him. "Arrangements."

"We will take care of them."

Cobalt walked at Matthew's side, unable to think, unable

to feel, encased in numbness. It wouldn't last; soon he would break open and have to face this anguish. His great dream was all he had left, but it had turned to ashes.

Eventually they came to the medical station. It felt unreal, a nightmare. Surely he would wake. But the nightmare continued. He found himself back at the tent. Inside, two bodies covered in shrouds were laid out between the jaguar braziers.

The physician was kneeling next to Varqelle with his head bowed. He looked up as Cobalt came in, and immediately rose to his feet. An unbearable sympathy showed in his eyes. Cobalt couldn't speak to him. He had no more words. He had given what few he had to Matthew and only silence remained. This physician had saved lives today, not killed the people he loved. Cobalt the Great. *Cobalt the Fool.*

Matthew and the doctor spoke in low voices. Cobalt couldn't hear, couldn't listen. Then they left, giving him privacy. He knelt next to Mel's body and pulled back the gauzy white cloth that covered her face.

His entire life, he had been outside the warmth. He had seen other children in loving, complete families, but he had known that could never happen to him. As a boy, he had once stood outside the window of a cottage that belonged to a groom from the palace stables. Cobalt had watched hungrily while the family inside laughed and talked. The father had hugged his wife and son with unrestrained affection. Cobalt had run home that night, too torn apart even to cry. He had no father, only Stonebreaker. Had it not been for Dancer, he would have broken into a thousand pieces, inside his heart, where no one could see. All during his childhood he had wanted that scene in the cottage. As an adult, he had secretly dreamed of a loving wife, but he had never had any idea how to catch that elusive dream, and eventually he had stopped hoping.

Then somehow it had happened, not the way he had imagined, but with the same intensity that he lived the rest of his life. Varqelle would never have been like that gentle, affectionate groom, but he had approved of his son, admired him. *Loved him.* And Mel. *Saints, Mel.* She had been more than he could have dreamed, beyond his hopes. She had filled the holes in his life, those empty places he had lived with for so long, he hadn't even realized they were there—until she took them away.

And he had killed her.

"I'm sorry." The words choked out of him. "I am so very, very *sorry.*" He closed his eyes and tears ran down his face.

A finger touched his cheek. "Don't cry, love."

Cobalt froze. He opened his eyes—and found his wife looking at him.

"Mel?" he whispered.

"I tried to help him." Her voice was so low he could barely hear. "I tried. I couldn't do it." Circles of exhaustion darkened her eyes. But they were alert. *Alive.*

The world quaked under Cobalt. Time seemed to stop. He drew her into his arms and cradled her against his chest. He said her name over and over and thought he would sit here forever, for he feared if he moved, this delusion would dissolve and he would be left with only his grief and her lifeless body.

Then she put her arms around his neck and leaned her head against his, holding him. "It will be all right," she murmured.

Cobalt cried then, tears running down his face as he rocked her back and forth, her body so fragile in his arms.

"Don't die." His voice shook. "Don't leave me, Mel."

"I won't."

"I thought—we all thought—you didn't breathe, you had no pulse—" He couldn't finish.

"I went into a mage trance. To heal…like that night in the Sphere Tower."

"Sphere Tower?" He couldn't take in her words.

"That night King Stonebreaker found me…on the floor…"

"I'm sorry," he whispered. "For everything."

"Don't worry, love." She held on to him and didn't try to talk anymore.

Cobalt didn't know how long he sat with her. Someone spoke to him and someone else tried to ease Mel out of his arms, but he refused to let her go.

Gradually he became more aware. The doctor was kneeling next to him. As Cobalt's gaze focused, the man said, "Shall I tend your wife, Your Majesty?"

Majesty? It was the wrong title. He shifted Mel so that she was curled against him, her cheek pressed against his chest, his legs extended on either side of her. He bent his head over hers and his hair fell forward, mingling with hers, black on corn silk. She stirred but didn't open her eyes.

"She's alive," Cobalt said.

"Did you bring her back?" The physician sounded subdued. Awed, even.

"No." The last thing Cobalt wanted was for people to think he could do such deeds. "Not me. She was under a mage spell."

"Ah." He sounded bewildered.

Cobalt lifted his head. "My father?" Even now, he hoped.

The doctor shook his head. "He is gone."

"You are sure?"

"Yes. It is not like with your wife. He shows all the signs of his passing." He let out a quiet breath. "I am terribly sorry."

Cobalt's voice caught. "We must see to his funeral pyre."

"I will begin the arrangements immediately."

"Not immediately." Cobalt held Mel against him. "I need to sit here. With them. For a while."

"I understand."

"Can you bring ale for my wife?" He didn't know what mages needed to help them recover, but ale often made him feel better.

The doctor smiled kindly and rose to his feet. "I will fetch some."

Cobalt nodded, grateful, and held Mel. When he was alone, he sat in the dimly lit tent and mourned for his father while he thanked every saint he had heard of for his miraculous wife.

They spread Varqelle's ashes across the hills north of the Azure Fields, in green countryside that had escaped the weight of the armies. Skybells nodded in the wild grasses, and patchy shadows scuttled across the land from clouds. The ashes drifted on the wind and across a hill below the ridge where Cobalt stood with Mel and Matthew. Cobalt had thought he might place them in an urn and carry it with him, but this was better, giving his father the freedom of the land he had made his own before he died, though he lived only moments to know his victory.

"Rest well," Cobalt murmured.

He wanted to stay there forever, high on a ridge under the clouds. But it wasn't possible. Much remained to do. He had taken this country and now he had to prove to Mel that he could be a good leader instead of a tyrant.

Cobalt turned to her. "How are you?"

"Well," she said softly.

She didn't look well. Her face was gaunt and she had confined her hair in a braid that fell to her waist. Her tunic and leggings were black to honor his father, an honor she freely gave, though Cobalt would never have asked for it after all that had happened. He didn't deserve this wife of his, but for some incredible reason he had a second chance with her.

He took her hand and raised it to his lips. Her knuckles felt cold when he pressed his lips against them. Since last night, when he had thought she had died, he kept wanting to touch her, to assure himself she really was alive.

"Ride with me," he said.

"All right." She squeezed his hand. Then she let go and walked slowly back to where Admiral stood among the trees.

Matthew spoke at Cobalt's side. "She is strong."

Cobalt glanced at him. Matthew sounded strange today. Perhaps it was grief for Varqelle, but it confused Cobalt, for Matthew had avoided the king and knew him little.

"What troubles you?" Cobalt asked.

"I'm just getting old." Matthew rubbed his eyes. "More aware of my own mortality."

Cobalt laid a hand on his shoulder. "You must not think that way. You're a fine, strong man. You will outlive me."

Matthew set his palm over Cobalt's hand. "I hope not."

Cobalt lowered his hand and smiled. "We should catch up with my wife before she rides away on Admiral. I will return to camp to find she has taken over my army."

Matthew tried to return his smile, but it didn't reach the sadness in his eyes. "She just might."

"Well." Cobalt stood awkwardly, feeling as if he should say more, but he didn't know what.

They crossed the meadow to the trees. Mel had somehow already mounted, though Admiral stood taller than most horses and usually tolerated no one except Cobalt to touch him when he was without a rider. Cobalt saw the tree stump Mel must have used, so he used it, too, to boost himself up behind her. Matthew swung onto his chestnut horse. Then they rode through the trees, following a trail that wound down a mild slope on the other side of the ridge.

Cobalt's mounted honor guard was waiting at the base of the hill, where they had kept people from interrupting the memorial. They maneuvered their horses into a hexagon around him and Matthew, and they all rode back to the camp. He wondered at the origins of that formation. Why a hexagon? Mel said it was an influence from Aronsdale, but that didn't tell him much, it just made him wonder about Aronsdale. Mages and shapes. He had to learn more about them if he was to understand his wife. But not now. He needed time. With his father's death, Cobalt was not only in charge of the army, he also ruled Shazire and Blueshire. He had to establish the Escar presence here.

Hundreds of tents were scattered throughout meadows north of the Azure Fields. Last night most of the remaining sixteen hundred men in the Shazire army had sworn allegiance to the House of Escar. Of the four hundred spearmen from Jazid, over three hundred had survived. Cobalt wasn't certain what to do with them. They had fought for Shazire, but they owed allegiance to Jazid, whose sultan hadn't surrendered to anyone.

With or without its spearmen, Jazid had a big army, three thousand strong. Cobalt's now numbered nearly seven thousand, but he knew the history of Jazid and Taka Mal too well to harbor any illusions. They had long been allies, and Taka Mal claimed an army of at least three thousand. If its queen united with the sultan of Jazid, together they would wield a formidable force.

Cobalt shifted Mel in his arms as they rode. Her presence calmed his agitation and helped him think. If he sent back the spearmen, it was a gesture of conciliation. Was that what he wanted? He and Varqelle had intended to ride on Jazid and Taka Mal, but he was no longer certain. Grief weighed on him too much to make such a decision.

They were passing the first campfire of the camp. A group of men and women, support personnel for the army, were seated on logs around it eating. They glanced up idly, then quickly rose to their feet when they saw the riders. Beyond them, a cluster of soldiers turned. When they saw Cobalt and his retinue, they too came to attention. Cobalt nodded to them and rode on—and everyone they passed also stood to face him. The soldiers saluted him. He wasn't certain if they were honoring Varqelle, Mel, or himself, but their tribute spread like a wave through the camp.

Mel spoke in a low voice. "I've never seen anything like this."

"Nor I," Cobalt said.

"At least they don't hate us."

"Apparently not."

"Cobalt?"

Whenever she said his name that way, he worried. "Yes?"

"What will you do with Prince Zerod?"

"What do you think I should do?"

"Send him to Jazid with the spearmen."

"It will make me look weak."

"It will make you look compassionate."

She was a dreamer. "I am not compassionate."

Mel leaned back against him. "You are wrong."

He frowned. "If I send him there, he will petition the sultan of Jazid for an army to defeat mine." As Varqelle had asked Stonebreaker.

"How is that different from what would happen anyway?"

Cobalt recalled when he had asked Varqelle exactly the same question. "It changes Jazid's stance from defense to offense."

"Why does it matter?" she asked. "Either way you are going to invade them, aren't you?"

Cobalt squinted at the top of her head. "You ask too many questions."

She went very still in his arms. "Does that mean you might *not* move against them?"

He didn't have an answer for her.

"If you execute Zerod," she said, "you will earn the enmity of the Shazire men. He is much admired by them."

"I already have their enmity."

She answered softly. "Look, Cobalt. Look around. They are all standing. They don't sit again until you've passed. Even the men from Shazire. This is not enmity."

"They honor you. And Varqelle."

"Then why are they looking at you? And saluting you?"

It was true. He didn't know why they were doing it, but he wished Stonebreaker could see such respect given to the grandson he claimed was worthless. He wanted to lean his forehead on the top of her head, but he couldn't with so many people watching.

"I don't know what I'm going to do," he said. "I need time."

"Come home with me."

He couldn't help but smile. "I cannot."

"Why?"

He answered wryly. "Mel, perhaps you haven't noticed, but I have acquired a kingdom." It was, he realized, why the doctor had called him "Majesty." Then he added, "And you are my queen."

She said nothing for a while, absorbing that. After they had ridden beyond all the campfires, Cobalt looked back, but they were far enough away now that much of the camp blurred. He took out his spectacles and settled them on his nose. Then he could see that his people had resumed their activities, breaking their fast, tending weapons and horses, preparing to ride.

"Cobalt?" Mel asked.

There it was, his name again. Turning forward, he spoke warily. "Yes?"

"Now that you have a kingdom, what will you do with it?"

"Check the tax structure first, I would guess."

"For saints' sake," she said. "What about the *people?*"

"What about them?"

"What are you going to do with them?"

"Nothing." He knew she wouldn't be satisfied with that answer, and would interrogate him until he put together many sentences. So he added, "The only real change is that they will pay their taxes to me rather than Zerod or Lightstone. Their armies will combine with mine. I will replace Zerod's top people with my people, both in the government and the military. But most people won't notice much change."

"'Not much change' doesn't equal 'no rebellion.'"

He rubbed his hands along her arms. "We will take things as they come. Perhaps the people will rebel. I don't know. But they were once part of the Misted Cliffs. Their history is part of me. I know this country in a way Zerod never could. That will make a difference."

Some of her stiffness eased. "I hope so."

He thought back to the scrolls he had pored over in the libraries at the Castle of Clouds and the Diamond Palace. He had never liked most of the studies his mother insisted he do, but history was the exception. He had inherited her passion for it. "The reign of the House of Zerod stagnated. They haven't badly misused the people or the land, but they haven't done a lot to help, either. I see much that could be improved."

"Irrigation," Mel said.

"Yes! You know this country?"

"To some extent." After a moment, she said, "Actually, rather well."

"Good." She would be a valuable adviser. He waited, but she asked no more. Relieved, he lapsed into silence.

After a while, she said, "And Zerod?"

Saints! He did not know what he was going to do with Zerod. "You ask too many questions."

She sighed, but she let it go.

They soon reached the tents where he had located his head-quarters. He dismounted, then reached up for Mel, worried for her health. Although she let him catch her as she slid down, but she stepped away and stood on her own as soon as she was on the ground. Her face was somber when she looked up at him, but then she suddenly broke into a smile.

Cobalt blinked. "What?"

She reached up and touched his eye—except his blasted spectacles stopped her finger.

"So different," she murmured.

Mortified, Cobalt quickly removed the glasses and stowed them in his hidden pocket. He had crushed more than one pair that way, forgetting he had put them there.

"It is no shame to wear them," Mel said.

"I don't really need them," he said gruffly. He didn't want her to think his strength less because of them.

Her smile shifted into something gentler. "To need help isn't a weakness." She put her palm against his chest. "The part of you that isn't a fighter is no less valuable than the warlord."

Cobalt took her hand and held it against his chest. He didn't know how to say thank you, beyond just the words, which by themselves didn't mean enough to express what she made him feel. And he feared to sound foolish. He squeezed her hand and her smile returned, so sweet he almost broke inside.

Matthew came up to them, leading his chestnut horse. "I can look after Admiral while you're inside."

Cobalt handed him the reins. "My thanks." It was so much easier to say those words to Matthew. He turned awkwardly back to Mel, uncertain what she would think of him, but she didn't seem put off by anything, neither his taciturn nature nor having seen him in spectacles. She continued to watch him with those luminous eyes of hers. It rattled him as much as it had the first time he met her, but he would gladly spend a lifetime perturbed in such a manner.

"Ready?" he asked her.

She bit her lip, but then she nodded. They entered the tent, Cobalt ducking his head to fit through the opening. As he straightened, the people waiting inside rose with a clink of armor and mail, and the scrape of chairs on the heavy rugs that covered the floor. Cobalt supposed he could have come in with more flourish, preceded by his honor guard. But he had never liked pomp. He preferred things simple.

Colonel Tumbler and several of Cobalt's other top officers were standing around a square table, impressive in their white over-tunics emblazoned with the Chamberlight sphere, their mail showing at the sleeves and neck. Each wore blue trousers tucked into boots and a finely tooled sword belt inlaid with sapphires, for they served the Sapphire Throne. Cobalt wore a similar outfit when he rode as a Chamberlight prince. Today, however, he had chosen black. All black, from his boots to his trousers to his tunic to his cape. For the House of Escar. For his father.

One other man was at the table: Zerod. Gone were his plumed helmet and bronzed armor. No sword hung at his side. His clothes were clean and well made, a russet shirt and darker trousers given to him by one of Cobalt's men, but it was the garb of a gentleman, not royalty.

Zerod inclined his head stiffly to Cobalt. His face showed no expression. If he was afraid, he hid it well behind his carefully composed features.

Cobalt went to the table with Mel at his side. They had only left one chair, for him, but Tumbler immediately brought another for Mel. No one dared question her presence. Zerod stood, his palms on the tabletop, his fingers tensed into claws, a man facing the specter of his execution.

Cobalt spoke to Zerod without preamble. "I have three hundred and forty-two spearmen from Jazid who served in your army. I cannot send them back to Jazid."

The emir waited.

"My men took Alzire this morning," Cobalt added.

Zerod went rigid, his strained muscles pulling his shirt. "And the palace?"

Cobalt knew what the emir was asking. "Your wife and son are in our custody. They have not been harmed."

Zerod's grip on the table eased but his shoulders remained tensed. "What will you do with them?"

A good question. Varqelle had planned to execute the entire family. Cobalt was painfully aware of Mel standing at his side.

"King Jarid let my father live," Cobalt said. "My mother and I were in the Misted Cliffs, so we also survived." Quietly he said, "You see the result."

"Let them go," Zerod said, his voice urgent, "and I will have them swear never to move against you."

Cobalt exhaled. "I know only too well how much—or how little—such a vow means to a son robbed of his father."

"I beg you." Zerod spoke with simple eloquence. "Let them live. Take my life. But not theirs."

Cobalt could feel Mel at his side. He remembered her words: *You live on the edge between your own darkness and light. What will drive you as you sweep across these lands? Will you become a tyrant?*

Cobalt spoke slowly. "I set you a task, Zerod of Shazire."

"A task?" Zerod asked, wary.

"Deliver this message to the sultan of Jazid," Cobalt said. "His spearmen are prisoners of war. They have two choices: go to my dungeons or swear allegiance to my army."

"I understand," Zerod said. Something flickered in his gaze, an emotion that went by almost too fast to read. Hope? Until now, Cobalt had given him no reason to believe the House of Escar wouldn't wipe out the House of Zerod.

By using Zerod as his messenger, Cobalt also hoped to send Jazid an unspoken message: the Midnight Prince had stripped the potentate of his title. Cobalt the Dark had such great power, he feared no one, not even a sovereign he had deposed. Cobalt did actually fear Zerod, but a plan was forming in his mind.

Letting Zerod live and travel freely implied Cobalt offered conciliation to Jazid, less than if he returned the spearmen but enough to suggest he might wish neutral relations rather than conquest. Cobalt no longer felt certain what he intended. Within one generation, his House would rule the Misted Cliffs, Harsdown, Blueshire, and Shazire, two-thirds of the settled lands, an empire larger than any single realm in known history. Jazid and Taka Mal had tried to achieve a similar goal two-hundred and six years ago, when they had attacked the Misted Cliffs, but they had failed. Now some of the damage of that conflict had been set right for the Misted Cliffs. It wasn't the empire Cobalt and Varqelle had envisioned—but perhaps it was enough. He needed time to think and to recover from his losses.

He spoke to Zerod. "You will also give him a document that you and I have signed together. In it, you will swear to leave Jazid after you deliver your message and never seek their help in bringing an army against me."

Zerod's expression became guarded. "Very well."

Cobalt didn't believe him for one moment. Had he been in Zerod's position, he would have said whatever was necessary to ensure the survival of his family and himself.

"To make certain that you abide by this vow," Cobalt added, "your wife and son will remain here as hostages, under guard at the palace." That had been Jarid Dawnfield's mistake; he had left the son free and the father in prison. Cobalt wondered if his father would have come for him if the reverse had been true. Had it been Stonebreaker, he didn't think so. But Varqelle? Yes, he would have, even if it took him years to raise an army.

Zerod spoke carefully. "I understand."

Cobalt could have stopped there, but he surprised himself. "If you abide by this agreement," he continued, "then in two years you may go into exile with your wife and son." By that time, his business with Jazid and Taka Mal would be done. Either they would have signed a treaty or he would have conquered them. He supposed it was also possible they might depose and execute him, but that wasn't an alternative he chose to entertain.

Zerod's shoulders visibly lowered. "Will you put that in writing about my family?" he asked. "Also your guarantee to grant me free passage to Jazid?"

Cobalt shifted his weight. "If I do that, it is a promise I will not attack Jazid while you take my message to them."

Zerod raised an eyebrow. "You intend otherwise?"

Cobalt frowned. The Shazire prince wanted him to sign a promise that, although temporary, could have long-term consequences. It amounted to the offer of a treaty he wasn't certain he wanted to make. He had little idea what the next years would bring.

He glanced at Mel. She met his gaze, and he knew what she would say: *Do this, and he will be more likely not to seek an army against you.* No guarantees existed, but Zerod was reputed to be a man of honor. Cobalt wished to be one as well.

He considered the emir. "I will sign a statement to this end, effective for one year, with the condition that I will abide by it only as long as Jazid makes no move against my lands. After one year, the agreement will have to be renegotiated, with no guarantee of continuance except in the pledge that you may rejoin your family in two years."

Zerod inclined his head. "I will carry this message to Jazid."

They wrote and signed documents that afternoon. Cobalt assigned Zerod an honor guard to accompany him to Jazid. When the honor guard returned to Shazire, they would escort back any families of the spearmen who chose to come here.

For now, Jazid and Taka Mal were safe.

22
The King's Brother

Part of Harsdown's southern border lay along the north-western border of Shazire, with Blueshire on the easternmost edge. Mel knew the moment their party passed from Shazire into Harsdown. Nothing delineated the border, but these lands were so familiar, she could draw that ephemeral line without a compass or guide. She and Cobalt were traveling with one hundred men from his army. In gentler times, she would have sung with delight, but today her happiness was muted. To the east lay the fields, stripped and trampled, where the Chamberlight and Dawnfield armies had passed only a few weeks ago. The countryside was already recovering, though. Spring had taken over the land and the fragrance of sweet-grasses filled the air.

They could visit her home only for a short time. The process of setting up a new government in Shazire might have little effect on everyday life there, but it certainly affected Cobalt. Patient work and constant diplomacy to avoid flare-ups wasn't part of his personality; he wanted to be out traveling, training, pitting himself against the world. Administration and negotiation wearied him until he paced the halls of the Alzire Palace like a caged wildcat.

So they had come to Harsdown to get Dancer.

Mel didn't wait until the horses went to the stables. As soon as the farmhouse came into view, she jumped off Smoke and thrust the reins at Cobalt, who was still on Admiral. Then she ran toward the front porch.

With one hundred men, their arrival was hardly unannounced. The company had spread itself out over the land and would set up their camp under the wary eye of the Dawnfield forces stationed here. Chime burst out of the front door before Mel even reached the porch. Her mother ran down the steps, and Mel barreled into her. They hugged hard, crying and laughing, and Mel felt as if she was taking a full breath of air for the first time in months.

A hand clapped Mel on the shoulder, and she turned to see her father. She went into his arms and hugged him, too, forgetting for this moment everything else but these two people she had so deeply missed.

After a while, they separated. Mel smiled and wiped her eyes. "It's good to see you."

"Aye," her mother said, her face wet, too.

Muller's voice caught. "Welcome home."

"I'm so glad to be here." Mel looked back at the gardens and the orchards beyond. She had ridden through them with Cobalt and their honor guard, and they were all waiting about fifty paces back, dismounted, Cobalt holding the reins for Admiral and Smoke. Matthew stood at his side.

Does no one else see it? Mel wondered. Matthew had the same cheekbones and nose as Cobalt. Their features weren't identical; Matthew had a gentler cast to his face and gray eyes. He also dressed in rougher clothes. But if one looked past the external signs of social class, his Escar heritage was obvious.

Cobalt was watching her with his shuttered expression, but she recognized the pain behind his control. Seeing her with her parents, he was remembering his father.

"Cobalt!" The woman's voice came from behind them.

Mel turned to see Dancer walking across the porch, her spectacles in one hand. As she descended the stairs, she nodded to Mel and her parents, then passed them, her attention on Cobalt. He handed the reins to Matthew and went to his mother. Their reunion was quiet. Restrained. Dancer lifted her arms as if to hug him, but she held back. Cobalt looked down at her with a gentleness he so rarely showed anyone. He hesitated—and then stiffly pulled her into a hug. For the first time since Mel had known them, they embraced.

They released each other after only a moment and stood awkwardly. Cobalt said, "You look well."

She seemed to light up from within at the sight of him. "That is because you are here." Her smile faded. "But Cobalt, you look tired. You must make certain to sleep enough. And are you eating enough? It is important that you do."

He laughed, evoking flustered looks from his guards, who had probably never heard him make such a sound. "Ah, Mother, I am glad to see you."

She patted his arm. Then he and Dancer came over to Mel and her parents. While the rest of their honor guard led the horses back to the stables, Mel took her husband into her home for the first time since their marriage.

Mel's dearest friend Shim joined them for the evening meal. It seemed ages since Shim had stood up for Mel at the wedding, though it had only been months. It gratified Mel that Shim still considered their friendship strong despite all the changes.

It wasn't until after supper was eaten and drinks shared in the spacious parlor that their guests departed and the household settled down for the evening. While Muller retired to his den to talk with his son-in-law, Mel spent some time with Fog. Then she wandered through the house alone and reacquainted herself with her home.

She found Dancer in the library.

The queen was standing by a shelf, reading a scroll about the matrilineal structure of Aronsdale farming households. She looked up as Mel came over to her. "This is astonishing! I had no idea." She showed Mel the scroll. "I've never had a chance to read so much about Aronsdale." Belatedly, she seemed to realize what she had done. Her face reddened and she lowered the scroll. "Good evening, Melody."

If ever Mel had felt her name didn't fit, it had been since she married Cobalt. It was good to see Dancer so animated, though. "Have you enjoyed the library here?"

"It is a fine collection," Dancer said with formality. Then her voice relaxed. "Your parents have so many books I've never seen."

"I spent many hours here as a child." Mel grimaced with the memory. "Always I had some studies or other I had to do."

"Learning is important." It sounded like Dancer was no stranger to admonishing a reluctant child to study.

"My parents said that, too."

"They are kind." Dancer paused. "They have treated me better than I expected."

It didn't surprise Mel. She suspected almost anything would be better than what Dancer had learned to expect. "I had hoped you would like them."

"Why?" Dancer seemed genuinely perplexed.

"They are your family now, too."

The queen hesitated. "They have invited me to stay as the court historian."

Mel thought it was a good idea, if Dancer would consider it. "It isn't a royal court like you're used to." She indicated the sunbask room around them. "No castle or palace. Just this farmhouse. But it is a good place to live."

"I love it here," Dancer murmured.

"I, too." The irony didn't escape her, that Dancer Escar of all people could come to live here, but Mel could never come home again, not to stay. Her fate was too intertwined with Cobalt.

Dancer returned the scroll to the shelf. She stood with one hand against its surface, her gaze averted. "And my husband?"

Mel answered in a subdued voice. "I'm sorry about his death." As much as she had disliked Varqelle, she did regret his passing, though mainly for what it had done to Cobalt.

"Ah, well." Dancer turned to her. "He and I have barely spoken for over thirty years."

"He died with his sword in his hand."

"It is what he would have wanted."

"Dancer?"

"Yes?"

"I wondered about Matthew——" Mel wasn't sure what to

ask. *Is he Cobalt's uncle?* She didn't have the right to pry. Dancer might not know, anyway.

"Why do you ask about him?" Dancer asked.

"I wondered if you would manage all right without him here. He has served your family for a long time."

Dancer walked over to a table where a yellow vase was filled with rosy box-blossoms. A delicate glass sphere stood on a stand next to it. She ran her finger over the vase. "Matthew has asked Cobalt if he may remain here, too, if I stay."

"Do you think you will?"

Dancer looked up. "If Cobalt allows Matthew, then yes, I will stay."

It gladdened Mel to hear. "Does Matthew know?"

"I have told him so."

Mel wondered just how close Dancer and Matthew had become over the decades. "He is a good man."

Dancer's expression softened. "Yes."

So. Matthew had been Dancer's closest friend at the Castle of Clouds. Did they wish it to be more? Dancer could wed again after a suitable time of mourning. In the Misted Cliffs, a queen couldn't marry the man in charge of her stables, but here it might be different.

Mel smiled. "He is also a handsome man."

Dancer's mouth curved upward as she touched the box-blossoms. "That he is."

Mel spoke carefully. "He resembles King Varqelle a bit."

"Do you believe so?" Dancer's face took on its closed expression. "I don't think so. He has a much kinder face."

Mel thought of Matthew caring for Dancer throughout the years, hiding Cobalt from Stonebreaker's rages, smuggling the boy dinner when his grandfather locked him in his room without food, always there, always helping. "Yes. He does."

Dancer sighed. "He and I are of an age, you know. A couple of old folks."

"Not so old," Mel said.

Dancer turned to her. "You have said nothing about the difference in our stations."

"There is nothing to say." Mel lifted her hand to indicate the library, but she meant all of her home. "This place is enchanted. Anything can happen."

Incredibly, Dancer laughed, a lovely sparkle of sound, a hint of how the queen might have glowed had her life been kinder. "You almost make me believe that."

Mel felt her own face gentle. "I am glad."

Crickets were singing in the night, and the music of a fiddle trickled out an open window of the house. Mel strolled through the orchard and tried to imprint it on her mind so her memories of this place would remain vivid.

She concentrated on the glass sphere she had brought with her from the library. Dim orange light filled it and then faded. It would be a while before she could perform any significant spell, especially with high-level colors, but she was recovering faster this time than the last. She hoped that eventually she could use her powers without knocking herself out in the process.

"It is a beautiful night, Your Majesty," a man said.

Startled by the title, Mel looked up with a jerk and saw a figure under an apple tree a short distance away. "My greetings, Matthew."

"May I walk with you?" he asked.

"Yes. Certainly."

They strolled together under the trees. After a moment, she said, "Dancer told me the two of you might stay here."

"Cobalt has given permission."

"I'm glad."

Matthew paused. "Mel—"

"Yes?"

He had an odd expression, one of sorrow and something else harder to read. Regret? "Cobalt treasures the memory of his father. And he values his heritage, both in the House of Escar and the House of Chamberlight."

"It means the stars to him," Mel said.

"I would have it stay that way."

Mel knew what he feared, that the more time Cobalt spent with her family, the more likely he was to hear ill spoken of his father. But they would never dishonor Varqelle's name to Cobalt.

"My family respects the memory of the deceased."

Matthew indicated a lawn seat under the trees, one of several set out in the orchard. He brushed leaves off the bench and they sat down together. Enough moonlight sifted through the trees for her to see his pensive expression.

"I would like to tell you a story," he said.

"Please do."

"You must promise to repeat it to no one." He spoke firmly. "Especially Cobalt."

"If my silence would harm him, I cannot promise it."

"Will you trust me if I tell you harm will come to no one as long as you never speak of it?"

Mel thought of all she knew about this man. He had given her many reasons to trust him. "Yes. I promise my silence."

He sat back in the lawn seat. Then he began. "Thirty-five years ago a beautiful girl married a king. Her husband mistreated her, but she knew of no other life, for she had lived with even worse in her home. She was like an injured dove."

He stared into the trees ahead of them. "Another man fell in love with her. He worked with the horses." His voice softened. "He wanted to take away her pain and show her that she didn't have to live without love. And incredibly, for one night in the loft of his stable, they shared that love."

"Ah, no, Matthew," Mel murmured.

"It was only one night." He looked at her. "Nine months later she gave birth to a son."

She stared at him. "A son?"

"Everyone believed the child was premature. It could be true."

"Matthew—"

He put up his hand. "The son looked like the king. Walked like him. Spoke like him. Paced the keep with the same restless spirit that never found peace. Like the king."

She spoke quietly. "Or the king's half brother."

"His bastard half brother." His gaze never wavered. "As the king's only child, and the only male heir to his mother's father as well, the boy was heir of two kingdoms."

Heir to two kingdoms—or dead. Mel knew the miserable laws; she had read thoroughly the history of this country. "In Harsdown, the sentence for a queen's adultery is execution for both her and her lover."

"And their child."

Saints above. "And the king suspected? So the queen fled?"

"Never. The king believed the boy was his." He spoke with difficulty. "And that may be true."

Mel had seen Matthew's kindness reflected in Cobalt, but never had she seen such in Varqelle. It might be because Matthew raised Cobalt, but now she wondered. "If the king didn't suspect, why did his wife leave him?"

Matthew put one elbow up on the back of the seat and

regarded her. "The king's mistress knew. She spied on her rival."

No wonder Dancer had been so unhappy. "The queen knew about the mistress?"

Matthew snorted. "Everyone knew. It was no secret."

"And the mistress threatened to reveal the truth if the queen didn't leave?"

"Yes."

It made an ugly sort of sense. Dancer's adultery had given her husband's lover the ultimate weapon. No wonder Dancer was bitter. Varqelle suffered no consequences for openly keeping a mistress, yet he could have killed Dancer, Matthew, and Cobalt with impunity for the one night Dancer and Matthew spent together. Nor did Mel doubt that Varqelle would have done it.

"Is the mistress still alive?" Mel asked.

"She died years ago."

Mel thought of Stonebreaker. "Couldn't the queen go to someone else besides her father?"

Matthew's hand clenched his knee, gripping the cloth of his trousers. "Her father wouldn't allow it. Finally he had everything he wanted, a male heir and a weapon to control his daughter—her fear of her husband. He gave her a choice. Either she stay with him or his army would return her to Harsdown."

Mel felt ill. It fit with what she had seen of the Chamberlight sovereign. "Did he suspect about her baby?"

"No one did. The child's resemblance to the king was unmistakable."

"Saints, Matthew. It is a terrible story."

"Ah, well." His face lost its harsh cast. "The ending is not so bad, at least for Dancer." After a pause, he said, "And who knows. Cobalt *could* have been premature. I might not be his father."

Mel laid her hand on his forearm. "In every way that matters, you were a father to him. You taught him, guided him, protected him." She couldn't imagine what Cobalt would have become without Dancer and Matthew. The tyrant existed within her husband, but his light had won over his darkness.

"Someday," Matthew said, "he must face Stonebreaker. They are not done, those two."

"He isn't ready yet." For all that the rest of the world saw Cobalt as invincible, Mel knew otherwise. "But someday."

"You are good for him." Matthew's face relaxed into a smile. "I am glad you came to us."

"I, too," she said, and meant it.

Mel was walking along a hallway when her father came out of his study. He stopped and waited, his face lit by a spherical oil lamp in a wall sconce. It comforted her to see him so perfectly arrayed, his buff trousers, polished knee-boots, gold brocaded vest, and snowy white shirt. His hair was gold and thick, with streaks of gray. He had the same slender build and long-legged grace she recalled from her earliest memories. As a small girl, she had liked to run around the yard while he and Chime pretended they couldn't catch her. It had delighted Mel that she could outrun them both even with her stubby toddler legs.

"Evening, Papa," she said.

His smile crinkled the lines around his eyes. "It is good to see you prowling about in the halls again."

"I am not prowling," she said, indignant.

"Ah, Mel." He chuckled. "We've missed you."

She hesitated. "So much has changed. I wasn't certain I would be welcome in Harsdown."

"You are always welcome here." He shifted his weight. "I cannot say that all of our people feel such about your husband."

She didn't doubt it. "I wish they knew him better."

"He and I talked for quite some time this evening."

"What do you think of him?"

Her father winced. "He's rather alarming."

She smiled wryly. "That he is."

"King Lightstone has made his home in Aronsdale. A refuge. If you ever need to come here—" He let the sentence hang.

"Thank you, Papa. But I'll be all right."

"Will you?"

She wondered at his mood. "What is wrong?"

"I have heard what people call you."

"Call me?"

He regarded her steadily. "They are saying you are the Dawn Star Empress."

"What!" She didn't know whether to laugh or be appalled. "I haven't heard that."

"You will, I'm sure." He studied her face. "Is that what you want, Mel, to have the world bow to you?"

"Saints, no." Softly she said, "No."

"Do you think this peace will last?"

She knew what he was really asking her. Would Cobalt be satisfied with what he had gained? She considered her words carefully. "He is driven. Nothing will change that. But it may be enough. And I do genuinely believe it is in him to be a great leader."

Muller put his hand on her shoulder. "Just take care. If his dreams become heady and seductive, remember compassion."

"I will, Papa."

Although he smiled, he seemed sad. "Yes, I think you will."

She hugged him then. He and her mother had taught her what she needed to remember, and she would always carry that with her.

Light leaked under the door of Mel's bedroom as she creaked the door open. A candle was burning on the windowsill. Cobalt lay sprawled on her bed, fully dressed, with his booted legs hanging over the footboard and his head against the headboard.

She closed the door and padded over to him. He stirred, restless even in sleep, and his eyelids twitched. He tried to turn over, but his arm hit the wall on the other side of the bed. Mel sat next to him and traced her hand over the plane of his cheek.

"Eh?" Cobalt grunted, shifted again and smashed his leg against a bedpost. "Damn it all," he muttered.

Mel smiled. "Good evening, my sweet-natured husband."

His lashes lifted and he peered at her with bleary eyes. "Your blasted bed is too small."

"So I see."

He maneuvered onto his side, almost knocking her over in the process. "I would invite you to share, but there's no room."

She toyed with his hair. "We could put the mattress on the floor."

"That would be much better." He looked relieved at first, but then he paused. "Maybe not. Your cat will walk on us."

"Is Fog in here?"

He pointed at the floor. "Under there."

Mel leaned down and peered under the bed. Fog lay with his front paws folded under his body and regarded Mel with large, gold eyes.

"You beautiful kitty," Mel crooned.

"No! Don't do that." Cobalt tugged her back up. "If you encourage him, he will jump up here and sit on us."

"He likes you."

"He walks all over me," he grumbled. "I'm supposed to be the Jaguar Emperor, not the kitty-cat king."

Mel burst out laughing. "Ah, Cobalt, I do love you."

He touched her cheek. "I have thought sometimes that surely you must hate me."

"No." She took his hands. "You alarm me sometimes."

"You terrify me." He sat up on the bed, swinging his legs over the side, and drew her into his arms.

Mel closed her eyes and held him around the waist. She savored the strength of his arms, the clean smell of his clothes, and the rough weave of his shirt against her chin. "Why do I terrify you?"

He answered in a low voice. "Because I've never loved anyone the way I do you."

"Ah, Cobalt." Softly she said, "And I you. It is a good thing."

He rested his head on hers. "Yes, I think it is."

They sat that way as the candle sputtered and melted in its glazed dish on the sill. In a few moments they would have to haul the mattress to the floor; in a few days they would return to Shazire; in the next few seasons they would send part of the Chamberlight army back to the Misted Cliffs and arrange for the protection of Shazire; and in the next years Cobalt would have to make hard decisions about what he intended to do with his new power and influence. And someday he would have to face his grandfather. The future loomed, but its complications no longer daunted her. They would manage, no matter how complex their lives, as long as they had each other.

She sat, content in his arms.

* * * * *

Will they rule an empire?
Look for more from the houses of Dawnfield and Escar next year.

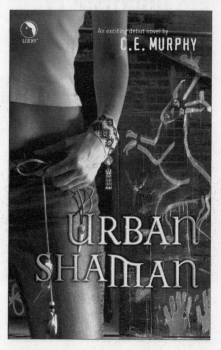

THE TEARS OF LUNA

A shimmering crown grows and dims and is always reborn. Luna has the power and gift to brighten dark nights and lend mystery to the shadows. She will sometimes show up on the brightest of days, but her most powerful moments are when she fills the heaven with her light. Just as the moon comes each night to caress sleeping mortals, Luna takes a special interest in lovers. Her belief in the power of romance is so strong that it is said she cries gem-like tears which linger when her light moves on. Those lucky enough to find the Tears of Luna will be blessed with passion enduring, love fulfilled and the strength to find and fight for what is theirs.

A WORLD YOU CAN ONLY IMAGINE ™

LUNA™

www.LUNA-Books.com

THE TEARS OF LUNA MYTH COMES ALIVE IN

A WORLD AN ARTIST CAN IMAGINE ™

This year LUNA Books and Duirwaigh Gallery are proud to present the work of five magical artists.

Last month, the art featured on our inside back cover was created by:

MARK FISHMAN

If you would like to order a print of Mark's work, or learn more about him please visit Duirwaigh Gallery at www.DuirwaighGallery.com.

DUIRWAIGH Gallery

For details on how to enter for a chance to win this great prize:

- A print of Mark's art

- Prints from the four other artists that will be featured in LUNA novels

- A library of LUNA novels

Visit www.LUNA-Books.com